SPLICE
The Hybrid Resurgence

Nathan Schnackenberg

With Zeke Wheeler

ACKNOWLEDGMENTS

This story could not have come together without the backing, research and insights of a few really smart people. My gratitude goes to Randall Niles, Chuck Border, and Dillon Lane for their wisdom and counsel.

Special thanks to Val Schnackenberg for the hours and hours of editing help, and to Chris Campion for his design work on the cover.

My wife, Liz Schnackenberg, was a steadfast encourager, even when the going got tough. Thank you for believing in this project.

Find other titles by Schnackenberg at

www.Amazon.com

FOREWORD

It was the spring of 2013. I was meeting with a friend at a Starbucks in central Colorado Springs. I expected to share some laughs, talk about sports, and catch up on family – the usual stuff. What I wasn't expecting, was to be given something that has since changed my life.

"Keep this stuff to yourself, for now," my friend said as we approached his vehicle. "I don't think it's for mass consumption yet…"

It was a bright sunny day, but the wind rolling off the mountains had a cold bite to it. He opened the back hatch of his SUV and leaned in. The box he pulled out was full of old books, pamphlets, article clippings, and personal journals. All of it had been given to my friend by a man named Zeke Wheeler.

I didn't know what the big deal was until I got home and immersed myself in Wheeler's wild and wacky world. At first glance, the pages of his journals looked like something out of the movie, *A Beautiful Mind*. There were maps, renderings of Sanskrit, quotes and passages from an array of historical and religious texts. An excited hodgepodge of lines and arrows zigzagged all over the place, linking one concept or *clue* to another. Getting into Mr. Wheeler's mind was a trip, and I couldn't help but lie awake at night and think, "Is this stuff really happening in our world today?"

In addition to the journals, the box contained newspaper clippings and articles about recent archeological discoveries. There were two articles about the sudden death of an individual who was close to the center of what Wheeler was researching, and then I found an obituary – which, due to its sensitive nature, is all I can say. That's when I knew I had stumbled onto something incredibly valuable.

A few days after receiving the box, I called my friend to process some of what I was reading. I started asking a lot of questions about the man, Zeke Wheeler. I was devastated to find out that not only could my friend furnish very little info, but that Wheeler had recently passed away – he died on April 15, 2011.

His last journal entry was penned on April 13, 2011. In it, the eerie words echo into the future, "blow the trumpet, now…"

My friend and I had more than a few follow-up meetings to talk about Wheeler's research. The stories Wheeler told and the linkages he made were indeed compelling, and the implications of his conclusions were downright frightening. We struggled with how to present his material for mass consumption.

For starters, we had a hard time independently verifying some of what he presented. Secondly, the material was so vast – spanning the ancient histories and beliefs of Sumerian, Hebrew, Greek, Persian, Roman and other cultures – that we were confounded by how to keep the reader engaged. In the end, we ruled out the possibility of presenting Wheeler's lifelong research in nonfiction form.

Having finished this first "fiction" book, I do believe we did his research justice. I hope so, anyway.

Wheeler was able to link the present and the past with cogent precision. He found connections that married polytheistic mythologies to monotheistic religions, everywhere. To Wheeler, the recent tech boom is not only beginning to support mythological and religious belief, but is the smoking gun that proves some of the most profound and frightening prophesies ever told!

Wheeler's conclusions often defy the imagination and assault the moral standard. If you ever read what's been posted online about Zeke Wheeler, you'll find him to be a truth seeker, believer in the tenets of the Christian faith (though apparently not a religious man), and a mystic. Having seen his research first-hand, I am convinced that he was somehow chosen by some extra-worldly, supernatural force, not only to shine light in dark places, but to mark this generation as one of extreme significance.

Zeke was convinced that the world is going to change in unimaginable ways. I now agree with his conclusions. A time of terrible turmoil approaches. The sovereign, so-called 'First World' will fall and freedoms will be vanquished. Wheeler believed it. I now believe it.

This book is a work of fiction. It's the first in my *Anno Domini* series of three. The second book is expected in late 2014. I sincerely hope you enjoy it, even if it makes you squirm a bit.

Nathan Schnackenberg

CHAPTER 1
A Nudge From Beyond

Monday, August 15, 2011

It was a spontaneous decision to check out of the Best Western a day early. Solomon Keys was close to wrapping up an emotionally charged week, but there was still one more thing he had to do.

Since he was an only-child, everything involving the settling of his mother's affairs flowed through him. There was the planning and attending of her funeral, the hosting and entertaining of the grieving family, the estate issues, the legal matters; all of it had landed square on his shoulders. In hindsight, those things were all pretty straight-forward. The death industry was an efficient one, if nothing else.

For Solomon, the emotionally draining aspects had to do with the guilt-ridden acquaintances that unexpectedly showed up at the functions. Like vultures to a corpse, a blight of sniffling, sobbing, *non*-friends arrived to pay their respects, and each of these uninvited "townies" required long sessions with her only surviving child. It was agony. Solomon knew they were each just seeking absolution, forgiveness, or some form of closure, but none of them had been good to his mom in life.

Only after death do the parasites conjure the illusion that they ever really gave a damn, he thought, as he popped a few Tylenol and swallowed them without water. After one final glance through the dimly lit hotel room, he grabbed his suitcase and headed to the lobby.

Solomon Keys stood 5'11" and carried 180 pounds on a slight but fit frame. His dirty-blond hair was cut and styled to his age – what he called "early-thirties chic". His jaw was firm, his eyes green and bright, and the evidence of his attention to physical appearance was obvious. Had he the temperament of a hound dog, he might have been a danger to the opposite sex. But he didn't. He was a contemplative man. He possessed a sharp mind and had great skill as an orator. He had the whole package of a young Beltway lawyer, and that package was responsible for his rising star in the world of law.

He checked out of his hotel a day early because he wanted more time to go through some of his late uncle's belongings. He'd noticed something odd in one of his mom's journals a few days prior, and it tempted his curiosity. Was it the lawyer in him that needed to dig deeper? Was it something else? Though his intellectual mind told him it was nothing – just an insignificant and odd series of events – he felt like something other than intellect was driving him to take a second look. It had become an obsession, as if somehow he was being nudged from beyond.

1

He'd phoned for cab 20-minutes prior, but it had not arrived yet. After glancing at his wrist watch, he found a comfy chair and took a seat to wait.

Solomon cared not about fate, destiny, superstition, or any such nonsense. In his mind, fate did not exist and destiny was merely the vehicle by which one attained, through hard work and determination, the spoils of wealth and success. He fancied himself a logical man, a down-to-earth pragmatist. In 1999, he received his JD from Georgetown University Law School with the full intention of exploiting the corporate/securities niche of VCs, IPOs, and mergers & acquisitions. He first joined a small firm serving entrepreneurs in the fast-paced technology sector along the DC Beltway. In a twist of fate, or in Solomon's case, *bad luck*, the tech sector crashed in the spring of 2000, leaving him unemployed by that summer.

Relegated to waiting tables at the 1789 Restaurant in Georgetown, he kept his eyes open for a new niche to exploit. One evening he served dinner to his new meal ticket; a hip young pastor caught up in a lawsuit with the ACLU for declining to perform a series of gay wedding ceremonies at his "lightly" taxpayer-funded *Church on the Green*. Although Solomon had no fondness for religion, and had no qualms with gay marriage, the *Church on the Green* had a legal defense budget, and that's all he needed to hear.

After some slick salesmanship, he grabbed the case to defend religious liberty and rather fell in love with it. Remarkably, the matter went all the way to the 4th Circuit Court of Appeals and Solomon won a high-profile decision. It was the launch he needed. Solomon became known as one the best First Amendment lawyers in the country, and with that newfound fame and cash, he opened a boutique "Con Law" firm in an old converted boathouse on the Potomac River. He was the only lawyer in the firm, Keys & Associates, but he employed a few paralegals that knew their way around the underbelly of DC politics, nonprofits, and lobbying.

The cab pulled up and he climbed in the back seat. There was a mounted digital clock on the dash. It read 10:41 am. It was peculiar because the meter also displayed the current time. "Why did you mount a clock when you have the meter?" The attorney asked casually.

"It was a gift," grunted the driver. As he pulled away, he flicked the radio dial and turned up the volume. Solomon cocked his head involuntarily at the abruptness and thought, *what a jackass. Was this guy at mom's funeral?*

As the cab whisked past businesses, subdivisions and random pedestrians, Sully (as Solomon was known to his genuine family and friends) noticed that the town seemed quiet for a Monday. Alton, Illinois had a quiet temperament anyway, but it was especially dead that morning. He noticed the churches; there were plenty of them. First they passed a sign for the Church of Christ, then the Beltline Christian Center on the left. A few blocks later, there was the Evangelical United Church across the street from the St. Ambrose Parish, and a competing sign that said,

"Gospel Tabernacle, Next Left!" Amused, he watched as the next mile of travel revealed the River of Life Community Church, Westminster Presbyterian, and finally, Hillcrest Church of the Nazarene. *Church is big business here, I guess. Strange, I hadn't noticed all these before now...*

The taxi turned right onto Boy Scout Lane and zigzagged into the subdivision. As they drew closer to his mom's home, an uneasy feeling came over him. It was brief, but clear, and in that instant he didn't want to be alone – like the world around him was trying to warn of an impending cosmic doom. But just as the feeling surfaced, it passed. It was like an ocean wave surging onto the beach with a roar, only to be sucked through the pores of the sand and disappear. Nothing was left but the testimony of a soapy residue... *What?* He stopped himself and shook it off.

"Ey, we're here bud."

The cabbie's drawl drew him back to the here and now, and he paid the $18.45 tab with a $50 and told the driver to keep the change. A look of embarrassment flashed across the cabbie's eyes and Solomon felt a twinge of satisfaction.

He entered the modest single-story home once shared by his mom and uncle, and put his Samsonite suitcase by the front door. Solomon had no intention of sleeping or showering before another cab would beat the rising sun and take him to the St. Louis Airport for his 6 am flight back to DC. He wanted to get as much time as possible with the stacks of file boxes in his uncle's old study.

His mom's home didn't have great natural lighting, so he flicked a few light switches as he passed a hallway on the right, and rounded a bend to the left, entering the living room and conjoined kitchen where he stopped short. The family who stayed in the home during the funeral services left a mess. Dirty dishes in the sink, newspapers on the counter, and trash overflowing the can. Sully half expected as much. He shook his head and mumbled an obscenity as he surveyed the damage.

With a sigh, Sully took off his blazer, rolled up his shirtsleeves, and started on the dirty dishes. It wouldn't take long. There were worse things than a cathartic activity like washing dishes, especially before jumping into investigation mode.

Juliette Bernard Keys, Solomon's mother, bought the house in 2003 and invited her brother Malcolm Bernard to live with her. Malcolm traveled so much for work that it made no sense to carry a mortgage of his own. Malcolm was the VP and Chief Technology Officer for TB Optics, a government contractor specializing in "next-gen communication systems to support U.S. military operations in Iraq." Most of the extended family thought this meant Malcolm made way too much money installing Facebook stations in soldier pubs and cafes throughout the Middle East. Of course, Solomon knew his uncle's expertise went much deeper than WIFI installs for homesick GI's.

Although he had no clue about the depth of Malcolm's indispensable role in the U.S. military-industrial complex, Sully knew that his uncle was brilliant. Over three decades, he achieved 18 patents in areas such as point-to-point optical systems, wavelength division multiplexing, laser isolation, and "meta-conscious frequency override algorithms." Most of this was lost on Malcolm's simple-minded family and friends. Since he was never the type to boast, nobody ever realized the extent of his genius.

The Bernard family hailed from Dekalb, Illinois, about 65 miles west of Chicago. There, Malcolm was simply known as "the IT guy." In fact, that's how he was listed in the official 1961 Dekalb High School 40th reunion program: "IT Guy, Malcolm Bernard."

In May 2006, Malcolm was killed by an IED, or so the Public Relations Officer at TB Optics reported. Juliette took the news at face value and lamented how Malcolm had only been home from Iraq a combined 18 days since she bought the house in 2003. Solomon remembered his mother calling him often around the time of Malcolm's death, but did not remember her being especially emotional about the news.

While cleaning out her home and going through her things, Sully came across his mom's 2006 journal. His sketchy memories surrounding Malcolm's death resurfaced. Until he read the journal entries, he too accepted TB's report of the IED at face value. However, after going through his mom's personal musings, a shadow of doubt loomed over the official story. That's why Sully checked out of the Best Western. He hoped one more visit to the house would provide clarity and closure. Did Malcolm truly die in a simple tragedy of war, or was there more to the story in Iraq? Not that any of this really mattered to Solomon, but his intuition and competitive drive compelled him to invest an evening. He loved the challenge of a case and he was good at sifting the evidence. Also, something kept tugging... He couldn't resist.

Having finished the dishes, Sully put on a pot of coffee and settled into the living room recliner with Juliette's 2006 journal. Flipping to the entries corresponding to May, he reread them one more time.

Friday, May 19, 2006 – *Today Optics rep Jacobi Maharashtra (Maharesta... Mharashta... God only knows how one would spell such a name) called to tell me that Mal died in a bomb attack. It was some kind of IED thing. He gave precious few details, and could not even tell me where it happened, claiming it was 'classified'. I'm so hurt. I'm so alone...*

Saturday, May 20, 2006 – *I left a message for Sully telling him about what happened to Mal. He hasn't bothered to call me back. My baby is preoccupied with his important job and girlfriend, Laila. Lala... Layla... What do I know? He's still never introduced us. Jacky and Bill were sweet – they came by today and sat with me for a while. Rex called. Rex is going to help me put together a service for Mal. Some sort of remembrance. Today is not much better. I feel like....*

Monday, May 21, 2006 – *Sully called! It was so good to hear his voice. He's still with that girl Leola Durand, and she sounds like a gem. He said he'd email me some photos too. She sounds beautiful and artistic -- a "perfect balance of allure and pulchritude," he said. My silly Sully, lawyer fit him like a glove. He doesn't think he can make the service for Mal, I sure do hope he can….*

Tuesday, May 22, 2006 – *The oddest thing happened today. I went to Eppel's Pantry for a few things. I got eggs and juice and some produce, and when I reached for my wallet to pay, I came across a note that had been slipped into my purse. The note was handwritten and says, "Malcolm Bernard was not killed by an IED, and it was not an accident. I'll contact you as soon as I can." I looked around the store but saw nobody interested in me. I'm still dumbfounded. I must have looked queer, Jenny even asked me what was wrong and I told her. I asked her if she had any cameras we could look at to see if we could identify the person who gave me the note and she says, "What, like a bank? I'm sorry we do not Miz Jules." Figures. I still haven't received a photo of Leola…*

Thursday, May 24, 2006 – *I'm busy today, feels good to be busy. I've been delivering flowers and programs to the Lifehouse and the guest list is beginning to grow…*

Friday, May 25, 2006 – *I'm trembling still. At the Lifehouse today while I was greeting the guests arriving for Mal's service, a man with bloodshot eyes, maybe a broken arm, and rancid breath came up to me and says, "Did you get my note?" At first I didn't understand what he was talking about, but then I remembered. Before I could answer he leaned forward and whispered something in my ear. I says, 'What?' because I wanted to clarify what I heard, but before I could ask him anything, at that very instant, Katelyn Riggs, that gossiping nag, if she didn't pull my arm and yank me away! To think she did it to introduce me to her louse of a mother; they went on and on about the husband she just divorced. Who cares! I was so mad! When the opportunity came, I looked everywhere for the man, but he was gone. As best as I could hear, he said, "I'm Will (Bill, maybe) Bates (maybe Gates, I don't know), and I worked with Malcolm. He found the WMD and, God help him, he decoded it," That's it. That's all he said…*

Friday, May 25, 2006, Second Entry – *I have been on the phone with TB Optics since leaving the service and nobody has heard of a Will Bates, Bill Bates, or any such name! No Bates, no Gates. I called Sully twice and he didn't answer or call back. I'm so alone and so tired. I want to believe the TB people are telling the truth, but something just isn't right. I feel like someone is watching me. Why is all this happening to me? I feel so alone…*

Sunday, May 27, 2006 – *Today I looked though Mal's study and realized that I don't know how to read the language he worked with. I haven't had a bite to eat since his service. I don't feel like eating. I told Jacky about what happened, and she started psycho-analyzing me. She said it was a figment of my imagination, and that the peculiar man with rancid breath was just my subconscious doing weird things. I was either going to punch her in the nose or prove she was wrong; so I tried to fetch the note he gave me and realized that either it never existed or I accidentally threw it away, because it's nowhere now. Maybe she's right…*

Splice

Monday, June 5, 2006 *– The sun is shining and the birds are chirping. It's nice to feel warmth on my skin again. I've been seeing a therapist, Dr. Monique Bagri. She's a godsend -- Big Negro woman with a huge smile and personality that goes all the way up and all the way around. What an angel she's been. The day is even brighter because Sully says he's coming with his Leola next month for a weekend visit. "Mal, rest in peace, as we choose to live and abide by peace ourselves." – the wisdom of Doc Monique.*

Pulling away from the journal, Solomon glanced at his watch, *5:52 pm.* He set the journal on the coffee table and thought about it. He could read *tech-speak* better than his mom, but having reread the journal entries, he now wondered if it was all a wild goose chase. Malcolm's study was full of boxes and he intended to go through them, but chances are he wouldn't find much insight into the events surrounding his uncle's death.

I'm hungry, he thought. *Wonder what Jasper's up to?*

His mind floated off and settled on that statement he made to mom: *a perfect balance of allure and pulchritude.* The five-foot, five-inch brunette, who toted that rare mix of attitude and class, was, at the time of his mother's musings, a 24-year-old aspiring journalist with a new internship at the *Post.* Solomon was enamored by her spunk in those early years, and for a season around the time of Mal's death, there was precious little beyond his own work and after-dinner plans with Leola that mattered. Admittedly, he never stopped to consider how his mom was doing with the death of her brother, and felt bad about it now.

Glancing a second time at his watch, he thought about calling her to check in. It was almost 7 pm in DC. Leola was now an Assistant National News Editor at the *Washington Times* and normally worked noon to 8 pm during the week. Things between them had settled into a nice routine. They were past the various dating phases and were now accustomed to doing life together. He figured they'd probably be together forever.

But early on, sometime after the sex-phase, but before the settle-in phase of their relationship, she wanted to get married and brought it up often. That's the season Sully now refers to as their 'fight-phase.' The topic of marriage always seemed to end in a fight. It even brought them close to separation on a few occasions. He never saw the value of marriage and argued they were a civil union, and that's all that mattered – legally. She argued that normal people who love each another get married. They were hopelessly deadlocked on the issue for almost a year, but one day after an ugly brawl, Leola agreed to stop bringing it up – for good. That was in '08. Since 2009, they happily shared an apartment in the swank Foggy Bottom neighborhood of DC, enjoying the smooth waters of relational bliss.

An IM jingle took his attention to the open Facebook page on his laptop. Solomon smiled as Jasper's message appeared. Known on Facebook as 'Jasper Magdasper,' it read, "Hey bro, sorry I missed the funeral. My wife was on-call and got summoned 30 min before it started. I had to stay home and watch little Brad."

Solomon had met Jasper at a Fourth of July dinner party in '06, during Leola's first visit to meet his mom. He and Jasper hit it off from the beginning. They both saw the world from the same vantage point. Both were politically independent, both enjoyed a bit of crude humor, both shared a love of Jägermeister, and both believed in the power of reason and logic as an answer to the "kooky nonsense perpetrated by all fringe elements of the media." Jasper's wife was secure, independent, and absolutely hilarious. Then, Jasper was a med student and his wife was a social worker. Now, Jasper worked the ER in one of Grace Hill's St. Louis campuses four nights per week.

"It's no problem, you guys didn't know her well," Solomon messaged, "What are you up to right now?"

"Nothing. The wife isn't feeling well so she's gonna hit the sac early. Why, what's up?"

"I was wondering if you want to come over."

"The hotel?"

"No, I'm at my mom's. I'm going through that stuff I was telling you about the other night. I got an early flight tomorrow, but thought if you weren't doing anything, I could use the help."

A few minutes passed. Then Jasper responded with, "Send me the address. She's gonna drop me off and I'll catch a cab home later, or whenever you go to the airport, we'll share one. Whatever."

After Solomon sent the address, he popped onto Google and searched for the nearest pizza delivery. He ordered a large Meaty Pizza and a 2L of Coke. He then stood, stretched, and poured himself a cup of coffee.

Malcolm's study was down the hallway near the front door – the first door on the right. Sully walked in and found, on the opposite side of the room, large dark draperies covering two medium-sized square windows looking out over the front yard and driveway. No light penetrated the thick drapes, so he flicked the light switch. A door along the back of the study led to an adjoining bathroom that also exited into the hallway further down. Along the wall nearest him was a large closet full of boxes. Juliette didn't rearrange the study much after Malcolm's death; his old desk and chair remained, and most of his belongings were boxed, stacked, and neatly labeled. Solomon had sifted through some of the boxes the week prior, but there were plenty more to inspect.

Sully's skill at efficiently processing and analyzing data had always been remarkable to those who knew him. It was part of what made him such a good attorney. In quick order he was able to garner a pretty solid understanding of the man's financials and net worth. He even pieced together quite a bit of information about what his uncle did for the government; though some of the technical jargon used in certain op-memos was still beyond his comprehension.

Almost an hour in, the doorbell jolted Sully out of Malcolm's 2006 'patent prosecution and status' files and back to reality. He stood, patted down his pant pockets to be sure he had his wallet, and opened the door.

Jasper Nadar, pizza box in one hand and a 2L of Coke in the other, stood smiling from ear to ear. "Hey bud! You order some pizza?"

"Yeah," Solomon said, suspiciously eyeballing the front lawn and driveway looking for the delivery person.

"The delivery gal pulled up the same time I did, so I paid cash. Hope you don't mind, I gave a slice to the wife."

"I don't mind. Did she leave?"

"Who, the delivery gal?"

"No, your wife."

"Yeah, she's not feeling well." Then, with his arms wide open, Jasper boomed, "DUDE, we're like the real life Hardy Boys! Give me some love!"

Solomon leaned in, gave a double-tap bro-hug and said, "Suppose so. Get in here, let's eat first."

He was about to follow Jasper into the kitchen when he felt it again. That feeling. Like something was askew, but out of his control to fix. It came, washed over him, weakened his knees for a minute, and then was gone. His friend took no notice and marched straight for the kitchen, jabbering about Batman and Robin and their designated roles as the dynamic duo. Sully peeked one final time at the front driveway and yard before closing the door and locking it tight.

Jasper was a rowdy, loud, slightly vulgar man who stood a hair over six-feet and weighed a pound or two under obese. He didn't mind being the center of attention, but often achieved it by poking fun at himself, thereby making everyone else in the room feel more secure. Solomon often thought that Jasper was probably a wonderful physician. He had a magnetism and charisma that people in general, but especially people dealing with traumatic circumstances, would likely find comforting. He truly loved 'the wife' and 'little Brad.' When conversations tapered off, he could always tell a funny story about the baby's bowel movements or the wife's irritation with him for some boneheaded decision he made. He took life's ups and downs with a smile. Sometimes he added a middle finger or a sly wink.

Whether he had it all figured out was debatable, but nobody could deny the joy he found in the little things.

Opening the pizza box, he slumped his shoulders and dropped it on the kitchen counter. "Oh man. It's got meat and cheese, I can't eat this. I'm a vegan."

"Shut up," Solomon chuckled, "Really? You're a vegan now?"

"What dude?" he turned and stretched out his arms in a confrontational pose, "You just call me a vegan? What's next, you gonna say I'm a queer?"

"Good lord, what's the matter with you?" Sully tried to hide his amusement, but did a poor job. He pushed past his fun-loving friend and snatched a slice.

"I dunno. Docs can't figure it out either."

Jasper filled two glasses with Coke and took a slice for himself before joining his friend in the living room. They talked and told a few jokes, had seconds, then Jasper had thirds. The grandfather clock in the living room chimed, letting them know it was 8 pm. They sat in silence, waiting for the clock to chime eight times and give them the floor back.

"Obnoxious thing," Sully said.

"I know, right? In the land of far-far-ago, people must have thought the grandfather clock was an iPad."

"Speaking of ago," Solomon stood, "You ready to go to work, Sherlock?"

"Sure. What are we looking for again?" Jasper followed him to the study, "Something about possible foul play in your uncle's death, right?

"I don't know. We're going through these boxes and I'm looking for anything you might find about Iraq, a discovery in Iraq, or anything marked top secret or classified. In fact, if you see anything with a date stamp of 2006, that could be interesting too."

The Hardy Boys lost track of time. It was just after 1 am when Jasper called Solomon's attention to a lab journal he found in a box marked, "Optics." The journal was hand-written, which was somewhat odd in a sea of type font forms and memos. The dates began in March of 2006 and ended abruptly with the final entry on May 3rd of the same year.

To the Boys, much of the journal was scribbled mathematical nonsense. However, the little book was also full of symbols, ancient markings, and some kind of cuneiform script. The math calculations looked 21st century, but the rest looked like something from an antiquities museum. *Wait…!*

In an instant, Jasper and Solomon stopped what they were doing. They heard the unmistakable sounds of scratching coming from the living room. "What is...?" Jasper started, when Solomon put his hand up and whispered, "Shhh."

"You expecting company?" he whispered.

"No." Sully mouthed the word and shook his head.

"I'll go see, it might just be one of your ma's friends or something."

"At one in the morning?" Solomon whispered, looking at his friend with an absurd gaze.

"I don't know dude," he raised his voice to punctuate his point of view, "Why are we worried? We're not trespassing, I'll just go see what's up."

His confidence cut the tension. Jasper left the study with casual nonchalance, humming the 007 theme as he went. Sully chuckled as his eyes fell back to the pages of his uncle's notebook.

Jasper bent and peered out of the front door's peep hole. He saw nothing. He was about to return to the study when he heard the scratching again, but this time he realized it was coming from the back door, which was directly opposite the front door on the other side of the house. He took a few steps toward the back door, but stopped short when he noticed the doorknob oscillating, as if the lock was being jimmied from the other side. In that instant, though he could not put a finger on exactly what, Jasper knew something was very wrong.

There was only a kitchen light and a hallway light illuminating the house. Jasper felt frozen in time, like he ought to do something, but what? He thought about calling to his friend in the study, but no words came. He thought about turning off the hall light, but for whatever reason, he couldn't move. He thought about going to the back door, but saw a premonition of the door being kicked in on him, so just stood there like a statue. It all happened so quickly. The back door creaked open, slowly at first. He held his breath. Then he saw a gloved hand grip the edge of the door. In an instant, the door swung open with one fluid motion. The last coherent thought Jasper had was, *is this what it means to be petrified?*

The sting of the bullets ripping though his midsection was so intense that he almost didn't hear the suppressed *pop-pop* of a 9mm handgun. Had he been hit once? Twice? He couldn't tell under the explosion of pain and confusion. Everything was a blur. He was gasping for air from flat on his back, when above him, a person clad in tactical gear from head to foot, appeared and hovered. It was fuzzy at first, and then his eyes cleared enough to lock with those of the assassin. He couldn't speak, but he tried to will the words, "Please, no, I have a family." The barrel of the assailant's gun moved into view. *Pop.* Lights out. Just like that, Jasper was gone.

Solomon heard the first two shots. He didn't freeze. That wasn't what you did in the courtroom when the opposition hit you with something unexpected. You had to adapt, juke, and jive. Looking around the room, he noticed the door that led to the bathroom was ajar. Quietly, he slipped in and crouched down in the dark and waited; his mind a haze of fright and confusion. How many people were in the house? He didn't know. Was Jasper dead? He didn't know. Just as he was wondering, he heard the third *pop*, and that's when he knew. His heart raced up his throat, his breathing became louder. He was panicking and needed to get control. Solomon closed his eyes and tried to focus.

"Kitchen and living room clear." One voice said, slightly muffled.

"This must be him." A second voice said. He seemed to have a German accent, but it was hard for Solomon to hear them over the sound of his own nerves. "Did we know he was here? Why didn't we know he was here?"

"It doesn't matter,' said the first voice. "Let's get the book and finish up." The voices seemed cold, emotionless, and very coherent.

The two proceeded to the study where the contents of the boxes were strewn all over the floor. "Looks like the Greek was looking for it too, eh?" the German voice said.

Solomon's skin was cold. *Who are these people!?* He knew he had to try and escape. Sooner or later, when they failed to find… he looked at the little book he was still holding in his hands. *The lab journal. Of course, this is it. This is what they're after.* He didn't know how he knew, but something told him so. He considered his options.

Solomon wasn't a wimp. Growing up, he always made courageous decisions and stood up for what he thought was right. However, this situation was confronting his courage in a bad way. While struggling to make a final decision, he considered approaching the trespassers and handing them the lab journal. But that idea, he knew, was presumptuous to a fault. Given the routine nature of the first execution, he quickly calculated the chances these thugs would let him live – under 25%. Regardless, it would have been the pathetic course of action, and that wasn't part of Sully's genetic makeup. He needed to try and escape, so he set his mind on that and looked around for options.

He stuffed the journal behind his belt, in the small of his back. He was beginning to think clearly. He turned the handle on the door that exited to the hallway and opened it silently. It opened inward, toward him. Once ajar, he peered down the hall toward the front of the house where he could see a man's shadow stretched across the hallway floor, illuminated by the bright lights in Malcolm's study. The two were talking, but Solomon was too focused to worry about what they were saying. He hardly heard them. He crept out of the bathroom and moved quietly, but deliberately, down the hall toward his mother's master bedroom, away from the intruders. All the lights in this section of the house were out, but he was familiar with the layout and furnishings. He navigated his way across the master bedroom and unlocked the window facing the side of the house. The window was stiff, but with enough force, it slid open. As it did, a light breeze kicked against thin drapes that hung loosely. He was sweating, and the breeze licked his forehead with a sudden burst of cool that felt oddly refreshing, given the circumstance.

"We may have a problem here."

Solomon heard those words as he turned to face the hallway behind him. Everything had been muffled until then, but those words were as clear as a bell. He knew what was coming next. "It looks like this isn't the Greek. His ID says, Jasper Nadar."

"Clear the rest of the house."

Damn it! Panic returned with a full assault on his senses. He whipped back toward the window and thrust his shoulder into it with all his might. It creaked open enough to have a go at it. As he hung both legs out of the window and positioned to hop the three feet to the grass below, he wondered if a third intruder was standing guard, watching the perimeter. *Doesn't matter now -- GO!*

Just before letting go of the windowsill, he saw the shadow of a man approaching the bedroom. Before he appeared, Solomon let go, fell, hit the grass, and lunged into the hedge that lined the property. Moving on all fours, he followed the hedge to the back of the property, where it gave way to forested land.

Before running into the forest, he turned to look for pursuers. Keeping quiet and motionless, he peered through the hedge, back toward the house. A sconce light hung on the side of the house, just above the window he used to escape. There, in that window, he saw the figure of a man dressed in tactical gear. He was leaning out the window and his head was cocked directly at Solomon's position in the back corner of the property. Ten seconds passed, then fifteen; the figure in the window stood motionless and continued his gaze at the hedge area where the young attorney held his breath and waited with strained anxiety.

I'm behind the hedge! How can you see me? I'm behind the hedge!! There was something wrong about the man in the window. For one, his neck seemed to stretch as he peered toward the back hedge. Solomon could have sworn it grew a foot or more during the standoff. Though his eyes were concealed behind a tactical shield, Sully thought he saw two points of red light marking the intruder's pupils. Solomon was terrified, and struck dumb where he crouched. He couldn't think or move, as if held captive to the will of the man who stared at him from the window.

For what felt like close to a minute, the assailant stood and stared with a malicious gaze. If he didn't know better, it seemed the intruder was looking at him *through* the hedge with some sort of x-ray night vision. Solomon wanted to make a mad dash for the forest, but was somehow petrified, locked in stillness under the eyes of this someone or something.

Then suddenly, the figure in the window nodded his head. It slowly bobbed up and down for a second or two, as though he was letting Sully know he found him, and then he disappeared into the house. As soon as he did, Solomon turned and ran like hell. He didn't need to think about it; all he wanted to do was run.

He never ran so hard in his life. He ran until the forest gave way to a clearing. There, rather than go into the clearing, he followed the forest line and kept running until he reached Pierce Lane. He followed that road south, toward St. Louis, careful to not let the occasional vehicle spy him along the way. Eventually, Pierce dead-ended at Delmar Avenue, and there he saw his salvation -- a MotoMart gas station that appeared to be open, less than 200 yards west of his position. In total, the trek was just over two miles, but Sully was hardly tired. Adrenaline had carried him like a gurney carries an unconscious soldier.

The MotoMart clerk was kind enough to let Solomon call for a cab using the station phone. Superficial fascination with popular conspiracy theories and gut intuition told Sully to avoid his cell. The cabbie arrived and was instructed to head toward the St. Louis Airport. Along the way, he thought about his Samsonite bag and had to assume it was compromised. Therefore, he had no choice but to forfeit his flight. He needed to think. He needed a cup of coffee. At the I-170 to I-70 interchange he saw a sign and changed his mind about the airport. "Take me to that Denny's please."

The cab driver, every bit the customer service pro that his colleague was the day prior, did not say a word; he just exited the Interstate and complied. Solomon paid the meter, entered the Denny's, asked for a seat in the back of the restaurant, positioned himself so he could see the front dining area, and took a deep breath.

He asked for some coffee and tried to maintain composure. He took an inventory of his belongings; all he had was his wallet, keys, cell phone, and Malcolm's lab journal. He needed to think, but he was becoming emotional. *Oh God, Jasper was slaughtered! Crap, what about Jasper's sweet wife and kid? Why was Malcolm's research such a target? Why am I even involved in this crap? I'm a frickin' First Amendment lawyer...*

Emotions tend to crowd out logic and reason. Sully knew he was about to lose it, so he ducked into the bathroom and locked himself in a stall. It was there that he let it out. The outburst was muffled in his shirt sleeve, but he let it all out.

CHAPTER 2
Invite

Friday, December 14, 2012

As the only son of a powerhouse couple on the world stage, Leonardo Khalpana's childhood was coveted by most. Leo's mother was Isabella Khalpana, sister of the renowned Spanish soccer icon known around the Premier League as Mateo "Lion of Aston Villa" Miguez. His father, Fedot Khalpana, was a Jordanian Ambassador and career civil servant.

Like the entire Khalpana family, Fedot was a very wealthy man solely as a result of his birth. There was an Arabic saying among Fedot's siblings, "Grandpa's money is enough for a dozen generations, so live and be well." Although no one in the family knew exactly how the late patriarch amassed such wealth, the "live and be well" beneficiaries never felt the need to ask too many questions.

Leo attended numerous schools for the children of social elites while Fedot served the Kingdom of Jordan as an expatriate dignitary in Damascus, Mecca, and Paris. While in Paris, Fedot's term as the Jordanian Ambassador to France was cut short due to scandal. Fedot tried to insulate his wife and son from the fall-out, but he could not.

By age 9, Leo was fluent in English, Arabic, and Spanish. He began learning French while his Papa was stationed in Paris, but on May 8, 1990, three days before Leo's 13th birthday, the scandal broke on the front page of *Le Nouvel Observateur*. At the time, Leo did not understand much. What he did know was Mama spent the balance of that year locked in her room crying, and Papa was no longer around. He also knew that only one boy ended up attending his 13th birthday party, and he was the son of a French Embassy employee. From May 8th until the day he and his Mama left France to return to Spain, Leo ate lunches alone.

He never knew how much he took his social status for granted; that is, until it was all ripped away. He never knew how badly it hurt to be silently scorned by those he admired; that is, until the disdain was an everyday reality. He was bullied, especially by the offspring of other prominent Middle Eastern expats. Mama told him to keep his chin up, and he did. But Mama was too busy feeling sorry for herself to see that Leo also cried himself to sleep each night, buried in the cold, unemotional comfort of his pillow. It was an awful eighteen months.

"What's the matter?" Alegria Khalpana's reflection appeared in the mirror. She looked stunning, dressed and prepped for the party. Leo waved a hand in frustration, gesturing toward the obstinate bowtie hanging loose around his neck.

She put her handbag on the sink and skillfully, with manicured fingers, tied and set it for him. She had tied many of these.

"I was just thinking," he said, smiling and trying to look as though it was nothing important. She returned his smile with one that said, *I know what you're thinking, baby.*

He shook his head in embarrassment. His wife knew him so well. "Okay, I was thinking about my Papa's scandal, and realizing that since it happened, this is the first time I've been invited to such an important event. I mean, we've been to our share of posh parties, but this is the big one. This is Abdullah Kahn."

"That's good, no?" her long fingernails lightly explored his neck. "2012 may be ending on a high note, don't you think?"

He nodded slowly. "Maybe it shows I've begun to make it on my own. That I've started moving out from under my Papa's vile shadow."

"Of course it does." Her smile grew a bit and it mesmerized him. "Baby, you have never had a thing to be ashamed of. You are a model of integrity and strength."

She grabbed a golden cufflink from the counter and started work on his right wrist. "Mama and you were put through hell by that sleaze. You kept your head high and you chose not to defend him. I'm proud of you, and I love you, and if you never get another invite to a party like this one, I'd still be proud to be the woman standing beside you. And I'd still be deeply in love with you."

Leo hit the jackpot with Ali. He met her while attending the University of Chicago. She also came from a well-to-do family and was attending Northwestern University on an exchange program. Their acquaintance was made when she dropped her textbook on the train one day and Leo was nice enough to pick it up. After some small talk, the physical electricity was obvious, and they soon realized how much they had in common. They were both from Spain, both in college, both 24 years-of-age, and both homesick. In addition, they both came from tremendous family wealth.

Alegria's father converted to Islam in the early 70's. For him, it was purely religion – nothing radical or political. In fact, he detested the violent behavior of what he called a 'fringe element of deceived evildoers' within Islam. Ali converted while she was a teenager, but she did it mainly for her father's peace of mind. He never forced his faith on her, but she knew it mattered to him. Like any girl, she wanted to please her daddy. However, she told him flat out, she was much too modern to acquiesce to certain rules about female attire, and pointedly refused to abide by any dress code whatsoever. Her father laughed, hugged her, and told her to simply live by the moral code set forth by the Prophet, and all would be fine.

Since her conversion, Alegria didn't think much about Islam. She cracked open the Book now and then, and when times were tough, she prayed more diligently –

more "religiously." However, for the most part, she was having too much fun living life, traveling, and enjoying romantic evenings with her handsome husband in exotic places around the world. She lived on a dreamboat and knew she was blessed beyond measure. That's why she always told Leo to live like there was no tomorrow – enjoy the people who make the days interesting and the nights exciting. But Leo didn't always see life through a pair of carefree goggles.

They were married in October of 2003 at the Bali Four Seasons Resort, Jimbaran Bay. It was a private, exquisite occasion. The tan and teal color scheme worked well with the aqua blues and leafy greens of the island paradise. At the time, Leo counted 41 individuals from his side of the family who declined to attend his wedding. It irked him. It was certainly not a money issue; the no-shows had simply flicked him and his family into the dustbin of history because of Fedot's sins. It irked him badly.

After one final image-check in the mirror, they decided it was time to go. In the elevator, Ali inched closer to Leo, and backed her body into his. Her silky smooth dress begged to be touched. Her skin begged to be caressed. Leo glanced at his gold-rimmed wristwatch and wondered if they had time to dip back into the room for some romance. They were staying at the Setai Fifth Avenue Hotel in New York City. Depending on traffic, the drive out to Long Island could take a couple hours. He frowned and put the thought out of his mind; there just wasn't time.

She wore a stunning, dark blue, sleeveless, drape front dress made by Donna Karen. Her accents included a silver tie around the midsection, a band of pearls around her neck, diamond earrings, and a diamond bracelet around her left wrist. She brought it all together with a pair of 4-inch Manolo Blahnik pumps from Barneys. Her long, dark hair was a messy updo, which she did herself (but would never admit that), and her makeup was sensational. With the heels, she stood 6'1", which was fine because Leo stood 6'4" in bare feet.

He wore a custom tuxedo from Alan David and a pair of Salvatore Ferragamo leathers. For this occasion, he decided to sport a manicured goatee that was disconnected at the corners of his mouth. His eyebrows had been tweezed at the spa a few days prior, and his hair was purposefully messy, typical of a trendy young celebrity. Ever since Fedot's sexual exploits that damned his access to the higher echelon of civilized society, Leo had been careful, even neurotic at times, about his appearance. He worked his body hard and watched his diet like his accountant watched his figures. He was muscular and had very little body fat. He had a wide bright smile and charming dark eyes, but a social demeanor that often bordered on desperate, especially in the company of those he idolized. The self-confidence issue was something he only admitted to Ali; something he was working to overcome.

Her fur and his Moreno wool coat hung over his left elbow as she backed into him even further. Now she was teasing. His hands ran down her sides; his thumbs hooked on her sash. She tossed her head back and he caught a tantalizing whiff of the scent she splashed on earlier. He couldn't help but kiss the bend of her neck. As he did, her body tensed ever so slightly.

Leo was a lucky man. For the most part, Ali was skilled at keeping Leo grounded and happy. Not only was she a source of encouragement and support, she was also classy, sexy, and confident enough for the both of them. She always knew when to put up a submissive front in the company of others. Her social dexterity was possibly her most valuable asset; she had an uncommon suave when in the public eye. Having grown up with powerful men all her life, this was something that came naturally to her. Maintaining a proper and respectful demeanor in public was important to every man she ever dated, but especially to Muslim men.

In reality, Leo and Ali were a power-couple. She knew it, he did not. Rather, he regularly chose not to even entertain the idea. Occasionally, he'd say something to make her think he was finally climbing out from under the shadow, but it was always a *two-step forward, one step back* sort of thing. She knew his healing would be a process, and she was willing to stand by him, no matter how long it took.

A black sedan was waiting for them at the valet. The concierge helped them with their coats before they stepped into the chilly drizzle of the December evening. Once situated, the driver whisked them away and into the busy hubbub of New York City.

Their destination was the Long Island estate of Abdullah Kahn, a Kuwaiti billionaire who married into his wealth by tying the knot with the sole daughter and sole heir to the Karafi family fortune. The Karafis were millionaire landowners until they realized that the bulk of their acreage was situated atop the supergiant Burgan Oil Field. Once that was exploited, they became billionaires.

The Karafi inheritance arrived eighteen months after the wedding, making Abdullah a very wealthy man. Six months after that, his dear wife suddenly died in a terrible accident. Her limo was hit by a huge semi-truck and knocked off the road, killing her and her driver instantly. Oddly, though Abdullah had been with her at a social gathering that night, a final business discussion forced him to take a cab home instead of ride with her in the limo. Any dimwit journalist could smell a story. Media controversy erupted within hours. But then, as quickly as things started, the reporting stopped. The matter was closed. In the end, the generally accepted conclusion was that Abdullah's wife had simply died in a tragic car accident; nothing more, nothing less.

Leo didn't care. Abdullah's family issues were none of his concern. What mattered to Leo was that Abdullah was not just a party-thrower to high-society; he was the power-party epicenter on a global scale. Anyone who's someone has partied with Abdullah, been to one of Abdullah's many homes, or spent time on one of Abdullah's yachts. Abdullah didn't know Leo, but Leo certainly knew about Abdullah.

Indeed, 2012 seemed to be ending on a very high note.

CHAPTER 3
A Chance Encounter

Tuesday August 16, 2011

A cocktail of fear and exhaustion trapped Sully in a box of numbness and confusion. He had no idea how long he was sitting in that Denny's booth, but his watch now read 6:12 am. He also had no idea how many cups of coffee he drank or which Slam breakfast now littered his plate. His only coherent thoughts pointed to the smallness of his life in a world that now seemed huge and complex.

He fondly remembered his fun-loving friend Jasper, but that prompted thoughts about little Brad, only four years old and now fatherless. Inevitably, that would stir thoughts about the woman Jasper adored, little Brad's mother. How would he face them? Could he ever... *Stop.* As soon as Sully's emotions surged too high, he would terminate these cycles of thinking. He refused to fall apart. Being locked in a box of numbness and confusion was better than falling apart; so for hours, that's where he lingered.

As the hours passed, however, he slowly regained his ability to logically process the events of the last day. Mom's journals and Malcolm's files definitely pointed to something bigger in Iraq. It was clear that whoever killed Jasper probably had something to do with the death of his uncle Malcolm. The simple party line about the IED now seemed improbable based on the professional attack he'd just endured. He thought it through again and again.

Mal had unique knowledge and access. Was he killed for technology? For special knowhow? Why? Did Mal stumble onto something else of importance and get killed because he knew about it? Or was he killed because he knew how to use it? What was up with that WMD reference? Who was that guy who tipped-off Mom? Somehow, all this ties into Iraq and whatever TB Optics was commissioned to do over there... But killing Mal wasn't enough. What's so special about the calculations and drawings in Mal's journal? After five years, why is that journal still special enough to kill over? Were those U.S. government agents? Killing in cold blood? Foreign agents? Damn it, professional hit men are looking for Mal's little book and my buddy Jasper gets murdered over it. Stop, don't go there again...

Sully's hand slid to the small of his back. He felt the lab journal firmly pressed between him and the warm vinyl of the booth. He sensed something deep... Something otherworldly. He remembered the foreign script lettering and complex mathematical equations that seemed to dance on the pages. When he and Jasper were skimming those cyphers, he knew they represented something profound.

Splice

The waitress offered to warm up his cup, but he placed a hand over the gape and smiled, "No, please. Any more coffee and you'll see me have a nervous breakdown over here." She returned his smile and walked away.

The restaurant was considerably busier than when he arrived. He looked around the dining area and realized that *they* might be watching him even now. His breath hastened just a bit as he inconspicuously glanced here and there, trying to catch a glimpse of anyone who might appear to pose a threat. He was becoming paranoid and on the verge of a full-blown anxiety attack.

There was a mid-40 year old who was facing him, reading a newspaper at his 11-o-clock. There was a 20-something sitting alone wearing a jogging suit and sunglasses perched at his 3-o-clock. *He seemed oddly placed, but not dangerous.* There were two women with six, no seven, kids at a large table in the middle of the bigger dining area. They were loud and carrying on about nothing. Many of that company had swimsuits on under their clothing; a clear indicator that they were heading to a lake or nearby waterpark. *These people are harmless.* There were two separate couples sitting in small booths near the front door...

His trembling hands massaged his throbbing temples as he closed his eyes and tried to get a grip. *Most likely harmless...? That's my assessment for two middle-aged women and their seven kids? Pull yourself together!*

He opened his eyes, and like an oasis in the desert, he saw a familiar face walk through the front door. *Father Abelemy?* Solomon stood up and waved in disbelief, wondering what the chances were that Father Abelemy could walk into this particular Denny's on this particular day. *What luck!*

Father Abelemy Dotson was Solomon's primary Eastern Orthodox Church contact during a discrimination suit, which Solomon litigated on the Church's behalf. Abelemy reached out to Keys & Associates in the spring of 2006 and promptly retained the attorney's services. The legal matter concluded abruptly, about six months after it began, when Solomon negotiated a nice settlement acceptable to the Church. The Father and Sully remained friends – even became close friends in the few years since.

The Father was an easy-going man. When faced with arguments or conflicts, he often wielded a well-timed (frequently stupid) joke to disarm everyone around him. He was not especially religious, which Sully wondered about from time to time. He even shunned the "Father" title and preferred to be called "Dotty" by his close friends. Over the years, Sully came to realize that one of the reasons he liked him so much was because the Father, by his life and actions, made Sully want to be a better man. The Father's general demeanor was humble, casual, and authentically light. He had a way of not taking life too seriously. His presence was like a drink of cold water in times of stress, and his presence now was a welcome drink indeed.

On approach, Solomon could tell he was serious. Even after they caught eyes and Solomon's wave was returned with a slight nod, it was clear that Dotty was in a zone. Solomon's smile faded as the Father deliberately looked at every patron in the Denny's. He looked at them as though he was analyzing risk and making assessment. He even scrutinized the women and kids. At that moment, Solomon realized that this meeting was no coincidence. Father Abelemy was somehow involved in everything.

He reached the booth and the two men stared at one another. The Father broke the silence. "Under the circumstances, you're probably wondering whether to hug me, kiss me, or punch me in the nose, huh?"

Sully chuckled, partly out of raw emotion overload, and partly out of relief, "You and your jokes; at least that's authentic."

"Of course. And what's also authentic is that I'm your friend, and I'm someone you can trust." The Father extended his hand and Solomon shook it. Sully then gestured to the booth and the two men sat.

"Coffee?" Solomon waved a hand over the plate of mutilated food, "Slam?"

"No, not for me thanks. We have a lot to talk about and I think we should jump right in." Solomon nodded as Dotty leaned on his elbows and started in a quiet, clear voice. "Okay then. You've had a traumatic night, and all of this is new, and let me start by saying that I believe the worst is behind you – for the time being."

Solomon breathed in as if to interject, but the Father put up one hand and continued. "This will work better if you save your questions for the end. We don't have a lot of time and I want to give you as much information as possible." Solomon exhaled loudly and nodded.

"Look, I am a Greek Orthodox priest – this much you know. But full disclosure here, while I was still in college getting my masters in biblical counseling, I was recruited by, and ended up working for, the federal government. I am a clergyman, but that's more of a cover than anything else. I'm not going to get into it, but I work for one of those divisions that doesn't get an official budget allocation, if you know what I mean." Being a DC lawyer, Sully knew exactly what that meant.

"So, after your uncle died, the clandestine power elites decided we needed a surveillance net over key marks, of which you were one. Some of your uncle's friends and some of his extended family were initially put under watch as well, but most of them have since been released." Solomon shrugged as if to ask, *why me?* The Father responded with grace, "We kept eyes on you because of your intelligence and profile. Your mom was kept on watch because of her proximity to Malcolm. The other family and friends were dropped within a year because of their, I don't know, ignorance and lack of intelligence, to be frank."

The waitress arrived, flopped down an empty mug, and filled it with black coffee for Dotty. After she had finished, she refilled Sully's cup. The two men looked at her and she said, "Oh, I'm sorry. You didn't want any more and I didn't even ask you yet. Good God Almighty, I'm losin' my mind here."

The patrons smiled as the Father reassured, "It's fine miss, thank you."

Abelemy sniffed the coffee and then took a sip. His fingers naturally and briefly inspected the bottom and sides of the mug as Solomon's mind recounted every CIA movie he ever saw. *This is absolutely crazy – I'm living in a real life spy flick!*

"Obviously, you now realize the discrimination suit was a fabrication," Abelemy concluded quietly as the waitress walked away.

"Yeah, clearly." Solomon looked like he might become sick.

"It was an easy way to make contact with you and keep an eye on you. You may not believe me, but this was done for your safety." Solomon scowled as his mind sprinted across the improprieties of what the Father was saying. "I was not involved with you or this case until after your uncle died. I was only brought in because my cover as a Greek Orthodox priest was an easy sell, given what you and your firm were known for in DC. After I came on board, I was briefed on your uncle, but not given the classified information in totality. I'm compartmentalized, like every other agent. There are still a lot of holes in the story. You'll just have to accept that because I don't know the answers to a number of your questions."

"What I do know is this. Your uncle was killed, but not by an enemy combatant's improvised explosive." Father Abelemy read Sully's eyes and slowed things down. "Wait. Let me take a step back. Malcolm was initially sent to Iraq for the purpose of developing and testing something the military called, LEMP – or 'Life-Essence Manipulation Protocol.' In layman's terms, it's where super-sensitive optic technology is used to monitor the essence of a person's existence. I know, freak show – this LEMP gave someone a snapshot of someone else's willingness to 'go on' in life. This was the next-generation of interrogation methods that was supposed to take over where waterboarding left off. I have no idea how it works technically, but the interrogators were evidently able to kill and resurrect a person's willingness to live by using technology your uncle developed. Somehow, he figured out how to speak directly to the soul of an enemy combatant and, how shall I put it… massage the 'jihadi-will' right out of them. It was explained to me as a cross between hypnosis and technology-guided telepathy. In the end, it would suppress a prisoner's ideologies and allegiances to the point where they would vomit anything they knew about anything asked. The LEMP was a non-invasive, non-torture technique to penetrate a man's soul. Crazy, huh?"

Solomon's mouth opened. Abelemy shrugged and sipped his coffee.

"So, WMD. We went to Iraq to neutralize their weapons of mass destruction, right? When we got there, we failed to find any mustard gas or nukes, but we did find something else at a place the military referred to as Alpha Kilo, or sometimes *Alpha Site*. I can't tell you what we found, because I frankly don't know, it's hyper-classified. What I do know is your uncle was brought in as one of a three-person team to analyze it, scientifically. A month or so later, everyone at Alpha Kilo – which was protected by the Army's Delta Force, mind you – was massacred. Your uncle was among the dead. There was no forensic evidence left by the perpetrators, so to this day, the perpetrators remain a bit of a mystery. In fact, they are now known in my circle as the 'Phantoms' for that exact reason."

Abelemy took another sip of coffee. "When Alpha Kilo failed to check in, a rescue team was dispatched to the site. Whatever the scientists were working on was gone and everyone was dead. Each victim – two shots to the torso and one shot to the head. We still don't know who did this. So, fast-forward a bit, we all watch and wait for years. Then, when you checked out of your hotel a day early, but made no change to your travel itinerary, I decided to come and have a look around. It was a hunch. We've all but stopped watching you this past year because nothing was happening."

"Anyway, this brings us to last night. I was there when Jasper and the pizza arrived at your ma's house. I kept an eye on you guys until around midnight when I went to grab a few hours of rest at the hotel and get some paperwork done. I came back at 4:15 am, but you guys were gone. I figured you went to the airport, but it seemed early. To be sure, I had the cab logs pulled and found out that nobody picked you up at your ma's house. I had a few additional surveillance protocols run, and eventually found another cab that dropped-off here about 2-something. That's how I found you."

The Father looked intently at Solomon. "Now, let me ask you something Sully. Where's Jasper?"

Solomon shook his head in disbelief. "Some spook, huh? What do you mean? He's lying in a pool of his own blood in the hallway of my mom's. Didn't you see him there?"

"He's not there." The corners of Dotty's mouth turned upward. "I looked."

"He's alive?"

"Doubtful. But it appears that the Phantoms have reared their ugly heads again. They don't always leave evidence of their activities behind, including the bodies of the deceased. It's part of their M.O."

Father Abelemy leaned back in his chair and stretched his arms above his head. He appeared to be thinking out loud. "Sometimes they do, but… why then would they…?"

Solomon took a deep breath and glanced around the restaurant nervously. The Father lost himself in thought for a minute. Then, abruptly, he leaned across the table and started again, "The Phantoms are a forensic investigator's worst nightmare. Since '06 in Iraq, we suspect they've struck over two dozen times, but the common thread is that they leave no shred of their own DNA evidence. No eyelash or eyebrow. It's actually quite remarkable. Sometimes they leave the victim at the scene, and sometimes not. If we find the victim, it's always deceased with two taps to the torso and one to the head. Sully, I feel like I'm missing something here, and I need to know what you saw last night, and what led you to your mom's house in the first place. Tell me everything."

Solomon explained his mother's journal and thought he saw a twitch of Abelemy's eyebrow when he said a man by the name of Bates or Gates made contact with her back in '06. He also explained his intention for checking out of the hotel a day early – just something inside drove him to spend some extra time exploring his uncle's belongings in pursuit of clarity, truth and closure.

"Did you find anything?" the Father interrupted, "Anything that corresponds back to his death in '06?"

"No," Solomon said, simultaneously wondering why he was lying and why his friend couldn't tell. "We were getting close to the end of those boxes when the intruders came. They picked the back door and snuck in. Jasper went to see what was going on, but all I heard were two shots, followed by a third a few seconds later. I ducked into the adjoining bathroom, waited for an opportunity to bolt, then did so as soon as I could."

"What did they say Sully. Did they talk?" The Father was stone-cold serious.

"I don't really remember. They were thinking that Jasper was 'the Greek' or something."

The old spook smiled, "Really?"

"Yeah, why?"

"The 'Greek' is probably a reference to me. What else?"

"Nothing. Why is it a reference to you?"

"It's a nickname of mine at the agency. Never mind about that, what else?"

"They said 'let's get the book and get out of here', or something to that effect. That's all I remember them saying." Solomon played with the handle on his coffee mug and hoped the questioning was over.

"Sully?" Solomon looked up to see his old friend's eyes staring a hole through him. "Did you find anything that might shed any light on your uncle's death? A book, a notepad, anything?"

Solomon willed himself into courtroom mode, "No Dotty. If I found something, I would have already handed it to you and asked you to fix this shit by now!"

There was a moment of uneasiness. Then, a few seconds of staring. Something did not fit, for either of them. Abelemy wondered about the Phantoms. Who was behind them, who funded them, and why were they so interested in 'the book' or Malcolm's death? Sully was a smart guy – What did he really know? What did he really learn over the course of the last few hours? Sully wondered why he felt like he couldn't fully trust the Father. How much of this saga was related to the U.S. government? Were the deaths of Malcolm or Jasper even, the CIA's fault? Was the government trying to hide something they botched in Iraq? Were these so-called Phantoms really just decked-out Seals? The Father lied about his identity before. What was stopping him from lying now?

Father Abelemy finally smiled and broke the thick air with one of his typical jokes. "How do you keep a moron in suspense?"

"I don't know Dotty, how?"

"I'll tell you tomorrow."

"You're an idiot." Sully said, chuckling. His weak laugh turned to a yawn. He was exhausted. "So, what's next boss?"

"Next, you get off the radar for a bit, while I try to piece some of this together."

CHAPTER 4
The Black Box

Friday December 14, 2012

The driveway must have been a half mile long. The sedan paused momentarily at a guard shack near the entry gate, then again at a secondary security post, where the guard asked for the Khalpana's invitation and verified their identities.

The security guard at the second stop wore a thick sheepskin coat and Russian Ushanka hat. He had an Izhmash/Nikinov AN 94 assault rifle slung over his shoulder. Leo spied two other guards posted about, although they remained inconspicuous. One was behind the door of the dimly lit guard shack, sitting in front of a computer monitor. The other was 75 yards up the road. Leo only saw him because he crossed through the sedan's headlight beams while their ID's were being checked. Ali squeezed his arm with excited anticipation.

After being waved through, it was only moments before the sedan pulled to a stop in front of the residence's grand entry, complete with Greek columns and a circular marble staircase that led to the front door. A servant boy, about twenty years old, wearing similar attire as the guards, sans the firearm, opened the car's rear door. The Khalpanas exited the car gracefully and proceeded up the stairs. At the top of the grand entry, Leo turned to look at the compound below. He noticed the headlights of other vehicles making their final approach to the mansion. The cobblestone drive circled around a huge water feature and grassy hummock, accented by 1920's style street lamps and iron fencing. Although dim, Leo thought he saw a botanical garden along the eastern side of the residence.

Upon entering the mansion, a short, white-haired, and rather peculiar looking man approached them and said, "Mr. and Mrs. Leonardo Khalpana, welcome to the Chanticleer la Deuxième, the New York home of Mr. Abdullah Kahn. My name is Mister Jones, and I am Mr. Abdullah's Hand. If there is anything I can do to make your time here more enjoyable, please do not hesitate to ask. Now, please give Katalina your overcoats and proceed to the main corridor down that hallway there to the right. Mr. Abdullah's guests are enjoying a drink and a bit of conversation in the library wing."

Mr. Jones was an odd fellow to say the least. To begin, his voice was an octave too high; it was almost jarring. He had a pale complexion with hair and eyebrows the color of snow, but his face was smooth and wrinkle free. He stood no more than 5'4", and Leo thought he detected a French accent. His elocution was sharp, and his welcoming monologue came across as though he were singing a song more than delivering a series of rehearsed statements. His lips were thin, his nose hooked down and came to a point, and his face was expressionless. Not expressionless because he lacked feeling or thought; rather, expressionless because competing feelings and thoughts seemed to be neutralizing one another. There was a cocky aura about him, as if this little man knew something that everyone else did not.

The Khalpanas proceeded forward and surrendered their overcoats to Katalina, who was a stick figure in a pretty gown. She did not look a day over 15, even though she was dolled up with makeup and an expensive outfit; she was probably even younger. Briefly, Leo wondered if Katalina had been trafficked. It was not uncommon for the super-wealthy elites like Abdullah Kahn to use bought-and-paid-for slaves, even in this day and age.

The couple locked arms and started down the enormous hallway toward the library wing as per the directions of the "Hand of Kahn." The hallway looked like a museum. It was loaded with antiquities and paintings, much of it renaissance era artwork from Italy and France, mostly of a religious nature. If Abdullah had to publically claim a faith, it was always Islam. However, most of his art would make nice additions to the Vatican. About half way down the hall, there was a door on the right. For some reason, this door caught Leo's attention.

The door was quaint and ordinary, almost as though it did not belong in this 'hall of splendor.' It was not what he saw in the door that caught his attention, but what he heard. Muffled, as though obstructed by distance and fog, he heard the sounds of... *What is that?* Smiting? Pounding? Not the sounds of a modern construction site, but the sounds of a Renaissance era marketplace. There were voices speaking in strange dialects and tongues; he could not make them out. Deep-throated rumblings, thick and powerful voices, unintelligible, yet authoritative. He also heard the sounds of quaking, as if a large tree was beginning to teeter under the strain of its own weight. There was laughing in the distance. He heard singing, but not to a melody or beat; it was as if the voices were chanting the melody and beat.

Leo stopped at the door. Something more than strange noises were grabbing at him. At first, he wondered if he heard the sounds of a television, but the noises weren't that scripted or organized. He scanned the area around the door looking for a speaker or some other source. *What's making that noise?* He thought, to which Ali replied, "What noise?"

He looked at her and blinked. Did he ask the question out loud? Hadn't he *thought* the question to himself?

"Nothing," he swallowed hard and his pulse quickened. "L-let's proceed." Arm in arm they walked slowly past the door. A few steps later, as though possessed by a strong compulsion, Leo was forced to turn and look back at the door one final time. As he stared, the sounds faded away.

Alegria noticed his fascination with the door and gripped him tighter. "You okay?" She whispered.

"Of course," Leo gently rubbed her forearm and smiled at her. He took a deep breath, put the door behind him, and said, "Yes, I'm fine. Let's enjoy this night."

Abdullah was nowhere to be found when the Khalpanas entered the library wing, but his servants whisked trays of delicacies and expensive liquor and champagne around the room with choreographed grace. Shelves of books, mostly old and expensive looking, adorned the walls. Some of the shelves were so tall that a ladder would be required to reach the top. The large library had a faint woody aroma to it.

Leo saw an acquaintance of his, the son of Zanzia Medina, a Spanish pop icon in Europe. He was with an exotic mistress. Eduardo Medina was laughing and carrying on with Jefri Bolkiah, brother of the Sultan of Brunei. He appeared to be with two women. Lady Zuma, daughter of the President of South Africa, was also there, speaking to one of the Williams sisters and three others, one of whom Leo recognized, but could not place.

Jill Kelly, the Lebanese-American socialite who became famous in connection with the David Patreus investigation, was in attendance. She was talking to a tall, rather young looking man, whose sporadic hand movements and facial twitches made for some amusement. *Speed. I bet that guy took some speed,* Leo thought.

"Notice anything, babe?" came Ali's voice in his ear.

"No, what?" he was surveying the room.

"There are an awful lot of children of rich and famous people here. That seem strange to you?"

"I don't know." Then he focused closer, and realized the same thing as his wife. There was Dylan Lauren, daughter of Ralph, there was Sasha Spielberg, daughter of Steven. Standing in the group next to them was Montana Fishburn, daughter of Lawrence, and across the room he saw Allegra Versace, Camilla Rockefeller, and Paris Latsis. The list went on.

"That's probably why they invited me," Leo mused. "Different generation. Scandals are relative to time and place and culture."

"May I introduce you to anyone, my dear?" Ali turned to see Cordova Gutierrez, an old friend from her childhood, standing behind her. The Gutierrez family made their wealth on four generations of countless patents and inventions.

"Wow! Cordova. How long has it been?" They kissed Spanish-style, "Fancy seeing you here. Cordova, please meet my husband, Leonardo Khalpana."

"Pleasure, sir," Cordova said as he extended a hand to Leo.

"Likewise."

The three exchanged some casual banter and enjoyed a few laughs while sampling truffle custards with crab, smoked salmon roulades, and cucumber and caviar canapes. Inevitably, the conversation bent down the path of old reminiscence between Ali and Cordova. Bored with the ruminations, Leo glanced around the room and looked for an escape. There were no more than 120 guests, and as the liquor and hors d'oeuvres kept coming, the room was getting noticeably louder and more carefree. His mind drifted back to the door in the hallway. He wondered again about the noises. Touching Ali on the shoulder, he gave her a light squeeze and said, "I'm off to find the lav. I'll be back in a minute." She nodded, but kept her focus on Cordova, who was animated about some wildly sensational story from their past.

Leo made his way back into the hall of antiquities and looked around at the collection, pretending to care. Meticulously, after eyeballing each piece, he worked his way back toward the door. He felt pulled toward it, as though *it* wanted to open to him and show him what magic it concealed inside. As he drew near, again he heard the sounds of that distant world, faint at first, then roaring louder. The languages were different than anything he heard growing up in many countries. There was power in the voices, a deep power that Leo seemed to feel more than hear. Then there were the peripheral sounds of work, community, marketplace, commerce, buying, selling, and constructing.

When he was within an arm's length of the door, he definitely heard the powerful sounds of commanding voices mobilizing a workforce of some sort. This gave way to the sounds of rhythm inside of song. It was musical, but unlike any music Leo ever heard. There were beautiful high-pitched voices; almost at a pitch inaudible, singing above the boom and ruckus of the world. Before he could stop himself, he gripped the doorknob and turned it. The door swung open. He glanced once to his right and then to his left to be sure he was alone in the hallway. He was. Taking a deep breath, he slipped in and closed the door behind him.

Inside, the light was dim and it took a minute for his eyes to adjust. He was now in a room, the size of which he could not guess because of the dim lighting. There was a fire glowing in a huge fireplace on the far wall. He saw two wingback chairs and two end tables in front of the fire. There was a lamp and an assortment of books on each of the end tables. It looked like Dracula's study. Between the two wingbacks was a beautiful marble pedestal. Leo was mesmerized; he couldn't take his eyes off of it. On the pedestal was something awesome, powerful – even magical. Leo felt pulled towards it.

The pedestal stood almost 5 feet tall. It was not unlike any other museum-quality pedestal that displays a Greek or Roman bust. This one, however, held a little glass cube with some sort of black material inside. Drawing near, he wondered if the little cube was some sort of speaker system. He knew better. It wasn't just physical sounds that mesmerized his every sense – there was indeed a metaphysical magic about the box that intoxicated him.

The sounds coming from the cube grew louder as he drew closer. It was thick and booming. Rather than plug his ears, Leo felt the need to grab his chest and brace for impact. The voices bellowed through his torso. When he was within a foot of the cube, he saw the dark material inside the glass. It was pitch black, yet somehow shone with specks of light, as though he was looking top-down on the entire cosmos from far away. A light, similar to black light, was being emitted from what he assumed was a very rare gem. The glass box itself was nine inches by nine inches, on all sides, and the speckled black material inside occupied most of the available space.

He looked closely and realized the material was pulsing. It actually seemed to expand and contract involuntarily. Now his nose was inches from the box and an aroma hit his senses too. At this proximity, the noises started playing on Leo in strange ways. Although hard to explain, it was like the musical elements of rhythm, beat, and harmony also carried emotional elements such as majesty, wonder, and suspicion. The deep-throated bellowing of earth-shaking voices also delivered power, persuasion, and force. Between the audible and emotional highs and lows was a complex mix of the stuff of ordinary life. If not for the unintelligible language, it was like the cacophony of the box represented the entirety of Leo's life.

Leo lightly sniffed the air. *What was that?* He could not identify it, but it was like a full menu of awful aromas. He breathed in the rather poignant smell of rot and garbage to try and identify it. As he inhaled, the air interacted with his psyche in a pure and life-giving way. He held his breath and suddenly felt an overwhelming sense of joy and elation, the likes of which he'd never experienced before. When he couldn't hold his breath any longer, he exhaled, and the aftertaste left a sour rank in his sinuses that caused him to sputter and spit.

After regaining his composure, he stood there in a suspended state. His desire to once again inhale that blissful scent fought against his resolve to never exhale that rot again. The competing desires left him stupidly statuesque for a full minute. He might have remained there for some time had it not been for a sudden interruption.

"What are you doing in here, Leonardo Khalpana, son of Fedot?"

Leo jerked his head around, trying to identify the source of the voice. He couldn't tell. It was as though the voice came from inside him. Finally, he answered, "Um, yes. Sorry. I was um, looking for the lavatory." He said it and rolled his eyes in mockery of himself. *What a stupid excuse.*

In the dimly lit room, little else was visible. In fact, the glow of the fire was all that illuminated his surroundings.

"Indeed," replied the voice, toned for playful skepticism.

From the dim, a man approached. He was an older gent, early 70's or even 80's. He had a short beard, and wore casual jeans and an un-tucked button-up shirt. Apart from his casual attire, Leo saw fierce seriousness in his face and eyes. His jawline was tight, as if he was biting down, and his eyes darted around in his head. He looked like a nervous fellow.

Though his mouth did not move, he said, "why is it that you decided to come into this room?"

Leo looked around. *Who is talking to me?* He thought.

"There's nobody here but me, Mr. Khalpana. Look at me." Leo turned back to face the man who now stood before him. The man continued speaking, though his mouth did not move. "In this room, we speak with extrasensory perception. When you have a deliberate thought, I can hear it as though it were audible, and when I have a deliberate thought, you can hear it the same way. Try it."

How is this possible?

The old man managed a slight upturn at the corners of his lips and looked at the glass box. "It's possible because we have this curious little item here. Not everyone has the gift of hearing it. In fact, you are only the second person who's ever heard the sounds from beyond. Do you like it?"

I do. It was as though the box was calling to me...

"Yes, it does that. The black matter called to me too, when I was in the deep."

Who are you?

"I'm Abdullah Kahn."

Leo looked puzzled. In the dark room he could not see the man's face very well.

"Come close. Look at me."

Leo leaned toward the man and looked at him by the glow of the fire. He saw the nose, eyes, and mouth that he remembered. However, Kahn had aged tremendously from the time Leo last glimpsed his face; he now looked rather decrepit, even frail, compared to what he should have looked like. There were scars around the crown of his head too, terrible, ugly scars. *It is you...* he thought.

"I aged quicker these past few months because of health, among other things. But I have been called to a mission greater than me, greater than any one individual. These days I rarely show my face. But my mission was set before me, and it requires only that I find the king at last."

Abdullah managed a full smile and gestured for Leo to sit. He had not yet used audible speech, and Leo wondered if he even could. Once seated in front of the fire, Abdullah leaned back, closed his eyes, and started speaking telepathically again.

"I have these parties, and I invite guests who I believe may be the key to the great questions of our human race. I invite the world's elite, and the offspring of the world's elite, to my home. I then put my box on a pedestal behind a closed door and sit in the dark, waiting for someone to come in. I've been doing this for months; three, sometimes four parties a week."

What is it? Leo used his mind to ask as he looked at the artifact.

"I cannot answer that right now, but you will know soon enough. I have a partnership that I must consult. When we so choose, we will contact you for further evaluation. I will tell you this – the black matter speaks only to a person of destiny. It ignores insignificant people. The fact that the box spoke to you means you are a man of significance. And this significance is much larger than you could possibly understand."

I want to be significant. I hope to be significant. No sooner had he thought it, he looked sheepishly at Mr. Kahn, realizing that his thoughts were heard loud and clear. The old man took no notice.

"We live in a changing world, son," Kahn continued. "We live in a world that sleeps on the eve of a final reckoning, where tired geo-political barriers will soon be erased forever. Mankind will not hold command over how the planet is appropriated next, but a king will preside." Abdullah looked at him with a hot gaze that sent a chill up Leo's spine.

"Go. Go back to Ali and the party. In a minute, my Hand will announce that I have come ill and will not be attending, and he will ask the party to move to the pool house. There will be live music and an open bar, and you are welcome to stay as long as you like."

Abdullah struggled to his feet, picked up the cube and cradled it like a newborn, turned, and shuffled back to the darkness from where he came. For Leo, the sounds of the cube drew faint, then vanished altogether. He stood up and waited a minute, trying to wrap his mind around what just happened. *Can you still hear me?* He thought, emphatically.

There was no answer.

CHAPTER 5
A Peaceful Drive Home

Tuesday August 16 2011

Rather than fly, they decided the young attorney would drive. Airline surveillance and airport security were a perceived risk, so Father Abelemy used his 'resources' to anonymously rent a midsize from a local Enterprise. It was a 13-hour drive back to DC, but frankly, Solomon was looking forward to it. He needed time to think. He needed some perspective.

He parted ways with Father Abelemy and hit the road. Sully was eastbound on the Interstate by 8:45 am. Though he started strong, he hit the wall by lunchtime. He was just too exhausted. On the southwest side of Indianapolis, he saw a sign marking a Holiday Inn Express. It was only a few miles ahead, just off route 267. *Perfect.*

He made it to the hotel in one piece and lumbered into the lobby. He paid the pimple-faced teenager with a pre-paid VISA the Father had given him. After finding his room, he plopped on the bed and fell asleep. He didn't even take off his pants.

When he opened an eye, the bedside clock read 5:18 pm. Solomon closed the eye and resolved to get at least eight more hours of sleep. A minute later, he sat up hungry. He walked to the window and opened the drapes. *Ouch.* He squinted tight as the bright afternoon sun assaulted his senses. He heard the AC busting hard in the background and noticed the area between the windowpane and curtain was sweltering. It had been a very hot day in Indianapolis. He stretched and walked over to the backpack that Dotty gave him and started removing the contents. Now that his mind was rested, he wanted a fresh inventory of his belongings.

Dotty had given him a pre-paid VISA loaded with $1,000. *I have $840 left after gas, food, and room. Say, $800 after dinner tonight.*

He also had a change of clothes, casual off-the-rack stuff from a Target department store. There was $120 in cash, a mini toothbrush and toothpaste, and a pre-paid TracFone with its battery removed and taped to the back. It was only for an emergency call to Dotty.

Finally the Father had given Sully an index card with an address and key code to a five-bedroom house in Edgewater, Maryland, south of Annapolis off Hwy 2. It was some kind of "safe house". Somewhere he could go if things got real weird.

"Use the place if things get dicey," Father Abelemy said. "It's totally secure – a buried resource we haven't used in a decade or more. There is an employee who comes by on Fridays to clean and keep up the yard. She won't ask questions if someone is staying there. If you ask her to leave, she will. That's part of her protocol. As soon as you have the chance, memorize the address and key code, and destroy the card."

Sully recalled some of the other pointers from Father Abelemy. "Remember, the safe house and the pre-paid cell are all just precautions. Actually, driving instead of flying was probably overkill. My assessment of this situation is that the Phantoms don't know about you, or don't care about you, and that's based on everything you've told me. Best thing for you to do is keep your head on a swivel and don't change your routines too much. If you're used to living hard and open, keep doing so. If you're a homebody, be a homebody. Changes in routine make people watching you – if they are watching you – suspicious. If you see something really strange, don't hesitate to make for Edgewater. Stock up on a little cash, and get a couple more pre-paids, just in case. Throw them in a little pack with a few personal items and go back to your life as a lawyer. But remember, if you ever do bail, leave everything but that pack behind. That definitely includes your phone, computer, and any other electronic devices."

He meandered to the bathroom for a quick shower. He noticed how cut-up he was along his left shoulder and both forearms, likely a result of the mad dash though the forest. His muscles ached a little, but other than that, he'd came through physically unscathed. *A lot more unscathed than Jasper,* he thought, and felt the twinges of guilt and anger resurface.

The mild-tempered CIA spook had given some direction about Jasper's wife as well: "You absolutely cannot reach out to her. My people will have the cab company's logs changed to reflect two cars dispatched, and two cars picking you and Jasper up at 5:20 am sharp. One took you to the airport and the other dropped him at his home. If she contacts you, be concerned, but affirm that he climbed into a cab at the same time as you. United's logs will be altered as well. They will reflect that you were on your DC flight as scheduled. This is all we can do for now, until we know more. It's not fair, but it's necessary."

After brushing his teeth, he slid into his new underwear, jeans, and a black t-shirt from Target. *Crazy how a shower and clean clothing can make anyone feel better about life.*

The sun was still high and hot. He grabbed the $10 pair of sunglasses he bought at a gas station near Marshall, and drove his rental car two blocks to a Japanese restaurant called 'Narita.' The place was busy, so he sat at the bar, where he sucked down a Sapporo and some so-so raw fish.

After dinner, he went back to the hotel and used the in-room phone to call Leola's office at the *Times* for the third time that day. She answered this time, "Leola Durand."

"Hey, it's me."

"Hi baby! Enjoying your trek across the US of A? I got your message earlier." Leola sounded genuinely happy to hear from him. He liked that.

"I am, sort of. I just wanted to call and make sure you got the message."

"Yep. Sure did. I'm curious about the family and all, but I'll save you from being pumped full of questions about it just yet."

"Thanks. I mean that."

"So, where are you?"

"I'm at a Holiday Inn outside Indianapolis."

"Wow." There was a pause. "Pacing yourself?"

"No," Solomon chuckled. "I just had a really late night. Actually, I didn't sleep at all last night, so I didn't get too far on the first leg."

"You didn't sleep, so then you decide to forego the flight and drive instead?" The twinge of agitation was obvious.

"Yeah, well, I'm not getting into it now, but I'll give you a play-by-play when I get there tomorrow. My plan is to get up around 5 and hit the road early. I should be back by 2 or 3 in the afternoon. You wanna get dinner together?"

"That'd be great. Wanna do the usual?" Any agitation was gone. Leola wasn't one to hold a grudge.

"It's a date. I'll meet you there. 8:30 work?"

"Yep. I'll call ahead and make a reservation."

"Okeydokey. I guess I'm going to get some shut-eye then."

There was a pause before she responded, "Baby?"

"Yeah?"

"Are you okay?"

"Of course, why?"

"I dunno. Just have a feeling. We don't need to get into it, but you'd tell me if something was wrong, right?"

"Of course. It's all gonna make more sense to you when we can sit down and talk tomorrow. I'll see you in, what, 24 hours, right?"

"Yes, 24 hours."

"I love you Leola. Sleep tight."

"You too."

Guilt gnawed at him a bit as he dropped the phone into its cradle. He didn't like keeping things from her, but a hotel phone in Indianapolis was not the place to start a conversation about what happened in Alton.

He found the remote control and turned on the television. He scrolled the on-screen menu until he found one of the cable news channels. The O'Reilly Factor was about mid-point on Fox, so he left it there. However, his mind was elsewhere. He thought about Father Abelemy and wondered again why he opted to keep Malcolm's lab journal a secret from him. It had been a spontaneous decision, one that in hindsight seemed foolish. *Father Abelemy, full of surprises,* he thought, chuckling to himself.

Dotty was in his early fifties and still rather fit. He was of Greek origin so his dark olive skin gave off an aura of vitality and health. He had thinning black hair, bushy eyebrows, and a cool, islander-type demeanor about life. Sully was certain the old spook couldn't run or jump like the younger field operatives, so he marveled at his longevity in an industry that requires such a sharp mind, body and spirit. *He has to be good at what he does, or he'd be pushing paper in an office somewhere at Langley.* Sully felt a bit reassured, even empowered. *I've got a Greek Orthodox Rambo covering my back.*

Even though he was tired, he had a hard time falling asleep. The bed was comfortable enough, but crazy thoughts kept coming in rapid succession. To fight the anxiety, Sully thought about Leola. Then his mind wandered to his rag-tag band of accomplices – the "paralegals" he employed back at Keys & Associates.

Phil "Rooter" Patchouli was a 46-year-old retired private investigator of Italian descent. Sully hired him in 2006 when he needed some shady material brought to light in a case outside the regular comfort zone. Rooter got his nickname from Sully when it became clear that Phil would stop at nothing to uncover the foul truth. His talents for slight espionage and "rooting about" for answers in the underground were amazing. This man was every bit the stereotypical P.I. He had greasy black hair, a goatee, and always wore a Hawaiian shirt, which was normally unbuttoned too far, exposing his hairy barrel chest. He was a hefty man and carried most of his excess in the neck and shoulders. By comparison, his legs were oddly small. He could be foul-mouthed at times, with a tendency to go overboard in social situations, but he was easily Sully's best friend. Lowbrow character traits aside, one thing was undeniable, he was the most loyal guy on the planet.

Though a Catholic, Rooter stopped associating with what he called "good Catholics" after his third divorce. Marriage never agreed with him. Under his own perceived failure to meet the minimum expectations of piousness within the parish, he now saw himself as a "bad Catholic," and wore that badge with honor. Ironically, he wore that badge while working on some of the biggest "freedom of religious expression" cases in the country.

Sully's second paralegal was known as "Con." He was a 27-year-old, African American, super-computer-whiz, who became indispensable to the team after a 2007 case involving illegal surveillance against a Keys & Associates client. Con performed a slight hack against the hackers, which locked the case for the "good guys." Con was truly brilliant and only Sully knew his real name. Most assumed his nickname came from his slightly underground past in computer hacking and whistleblowing. However, Sully knew it came from the Latin word, *Conscientia* – meaning, "knowledge." Actually, never had a double entendre nickname been more appropriate.

Con was a skinny man with a medium-length afro. For the most part, he was quiet. Occasionally, if the opportunity presented itself, he could deliver a zinger, but he preferred to stay away from the office gossip and nonstop jazz that went back and forth between Rooter and the others. Con's favorite place was 'under the headset,' lost in his own world, jamming on his expensive computer system, doing god knows what. He understood algorithms, filters, and codes. Given enough time, he could always figure out how to manipulate proprietary applications. Outside of work, he ran with a shadowy crew of computer geeks. Unknown for sure, Sully suspected a loose affiliation with Anonymous.

The fourth and final member of the team was Annette Boyle, a 26-year-old blonde from the Midwest. Although she could play the girl-next-door, she knew her way around the legal world. In fact, she could match brainpower with Solomon in many areas, including, most importantly, legal research. Anny graduated from the University of Kansas School of Law and passed the Bar in her home state. Although 'lawyer' wasn't her formal role at Keys & Associates, Sully occasionally needed the extra coverage in the courtroom for a double-booked hearing or motion. The relationship worked great.

However, Anny's value to K&A extended beyond her legal acumen. Often in DC, the more access you have to the back room, the more you really understand about what's happening in the headlines. Rooter and Con were nowhere 'swanky' enough to get behind-the-scenes access to the heavy hitters in and around the Beltway. However, this is where Anny excelled. She was smart, quick on her feet, and loved playing the slightly dumb socialite for sensitive information. She was good at it. And she had the body to match.

While Anny was willing to use her looks for attention and access, she held fast to a strong moral position about not crossing a line her "daddy in Kansas would disapprove of." She often reminded the K&A crew that she never had sex in the pursuit of Solomon's coveted information, and she never would. Frankly, she didn't have to. She was *that* good.

Solomon started drifting off to sleep. He loved his K&A team. They were fast, loyal, and enjoyed their work. They made coming to the office fun. Sure, Rooter and Anny fought like siblings, but they never held a grudge. Sure, Rooter's behavior often bordered on sexual harassment, but Anny never even thought about complaining. To an outsider, there was some obvious dysfunction. To Solomon, he had the dream skillset for a boutique law firm in DC. Together, they were a band of four who could chase any case, crack any code, and challenge any opponent. Most importantly, each of them knew the team had their back.

CHAPTER 6
We Are In this Together

Wednesday August 17, 2011

Solomon got the call he was expecting from Jasper's wife during dessert at *Urbana*, a contemporary fusion restaurant he and Leola adored. He had no desire to answer the phone, but knew that if he ignored it, he could arouse unnecessary suspicion. Reluctantly, he excused himself and took the call.

Taking a call during dinner was not unusual, nor did it bother Leola, whose dark complexion looked dazzling in the soft light of the restaurant. She smiled at him as he apologized and stepped away. She was with a lawyer after all, and knew that untimely conversations of a confidential nature were part of the package. As a journalist, she was also beginning to develop a hefty Rolodex of sources and informants, so she also took calls at inopportune times. It was a mutual understanding.

She was a confident, sassy woman of mixed ethnic background. As soon as her man stepped away, predictably, the wandering eyes of male patrons found her sitting alone. She didn't really mind, unless the stare came from someone wearing a wedding band. That peeved her like nobody's business. Having come straight from work, she wore a classy skirt and top. Her hair was up, showing off a pair of dangly, sparkly, expensive-looking earrings.

In an act of defiance aimed at two middle-aged hound dogs sitting at the bar, she adjusted her posture, crossed her legs in their direction, and dismissively nibbled at her favorite sinful pleasure, *Pots du Crème*. A year or so prior, she tasted it for the first time. She grinned as she recalled promoting it to her colleagues at the paper.

"It's an *Urbana* masterpiece, if ever there was one. Dark chocolate crème, whipped hazelnut anglaise, and hazelnut biscotti. Voila." She had punctuated the sentence by dramatically kissing her fingers, "A triumph of culinary art and chocolate deific bliss. Ladies, if you never knew, now you do. Pots de Crème must be on every sane woman's bucket list, I'm just sayin'."

The waiter came by and folded Sully's napkin. Leola popped open her purse and pulled out a small mirror, more for something to do than anything else. While checking her makeup, she noticed a guy at her four-o-clock checking her out from behind. She winked. When he realized she made him, he looked away embarrassed.

She laughed and shook her head. Men are so predictable.

Leola only stood 5'5" but always wore stilettos, so not everybody knew she was that short. She had a thin waist, full-breasted front, an oval-shaped face and deep, engaging brown eyes. It all came together under her magnetic personality and over-the-top flair for the dramatic. Maybe her most attractive characteristic was that Leola liked Leola. She was proud of herself; proud of whom she had become both socially and professionally. She had the unique ability to see her shortcomings through the lens of her charm and virtue, and because of that, others did too.

When Sully returned, she could tell the phone conversation stressed him out. He was now disconnected, lost in some other place. He sometimes got this way before critical points in cases. He was good at dealing with the unforeseen, unexpected issues that invaded his life at the spur of the moment. However, he was not particularly good at dealing with matters of the heart. She wondered what was bothering him. A few minutes after his return, she tried digging a little, but immediately regretted it. Clearly, he had no intention of discussing whatever was on his mind.

Frustrations began to pile up. She had not seen him for over a week and he was purposefully vague about his time in Alton. This bothered her to some extent. She learned from past experience that pushing him too hard rarely worked in the end. She could pry, but he'd dodge. She might then get frustrated and feel like she was second-fiddle to whatever he was keeping from her, and that would often lead him to stonewall her. His emotionally blasé act would infuriate her and that's when she'd yell at him, to which he'd respond emotionally and say some things he'd later try and take back. That cycle was tested ad nauseam early in their relationship. It was not something she liked. So she decided, on this night, to let it go and live to pry another day. After dessert they left together in Leola's Toyota Camry.

Earlier that afternoon when Solomon drove into town, he went directly to his office where Rooter brought him up to speed on the Nationals ongoing sub .500 season, and a new gal-pal he had met at the local bar. "Yeah boy, haven't got her in the sack yet, but the Rooter's a rootin', know what-a mean?" Anny's expression had been priceless. She glared at him with a disgusted look as Sully nodded his understanding and put a hand up as a gesture, saying, *Too Much Information.*

"I just threw up in my mouth," Anny muttered, before turning her attention to the boss, "Now that the important updates have been delivered, you want to hear about the Willow Canyon case, or would you prefer I drop it in an email?"

Rooter knew that was his cue, so he stood up, stretched his back, and left the room with a middle-finger salute in her direction for good measure. Sully shook his head in amusement. What love! He missed his K&A team.

"No, I'll take it. I got some time to kill…"

Rooter and Anny left work at around 5:15 pm. He heard them bickering until their voices faded from earshot. Con, who said precious little since the boss returned, was still under the influence of his headset, jamming away on the keyboard of his 'super rig.' Sully had only seen him take the headset off once to use the restroom; the evidence of it was a permanent indention in his otherwise frizzy hair. He was clearly in the zone.

Con was oblivious to his presence in the building, so the attorney took the book he liberated from Malcolm's study and began making photocopies of each page. After finishing, he folded the loose pages and put them in his back pocket, grabbed his backpack, and shoved the book back in. It was nearly 6 pm, so he said goodbye to Con (who did not answer him, but might have put a hand up, Sully wasn't sure) and drove to Reagan Airport and returned his rental car. He took the Metro to the Bank of America on the south side of Dupont Circle, just two buildings from *Urbana*. At the bank, he was relieved to find that safety deposit box access and rental was 24-7. He promptly rented a box and surrendered the book. By this time, it was almost quarter past 8, so Sully meandered over to the restaurant. He found an open barstool and ordered a Hendricks & Tonic while he waited for Leola. She walked in about five minutes later.

After dinner, the couple drove to the valet at the Colombia Plaza Apartments and walked into the main lobby of the residence. The on-duty officer was Willis, who greeted them both by name. As the couple was about to get on the elevator, Willis called to them, "Oh, Mr. Keys. I have a message for you. 9:55 am, this morning, a gentleman caller came by asking to see you. He was told you were not in, and he asked if you had returned yet. We repeated and told him that you were not in, and he left."

"Really?" Solomon stood silent for a moment, looking at Willis blankly. The elevator opened, and then closed again. "Who was on duty this morning?"

"Bill Jackson, sir."

"Bill say anything else?"

"Sir, he did. He told me the man was peculiar. What was the word he used…? Flat. He said the man had a flat affect, and that he never seen him before. He was tall too, around 6-foot-8." Yep. That's about it."

"Okay, thanks Willis. Bill in tomorrow?"

"Yessir, he is. 8 am, sharp."

"Okay then, goodnight Willis, and thanks for the message." Sully waved goodnight as the elevator dinged and opened a second time.

"My pleasure sir. Welcome home."

When they got into the apartment she grabbed his face and kissed him. It turned into a long kiss, a passionate kiss. Sully felt her body through the blouse. He'd missed this. Then, abruptly, she pulled away, cupped his cheeks, looked into his eyes and said, "I'm glad you're home, but you're not off the hook. I want to know how Alton went, but it can wait until tomorrow. I'm going to bed."

With that, she turned and walked back toward the bedroom. Sully followed a few seconds later, a bit dejected. He knew this one was on him. Had he been just a little more forthcoming about his time in Alton, their clothes might have been littered across the floor that very instant. Now, best case, he'd have to wait for tomorrow. It might have been worth it though, the more he thought about it.

Simply, he was unsure about what to disclose and what to hide. The long drive from St. Louis only confused him more. He did not want to worry her unnecessarily, but he also did not want her to be caught off guard should his brief history in Alton catch up to him. What's more, he couldn't help but wonder about his safety, and by extension, hers.

And who came and asked about me today? That's weird. Who knew I was supposed to get home this morning? It wasn't one of my crew. They would have mentioned something at the office. And last time I looked, they were all far short of 6'8".

Sully put the photocopies of the book in a large envelope. He walked to the desk in the corner of the bedroom and tossed the envelope in the top left drawer.

"What's that?" she asked as she brushed her teeth.

"Oh, these? Just some docs from the office." She nodded and walked back toward the master bathroom. He undressed to his boxers in their walk-in closet. He was tired, happy to be home, and ready for his own bed. It had been a long few days, and even though he was anxious about the news from Willis downstairs, his exhaustion won. He fell asleep almost the instant his head hit the pillow.

Sully woke up to the sounds and smells of a hot breakfast. Thursday, August 18, 2011, started for Sully at 7:52 am. *Any day that starts with bacon and eggs is poised to be a great one,* he thought as he threw on a t-shirt and walked into the kitchen. Leola was also wearing one of his t-shirts. It came half way down her bare thighs.

"Good morning," she said and leaned in for a quick kiss. "You sleep okay?"

"Yeah," he said, stretching. "I think I slept hard. Body feels a bit stiff."

"Probably that long drive." She reached for the island countertop and grabbed that morning's *Times*. "Page six, 'Investigating S&P', the article I was telling you about."

Sully nodded, took the paper and sat down at the kitchen table. She poured a mug of coffee and brought it to him. They chitchatted until the eggs, toast, and bacon were ready. They each grabbed a plate of food and moved to their private balcony overlooking the Potomac River. The morning was bright and already hot. The sounds were those of DC waking up to another day. During breakfast, Sully gave what he felt was a satisfactory account of his mother's funeral and his interactions with the family from North Illinois. He even tackled the reason he was distraught after taking the phone call at *Urbana*.

"I was quiet because Jasper, evidently, never went home that morning. I'm worried something might have happened to him… and his wife, poor thing, sounded terrified and exhausted." He did not like lying, but until he knew how much to disclose, it would have to do.

To his thankful surprise, his girl never did ask why he opted to drive home instead of fly, or why he had no suitcase, or why he was so vague about his ordeal, or why he never slept the day before his drive. She just sat in her chair, knees at her chest, sipping her coffee and listening quietly.

After breakfast Sully excused himself and rode the elevator down to the security desk where he intended to ask Bill Jackson a few questions about yesterday's visitor. Random residents galloped through the lobby toward the Valet pickup stand, en route to their workplace. The employees were typically friendly, and greeted the people by name as they hurried past. On his final approach to the security desk, Sully caught a glimpse of one neighbor emerging from the elevator with her dog on a leash. Ms. Appleton was a single, middle-aged lady who liked to meddle. She was the prototypical busybody, and Sully avoided her at all costs. He turned his back and hoped she'd pass by without noticing him. An employee who was wiping down the business desk saw his reaction to her and grinned at him.

"Mornin' Sully." William Jackson IV said with a smile. "Welcome home. I trust your trip was good."

"Good morning, Bill. Yes, it was fine. Thanks." Sully shook the security guard-turned-old-friend's hand. "Say, Willis mentioned I had a caller yesterday and that you interacted with him."

"Yes, odd fella. What do you want to know?"

"Did you catch a name?"

"Tried, he just looked at me, odd like, if you know what I mean." Sully stood, puzzled. Bill did his best impersonation of the man and gawked at Solomon with his lips pressed together to a point. "He spoke clear, but he was not friendly. He had an accent, but I couldn't place it. He wore dark sunglasses, jeans, and a long-sleeve shirt and a light jacket, like a golfer's windbreaker. That was strange, cuz you know how hot it was yesterday."

"What else?" Sully asked.

"I don't know, let me think." The guard squeezed his eyes for a second, "He wore a black ball cap, I think. He was a tall dude too. Willie mention that? Goin' on 7-foot, maybe. Wasn't no rail either, had some meat on his bones."

"Ok. What was he? Black? White?"

"Hell if I know. He looked sort of like a white guy, I guess. Hairy too. He had dark hair, I think." Bill paused again, "Look, everything about this chap was strange. His skin was closer to pinkish than it was white. He had meat on his bones, but his cheeks were sunken. He was clean-shaved, but almost like he had a smaller than normal face – like it didn't fit well on his big frame. He spoke clear enough, but his mannerisms were weird. When he heard things in the entry area, he kinda twitched toward the sound, like sounds startled him. But these were general lobby sounds, the type of thing you always hear, not as though someone dropped a lead pipe or anything."

"Ok." Sully shook his head and smiled, "I swear, I can't place this guy. Anything else you can remember?"

"That's it." Bill put his right hand over his heart in a gesture of humility and apology and said, "Sully, I'm terribly sorry I didn't get more. He wouldn't give a name and I tried to get him to leave you a message, but he looked at me like he didn't know what a phone was. I swear. This dude was a bit super-freak."

"Nah, it's fine," Sully smiled. "We'll ID him soon enough, and maybe we can all have a laugh about it when we do. It's probably Bilford from the DA's office. That dude is tall and a bit of a super-freak, as you call it."

They laughed and exchanged a few other pleasantries before Sully was back in the elevator. Alone, his pulse began racing. The elevator opened and he walked the hallway to his apartment, remembering the Father's words… *"If you see something strange, get to Edgewater." Does this constitute something strange? Am I being hyper-sensitive?*

He reentered the apartment and heard the shower running in the master bathroom. *Good, she's taking a shower and I need to think. This has to be about that goddamned book.*

He walked to his desk and pulled opened the top left drawer, but the envelope containing the copies was gone. He opened the other drawers, wondering if he misplaced them, but the copies were definitely gone. His nerves were on-edge. He started to panic.

Where were the copies? He scanned the room frantically. He went to the walk-in closet and found yesterday's jeans in the hamper. He checked the pockets, but no photocopies. In Leola's hamper he noticed his shirt, the one she wore at breakfast. Something was odd about that, but he couldn't place it. He was about to interrupt her shower and ask if she saw where he put the copies, when his phone rang. It was his office.

"Hello?"

"It's Rooter, bud. Got some bad news."

"What? I'm busy," Solomon said, as he checked the nightstand.

"Yeah, well, you may wanna get down here boss. Place was broke into last night."

With those words, Rooter sent everything in Solomon's world into hyper-drive. Everything that happened during the last few days, especially those involving Jasper and Dotty, pin-balled around in his head. His mind began concocting wild contingencies. A blitz of questions overwhelmed him. "What? Where? I mean, how do you know?"

"Yeah. I'm the only one here, but it looks like whoever came in was diggin' through your desk and files, lookin' for something." Rooter paused and Sully could hear him rummaging around the office. "Strange though boss, looks like they didn't take anything of value."

"Look, Rooter, you gotta get out of the office and wait for me. I don't want you to call the cops just yet. I have a hunch I know who did this, but I want to talk to you about it when I get there. Just hang out on the docks and keep the others out of the boathouse 'till I get there, will you?"

"Yeah, sure thing boss."

"Ok, see you in a few." They hung up.

Sully pulled his hands though his hair. Now he was sure this all constituted 'strange' according to Father Abelemy's warnings. *Ok, think Sully. Think. They went through the office trying to find the book. They weren't able to find it because it's in the safety deposit box. I can't find the copies. Did they take the copies? Wait, were they in the apartment last night?*

Slowly now, Solomon walked back into his walk-in closet and grabbed his Beretta PX4 from its case on the shelf. Cla-Click – *that's odd*, he thought, as a 9mm cartridge flipped out of the chamber when he pulled back the slide. That meant he kept one in the chamber after the last visit to the shooting range – something he never did. He started checking the bedroom and looked under the bed. Then, more frantically, he went to every hiding place he could imagine. Then he advanced to the kitchen, then the living room. He checked the balcony and the front door locking mechanism. All was normal, operational, and everything seemed fine. *Am I losing my mind? But where are the damn copies!* Sully's head started beating like a drum.

"Honey! You see where I put those photocopies I brought home last night?" Leola had been suspicious of him, so maybe she took them and grabbed a peek after he fell asleep. Not waiting for an answer, he looked through the pile of mail on the kitchen counter.

"Hun? You hear me?" Agitation was obvious in his tone. When again he didn't get an answer he walked back to the master bathroom and opened the door.

"Honey, did you hear me?" No answer. He ripped opened the shower curtain.

Leola was on her back, slinked into the tub, naked, with startled eyes wide open as the water spray cascaded down onto her face. She was shot – twice in the chest and once between the eyes. With a gaping mouth she stared back at Solomon, emotionless. There was little blood because of the running water.

Sully's knees gave way. He fell forward, lost his breath, and started hyperventilating under the weight of shock. A few seconds later, he just screamed uncontrollably. He reached for her and cradled her head, the water soaking his shirt from above. He slapped at the handle and shut it off.

"Baby. Baby, no. No, no, no," he whispered through clenched teeth, pawing and wiping the water off her face and neck. "Come on. No, no, baby please, you're okay. You're gonna be okay."

His mind knew she was gone, but his heart forced the issue. He tried in vain to rouse her. He searched for a hopeful sign even as he talked and shook her gently, but nothing. When hope lapsed altogether, he screamed again and started crying. When the desperation hit a second time, he tried to sit her up, as if sitting her up would bring her back. His crying turned to wailing. Nothing going on in his mind was coherent; everything was a manic reaction to the shock and confusion that assaulted his every sense.

Before he knew it, his breakfast came up like water from a fire hydrant. He lunged for the toilet and made it just in time. Tears, snot and vomit all surfaced at once. He was out of control. In that instant, Solomon was a mad man. Between heaves he screamed with unintelligible groans and moans.

Some time passed before he finally pushed away from the toilet and went back to his precious Leola. His stomach was settled a bit, but his eyes were bloodshot and wild looking. He picked up the Beretta. With sick dismay, he now knew why the gun was chambered. He racked the slide of the semi-automatic handgun back and counted as each rack dispelled another bullet. *Nine, ten, eleven, empty. Fifteen round mag. Bullet twelve is on the floor of the walk-in; thirteen and fourteen are in Leola's chest and fifteen is in her head. My God, they used my gun to kill her.* Rage welled-up. His breathing got louder and more deliberate. *What evil is hunting me?*

Though the shock wore off, Sully found it hard to keep his composure. His mind was going all sorts of dark directions. His cell phone rang and pulled him out of the shadows. It was Rooter again. He checked the time and it was now 10:12 am. He decided not to answer. Instead, he went to the backpack and found the TracFone he got from Dotty. He loaded the battery, turned it on and called the Father instead.

"Oh no, this can't be good," is how Dotty answered the call. Sully couldn't manage a response at first. "Ey, Sully. You there?"

"Yes," He finally managed, in a raspy voice.

"Ok. What happened? You at the place?"

"No."

"Stand by buddy. I'm going to call you right back with another phone."

A minute or two passed. Sully wiped away another stream of tears. *I didn't protect her. I let her die. Why didn't I tell her the whole story? Why didn't I warn her?* Self-accusation flooded his senses. He walked to the linen pantry and pulled out a sheet. In the shower he draped it over his lovely Leola. Again, he lost his composure and felt weak at the knees.

The TracFone rang six minutes later. Sully answered it, sniffling slightly, but holding it back. "This channel is clear. What happened?" Father Abelemy strained.

"They killed my girlfriend. They did it with my handgun, and they left her in the tub. It happened while I was in the lobby talking to the security guard. I wasn't gone for ten minutes."

"Shit. Ok. Ok. I'm so sorry Sully. Really I am." The Father paused for a moment and listened to his friend struggle to contain his emotions. "Bud, I need to be frank and this may not be easy for you, but you have to listen carefully. Tell me when you're ready."

Sully took a deep breath and left the bathroom. "Ok, give me a sec."

He put the phone down and walked out on the balcony to get some air. He came back two minutes later and picked up the phone, "You still there?"

"Yes. You OK?"

"I'm okay."

"We need to keep this brief. Who can you trust Sully? You need help and I can't be there for a day or two."

"I trust Rooter." Sully said, quietly.

"That filthy-mouthed PI I met that one time? Really?" The words just came out and after they did, the Father felt bad. "Um, sorry about that, just surprised me is all, that Rooter is your trusted first choice."

"The guy has got his hands pretty dirty for me in the past. I trust him with my life. Are you saying I shouldn't now?"

"No, nothing like that. It's fine. Listen, do we know it was the Phantoms who did this?" The Father knew this would upset him, but he had to ask.

"No, it was her editor!" he retorted with rage, "Of course it was."

"Ok, take it easy. How do you know?"

"Same thing as what you said at breakfast. Two to the chest and one to the head." Solomon's words tapered off at the end.

"Ok then, listen. You need to get Rooter over to your apartment. Call me when he gets there and we'll go from there."

"Okay."

"Sully?"

"Yes."

"I'm not going to tell you a joke. You're going through hell right now and it would be inappropriate. But I will tell you this. We're in this together. It's important that you know that and not lose hope. Whatever's going on is much larger than you or me. I can't get into it, but I think it's bigger than even our nation. We've stumbled into the hornets' nest and we need to stay focused, stay calm, and keep a clear head. Under the circumstances, I know that sounds uncaring and insane. But do this, and we'll get through it together. Okay?"

"Okay." Dotty's frankness was somehow soothing, and brought Solomon a sense of comfort. Part of the agony of that moment was in the randomness of the Phantom's actions. That there was some rhyme and reason to what was going on; even though he didn't know what it was yet, brought some relief and stability to his senses.

"Call me right away when your crazy friend gets there."

"I will," he said, and disconnected the call. Before he could do anything, Sully needed a drink of water. He had a terrible case of cottonmouth and the onset of a pounding headache was inevitable. Under an exhausted posture, he slowly walked to the kitchen and filled a glass of water, and took it down with a single shot.

CHAPTER 7
We Got It

Thursday, August 18, 2011

The Hand of Kahn boldly opened the door and stepped into the billiards room, where Abdullah was sitting with the outspoken environmentalist and clean energy advocate, Robert Hayes. His interruption was not inappropriate, and it irked Abdullah enough that he purposefully ignored the pale associate, and carried on with his guest.

The two were enjoying a mid-afternoon smoke and some casual conversation. Hayes was there for an environmental recap meeting with participants from the 2011 Rio+20 Summit. Kahn was there because he was a heavy-handed gambler who had succumbed to the pressures applied by his MGM Grand Casino Host.

A $10k per hand blackjack player, Abdullah carried a two-million dollar marker with the Casino. In the business of high-stakes gambling, the Casino Host is to the player, as grapes are to wine. Without the host, the player is anobody, regardless of how much money he might spend on the green felt. It's the host's job to assess the player's worth to the casino, and sell the casino's value to the player. Abdullah was considered a top-echelon guy, so it was right that the MGM sent the Cessna to pick him up, "comp" his villa for a seven-night stay, and give him front-and-center access to whatever show or event he wished to attend.

Though he was on vacation, and though the temperature outside was pushing 115 degrees, Abdullah shunned the idea of short-pants and sandals in public. He was much too important to dress like a tourist. Only in the protective confines of his private pool would he ever dare going shirtless.

On this occasion, Kahn wore a patterned blazer and brown slacks. His button-up was loose at the collar and his expensive shoes were made of soft, two-tone leather; what he called his 'Vacation Treads'. Such was his version of casual. Hayes looked touristy by comparison, wearing a nice pair of khaki shorts, shoes, and a polo-style shirt made of thick-thread cotton. The Polo caused Kahn to grimace when Hayes first entered the Villa. *Poor Bubba.*

The Hand, still standing in the corner, finally cleared his throat to draw their attention. Kahn decided to forgive his abrupt intrusion a few minutes earlier. "What is it, hand?"

"We got it, sir."

Suddenly appearing to be stunned, Abdullah stood involuntarily, "We got it?"

"Yes sir." The Hand's thin lips curled into a prideful grin. He'd been waiting five long years for this moment.

"Jonesy," Abdullah's look was one of disbelief. "Jonesy, come have a drink with us. You've earned it."

"Yes sir, I believe I have," said Mister Jones, his words dripping with conceit.

They poured a round of Courvoisier L'Esprit and took their seats. Abdullah raised his glass, looked at his pale servant and said, "You, Jonesy. You have done it."

The Hand smiled and nodded as the men drank to his achievement, but Abdullah fell into thought and rubbed his tightly manicured, full-faced beard with his free hand. *It has been found!*

He was a handsome man in his mid-sixties. Energetic. Passionate. His hair was more salt than pepper, but nobody knew that because he colored it regularly. He even colored his eyebrows to match. His skin was the color of dark mocha, and he spoke with an eastern-European accent, though he originated from somewhere in the Middle East. Kahn's early history was a matter of intrigue. In fact, nobody knew the whole story except him. Those who might have known his tale had died long ago. In his thirties, Kahn made the choice to ditch the past and alter the course of his own destiny, and he'd certainly accomplished that.

Life was now a game to him; a game of excess and pursuit. With his excess, he pursued any rule, boundary, or status with every intention of breaking, exceeding, or resetting them accordingly.

"Hayes, you know this boy saved my life once?" Kahn leaned over and rubbed the little man's shoulder. "Yes he did. There was a very difficult event that took my late wife's life, and this one came in when I needed some guidance, at my lowest point, and he saved me."

Turning his gaze onto Mister Jones, he continued massaging his shoulder and said, "And today, you have given me immortality. You truly were a Godsend to me, my Hand." The pale man-servant gazed back at his master and the two locked eyes, not speaking.

Hayes felt like the third wheel. It was an awkward moment. So awkward in fact that he leaned forward in his chair and interrupted, "If I may, what is it you believe you've found?"

To answer the question, Abdullah turned his attention to Hayes. When he did, the Hand frowned unashamedly and drove his little fist into his own leg, as if he just lost the finals at Wimbledon. Hayes was surprised by the reaction and cocked his head. Abdullah didn't react at all.

The environmentalist found the whole scene rather creepy, but disguised his feelings and listened as Abdullah answered, "We have found a blueprint. An ancient scientific key that we think will dramatically change everything – indeed, even our lives. In it, there may be many applications, but one is atmospheric energy – free, abundant energy for the whole world." He paused and glanced at the Hand again. They shared another brief stare before Abdullah continued.

"It's a find long overdue. Robert, remember back when you worked for the Clinton administration? You used to tell me that you believed renewable energy was there, and science was on the cusp of unlocking its power and potential?"

"Yes, of course. That's why I founded Wave International. It's been my lifelong pursuit. Is it the Torus? Have you found the Torus energy field?"

"Not exactly," Abdullah sipped his drink. "I do believe this find brings us one giant step closer to it though. We could be a matter of months out."

"Really?" Hayes was stunned. The Hand smiled again, as if taking full credit for the discovery *and* Hayes' astonishment. "Really!" Hayes repeated, this time to himself, as his mind raced.

"We won't know the full extent of what we have until we conduct more investigation and analysis. Right now, the goal must be to mobilize the team, and recruit those we need."

"I understand," said Hayes. "What can I do?"

Abdullah ignored Hayes and turned back to the Hand, "Hand, is the Greek still a problem?"

"Yes, likely." The Hand sat up straight and spoke with precision. It was as though he went into key employee-mode. "Unfortunately, the final retrieval operation involved someone that the Greek is fond of – actually, the nephew of the Wizard in Iraq. Not just that, but a copy of the key is still at large, and though we do not think the Greek has it, he will certainly be looking for it."

Abdullah was visibly perturbed by the news. Hayes listened closely, but did not know what the two were talking about.

"It's these idiots all over the Hill, the Pentagon, and at Langley. I've shelled out millions to them to protect these operations, and they can't keep one inquisitive Greek asshole out of my way?"

"Perhaps," the Hand said, holding his glass an inch from his mouth, "Is it time to take Greek matters into our own hands?"

Kahn glanced at the environmentalist and was about to shut that line of talk down, as he did not fully trust Robert Hayes, when Mr. Hayes boldly piped up, "Perhaps, I can be of assistance."

Abdullah looked at Hayes with a cold stare from under his bushy eyebrows. Nobody spoke, so Hayes continued, "Administrations change, but the power brokers who run the government are the same today. Actually, much of the power structure remains even from the Carter administration. I worked in that town. I still work in that town. I know many of the real players personally. Perhaps I could deliver a message for you?"

Abdullah smiled and nodded. He then suddenly stood up and extended his glass to the overzealous environmentalist. "Mr. Hayes, perhaps I'll give that some thought and be in touch. But for now, know that we are close. Very close indeed to a world full of free, nonhazardous, abundant energy."

Hayes and the Hand both stood and the three clinked their glasses in salute to their accomplishments, and drank to their secret. Comically, though Hayes drank, he was oblivious to the secret part. He really had no idea what just happened.

After Mr. Hayes left the villa at the MGM Grand, Abdullah sat down with his trusted servant by the private pool, now dressed to swim, and gave some orders. "I think your assessment is correct. It's time to take the Greek issue into our own hands. Go ahead and take care of it." The Hand nodded.

Two young women walked out of the villa stark naked and jumped into the pool with a ruckus of giggles and splashes. The Hand smiled at them while Kahn took no notice and continued, "You said there is a copy of the key. Am I getting the original or am I getting copies?"

"Copies," the Hand responded reluctantly.

Abdullah put his head down in a gesture of disappointment. This angered him greatly. The girls splashed some water on the stone walkway near them, so Mr. Jones put up his hand in a gesture for them to calm down, not wanting the situation to worsen. Abdullah's jaw clenched and he balled his hands into fists.

"That won't do at all, will it?" he finally snarled. "I'm supposed to recruit brilliant men to join our cause, and ask them to help unlock the key to humanity's survival, with a bunch of fucking photocopies? Damn it, why does something always go wrong?"

The Hand shrugged nonchalantly, "Photocopies are better than nothing, and nothing is what we've had for the past five years."

Abdullah nodded reluctantly, as his eyes drifted to the pool. They watched the girls play for a few minutes. Their arrival had kicked up the smell of chlorine and Coppertone.

"Ok, let's do this. I want to meet the Cardinal, the General, and the Scientist next month. Keep it quiet though. Let's keep it to just those three. Set it up as early as possible." Kahn looked at his watch. "It's August 18th. I want this thing scheduled to happen before the second week of September."

The Hand nodded and said, "It will be done. Where?"

"The Vatican," Abdullah grinned. "Tell that old Roman Catholic to open up a conference room and let us heathens in."

"What about Hayes?" The Hand asked with a snicker, knowing the response he'd get.

"Please!" Kahn threw his head back in amusement. "That urchin knows people, right? He worked in the Clinton administration and that qualifies him to help us? Clearly this man has no idea who he's talking to. But he's a respected environmentalist and lobbyist who's been around the block, and we'll need him when strange things start happening. He understands energy. He understands the atmosphere. Just wait until he sees what's coming! Yup, let's keep him on the line – we'll need someone like him to communicate with the media and bureaucrats."

Abdullah paused and considered how best to keep Hayes interested, feeling important, and ready to mobilize. "Reach out in a week or so and let him know we've been able to neutralize our Greek issue, and thank him again for his offer. Ask him to develop an eyes-only list of people who share his beliefs about the Torus-design energy potential. That's enough for now."

"Okay. Anything else?"

"Yeah," he licked his lips and looked at the pool. "Give me a little privacy with these two, will ya?"

CHAPTER 8
Messy Business

Thursday, August 18, 2011

"Sully, it's about damn time. You've had us sittin' on the docks two hours already. You getting close or what?" Rooter sounded miffed. Solomon was moving as fast as he could, but found it difficult to process basic information.

"Hey, yeah, I'm sorry Rooter. Tell the others too. So, um. Well, look, I need to ask you a favor."

"Okay. What?" Rooter rolled his eyes as Anny and Con watched him from under the relentless assault the hot morning sun. They were all used to an efficient boss, one that made appointments and showed up early. This struggling, bumbling, scatterbrain replacement would not do at all.

"Can you come to my place? I need you here right now." Solomon paused, but got no response. "Ask the others to go get some coffee or lunch or both. Just tell them we'll check in later this afternoon. I don't know. Give 'em the day off maybe. It doesn't really matter. Hello?"

"Yeah, I heard you. I'll let 'em know and see ya in 20." Rooter disconnected the phone without a goodbye. That wasn't atypical.

Sully put on a fresh pot of coffee and sat at the kitchen table, fidgeting, and looking around the apartment. He glanced at the newspaper again. There was Leola's name, above the article she mentioned earlier. Tears trickled down and splotched the cheap newspaper ink.

Lobby security knew Rooter, so they let him right up. Rooter rang the doorbell, and then let himself in. "Jesus H Christ, Sully. You look like shit."

Solomon managed a wry smile. "Come on, let's sit on the balcony for a sec so I can tell you about Alton and catch you up on what the hell's going on."

Solomon delivered it all. He told Rooter about his extended family, the funeral, and even got into the details surrounding a planned estate sale. His mind was all over the place. Rather than try to keep him on task, Rooter felt obliged to sip his coffee and listen to what his distraught boss had to say. Sully got to his mom's journal entries and rattled them off in chronological order – he had nearly committed them to memory. He explained his interest in Malcolm, why he checked out of the hotel early, and how Jasper came over to help and hang out. However, when he was about to get to the gritty stuff, he stopped, refilled their coffee mugs and once they were situated again said, "Before I tell you what happened next, I need to know you are 100% loyal to me. Based on our track record together, will you support me, no matter what?"

"Yeah, course. So what happened?" Rooter waved him on. The story was picking up and Rooter had by this point, forgotten he was miffed at Sully for his absenteeism that morning.

"I'm not bull-shittin' you Rooter. I need to hear you say it." Solomon was rigid in his chair, bent slightly forward and very serious. Rooter cocked his head, feeling surprised and sobered by his boss's intensity.

"Oh man. Something bad happened, didn't it?" Solomon nodded, slowly. "Yeah boss. Yes, you can trust me and I'm with you. Now what happened?"

Solomon told him about the lab journal, the intruders, the murder, the escape, and his eventual run-in with Father Abelemy. Rooter listened intently until the Father Abelemy part, where he put up a hand and said, "Wait just a minute. You mean to tell me that goat-banger was behind all this?"

Solomon stopped to reflect on 'goat-banger', tried to wrap his mind around the insult, and then shook his head in disbelief. "Hang on. I just told you about the cold-blooded murder of my friend and your interest peaks at the mention of Father Abelemy? Do you two not like each other or something?"

Rooter sat back defensively and spread his arms, "Why you ask? That zorba-bastard say somethin'?"

"For God's sake, man!" Getting frustrated now, he raised his voice and punctuated his words, "It's not about him. The story is about me!"

"Yeah, right," Rooter gestured for his boss to calm down. "Sorry boss. Nothin' personal, just he and I never really saw eye-to-eye on things. Anyway. Continue."

Rooter lit a cigarette as Sully told him about the Father's real job with the CIA, gave some brief notes about the drive home, and then told how he made copies of the book when he got back to the office. He explained how he put the copies in a drawer in the bedroom desk. He mentioned the giant, anonymous visitor who showed up looking for him. Then he slowly recalled his visit with the security guard downstairs earlier that morning.

As he spoke, Rooter was impressed by how well he'd kept composure yesterday. He'd given no real indication that he'd undergone such a traumatic event in Alton. Rooter wondered if Sully was that good of an actor, or if he was just losing his edge. *There was a day, not too long ago, I'd have pegged that something bad happened!*

"I got back to the apartment and that's when I realized that the copies were gone. You called to tell me someone broke into our office, and that's about when I realized that someone had been here in this apartment too. At first, I figured someone must have entered while we were asleep."

Rooter's mouth was agape, as if stunned. With the hand holding his three-quarter burned cigarette, he lightly scratched the exposed area of his chest, under his mostly unbuttoned Hawaiian shirt.

"Once I was sure nobody was in the house, I called for Leola. I heard the water running, so I knew she was taking a shower. But she didn't answer." Rooter blinked with a shocked gaze as he began to put it all together. Sully shook his head in disbelief and held back some more raw emotion.

"I wa-went, went in there," he finally forced the words, but only managed a wrenching whisper, "and I found her dead. Two bullets to the chest and one between the eyes, just like what happened in Iraq, just like what happened to Jasper."

The two sat in silence for a few minutes. Rooter even felt the tug of emotion. He loved Sully, and by proxy, loved Leola too. "She…" he coughed to get his voice back, "She still in the tub, boss?"

Solomon nodded. Rooter sat still as stone and blinked. As if in slow-motion, the ash of his forgotten cigarette fell under its own weight and broke into thousands of specs on his cargo pants.

"It gets worse," Solomon's head was downcast. "Whoever did this, used my gun."

Rooter stood abruptly and knocked his chair over in the process, startling Sully. The noise of city hubbub below meshed with the faint echo of sirens in the distance. The sun was beating into the patio space and the wind was barely noticeable, so the air felt hot and muggy. "Sully, you know I love you. But I don't think that's something that I am prepared to believe right now."

"Which part?" Solomon asked without looking at his friend. The question was rhetorical. The whole story was hard to believe and Solomon knew it. He buried his face in his hands and kneaded his forehead at the hairline, as if trying to rid himself of an awful headache. "Look, I know how crazy this sounds, but I didn't vandalize our office, and the tapes will prove that. And I didn't kill my girlfriend, but you'll need to talk to Dotty for yourself. He'll tell you I'm not making this story up. Then, you'll just have to trust me."

"Why'd you call me, Solomon?"

"I called Dotty to let him know this crazy shit was happening. He told me to call one person I knew I could trust, so I called you. We're supposed to call him back."

Rooter nodded, then grinned and shook his head in disbelief, "That olive-picker freak-out a little when you told 'em I was your man?"

"Actually, you're much more of a prick than he is."

"Yeah, it's just a thing. Greeks and Italians haven't always seen eye-to-eye on stuff. If he's CIA, and he's been up on this thing from the beginning, then I'm glad he's in our corner."

"I dunno, I guess so." Sully was clearly out of it, not himself. Glancing up, he repeated, "Dotty said to call him back once you were up-to-speed. That's about as far as I've tried to figure this mess out."

Rooter pulled a pack of Reds out of his pocket and lit another cigarette. Beads of perspiration were taking over his forehead. There, standing next to his friend, he figured he had two options. Option one: He could bail out and leave his friend on a balcony alone, hopeless, and depressed. Option two: He could accept his destined role in this crazy saga and do whatever was needed to help his friend. In his heart, he knew Sully couldn't murder Leola. That just wasn't part of his genetic makeup. Though he was risking much, he decided to be the friend that Sully bet he was when he called. Two-thirds of the way through his smoke, he took a deep breath and looked at the attorney, "Okay then, let's get Yanni on the phone and see what's up."

Once inside, the TracFone was used to call Dotty. They quickly disconnected while Dotty did whatever he did to get a new connection over a secure line. When the Father called back, Sully put him on speaker and they launched straight into the business at hand. Rooter had a lot of questions, but Dotty reminded him that the channel was not *that* secure, so the bulk of the questions needed to be discussed in person. The conversation lasted just a few minutes.

Dotty relayed cleanup instructions for the apartment. He spoke fast, but his language was sharp and to the point. He told them how to get into the Edgewater safe house, and gave the general gist of their cover story. Whether they liked to hear it or not, they needed to go dark, so Dotty instructed them to hope for the best, but plan on being out of commission for a month or more. They agreed to not talk again until Dotty arrived at the safe house on Saturday. The Father encouraged them to be smart, get to the safe house, and stay put.

Just before the call was over, Rooter asked, "What about the book?"

Sully put his head down, then looked at his friend horrified and mouthed the words, "I never told him about the book."

The phone was silent for a second. Then Dotty said, "Don't let it out of your sight. I'll see you guys in two days. Stay safe."

Once disconnected, Rooter defensively asked, "What? Why didn't you tell him about the book?"

"I don't know frankly," Sully shot back. "He had just come clean about playing me since '06, and I didn't know if I could trust him, I guess. He took it okay though, right?"

"He didn't have a choice," Rooter grunted as he headed toward the balcony.

"Where are you going?"

"I need a smoke."

Sully followed him outside and gestured for one.

"You smoke?" Rooter asked.

"I do today." They lit up and stood in silence, listening to the sounds of the Capitol below.

"I'm sorry I spilled the beans on that, boss. I shouldn't have assumed you told him about Malcolm's journal."

"What's done is done," the attorney said, as he winced and coughed lightly. "I might have mentioned it as well."

Rooter had a strong stomach and less of an emotional connection to Leola, so he took the duties in the bathroom. He first removed the sheet Sully that was draped over her and investigated the entry wounds. He found that one bullet entered her right side ribs, one entered just below her sternum, and one entered right between her eyes. Hoisting her into a seated position, he checked her backside to see whether the bullets exited. The one to the head did, and the one to her sternum did, but the rib shot was lodged. He found broken tiles in two locations, one at the rear of the shower about 3 feet off the floor, and the other just above the lip of the tub along the seam. He found brain and bone matter in the cracks at the seam of the tub. There were no holes in the shower curtain.

He surmised that someone likely entered the bathroom, opened the curtain, shot her twice in the torso, then once between the eyes after she fell. The damage to the tile and tub was consistent with this theory. Draping her right arm over his shoulder, he hoisted her limp body up and ran his hand along the tub floor underneath her, looking for the spent rounds. He found one, but not the other. He searched the rest of the bathroom meticulously, trying to find any other damage that might be the result of a ricochet, but he found none. He found all three casings, and dropped the evidence in his pants' pocket.

Fixated on the missing bullet, he wondered if it might have gone down the drain. He checked the diameter of the drain against the crushed bullet he found and calculated the distinct possibility. After replaying the scene in his mind again, he decided it wasn't just possible, but likely.

He went back into the living room where Solomon was dusting like a mad man. "I found the casings and one of two bullets that exited. Need to get the other. Got any tools?"

Solomon looked at him and silently thanked God that Rooter was there. *If this man wasn't best friend material before this, he has been immortalized from this day forward.* Sully pointed to a coat closet near the front door. "There's a tool chest in there. Don't put a print on it though. I've already dusted over there."

Rooter returned to the tub with a pair of needle nose pliers and went to town on the entry wound just below her right breast. It took a few minutes, but he eventually found the bullet and pried it out. He repositioned her roughly the way he found her, eyes open, mouth open, lying face up in the tub. Having recreated her basic position and appearance, he sat on the lip of the tub and reexamined the scene. Anger returned. Hatred welled. She was so beautiful and innocent. He clenched his jaw and looked away to regain composure. He then bent down one last time, kissed his fingertips, and pressed them on her cheek, whispering, "We'll get 'em sweetheart. We'll get 'em."

Rooter returned the sheet to protect her dignity and Solomon's sanity, while the two men started cleaning the bedroom and bathroom together. They were not able to dispose of the body, so the idea concocted by the Greek was to break open the safe that Solomon kept in his end-table by the bed, but leave the contents. Doing so would make it look like the work of the Phantoms. If they did a good job cleaning up the ballistic evidence meant to frame Solomon, and left no DNA evidence of their efforts, combined with what's been deemed the Phantom's assassination call sign -- double tap to the torso and one to the head -- the spook was sure he could override local jurisdictions and take the case to the FBI.

The rest would get figured out when Father Abelemy arrived at Edgewater in two days. The FBI did have a task force assigned to investigate suspected Phantom incidents, and the Jasper case had already been handed over by Dotty. Once the FBI agrees to add this case to the task force, Father Abelemy would be compelled to keep Solomon in witness protection until his safety could be reasonably guaranteed.

After the cleanup job was complete, Solomon packed a suitcase while Rooter broke open the safe with a grinder. Solomon also retrieved the backpack and tossed in the handgun. Then Rooter removed the sheet from Leola and stuffed it into a garbage bag and tied it closed. Before they left, Solomon asked for a few minutes alone. Rooter sucked down another few cigarettes on the balcony and waited patiently. Sully was in the bathroom for 20 minutes before he came out with red, puffy eyes.

By that time it was almost 7 pm and the sun was descending over the Potomac River.

The two men left together. When the valet brought Rooter's 2003 Lincoln Navigator to the entry, he tossed the garbage bag, suitcase, and backpack in the rear and they pulled away. Their first stop was the bank, where Sully retrieved the book and prepaid VISA card from the safety deposit box. When he climbed back into the Navigator, Rooter was on the phone. The PI shrugged his shoulders at Sully, as if looking for direction on how to handle the caller.

"Whatever, just shut your pie hole for a sec and let me find out," Rooter finally blurted and cupped the phone's mic.

"Who is it?" Solomon asked.

"It's Anny and she's pissed. She's worried about us. Well, you, in particular. She said she's with Con at the City Tavern on M Street. What do you want to do?"

"I don't know." Sully rubbed his free hand through his hair, "I could use them if we're going to get to the bottom of all this, especially the importance of this book. We're like the dream team when it comes to this stuff."

Sully looked at his uncle's journal. "Then again, I'd feel like I was putting those kids in harm's way." He was thinking out loud. Frankly, he didn't have the psychological fortitude to make this decision right now. After a minute, he looked at his trusted advisor inquisitively.

"If you're waiting for an endorsement from me, I couldn't give a stronger one for those two. That hot piece of ass isn't all legs and curves, she's got a helluva brain too. And Con, well, he makes us all look like dummies. I think we'd be stupid not to get them in right now and use 'em for the God-given skills they got. Boss, they are as loyal and trustworthy as me. I think they'd never forgive you if you kept them out in the cold on this."

"Yeah?" Sully smiled at his friend, relieved.

"Yeah. Absolutely." Rooter's mind was made up. He pulled the lever and put his rig in gear, flipped a U-turn, and headed east on P towards Georgetown, and the City Tavern.

Once they were moving he put the cell back to his ear and said, "We're coming to get you. Be there in five. Be out front woman, or you'll be S.O.L., and be sure Spock is with you."

He hung up and smiled proudly, then looked at his boss in the passenger seat and winked. Rooter wore the 'chief' attitude well, and under the circumstances, Sully was thankful he had his wits about him.

Before driving to Edgewater, they'd need to bring the other two up-to-speed and assure that they were on board with the plan to go dark. They would need to craft a couple of lies, shore-up some loose ends and go underground for a few days, maybe a few weeks. Surely the Father would get to the bottom of what was going on and they'd be able to return to life within short order. *Right?*

CHAPTER 9
The Cardinal, General, and Scientist

Friday, September 9, 2011

The Hand sat opposite Abdullah Kahn, sipping what remained of his nearly empty glass of rose. They had just finished lunch at Da Paolo, a casual, touristy restaurant across the street from the Vatican Museum. The man known as "The General," Viktor Dultsev, sat between the two, cradling a cup of lukewarm Mochachillo. Though he tried to ignore the endless parade of pedestrian traffic that kept bumping his chair as they passed, he was beginning to get irritated.

The sidewalk was bustling with happy tourists speaking an array of languages. The men watched from under their dark-tinted sunglasses as some Italian nationals, but mostly foreigners, hustled their way along Viale Vaticano, snapping pictures with their phones and carrying on without a care in the world. The air was hot and sticky, and about every tenth tourist to pass by their tiny table reeked of body odor. Had they arrived twenty minutes earlier, they might have secured a table in the dining room, but the restaurant was popular. The patio, which was merely a series of small tables along the outer wall of the restaurant, was their only option. The Hand's pale complexion was now blotchy and pink under the relentless sun. They were all rather uncomfortable.

Viktor Dultsev was a Polish National who held a Doctorate in Military History from Duke University. His parents moved to the U.S. and were granted political asylum in 1951 after covertly working against the USSR's puppet government that controlled their home country. Because Communist Poland fell in 1952, the Dultsev family's need for asylum was short-lived. Though they ended up returning to their homeland on numerous occasions to visit family, their official home remained in North Carolina.

The only intelligence services that maintained active dossiers on what each government now referred to as "The Phantoms" were French DRM, British MI6, and American CIA. The 2006 Alpha Kilo incident in Iraq was the first known operation perpetrated by the illusive outfit. Although the U.S. military had jurisdiction over Alpha Kilo, DRM and MI6 both gained operational knowledge of the incident because Dr. Claude Galois, a French forensic microbiologist, and Dr. Gill Spates, a British cosmologist and theoretical physicist, were on the scientific team with Dr. Malcolm Bernard. Notable to the intelligence services, all the bodies at Alpha Kilo were recovered except Dr. Spates.

In 2001, the General became an advisor to the Polish Defense Minister, Jerzy Szmajdzinski. In 2003, as a result of strong self-advocacy efforts (and back-channel string-pulling by his friend Abdullah Kahn) he secured a post as a special advisor to NATO Deputy Secretary General Alissandro Minuto Rizzo. That post gave him access to classified information, which is how he came upon knowledge of Alpha Kilo during Operation Iraqi Freedom. It was this confidential knowledge that became the driving force behind Abdullah Kahn and his team in recent years. It was this special access that allowed Viktor to orchestrate the assault and massacre there in 2006. It was the ultimate success of the operation that established Viktor's nickname – "The General" – throughout the "Phantom" outfit.

Amid the hustle and bustle of tourist-central Rome, the three men sat patiently waiting for Professor Mikel Maldaceto, the 65-year-old Egyptian they now called, "The Scientist." Professor Maldaceto was a celebrated scholar, author, and theorist known affectionately throughout the scientific community as the "Big TOE." TOE referred to the "Theory of Everything," an illusively simple, self-contained, mathematical formula that harnesses all the fundamental forces and forms of matter into a singularity. Like popular theoretical physicists Stephen Hawking and Edward Witten, he believed string theory was foundational to a more complete understanding of physics and the laws of nature. He disagreed with the notion that one item, such as black-hole thermodynamics, could ever be accurately explained or understood outside its interplay with the other fundamental forces common to the cosmos as a whole. Hence, the TOE – the Theory of Everything – the cohesion of all things micro and all things macro – a glimpse into the mind of God – this was his decades-long passion.

"I regret losing that man, Malcolm Bernard, in Iraq," Abdullah said, glancing at the General briefly before returning to the tourist pamphlet he was reading. "Maldaceto had five years to figure out what Bernard knew, and now we are here to spoon-feed him the answers that he failed to realize on his own."

The General nodded contemplatively as he balanced the tiny cup of coffee on his barrel chest. He still looked like a stereotypical Eastern European Communist from the Cold War era; thick bone structure, hard jawline, wavy dark hair, and dark stubble along his neck and face. No matter what he wore, it looked like a cheesy uniform. He carried too much weight, but didn't care at all. He gave up trying to attract female companionship long ago. When he needed sex, he was happy to pay for a hooker. He preferred life simple and overindulgent.

"Bernard was too smart for his own good. He caught us all by surprise when he blew himself up," the General mused, mostly to himself.

"As if your hybrid militia can actually *be* surprised," the Hand snorted. "Fact is you should have seen that coming."

"I should have seen what coming, Pink Casper?" the General shot back. "I should have seen a wimp scientist muster the moral conviction to blow himself up to protect his secrets? Please. It wasn't quite as obvious as your sunburn or squeaky little voice, midget."

The General stared down his wide nose at the pale man who sat undeterred with an arrogant grin. Fueled by the annoyance of being bumped by yet another passerby, the General continued his rant, "Within 72 hours of finding out about Alpha Kilo, I had the site secured. On average, it takes me less than 72 hours to mobilize my forces on a target you identify, worldwide. Other than death, shall we talk about what those operations have yielded over the last five years? Nothing. Spare me the lecture, little finger. Five years to find a goddamned book; this is the extent of your resume? If I were you, I'd have resigned in shame years ago."

"Watch your tone Mist…"

"Take it easy," Kahn interrupted. "We're not starting a blame game. We're here now on this lovely September afternoon in beautiful Rome. Our fortunes have changed and we are back on track. I just pray the Scientist can read Bernard's chicken-scratch. You both should pray the same thing."

The Hand fumed with a clenched jaw as the General chuckled, the tiny Italian-sized coffee cup bouncing up and down as he did. The General won that little spat and he was pleased with his performance. Occasionally, he felt bad for the one they called, "The Hand." He was frail, pale, and ugly. In public, he appeared socially awkward. To confident men and women, he was pitiable. However, unknown to most, the Hand was a master manipulator. He was as sly as a fox, and used everything, even a spat with the General, to his ultimate advantage.

After the assault on Alpha Kilo, the General resigned his post as an advisor to the NATO Deputy Secretary, Alissandro Rizzo, and began overseeing Kahn's paramilitary objectives at a private facility on the outskirts of Rio de Janeiro, Brazil. The facility originally opened as the Genome Research Center of Brazil in 1987. Then, it was a state-sponsored animal and agriculture genome mapping enterprise. However, things got too controversial at the Center, and the associated universities providing scientists lost too much of their funding. The facility was forced to close in 1994.

Kahn bought the facility in 1996 at a huge discount and renamed it the Bio-Systems Academy of Brazil. BSA, as it's known to the Phantoms, is the unholy place that the General has called home ever since leaving NATO and joining Kahn's pursuits full-time.

Over the years, leading researchers who lacked moral compassing flocked to BSA. Government oversight was nonexistent and medical ethics took a backseat to utilitarian progress and the pursuit of transhumanist knowledge. With huge funding and no political barriers, Bio-Systems Academy scientists were among the first to successfully alter a person's genotype for the purpose of manufacturing specific phenotype traits in adult humans. However, this was never publicized. When the assault on Alpha Kilo took place in 2006, the phenotype enhancements among the assailants included improvements to things like strength, hand-eye coordination, hearing, and even extra-sensory perception. This was the start of "super-soldier" modifications only dreamed about in science fiction novels.

Kahn hadn't visited BSA since 2002, and hadn't funded operations there since 2004. BSA's Chief Administration Officer was amazingly adept at soliciting backdoor grants and foundation money from a wide range of international sources. Of course, no government could ever get away with allowing a facility like BSA to operate within its borders. The old Genome Research Center in the midst of Rio's crime-ridden favelas was perfect cover. Simply, no one asked questions, and no one really cared.

The money flowed to BSA through quiet back channels of government, banking, and business. When research successes were achieved, BSA would slip certain discoveries to the big military, pharmaceutical, and agricultural interests that were waiting for a return on their investment. Occasionally, leaked documents or pictures would surface on the Internet. One of the last incidents involved an image of a hideous human-pig hybrid lying naked in some sort of clean room environment. Within 36 hours, the image went viral through RealCrazyTruth.com. A half-day later, it was over. According to protocol, BSA tapped its access to some big media machinery and successfully trivialized the image as the photo-shopped fantasy of conspiracy theory loons. Marginalizing truth with big money and big media works every time.

A few donors were most interested in the bio-warfare ramifications of research at BSA. Although the World Health Organization and its subsidiary agencies were adept at monitoring a large sector of the bio-research industry, well-funded and well-buried operations like BSA made total surveillance impossible. Also, WHO-endorsed research centers were always at a real-world disadvantage because of oversight and ethical compliance. So, while big government and big NGOs aligned with WHO-compliant research centers publically, those with the means also secured their place in line with facilities like BSA.

The General had seen it all. He'd witnessed so many genetic catastrophes on the gurneys at BSA that bad dreams were likened to a picnic. He eyeballed the Hand over his Mochachino and mused, *I wonder if this Mister Jones came out of a test tube at BSA? He sure is a weird looking thing.*

Abdullah saw the Scientist maneuvering through the tourists and stood up to greet him.

"Sorry I'm late," Dr. Maldaceto said.

Abdullah nodded to the Hand, who stood up and stepped away from the table to make a cell phone call. The Scientist sat down in the vacated seat. "Did I miss anything?"

"Yeah, lunch. If you need something, get it to go." The General grunted, and shot the last swig of his coffee drink.

"I'm fine. Thank you, though, for that warm welcome, Viktor."

Kahn nodded at the Hand, "He's calling the Cardinal. I'll present what we found when we're all together."

The Scientist was a slender man with a long neck, pronounced jawline, and sunken eye sockets. He parted his hair down the center like a real gomer. Not like Bradley Cooper in *The A-Team*, but like a throwback nerd with long bangs hooked around his ears. If his pants were not an inch too short it wouldn't be worth noting, but God love him, they were. Beads of sweat formed under his pointed nose and he dabbed his forehead nervously with a paisley-patterned hanky. He used his hand to block the sun from his eyes while he talked to his comrades. Like the Hand, the Scientist was also socially awkward and something of an embarrassment to the self-righteous General. But Professor Maldaceto wasn't there for his good looks or his social charms. He was there for his brains and the General knew it, though he still couldn't figure out how he stumbled onto the set of Howdy Doody.

The Hand gestured for the group to join him.

The three men crossed the street and met up with Cardinal Mahmood Salah, Patriarch Emeritus of Babylon. He stood a solid foot taller than the Hand and many shades darker. He wore the traditional black cassock with a shoulder cape accented with amaranth lining and a purple fascia. The poor man looked dreadfully hot under the robes.

Though in his 70's, the Cardinal had keen eyes and relatively unwrinkled skin. He was a handsome man who carried an aura of authority and esteem. From his youth, he followed a rather typical path as a holy, devout Catholic in the "Eastern" Catholic Church. He was ordained in 1966, consecrated in 1989, and appointed a Cardinal by Pope John Paul II in the Consistory of February 21, 2001.

Cardinal Salah was a fierce opponent of Christian persecution in the Middle East. His friendship with prominent Islamic leaders undeniably helped curb a clear uptick in violence toward Christians in Syria, Iraq, and Egypt in the early to mid-2000's. Observers on both sides of the religious conflict, in fact, gave him much of the credit for recent diplomatic inroads.

The Cardinal viewed himself as a divinely appointed nurturer of these social reconciliations. In fact, he strongly believed that his work to bridge Islamic and Judeo-Christian relations was the reason he was born. It was a noble pursuit. He was a good man of impeccable moral fortitude. He was compassionate and genuinely loved all people. He was, in essence, a perfect ambassador for peace in the Middle East and around the globe.

Privately, Cardinal Salah knew he was advancing in age and was concerned that some of his brethren at the Vatican, men with considerable influence, held a more militant and dogmatic view about non-Catholics. He was troubled by the possibility that the bridges he worked so hard to build might be burned after his death. This was such a fear that much of his private time in recent years was dedicated to identifying other Cardinals who shared his views about pursuing reconciliation and peace, first with Islam, but also with the Eastern Orthodox and Evangelical churches of the world.

"Your Eminence." Abdullah Kahn said in a rare moment of humility, as he bent at the waist to kiss the Cardinal's ring. "Thank you for meeting with us today." The Cardinal responded in kind.

General Dultsev nodded respectfully as he said, "Cardinal Salah, good to see you again," to which the Cardinal smiled and said something in Italian, or Latin – none of them knew.

Professor Maldaceto, the Scientist, just waved awkwardly and said, "Hi," to which the Hand rolled his eyes and suggested they make for the Vatican Museum.

He was not a pompous man and preferred they address him as Cardinal Salah and skip the super-formalities. They had all met previously, but the Cardinal would only refer to them as 'casual acquaintances' in public. He was still wary of Abdullah Kahn. He knew that Mr. Kahn was actively involved in some controversial endeavors, but the details of those activities remained something of a mystery to him.

Together, they entered Vatican City at the Museum entrance. They zigzagged through a few corridors to a private door that exited to a parking lot. There, a large golf cart and driver were waiting. The men climbed aboard and the cart zipped toward the Vatican City Gardens. It stopped at the building that housed the Pontifical Academy of Sciences, where the men disembarked.

Cardinal Salah met Abdullah Kahn in 2002, while Kahn was serving as a relational attaché to Mullah Omar She'kah Rahim, a powerful Islamic cleric in Iran. Kahn was responsible for introducing the two religious thinkers, and because they hit it off so well from the beginning, the Cardinal used Kahn to set up a few other appointments with other high profile Mullahs. Over time, the Cardinal took a casual, distanced interest in Kahn and some of his other pursuits around the world. He even got Abdullah to sponsor two Middle East 'reconciliation tours' during the summers of 2004 and 2005.

However, it was a super-strange twist of fate that created the ultimate bond between these two very different men. Remarkably, it was their belief in extraterrestrial life and their mutual fascination with alien technology that kept bringing them together now.

The Cardinal stumbled onto such notions by accident. While conducting research for the "2005 Middle East Ecumenical Conference on Science, Religion and the Metaphysical Bridge," he spent countless hours at the Academy of Sciences delving into the scientific evidence supporting concepts of multidimensionality. In that season, he found that though proponents of the natural sciences often reject the supernatural claims of religion, more than a few scientific theories actually point to multiple dimensions outside the four measurable ones within our own space-time. Not religion, but science, was now making claims in support of multidimensionality.

During one late night of research, he stumbled upon an entire shelf dedicated to a telescope operated by the Jesuits atop Mount Graham in Arizona.

Incredible, the Catholic Order of Jesuits operates the Vatican Advanced Technology Telescope, one of the most powerful and advanced telescopes in the world. Seriously, what is this all about?

Later, he learned how ambitiously certain elements of the Vatican were pursuing 'deeper knowledge about alien life forms', and how doctrinal changes to the Catechism had been suggested in order to prep for a time when 'modern scientific advancement brings irreconcilable issues to the Church's doorstep.'

Cardinal Salah asked around, and one Jesuit put it this way over a cup of coffee at a nearby eatery. "Whether we are willing to admit it or not, science is about to research its way right out of the material world. Then what? What becomes of the faith? …"

Without fanfare, the Cardinal realized that the Jesuits believed the telescope to be a window on the coming 'bridge.' At least, that's what they hoped it would be.

By the mid-2000's, Cardinal Salah himself was a full-on advocate. He adopted the belief that sooner rather than later, a quantum physicist, molecular biologist, or some other super-smart person with a powerful computer was going to research this world straight into a new reality. But what would that reality be? Maybe a quantum fold that essentially *unfolds,* bringing us somewhere new? Would it be extraterrestrial? Extra-dimensional? Supernatural? Or do all of these concepts really mean the same thing?

There were so many questions and so few answers. Some of the Cardinal's brethren had committed to re-reading the Holy Scriptures under the paradigm of extra-terrestrial life. Others, especially in the Jesuit community, had poured millions into astronomy and academia. Still others, like Salah, were keeping a close eye on the scientific community and trying to connect the dots. There was really no telling how it would play out, but privately, the Cardinal wondered, *What if these celestial benefactors are merely helpers, created by the same Father God that brought life to earth in the first place through Adam and Eve? What if their existence didn't usurp the faith at all?*

One could only hope.

Splice

The men entered a hallway and walked down a corridor, then took a left, and another left, and found themselves in a private conference room. This area was considered 'back of the house' and had very little in terms of religious relics, art, or other appointments. The conference room had a medium-sized oval table in the middle, a white board on one wall, and folding chairs stacked in the corner. For the Vatican, it seemed remarkably unremarkable.

After they were seated, the Hand pulled five bound and reconstructed versions of Malcolm's photocopies out of a briefcase and passed them out. They all perused the pages, pretending to have a clue about what was written, but only the Scientist, Professor Maldaceto, actually had some immediate perspective.

"Okay," the Scientist said after a few minutes. He looked up at the group, seeming to wonder if it was appropriate for him to speak. The Hand gestured impatiently and he continued, "Okay, this journal is much more than a map of his optical frequency algorithms, although I suspect those are contained in here, at least enough to guide us in reconstructing the extrasensory optic device. I hope."

He looked up again and smiled sheepishly. He was clearly nervous.

"Mikel," Kahn said. "We cannot read this. If you can read any of it, you are well beyond us, and that is frankly why you are here. Take your time, look at it, give us your initial impressions, and we will go from there. You have the floor, sir."

"Yes, okay." The Scientist straightened his posture and cleared his throat. "My initial impressions are that this book contains three separate elements. The first is obviously focused on these mathematical equations, which I believe speak to the technical specs of the component Mr. Bernard used to manipulate the life essence, or soul, of a human. My colleagues and I will be able to get to the bottom of these together, in a matter of days or weeks, probably. They do not look overly complicated, just very technical. Then there is the next section, you see how the writings and markings change?"

The Scientist looked up momentarily as he flipped a few pages of the journal. He then began talking about the section where cuneiform and a series of numbers all collided in an archaic hodgepodge. "These pages are very odd. The numbers are coordinates, clearly, but the cuneiform and pictographs, I think, are Sumerian or Akkadian or some early Mesopotamian. I wonder if he added this cuneiform script to the journal for later analysis. If it is some kind of ancient Sumerian, he might have pulled these markings from sites in Iraq and around the southern Euphrates corridor. This style looks consistent with Southern Mesopotamia in the 3rd millennium BC. I can't say for sure, though. Maybe the coordinates will help us understand. I have two linguists on our team who can verify all this. Again, give me a few weeks on this too."

He then flipped a few more pages to a longer section and swallowed hard. Kahn saw him do it and felt a sinking sensation in his stomach. The Scientist coughed again and cleared his throat nervously, "Here, there are many pages of…" he paused and looked closely at the script for a full minute or more.

"I don't know. It looks like it could be a dead language. Eteocypriot is what comes to mind. I spent a couple years playing around with these ancient languages when I was analyzing the Giza cyphers at Cairo University. In the end, it looks like Dr. Bernard just started logging his activities in a crazy, ancient, encrypted language." He looked up and shrugged helplessly. "I have no idea how an optics guy would be able to write this stuff."

"What the fuck is an Et. Eteo. Eteocp…" The General stopped short and looked at the Cardinal, "Please excuse me Cardinal Salah. That was terribly inappropriate."

The Cardinal smiled graciously and turned his attention to the Scientist, "It's okay son. What do you think it is? And please use language we can all understand."

"To be frank, I really don't know what this is. But to my partially-trained eye, this script looks a lot like a language that went extinct around the 4th Century BC, called Eteocypriot. Eteocypriot is a pre-Greek language that nobody on the planet has translated. It would be impossible for Malcolm to write this without knowing the language, and nobody knows it, if indeed it is Eteocypriot."

"Somebody knows it," Abdullah blurted. "You're sitting here telling us about it, for God's sake!"

"No," the Scientist said in a moment of assertive confidence. "We've seen it. Eteocypriot makes up half of the inscription that was found on a tablet on the Island of Cyprus, on the Acropolis of Amathus, in 1912, 1913. The other half was written in an Attic dialect. That's a form of ancient Greek."

Grinning, the Scientist looked at the Cardinal and said, "Eteocypriot is as mysterious as the Voynich Manuscript. We know next to nothing about it. Maybe the Cardinal can talk about why this might be interesting?" Clearly, the Scientist was using this moment to wryly inform the Hand, the General, and Abdullah Kahn that he and the Cardinal were far more indispensable than the team realized. For the moment, it represented an odd and rather gutsy shift in persona.

"Cyprus was the home of Aphrodite," the Cardinal said, almost to himself, "the goddess of love and pleasure in Greek mythology. There was a cult of Aphrodite worshipers that lived there in ancient times. Some suppose the only people who ever actually knew the Eteocypriot language were members, or possibly high-ranking leaders, of the cult itself."

The Cardinal grinned and nodded as his mind began connecting a few dots.

"All mythology has this in common -- stories of gods fighting other gods, and tales of their interplay with humans. If it is Eteocypriot, the Scientist is right. Nobody knows this language anymore. It died on an island a couple thousand years ago, an island known for its ties to Greek demigods. But our Dr. Bernard was at Alpha Kilo in 2006, and suddenly learns a language not known by our human race since the supposed life of a mythological goddess named Aphrodite. So this begs two questions. One, is there more truth to ancient mythology than we understand or acknowledge? Two, what happened at Alpha Kilo that gave an optical scientist access to a language of the gods?"

There was a long pause. Then Kahn turned and looked at the Hand. "He really did open the portal! That's the answer. As we've suspected all along, Alpha Kilo sits on the site of the ancient ziggurat, the Tower of Babel. The portal at Babel – that's the real treasure buried at Alpha Kilo!"

The Hand nodded with a wide smile, "That crazy Dr. Bernard did it – this means the ancient portal is, or at least was, active once again!"

CHAPTER 10
A Thing of Destiny

Weekend of August 20, 2011

The five-bedroom safe house was pretty nice, especially considering its multi-year vacancy. It was all on one floor and had a detached garage big enough for three vehicles. The Keys & Associates crew each created reasons for their sudden disappearance from DC, and circulated that information to their close friends and family. They didn't know how long they'd be 'off the grid' so the work project and vacation alibis were crafted with that in mind.

Con didn't have close friends so his was rather straightforward. He told his mom and sister that he was chosen for another confidential programing project. He had worked on these before, and sequestration of the team was normal during sensitive projects. It was totally believable because of Con's notoriety in the computer-programming world. Since proprietary code was often a matter of severe paranoia and scandal within the industry, compartmentalization and sequester of the team was business as usual. It took him all of about three minutes to iron out the details of his story and deliver it to his family.

Anny's friends were used to her dropping off radar from time to time while she got to 'know' someone who Sully had marked for information. Sometimes she was out of relational commission for weeks at a time, so her cover was also an easy sell. Her mom and dad lived in Kansas and were used to hearing from her once or twice a month, but didn't tend to worry if she went a couple months without calling. Anny called her two best friends and let them know that her next 'project' was now living in the UK, and that she rented a flat there for the next couple months. They bought the story with little thought or concern.

Rooter had more people in his life. Not just that, but the people he associated with were similar to him and had skills at sniffing out things that failed to make sense. In a past life, he served as a cop on the Boston PD. He was fired from that job for going outside the boundary of *ethical behavior* when he fabricated a story that landed him on the front porch of his girlfriend's ex-husband's house. That incident ended with the ex-husband lying dead in a pool of his own blood and Rooter on administrative leave pending internal review. The internal review didn't go well for him, but formal charges outside PD discipline never came.

After getting fired he got dumped by his girlfriend, and then moved from Boston. He landed a security job working for an up-and-coming diva singer-songwriter, Claire Leeland. She was a teenager, regionally popular in the Pacific Northwest, and had a 46-year-old stalker causing major problems. He worked for Claire until her fame and career fizzled out a few years later, and that's when he moved to DC to work as a private investigator for-hire.

A few years after moving to DC, Rooter met Sully. That's when his life got on a much better track. Rooter hated the business side of his PI firm. He hated the accounting, taxes, and logistics stuff so much that he was eager to dissolve his successful business and work for someone else. He hit it off with Solomon almost immediately after meeting at a Senator's dinner party. Within months, Rooter took a pay cut, shut down his own business, and joined Keys & Associates. He exchanged pay for peace, and never regretted it.

Rooter came up with two stories and circulated them to the appropriate parties. First, for his seedy, fellow PI or ex-cop friends, he basically told them the truth. He figured, anything short of that would not pass the scratch-and-sniff test. He told them he was moving into a safe house with a client who was being put into the witness protection program for organized crime-related issues he couldn't discuss. The second alibi was concocted specifically for his aging mother who lived in Maine and his siblings who both hailed from Connecticut. He told them that he landed a job with a government contractor and was being shipped off to the Sudan to provide security at some sort of refugee camp. The money was good. He'd check in when he could, but he had no idea what the conditions would be. He told his family it could be months without phone service. It was hard, especially for his mom, who was used to getting a call every Friday evening at 6 pm.

Keys & Associates only had two active cases and both were on multi-month holds for court-scheduling reasons. Sully advised about a dozen organizations on retainer, but activity there was rather quiet too. For all things legal, Solomon assigned the firm's docket to his law school roommate, Jordan Gains. Jordan handled constitutional law matters at a mid-sized firm in DC with a strong reputation. He was a rising dynamo at his firm and loved the opportunity to feather his cap with some K&A slam dunks. Covering cases within the Georgetown network was part of the routine – Sully would get some nice referrals back from Jordan another time.

When the crew first pulled up to the safe house, they found a thick wire cord strewn across the driveway. Sully had memorized the code from Dotty, which unlocked both the padlock on the cord as well as the front door. It was a simple barrier, but effective at keeping vehicles from driving onto the property. The house also featured an 8-foot privacy fence that covered three sides of the property, enclosing the house and backyard completely. A more decorative picket fence and thick shrubbery lined the front of the property along the road.

The grounds were well kept. In the backyard there was a brick patio and awning that came off the house. There was a gas grill, two tables, and a bunch of mismatched chairs. Beyond the patio, the backyard was an expansive grassy oasis, with two large trees right in the center. Between the trees was a handcrafted, slightly elevated gazebo. The grass was manicured right up to the edge where the fence marked the boundary, and the whole place was on automatic sprinklers.

Beyond the backyard fence was Glebe Bay and the Atlantic Ocean, with two larger properties cattycornered just off the right and left.

The house was laid out in almost a perfect square, with the front door just a hair off center to the right. Walking into the house from the front door, there were two bedrooms and an adjoining bathroom that occupied the far left third of the dwelling. One bedroom was considered the master and the other was quite small, maybe an office. In the center third of the house was a kitchen, dining table, spacious living room, and the back door. On the right third was a hallway that led to three guest rooms and two bathrooms, along with a rather large laundry room. Except for the thick carpet in the living room, the entire house was covered in hardwood flooring.

They arrived to a musty smell and evidence of mold, but nothing that couldn't be cleared out with a little effort. They spent that first weekend organizing, shopping for groceries, and running a couple shuttles back to DC for clothes and equipment. Most importantly, Con and Rooter made a late-night visit to the office to shut things down, transfer calls to Gains, and grab the computer gear. By the end of the weekend, everyone and their vehicles were back at Edgewater for good. The safe house was clean, stocked, and secure.

"Think he's gonna be okay?" Anny asked as she poured two glasses of iced tea. "He's been in his room for like two straight days."

She handed one glass to Rooter who sat on a kitchen bar stool wearing shorts and an unbuttoned Hawaiian shirt, exposing his dark hairy chest.

"He's gonna be alright. It was a pretty nasty scene over there. Hard enough for me, not knowing that kid very well. Must have been hell for him."

"Yeah, I meant to tell you," she said after sipping. "You're a saint for doing what you did."

Rooter chuckled, "You'd have done it too."

"Hell no, I would not!" She shot back. "I wouldn't have done that to a dead animal. There is no way I could have picked the bullet out of a human. Especially someone I knew." She shivered at the thought.

"Hey gang," Solomon said, walking into the kitchen from the master bedroom. "What are y'all talkin' about?"

Anny looked away, hoping the question wasn't aimed at her. Rooter fielded it, just as cool as ever, "We were just talking about how much better a person I am than her."

"I don't know about that," Sully said, oblivious.

"Oh no, boss," Rooter snorted, looking at Anny whose back was to them. "At this point, it's a foregone conclusion."

Anny leaned forward and looked out the window above the sink. As she did, her blue striped tank top crept up just enough to drive Rooter into his depraved little world: *What a glorious peek at the red hem of her thong coming up from under those perfectly low-cut, tight fitting jeans she always wears.* He nodded in Sully's direction, beckoning him to take a look at the precious find, when he realized that Sully was also staring out the window.

"What is it?" He was only slightly embarrassed that Anny's underwear distracted him from whatever his less shallow friends had noticed. "What do you see?"

"Father Abelemy," Sully said, turning and marching toward the front door. "Looks like Father Abelemy is here."

That was the first time Anny and Rooter saw Sully smile in days. After he left the room, Rooter winked at her and assured, "He'll be alright."

"Hello, hello, you all made it here in one piece," the Father said as he walked in the house and swiftly shut the door behind him. Con took his headset off and joined the others in the foyer area. "Wow, you brought some friends, I see."

"Rooter and I thought it might be a good idea. You remember Anny and Con?" The Father nodded in their directions as Sully continued, "These guys are loyal, committed, and investigate things for a living. How could two of us just leave DC and not create bigger issues? Figured it was just easier to bring the whole team in. Plus, I love these guys!"

"Yeah, good," the Father was as cool as ever. He was shrewd like a Wall Street executive, but cool like a California surfer. The Father oozed a soft and smart charisma wherever he went. With the exception of Rooter, everyone was very fond of him. If Anny and Con's presence at the safe house was a concern to Dotty, he hid it well.

Turning suddenly to Rooter, he said, "Quick question then, is there room in the garage for my vehicle? I'm a little uneasy about leaving it out in plain sight."

"Yeah sure. Pull it in. I'll open the third bay for ya."

In the short walk between the front door and garage, the sun and steamy air assaulted Rooter. His silk shirt stuck like plastic wrap to his back and he began perspiring at the forehead, cheeks, and upper lip. He hoped the thick blast of muggy air meant rain was on the way.

The Father pulled his vehicle into the garage and they both walked back to the safe house together. Dotty had a briefcase and duffle bag. Before they got to the front door, the Father stopped Rooter and asked a few pointed questions about the crime scene. He also verified some specifics related to their cleanup job at the apartment. Satisfied with Rooter's recap, they entered the house together and found the others sitting on the sofas in the living room. There was a pot of coffee steeping in the kitchen and a pitcher of iced tea on the coffee table.

Though they returned to the glorious air conditioning, Rooter took his shirt off as he advanced to an open seat next to Anny.

"What are you doing?" She asked, miffed.

"What? I'm hot."

"You'll cool off, huss. You were just out there a few minutes."

"What is it hun?" He smiled as if trying to empathize with her struggle. "My chest? It makes you want me? My sex appeal is too much for you? Does my nudity make it hard to concentrate? I get it, really I do."

"Ugh," she rolled her eyes.

"It's too much for me," Con spouted with a mouth full of banana. "Way too much."

"Seriously," Anny interjected. "It's a silk shirt. You're not going to cool down by taking off an already unbuttoned short-sleeve shirt. I mean, why can't you just be normal?"

"This is normal hun," he said as plopped down next to her, flinging the shirt over the arm of the sofa. "I'll put that thing back on when I cool off a few ten-to-twelve degrees."

"You disgust me."

"You know what they say," Rooter grinned. "If you can't beat 'em, join 'em. Why don't you just dress to match me?"

"Okay, that's enough," Solomon piped as Anny, mortified, mouthed an apology to the Father, who took a seat across from her.

Drinks in hand, the Father asked for the story to be rehashed from the beginning, starting at the point when Solomon first saw his mother's journal. Hearing the entire timeline was crucial for everyone, since Solomon hadn't really talked much in the last couple days. The K&A crew were largely in the dark on what happened in Alton. The details surrounding DC on Wednesday and Thursday were of particular interest to the Father. He also wanted to know what Solomon did with Malcolm's lab journal.

"So this, what, lab journal you found? Where is it now?" The Father asked. He was gracious with a hint of agitation.

"Here," Sully pulled it from his backside and tossed it to the Father. "Again Dotty, everything happened so fast. I should have told you about this in St. Louis. I'm really sorry."

The Father waved his hand as if the wrongdoing wasn't even worth a pardon, and took a few minutes to thumb through each page. The rest of the team sat quietly while he did so. Having finished, he set the book on the coffee table and retrieved a file from his briefcase.

Holding the file in his lap, Dotty began, "You hid the book from me, and I told you that the worst was behind you. We were both fudging our assessments. There is nothing we can do about it now, so let's just move forward from here." Sully nodded as he continued, "Two things stuck out to me after our time at Denny's. First, I realized that somehow, and for some reason, I was being watched. Second, I realized that what I didn't know about Malcolm was going to get people killed."

"To the first point, I needed to know if I was being watched by an agency outside of the CIA, or if I was being watched with the help of a mole inside the CIA, or even by another federal agency of a clandestine nature."

"Hang on," Rooter interrupted. "How did you know you were being watched?"

"I didn't, I just assumed. Sully heard one of the assassins refer to Jasper as 'the Greek.' That's what my case officer calls me. At this point, long story short, I think it's a mole. I did a little saber rattling of my own, threatened to blow the top off what happened in Alton and involve the Deputy Director. That got me a couple meetings with the guys that are overseeing the Alpha Kilo file at the Bureau. Their information liaison is a foggy fellow named Miller, who I do not trust in the slightest. The only thing these meetings revealed was that this guy was withholding information between CIA and FBI. Miller got a slap on the wrist, but more importantly, I know he's not working in the best interests of the United States. He's got another employer."

"What are you saying? That the people watching you are the people who killed Malcolm and Jasper, and these folks have infiltrated Central Intelligence?" Solomon asked, leaning forward.

"That's my working assumption at this point. In the process of making a stink over there, I was also granted additional access to Malcolm's file and given clearance to more updated information about the Phantoms." He tapped the folder on his lap, "This file contains the FBI's summary findings on the Phantoms. We can make a copy here on your printer, but be careful to keep it secret like everything else. They didn't want to give this to me, and though I'm certain it's not the complete file, it's a good start."

He handed the folder to Con, who disappeared into his room to run it through his scanner.

"After I felt sure that I'd identified the mole as that Bureau liaison Miller, I went to my C.O. about everything and brought him in the loop. I'm glad I did. I asked him to take this safe house off line, and he did. I asked for some case cover, and he delivered. Then earlier today, he made contact with me while I'm on my way here. He told me that an NSA surveillance satellite just went hot, following a digital signal emitting from something on my person. I pulled over and found a pretty sophisticated tracking device in my briefcase."

Rooter and Sully's eyes widened as Dotty leaned back and raked his fingers though his salt-and-pepper hair. "It's a big deal. It's impossible to program surveillance protocols on these types of systems without high-level authorization from Homeland Security. Miller couldn't have done this. There must be others, and they must occupy high levels of authority. It's frankly a scary thought."

Con returned and handed the original folder to Dotty. Solomon was visibly nervous, his heel twitching up and down as he nibbled at a finger. Anny asked if she could refill Dotty's mug and he took her up on the offer.

"So, why did they kill Leola?" Sully asked. "What good did that do? She was in the shower for Christ's sake. Why not just take the photocopies and leave? And for that matter, why didn't they wait for me to get back and kill me too? You got a theory on this?" The pitch in Sully's voice revealed his stress.

"I had a thought about that," Rooter chimed-in. "Does Leola undress in the bathroom before taking a shower, or somewhere else in the apartment?"

"The bathroom. Why?"

"There were no clothes in the bathroom. In fact, there were no clothes on the floor anywhere in the apartment except for in the walk-in closet around the hamper."

"What are you getting at?" Anny asked.

"It was just odd, that's all." He looked at Sully and continued, "You said yourself that she was on the balcony finishing her breakfast when you went down to talk to the security guy, right? You were gone, what, five minutes, tops?"

Sully nodded slowly.

"So, in five minutes an intruder came in, knew exactly where to find the copies, shot your girl, moved her clothing for some reason, then left? Just doesn't add up."

Sully dropped his head and remembered the t-shirt in her dirty clothes hamper. At that point he also remembered that she asked him about the copies the night prior, when he had put them in his desk drawer. Rooter started to say something further, but Sully cut him off.

"You're right, she gave them the copies. Then quickly, they had her strip down in the walk-in, get into the shower, and they shot her in cold blood with my gun, which they found in the walk-in as well. That's how it must have happened because she knew I put the copies in the desk drawer."

After a moment, Dotty surmised, "They killed her because she was a witness. They may not have known how long you would be, so they killed her in a manner that would implicate you. They probably figured that by doing so, they would neutralize you in the process. It all makes pretty good sense, actually."

"What are we doing?" Anny asked awkwardly. "I mean, I'm not trying to change the subject, but what are we doing next? Is it safe to go home? Is it not? What happens to us now?"

Dotty looked at her with empathy. He leaned forward and took a moment to look directly at each of the K&A team. He took stock of their confusion and fright, "Had you asked yesterday, I would have visited just long enough to confiscate the professor's journal and head back to Langley. I would have told you all to hang tight for a few weeks while we sort the danger out. I would have alleviated your remaining angst by promising to be in touch. But after the NSA satellite thing today, and a lengthy discussion with my case officer, we've decided to abort that plan. Something just isn't adding up here."

"We don't know how high this scandal goes, but tapping an NSA spy-bird is no joke. Basically guys, we've decided to leave the journal here with you. I could put together an investigation team, but the fact is we don't know who's been compromised. I'd be playin' Russian roulette with the only piece of hard evidence we have. It just so happens that you guys are pretty secure here and pretty adept at researching this sort of thing. Somebody's watching me, so, let's keep it that way. You guys stay here and analyze the journal. It was my C.O.'s concept."

Rooter chuckled and Solomon blinked in amazement.

"You've got to be kidding me. What the hell do you expect us to do with this book?" Anny blurted.

"Yeah," Rooter agreed.

"It's actually sort of ironic," Dotty said, smiling now. "I was going to ask you guys to involve Anny and Con here, because as a team, you have about as good a shot at getting to the bottom of it as anybody I could put on the case. Look, I'll support the effort however I can, but we just don't know who we can trust. At this point, only six people on the planet know where you are, and that's a really good thing. Nobody at Langley has the ability to uncover this safe house now that it's off-line. You're safe. You're hidden for now, and I'll aim to keep it that way. This is a perfect base of operation."

"What about Leola? The apartment?" Sully asked.

"The firm too. I mean, how long are we going to be here doing this?" Anny jumped-in. "I'm not particularly fond of the idea of bunking down with the boys from work for God-knows-how-long."

"And money too, where's that comin' from?" Rooter wanted to know.

Dotty put up a hand, "Take it easy guys, we need to do this one at a time. When I brought the C.O. up-to-speed, he flagged the FBI directly and let them know that the case needed to be added to the Phan-Group file. Leola's already been picked up, and for now, you'll need to let us handle the notifications to her family. As far as you guys individually making rent and paying for utilities and all that stuff, nothing changes. The government will be making electronic payments as your "Orthodox clients" every month. You guys keep getting your individual salaries. Nothing changes. Just, if it's not already set up electronically, you'll need to do that."

"But what are people going to think if I'm not around for things like her funeral?" Sully asked.

"We've let her family know that you are in a protective custody program until we can assure your safety. Look, you can't worry about what people think. This thing is big and for whatever reason, you're all in the middle of it. What we can do is work the problem, play the odds, and take each day as it comes."

The five sat quietly for a minute, each pondering the Father's words from a self-centered perspective. This was quickly becoming a very unwelcome intrusion in their lives. Eventually, all their eyes settled on Sully, as they naturally looked to him for direction.

"Okay, so we're reopening the case with your shell organization then, and you'll be compensating us though that vehicle?"

Dotty nodded, "Yes, but only pay for your rent, utilities, insurance, and stuff like that with these automatic deposits. I'm going to be sending you cash for your expenses here. Cash is hard to trace and a lot safer. We need to create the illusion that you guys are doing your law firm thing, working a case from outside DC, living life rather normally with cash flow to your accounts, and all that. As far as this safe house, the gal who will be our drop-person is named Beatrix. From this point forward, she's going to be the go-between for communication and everything else."

"Who's Beatrix?" Anny asked.

"Housekeeper," the Father replied. "She's been looking after this place for years. She's an employee. She knows nothing about our op and it is probably best if you don't give her your names or get too close. Keep private docs private when she's around, for her safety as much as anything. She'll come by and drop off cash, pick up receipts, and occasionally carry correspondence from me. She's a good lady, but she's a civilian and not much use to you outside of delivering money and info."

"When does she come each week?" Anny followed up.

"It varies. I don't really know. She's not on a set schedule."

They were each absorbing the details, and each coming to grips with the situation in their own ways. Anny was the most visibly apprehensive about bunking down in an off-the-grid safe house with the others, Rooter was the most visibly casual toward it. Con's disposition was flat. Solomon was still a mess of raw emotions and didn't much care where he stayed, so long as it was somewhere other than his apartment in DC.

There seemed to be nothing else to discuss. After a heavy pause, Dotty finally said, "Look, you guys need to think about all of this and make a decision. I'm leaving after dark tonight and I won't be in touch again for quite some time, at least not directly. I need to know where you stand by the time I leave."

Rooter stood up. "After dark, eh? So you stayin' for dinner?"

"If you don't mind," he said. "But before that I need to go over some tech security and Internet routing stuff with Con. Probably take an hour or so."

"I don't mind," Rooter said. "I'm gonna barbeque."

Con led the way to his bedroom where his computer rig was already set up and humming. They reviewed the latest elliptic curve cryptography cyphers and associated security protocols tied into the safe house. Con was in geek heaven. The safe house had been set up and periodically updated to assure that voice and data communications in and out of the home were surveillance-free and tamper-resistant. While they were going over the protocols, each reminded the other that no system in the world is totally hack-proof. However, both were pretty happy with how this little house came equipped.

Meanwhile, Rooter started chopping veggies for a salad in the kitchen. Anny got up and moved to a seat next to Sully, "What are you thinking?"

"I don't know. It's hard for me to believe that a powerful government agency is asking us for help on this. They are the CIA for God's sake. I don't know. My mind is twisty spaghetti, my heart is shattered glass, and my gut feels like it's full of woodpeckers." He looked at her and gave a weak smile. "I really don't know what to think, Anny. What about you?"

"What about me?"

"I don't know," Sully shrugged, "how are you doing with all this?"

"I guess it's alright. I'm not so apprehensive about the task, I just didn't like the idea of being a bachelor with you guys. It would be different if there was another girl, you know?"

Sully wasn't really listening to her. She knew it, but didn't mind. He'd been through a lot. They sat in silence for a minute, and then Sully looked at her. When they locked eyes, something happened. It was a moment of intensity, as though something stirred in their souls. She grinned with slight embarrassment. She wondered if it was her imagination, or if he'd felt it too.

As if suddenly realizing he was staring into her eyes, Sully looked away abruptly and adjusted his posture. Anny took the hint and got up.

"If you need anything else," her voice was loud enough for Rooter to hear, "let me know. I'm going to go help Guido with dinner."

"I heard that ditz," Rooter retorted from the kitchen. "Who said I need help anyway? Women need to stay out of the kitchen when we're talkin' barbeque…"

To Sully's ear, their conversation tapered off. He could hear them just fine, but he let his mind to drift to a place less complicated. Once again, he found himself inside a protective box of numbness, while the world outside whipped around with gale-force ferocity. He needed to lie down. He walked to his bedroom and closed the door without saying anything. He was happy to shut out the mutual jazz and low blows that flew between Rooter and Anny. He closed his eyes and immediately floated into a peaceful sleep.

The knock at his door startled him and he sat up. Dotty cracked the door, "Can I come in?"

"Sure."

"Beer?" Dotty offered a Bud.

"Yeah, sure."

"How are you doing?" Dotty asked, taking a seat on a nearby chair.

"Okay, I guess."

"You got a good team here. I even like the Centurion." He chuckled and took a pull on his longneck.

"They are pretty special, aren't they?" There was a great aroma in the air – the smell of steak and sautéed mushrooms and asparagus. "Smell's good out there. Dinner about ready?"

"It is, but I want to talk to you first."

"Yeah? What about?"

"About doing this job for me, looking into the book, and seeing if you can get to the bottom of this intrigue surrounding Malcolm. I don't mean to be overdramatic, but I think it could be a thing of destiny."

Sully gurgled a swig of beer. "Why would you say a thing like that?"

"Because you don't know what I know, kid. If you jump into this thing head first, you'll see. The world as we know it is going to start changing, rapidly."

"I don't have much of a choice do I?" he wondered out loud.

"You do. You could stick your head in the sand like the rest of the USA and pretend that Hell's not rising. Or you could take a look at what's really going on and see for yourself. Maybe even do something about it, before it's all over."

"Do we even have the ability to get to the bottom of the book? I mean, do we have the skillset?"

"I think you do. It's all about inquiry, research, and analysis. It's really no different than anything else you do, for any other case. And you've got my help. If you need an astrophysicist, I'll find one. If you need a guy with expertise in nanotechnology, I'll find someone. Between you four and the resources I can provide from the Federal apparatus, it's as good a team as I could put together."

"You say, Hell's rising," Solomon shirked. "Can we hope to stop it?"

"I doubt it." Dotty took another long drink. "But we can have a front-row seat."

"Dinner's served," Anny's voice hailed from the back patio.

Solomon looked deep into the Father's experienced eyes, and finally said, "Yeah okay. We're in. Can't promise anything, but we'll do the best we can."

Schnackenberg

CHAPTER 11
Bio-Systems Academy

Tuesday, September 20, 2011

Bio-Systems Academy was housed in an expansive but inconspicuous building in the city of Niteroi; a subsection of metropolitan Rio de Janeiro, Brazil. From the outside, it looked like a gated warehouse facility in the center of Niteroi's business district. BSA was a mile and a half north of the famous Museum of Contemporary Art, or what the locals called "that terrible looking space-aged ugly thing."

After passing security, the limousine carrying Abdullah Kahn and his trusty Hand came to a stop at the main entrance. There, they were formally greeted by Dr. Michael Monroe, BSA's Chief Administration Officer, as well as the General, Viktor Dultsev. Both men looked sharp, wearing freshly pressed, hand-tailored suits and shiny shoes. Even the General appeared thinner and more sophisticated under his sleek pinstripe.

Monroe treated every VIP visit the same. It didn't matter if the visitor was the official representative of an entire nation or the middleman courier delivering funds from a nondescript NGO. He always met them up front with a level of formal pomp. He proudly chaperoned guests through the facility, served refreshments, and openly answered questions with legal precision.

Normally the General did not accompany Monroe in the function of playing host, Viktor merely lived and worked there. But since their recent meeting at the Vatican, the General had become the primary BSA liaison pertaining to issues involving the discovery of Malcolm's lab journal.

"Gentlemen," Monroe said with a million dollar smile as they stepped out of the limo. "Welcome to BSA. Mr. Kahn, it's been much too long since you were here last. Why have you abandoned us to our own devices these past, what, eight years?"

"It's been nine, actually," Kahn said, shaking the administrator's hand. "And it was not you I abandoned, it was the smell of rot in this city that hangs at nostril level like a cloud."

"Ah yes," they all had a chuckle, "the scent of Rio's favelas. Visitors are taken aback when they first arrive, but as I like say, 'it's a small price to pay for a location where anything goes in the name of science,' know what I mean?"

"True statement."

"So, how long do you plan on staying in Rio?"

"Just a day," Kahn said, as the General swiped his electronic keycard and held the front door for the others. "The science seems to be speeding up and we're interested to see what you're all working on."

The portion of the facility that was visible to onlookers from the outside was only two stories and roughly 30,000 square feet. This is what Kahn paid for when he bought it out of foreclosure, but two large expansions dramatically increased the size in later years. The first expansion occurred in 1999, when engineers figured out how to extend the back of the original structure deep into the hillside behind it. The second, more challenging expansion ran from 2004 to 2007, which added two additional floors in a larger section of the hillside directly behind and above the '99 addition. The facility was now over 155,000 square-feet and boasted four separate security levels, which employees referred to as 'wards.'

The first ward was mostly for show and fully accessible to visitors, provided they had a BSA supervisor as chaperone. Within this security designation, scientists, interns, and university students studied microbiology and applied microbiology, with a heavy focus on pharmaceutical microbiology.

Access to the second ward was reserved for VIP's who were accompanied by a department head or higher. This sector housed the genetics labs where BSA personnel experimented with genetic engineering and genetic mutation theories. Any scientist working in the second ward was required to undergo an extensive background check and vetting process. They were also subject to third-party surveillance and verification related to the maintenance of confidential information.

The third ward, also known as Max-Sec (Maximum Security), housed the chimera lab. Access to the third ward required BSA board approval and was frankly unusual. This super-secure area was home to BSA's applied para-human sciences division, and what the General called, 'our little house of horrors.' In Max-Sec, scientists focused their efforts on adaptation sequencing of human and animal genetics for the purpose of developing para-human beings with specialized phenotype attributes. In laymen's terms, the geeks were trying to mesh certain animal characteristics into a human body or brain. Like a dog's sense of smell or a cat's twitchy reflexes. Using the science, they were trying to engineer humans with super-human capabilities.

As far as most BSA employees were concerned, the 4th ward did not exist. 4th ward personnel entered the facility from a private residence owned by one of Abdullah Kahn's shell companies, which was located on the southwest side of the hill. A secret tunnel at the back of the residence took authorized workers to the 4th ward through the hillside. The residence had armed guards and surveillance 24-7.

The 4th ward was primarily as a site-secure living facility. In actuality, it looked more like a nice hotel then a medical lab, and it housed both employees of the 4th and residents alike. While employees had their own individual quarters, the so-called "residents" lived in communal bedrooms and shared bathrooms, kitchen and laundry facilities.

Residents of the 4th lived under one of two possible classifications: A *new arrival* or a *para-human*. Generally, new arrivals consisted of teenagers and young adults trafficked in from overseas. Most often, they were boys and girls "rescued" from the international sex trade. As a newcomer, initial classification was new arrival, and they lived among other new arrivals while they waited for testing, experimentation, and augmentation. After genetic augmentation started, their classification changed to para-human and they would get transferred to the para-human living quarters.

Kahn had kept up with the facility additions over the years, and knew BSA's general layout. Through BSA's front door, the men came into a nicely appointed lobby. There were flat televisions built into the walls showing US cable news, a beautiful water feature in the center of the room, and plenty of leather furniture and sectional rugs scattered throughout. A dazzlingly attractive woman wearing a headset sat behind the information kiosk desk. As the men approached, the info-gal smiled at them and stood.

"This here is Catalina," Monroe said. "We don't tell everyone this, but she's received some genetic engineering and enjoys youthful radiance as a result, as you can clearly see."

"Hey look," the General elbowed Kahn in a playful way. "There may be hope for your Hand here after all."

The others laughed, while the object of their ridicule scowled at the General.

The young woman pushed a button that buzzed, and a large iron door slid open. Monroe led the way and they entered the administrative wing of the 1st ward. All of the department heads had well-appointed offices in the admin wing. This area looked like a business office with a healthy bottom-line. They passed the offices and came to a rather inconspicuous door at the back with attached thumb pad and retinal scanner.

"We've made a lot of technological improvements to the security systems," Monroe said as the General manipulated the thumb pad and scanner. "At this point, I'd put our facility up against Fort Knox. It's all controlled from a room in the 2nd ward we call 'the bunker,' and the entire enterprise can be locked down from that control center if we experience a security breach."

The Hand entered last. As he did, the General pointed to the height of the retinal scanner and said, "Hey, if you get a security clearance, remind me to get a stepstool installed, K?"

The General was relentless, always picking at the smaller man. The Hand pretended to not hear the jab.

"First ward, macrobiotics," the Doc announced up ahead. "You'll see the major changes since you were here last are cosmetic. We made it look and feel very academic, sterile. We focused on enhanced Feng-Shui for the purpose of successful funding solicitations. This place is a knock-out. Would-be donors tend to leave in awe."

"Speaking of finances, how are we doing these days?" the Hand asked.

"Well, between ongoing cash-flow from funding partners and royalties from numerous patents, we're valued somewhere around the eight-billion mark. Not that any financial exchanges really know or care. Annual operations are holding steady at seventy-six to seventy-eight million; that figure hasn't changed much recently."

"Well done," Kahn patted him on the back. "Last periodic report I read was a while ago and we were nowhere near that mark. What changed?"

"How long ago did you see a periodic report?" the Doctor asked, slightly agitated. The encrypted periodic reports were a specific request made by the Board, of which Abdullah was the chairman. Since only a few people in the world saw them, Monroe viewed the four-time-per-year-drudgery as a colossal waste of time.

"I don't know. I suppose it's been a while, huh?"

"Yes, well, at the request of the board, we did an internal valuation in 2009, and that's what I'm basing the bigger number on. I think the big pop was our 'fat boy slim' patent, which came out of the 2nd ward, with a few off-the-record findings from the 3rd. We used a PTGS process to wipe out fat producing proteins and got the result packaged in a one-time-per-month injection. The tech existed – it was the delivery system everyone was clamoring for. Anyway, it's been approved for human trials in the States now. Little do they know we've already done those," Monroe winked at the Chairman.

"I'm sorry, TG-what?" Kahn interrupted.

"PTGS – it stands for posttranscriptional gene silencing. It's also called RNA Interference. It's essentially a biological process that serves to inhibit gene expression." That explanation only confused them further, so the Doc dumbed it way down.

"It doesn't matter really. Basically, fat people who don't want to give up cake will soon be able to get a prescription for a one-time-per-month injection that will keep their taste buds happy and their waistline slim. We came up with the delivery system so we've been booking lucrative distribution contracts lately."

"Ah, got it. Why didn't you just say that?"

"I should have," he smiled graciously, "Sometimes I get caught up in my own bubble here and forget that the world doesn't necessarily operate the way we do." Monroe was a skilled host and administrator, and Abdullah knew he scored big the day he recruited him. With Monroe at the helm, concern for the future financial viability of the BSA enterprise was ancient history.

They maneuvered through the first ward, dodging lab techs and university students in white jackets who were hustling this way and that. Eventually, they made it to the elevator in the back that connected all four floors. Inside, the Hand observed that the elevator only had three buttons. Monroe saw him looking and fielded the implied question as he tapped the button marked 3.

"You both know the 4th ward is primarily accessed by the residence on the other side of the hill, right?"

The hand nodded as he remembered that detail.

"Well, a few years ago, we added 4th ward access by this elevator, but chose not to add a button. From this lift, the 4th ward is only accessible by keypad entry. Most people don't even know it exists so that's why we didn't bother adding a button for it."

The elevator lurched into gear and began ascending. "We're now on our way to the 3rd ward. Nothing has changed in the 2nd since your last visit Abdullah, so we'll begin the tour in our Max-Sec area."

"Gentlemen," the General said as the elevator reached its destination, "this ward can be upsetting. If you feel queasy or need to get some air, let me know and I'll walk you out. Some of what you are about to see is, frankly, disturbing."

CHAPTER 12
Betty

Sunday, August 21, 2011

As promised, the old Spook left under cover of darkness. After such a blitz of information, the team decided to table discussions and go to sleep. It was a restless night for everyone, as each battled personal demons of fear, sadness, apprehension, and uncertainty. Suddenly, the world was an unrecognizable place, an alien land where the seemingly impossible was now real.

At around 7 am, Sully stumbled out of his room. He started a pot of coffee and poured himself a bowl of cereal. Before long, Con emerged from his room, holding Malcolm's journal and a printout of the file Dotty gave them. He didn't say anything, just tipped his eyebrows as he passed the attorney. Wearing black sweatpants and a plain white t-shirt, he shuffled to the pantry for a bag of oatmeal mix. Con was not much for small talk, and he looked especially sleep deprived, almost hung-over.

Ten minutes later, Anny appeared. She was alert and attentive, and looked much more put together than the guys. She had showered, thrown on some makeup, and put her hair in a ponytail. She wore white shorts that showed off her tanned legs and a black spaghetti strap tank-top with the letters K U in blue across the chest.

"What-up boss? Con-man, good morning to you as well." She touched Sully's shoulder as she passed by and he returned the gesture with a smile. Con gave her the exact same treatment he gave Sully, an eyebrow salute.

"You look like you've been up awhile," the Attorney noted. "How'd you sleep?"

"Okay, I guess," she was lightly squeezing the fruit. "It's always better in your own bed, but I can't complain. I did a little searching on TB Optics last night and again this morning. We may have a mark."

"Oh yeah? Who?"

"Their CTO – a guy named Kyle Rasmussen."

She sat down next to Sully and began peeling her orange. A citrus squirt caught her in the eye. "Ahh," she grimaced, "I'm pretty sure he's single. He'd probably kill for a date. He's one of those, you know."

"A geek, huh? That's a great find."

"Doesn't have to be a geek. You know, I can handle anyone."

"You haven't attempted a star athlete or Hollywood A-lister yet, have you? You think you'd be as effective with those types as you are with tech-boys and old politicians?" He smiled. It was never too early for a little jazz.

"Yep." Simple response, delivered with utter confidence. Sully believed her, and Con shrugged with mutual approval.

Boom. They heard a thud, like the sound of a heavy book bag falling to the floor. It came from Rooter's room. A minute later, Rooter emerged, bare-chested, in only his boxer shorts, scratching his stomach and yawning.

"Morning to you, mainframe, hot chick, and the boss that shall get me killed. I hope you all slept well. I for one did not." He approached the table, stopped short of it, stretched his arms up above his head, and choreographed a little jig to a fart.

Con laughed, Sully shook his head in disbelief, and Anny said with disgust, "Christ, you're an animal."

Rooter looked puzzled, as though he was trying to come up with a comeback. Con, not missing a beat, tossed a banana from the fruit bowl, which struck him in the chest and fell to the floor.

They had a good laugh and ate breakfast with a kind of playful camaraderie that was the hallmark of the K&A team. After breakfast, Rooter insisted he be allowed to participate in the day's functions with just his boxers, and suggested Anny dress to match as a show of solidarity. When the conversation deteriorated, Sully instructed him to put some clothes on. They would reconvene in the gazebo in 30 minutes. The weather outside was unseasonably cool and pleasant; it was perfect weather for another crazy meeting.

Fuzzy seed-spore things hung in the windless air. The dawn was beautiful, and might have garnered a few comments, but everyone was intensely focused on the task at hand. In the gazebo, there were two sofas and two love seats, all configured around a square glass-top cocktail table, which got a good wipe down from Anny before the meeting. The furniture was made of wicker and might have been uncomfortable had Con not found the cushions in his bedroom closet on the first day of lock-down. Anny, who tossed on a hooded sweatshirt, sat with her legs tucked underneath her. Rooter did them the courtesy of an unbuttoned Hawaiian shirt and shorts, and sat back with his feet on the coffee table. He started the meeting with the first obvious question, obviously directed at Con.

"So, my black brutha from anotha-mutha, what do we know about the book?"

"I see three separate sections. In the first section, I think there are math formulas and engineering specs that I bet go to a piece of machinery. I'm not a mechanical engineer so I can't tell you much else. Second section here is full of pictographs and cuneiform writing. I am thinking this tells a story or a history of something in the context of geographic locations. That's just speculation, but there appears to be a chronological component with connected GPS coordinates. Therefore, we have a story with a terrestrial component as well. I mean, actual locations. This is a cool puzzle, and I think I can crack it with a little help."

"How do you know all that?" Anny asked.

"All what?"

"All that, what you just said?"

"Oh, I stayed up last night and found a lot of these images on the web. I cross-referenced the coordinates and found out basically what I just said, that the journal is telling a st..."

"What do you know so far?" Sully interrupted. Con leaned back. He got nervous when confronted in such a direct manner.

"That the story is about something mythical, or mythological, or what we believe to be mythical in our enlightened, postmodern era. What's interesting about it though is that the book doesn't center on any one mythology. There are references to Greek and Roman myths, as well as lots of stuff pertaining to Egyptian and Babylonian lore. Anyway, that's all I really know so far. But it's kind of cool to see technological language meshed with ancient language. I don't know, maybe it's the hacker-geek in me."

"What's the last section?" Anny asked.

"Last section is really weird. I tried uploading some characters and running an image recognition filter and it returned nothing. I did this five separate times with various sections of the text, and on two occasions, I got a possible match to a script known as Eteocypriot. Another time I caught a reference to the track left by a Desert Cobra, native to the Middle East. Evidently, the tip of its tail comes off the dirt and can make squiggles like the ones in the book. I don't know."

Con set the book on the cocktail table, "My feeling is that we need a lot of expert help to understand the last part of the book, and honestly, I wouldn't even know where to start. Last night, I read that Eteocypriot is a dead language that nobody can translate. There are no contemporaneous language keys in existence. This is unlike cuneiform, hieroglyphs, and all those other ancient scribbles where we found roots in a language like Greek."

"What were you saying about the potential mark you found online last night?" Sully returned the question to Anny, signaling a sudden change of direction in the meeting.

"Yeah, I was thinking more about it this morning, and this guy Rasmussen..." She saw Rooter was lost, so she backed up and gave some filler, "He's the TB Optics' Chief Technology Officer. I found him online and identified him as a potential mark, but the more I think about it, I don't think I need to go get in deep with the guy. A better play might be to just introduce myself as a member of the family, say, Malcolm's illegitimate daughter or something. I could just ask some questions as a kid trying to understand her estranged, late father. I'll sprinkle in some intelligent flirtation, you know, and I bet he'll sing like a canary. If he doesn't, I'll go deeper."

"What can he tell us?" Rooter asked, almost defensively.

"He would know about the first section, certainly." Con said.

"That's where I'll start," Anny said, pointing at Con. "I'll feel him out and see if he's game to help us. If he is, we might be able to bring him in on some of this other stuff. If not, I'll get as much as I can from him about the mechanical component Dotty referred to, and we'll just have to go from there."

"Where is Rasmussen? Chicago?"

Anny nodded.

Rooter tilted his head down and peered over his sunglasses at the others, "So, Miss Fleezy-McEasy is fieldin' section one and the abacus is off to crack the ancient riddle in section two. That leaves two Joe jerk-off all-Americans with six-packs and the dead language section. I think I'll take this opportunity to volunteer for security detail, if it's all the same to you."

Anny rolled her eyes at the self-reference to having a six-pack and Con chuckled at the notion of Rooter taking a stab at section three.

"Yeah right? I'm with you. If these guys can't even figure out what the last part is pointing to, we'll have to find our use in some other way."

"I could use help, actually," Con said. "We are pretty secure here, but it's more secure if we're not camping out online. If we gather the pages we need in a short amount of time and do most of our reading and research offline, we'll increase our chances of not being detected by anyone who may be trying to find us."

"Right," Sully jumped on the opportunity to volunteer Rooter for something other than watching TV. "In that case, why don't you set Rooter's laptop up on the secure system so he can help you."

"Since I'm working the family angle with Rasmussen, why don't you go with me?" Anny added.

"Wait-a-minute…" Rooter started, but Anny interrupted him.

"Perfect right? We'll get dinner at that restaurant I love, the Parthanon!"

"Wait just a minute there…"

"Yep, and we'll hit Gene and Georgette's one night for steak," Sully followed, knowing that G&G was Rooter's favorite Chicago dig.

"We should stay at the Drake too." Now they were being mean.

"Now just wait a goddamned minute!" Rooter bellowed. "We should discuss this, I think I should go with McEasy. No offense, Con."

"None taken, but what's the matter with this plan?" Con said, grinning, "I'm going to be too busy researching the book to do things like cook and clean, so there will be plenty for you to do here."

"I'm the housekeeper now?" Rooter stood up in a huff, just as a woman's voice came from the back door and stole their attention.

"No, I'm the housekeeper gorgeous." Standing just outside the back door was a short, stocky black woman with a great smile. She limped over to the gazebo, favoring her left leg. "But y'all can call me Betty."

"Somebody's tell you I was stoppin' by from time to time, didn't they now?"

"Yes Ma'am," Sully answered for the group.

"Good. What'd y'all need then?" When she got to the gazebo, having not been answered, she pointed and gave each person a number starting with Sully, then Anny, then Con, and finally Rooter. "You're num'er one, two, t'ree 'n fo."

When she got to Rooter she smiled wide and took a minute to look him up one side and down the other, as if eyeballing a juicy steak. She then hummed a moaning sound and moved her hips ever so slightly.

"Mmm-mm, damn. Numba fo. You a sexy stud with that chest all up in my biz'ness. What'd you need? Something I can provide? In private maybe?" she winked and puckered her lips, causing a chorus of laughter from the others.

After composing himself, Sully extended his hand to shake hers, "Ma'am, Betty, I don't think we are in need of anything right now, but thanks."

"Yeah? Good."

She climbed the steps up into the gazebo with some strain. This woman was small in stature, but Sully reckoned her a giant by the space her character enveloped. Anny watched with amusement as the woman limped over to Rooter's sofa and gestured for him to scoot over so she could sit next to him. He obliged and quickly began buttoning his shirt as she nudged him and said, "Ey numba fo, you ain't gotta go there. Leave it open."

He went there. He buttoned it all the way up to the neck and started to sweat at the forehead as his three companions watched the awkward interplay. Betty had skill. She actually quieted and neutralized Rooter's dominating personality with just a few words and one little obscure sexual innuendo. She was good, and Anny in particular knew she liked this woman from the get-go.

"What'd y'all standin' there fo? Sit. Sit." She said, gesturing, "I got somthin' fo y'all."

She reached into her shoulder bag and handed '#4' two large yellow envelopes. One was rather thin and the other was fat. Rooter, who was as flustered as anyone ever saw him, quickly passed the envelopes to Sully, and pretended nobody noticed when Betty patted his thigh and whispered, "Shhhhh, you're okay."

Laughing, Anny blurted out, "Betty, can you stay for dinner?"

Rooter shot her the death angel stare and cleared his throat nervously. Betty saw what was happening and played along like a seasoned veteran.

"I don't know. I don't drive aft-a dark. If I stay fo dinna, I prolly need 'ta stay the night." She squeezed his thigh and winked at the others.

Rooter glanced at her and she stared right back, longingly, awkwardly. At this point, Con was laughing so hard he slapped his own knee. Flustered, Rooter excused himself, claiming he needed to use the restroom. As he marched down the few steps to the grass, he heard Betty say in a wildly sarcastic tone, "Don't go, please."

Betty and the three that remained sat there and made fun of the PI, much to Anny's enjoyment. For a good 15 minutes, Rooter watched from the living room window. He dare not venture back outside. He was going to have to get this old woman back, but he didn't know how. He'd think of something. With arms crossed, he watched them from afar and worked on revenge options.

Eventually, Betty got up and announced that she needed to leave and asked if the team had any messages they wanted to send to their "Handler." Sully said he wanted to give an update on their plans and asked for five minutes while he jotted down a quick letter. She handed him an empty envelope and he went to the house to grab paper and pen.

He found Rooter in the living room, sitting casually on the sofa and pretending not to care about what happened. "Why didn't you come back out, bud?" Sully was grinning from ear to ear.

"What? So that jijjiboo can keep on taking shots at me? Nope. I'll tell you this though, she's gonna get hers."

"Take it easy, she was just playin' around."

"Yeah? Why did she target me? For my sex appeal? I'll bet."

Sully was laughing now. "Who cares? It was funny. You'd be in stitches if she'd done that to Con."

Rooter didn't answer and pretended to be fixated on a SI.com article on his PC. Sully took the hint and grabbed paper and pen. He jotted a note to Dotty explaining their initial plan. A few minutes later, Betty walked through the house on her way out the front door and blew a kiss to Rooter as she passed. He ignored her completely.

As soon as Betty left, Sully opened the envelopes and found the fat one contained just under $5,000 in small bills. He gave a few hundred to each individual and put the rest in a kitchen drawer. The second envelope had a letter in it. The letter was very brief and said, *Wanted to send you a little grocery money, let me know when you need more. Also, forensic investigation at your place complete, do not return until you have a green light to do so. In fact, avoid DC if you (Sully, in particular) can. Finally, do you own a cat?*

He looked up from the letter with a puzzled gaze. *A cat? Why would he ask a thing like that?*

After thinking about it for a minute, he raced outside to see if he could catch Betty before she left, but she was already gone.

Anny picked up the letter and read it aloud. Then, as he came back in the house, she asked, "Do you own a cat?"

"No, Leola hated cats."

By lunchtime, Rooter's Hawaiian shirt was back to being unbuttoned and he was back to being his jovial self. He was even able to find a little humor in how Betty had accosted him earlier. During lunch, it was decided that Anny and Solomon would drive to Chicago the next morning, bright and early.

CHAPTER 13
The 3rd Ward

Tuesday, September 20, 2011

The elevator door slid open, revealing a brightly lit, square room. It was empty and windowless, with a metal door on the far wall. The floor, walls, and ceiling all appeared to be concrete. The lights were built into the walls and set behind metal grates. They wrapped around the entire room about a foot below the ceiling. After the elevator shut behind them, a voice over an intercom said, "Buzzing you in now, sir. Stand by." A few seconds later, a loud *clack* sounded and the thick metal door slid open.

That open door revealed a wide hallway that extended into the mountain. This hall was as sterile as the room they just passed through. There were no decorations of any sort – just white walls, white lights, and glass windows and doors opening to individual laboratories and conference rooms. At about the midpoint, a second, longer hallway stretched perpendicular to the right, as if forming a capital 'T'. The men walked together as Dr. Michael Monroe explained the ward's configuration.

"All of our cleanrooms are behind the glass to your left. From inside those labs, this hallway appears to be blue. We use a special filament on these windows to keep the cleanrooms free from unwanted light waves. Each sliding glass door you see represents only the first of a 3-stage transition into the rooms. We also employ airlock and air shower chambers, which follow after the technician changes into cleanroom coveralls. Here on your right, behind these doors, are various offices and meeting rooms, as well as labs that do not require such strict control of airborne particulates. Past that hallway, you'll find our small, medium, and large holding quarters for bio-genetic specimens."

"The cleanrooms only extend two-thirds of the way down. What's on the left, past the glass wall there?" asked the Hand.

"Down there we have three state-of-the-art operating rooms and a recovery room. We loosely refer to that section of the ward as our hospital."

"And what about this hallway to the right? What's down there?" asked Abdullah.

"Down there are a series of holding cells and what we call the morgue. Occasionally, when experimentation goes poorly or ends up being unsuccessful, that's where we dispose of deceased organisms."

"I see. Call that the ugly side of BSA, right?"

"Indeed," the men stopped where the halls converged and the Doctor asked, "So then, what would you like to see first?"

"You're the tour guide, you tell us."

"Monroe to Spencer," the Doc said into a handheld walkie-talkie.

"Spencer here."

"Meet me at the 3-w junction please."

"On my way."

Turning to his guests, he explained, "Spencer is the third ward supervisor and knows our residents the best. I'll have him show us around and make a few introductions."

A minute later, a male with lanky features who looked mid-twenties approached them from the morgue. On closer look, they realized he was quite a bit advanced of his twenties.

"Gentlemen, may I introduce Spencer, our first successful chimera."

"Pleasure to meet you all."

"He looks perfectly normal," the Hand observed.

"Yes indeed," said Monroe. "He is perfectly normal, except for the fact that Spencer is a human containing animal material, which makes him a chimera. A chimera is an animal-human hybrid. You see, Spencer here used to be a university student working on his doctorate back around the time we launched. After finishing his education, he joined us full-time. He is a pioneer in genetic manipulative technologies and stem cell research. He is also our resident expert on engineering what we call 'artificial life' at the molecular level."

"Wait a minute, you don't look a day over twenty-five," observed Kahn.

Spencer smiled, "Add 32 years to that and you pegged me."

"No," The Hand exhaled with disbelief.

"It's true. I'm a Picasso. I've been using my body as a canvas for this stuff for a long time."

"You're not *a* Picasso, you are Picasso," the Hand said.

"On behalf of my pale little friend," the General grinned, "I'd ask if you could help him with his physical abnormalities, but I'm sure even Picasso has his limitations, right?"

The General had expected the others to laugh, but nobody did. An awkward silence filled the corridor before Monroe cleared his throat and continued.

"Six, maybe seven years ago, Spencer decided to exact an experiment on himself. In this experiment, Spencer had stem cells taken from his jawbone. Here, why don't we show them?"

Spencer lifted his head and showed them his scars, which extended from below his ear along the jawline for about two inches on both sides. Because of their location, they were rather discrete. The doctor pointed and continued his explanation.

"In two separate operations, Spencer was able to get mesenchymal, multipotent stem cells from the inferior maxillary bone – the jaw bone here – as well as tissue-specific stem cells from his oral mucosa, which is the inner cheek. He took these cells to the lab, and synthesized them with stem cells from a cobra snake's jaw region, to engineer a thing we call an 'induced pluripotent stem cell.' He then used a biolistic particle delivery technique to insert the new strand into the host, which was his jaw. After that, he broke his own jaw and allowed the new DNA to repair the break, which effactually gave him a double-jointed jaw, just like a cobra."

As the Doc finished with the explanation, Spencer opened his mouth in a manner that shocked both Abdullah and the Hand, to the point that the Hand looked away momentarily, startled.

"That's fascinating," said Kahn, who peered into Spencer's mouth cavity, which now had a diameter of just over seven inches. He chuckled nervously when he saw a second split-tongue near the back of his throat. "You have a split tongue in addition to your human one?"

Spencer closed his mouth and said, "Yes, it was a secondary genetic mutation. It doesn't bother me at all so I left it. The strange thing about genetic engineering is that for every successful mutation, there are frequently other, non-expected mutations that tag along for the ride. A good example is found in the news today with the goats that produce spider silk."

"I heard about this. I saw it on the BBC."

"That's right. Scientists are harvesting spider silk from goats, which were engineered to carry the specific protein needed for silk. Occasionally, every so often, a goat is born with an additional mutation that's hard to explain. In the case of those goats that are being used to harvest spider silk, some ended up producing venom-glands because the genetic splice was from a black-widow. I understand they ended up changing the source species gene to a non-venomous alternative, but you get the point. Whether the unexpected mutation is visible or not, they are peculiar because they seem to accompany the primary, sought-after mutation randomly, though we ideally don't change the recipe, so to speak."

"Do you crave mice and bugs and shit too?" the Hand asked nervously, lost on the larger explanation of primary and secondary mutations.

"No, I don't," Spencer chuckled, "but you bring up a good example of how tweaking the recipe can lead to a more exact outcome. You see, I conducted this jawbone experiment on a hamster back in the '90's. The first time I did it, the rodent developed bumps where the Cobra's venom glands were supposed to be, although the venom never formed. Anyway, I redid the experiment using an additional stem cell from the rodent in the synthesis of the induced pluripotent cell – as a counterbalance – and, blah-blah-blah, point is, eventually we got the recipe right and I was so certain the venom glands would not form, I conducted it on myself."

"Good on you for having the guts to do it, I suppose," Kahn nodded in admiration.

"The more we do it, the more exact the science becomes. When I used the bio-ballistic technique five years ago, nobody else in the world had a clue. We've moved on from those days and are now pioneering things that would shock the editors of *Popular Science*, but I'll save you from more of my boasting for the time being."

"No, I want to know. Such as what?" asked Kahn.

"Put it this way. I was what we call a secondary hybrid, or first generation chimera. I was in my 30's the first time I genetically engineered myself. Primary chimeras are specimens born with their genetic alterations intact. Back in the '90's, we were running thousands of tests per year, on both animal and human subjects, in vitro, for the purpose of adding, removing or exchanging specific genetic sequences at various spots in the subject's genome. For every thousand experiments that failed, one succeeded. Eventually, we brought primary chimeras to term and a healthy birth. The reason we refer to me as a first gen chimera is because the scientific procedures to accomplish double-jointedness are isolated, small, and procedurally much easier than what we were attempting to do in vitro."

"So, you are raising hybrids then?" the Hand asked.

"No, we're past that. We are still experimenting, researching, growing, and developing chimera, yes. But the molecular biology is pointing us toward *Zoe Ginosko*, what we call *life-essence realization*. The technology involving chimera is interesting to be sure, but the science that orbits what some around here are calling *the soul of a human* is exceedingly fascinating. To my knowledge, we're the only lab in the world that's delving into these waters."

"I think we may be getting ahead of ourselves," Monroe interjected. "Gentlemen, if you would, please accompany me to the holding quarters. We'll start with the small specimens."

Some distance past the perpendicular hallway they came to an iron door on the right with the words *Small Specimens* on a plaque just below a window. The window was only a foot by a foot, but large enough that Abdullah saw a number of employees in white lab coats working inside. After swiping a keycard and entering a six-digit numeric code, the door clicked open. They walked into a rather large room with compartments built into the concrete walls. The compartments varied in size, from less than the size of the window in the door to roughly three-by-three feet. In the center of the room were numerous tables and a half-dozen lab techs working under bright lights.

This room housed hundreds of very small samples in petri dishes. Many of the samples were synthesized chromosomes that had been mixed and meshed with both animal and human DNA. If visible to the naked eye, these items looked a lot like mold. Doc Monroe and Spencer both rambled on about the various scientific breakthroughs that BSA was researching in those petri dishes, and most of it made little sense to Kahn or his sidekick. However, in the larger compartments, mice, rats, and hamster-sized rodents were plentiful, and many of these looked rather strange.

As a result of genetic engineering, one hamster had a crazy hair pattern, one rat had eight legs, and one caterpillar was over a foot long with a six-inch diameter. It was an ugly monster to be sure.

All of the animals were recipients of forced genetic mutation. Every live animal in the Small Specimen Room was a hybrid animal-animal or animal-synG (fully synthetic double-strand DNA molecule) of some sort, except the hamster they referred to as Third Boyd. He was named for the third attempt that succeeded. Third Boyd was an actual animal-human hybrid, which looked just like a hamster in every way, except for the human eyebrows, human eyelashes, and human hair on his head. The crew got a laugh when Spencer parted it like Mr. Rogers.

Third Boyd was rather cute. He could use facial muscles to move his eyebrows like a normal human, and this gave him the ability to display a wide range of facial expressions uncommon to hamsters. After a tech gave a short briefing on the scientific importance of the Third Boyd hamster-human chimera, the men left the Small Specimen Room and entered the Medium Specimen Room further down the hall.

The Medium room was roughly the same size and similarly structured. Only two techs were working when the visitors entered. It had 66 holding compartments, and no compartment was smaller than three-by-three-by five foot deep.

The residents of this room were primarily monkeys and baboons. Of the 66 compartments, 54 were occupied with specimen-residents, eleven of which were animal-human hybrids.

One baboon had the mouth, teeth, tongue and lips of a human and was able to contort its mouth to form human expressions. The staff technician referred to it as the "bearded woman."

Three chimera specimens had no visible physical alterations, but had inherited human phenotypes. One had human immune characteristics, one had the testicles of a man, and another had a dual – one monkey, one human – liver, although the human liver was non-functional.

The oddest looking chimera in the bunch had human feet and human hands, and the techs were fascinated by the tactile functions of those hands, and how preoccupied the specimen was with the touch sensation of its fingertips and toes. The chimera spent the bulk of his day touching the walls and floor in his holding cell, seeming to enjoy the sensation it caused.

The Large room had 25 holding compartments and was almost twice the size of the other two rooms. Rather than a series of tables and lab equipment, there were two metal poles in the middle of the room with thick, two-inch chain-link attached at various points. At first glance, this room looked like a sterile torture chamber. However, the chains were only used to restrain a specimen when it became agitated during an evaluation. At present, 21 of the compartments were occupied.

The group watched in awe as the Doc ordered two techs to do a demonstration with specimen 'J', a wolf-human hybrid. One of the techs aimed a chemical dart gun at J while the other gave the chimera a few simple commands, to which J complied for fear of the dart. They explained that the dart gun was a deterrent, and used to condition J to respond to simple prompts in a mild manner.

J walked like a human, had the torso and head of a wolf, but the penis, buttocks, hips, legs, and feet of a man. J had opposable thumbs, but short, hairy arms that bent downward like the front legs of a four-legged animal. Because he had opposable thumbs, J was ordered to extend his hairy hand and give Abdulla a handshake. The visitors were awestruck. J was a menacing thing. He stood just over six feet tall when fully erect, with razor-sharp wolf teeth within his oversized snout, which he'd show on command. After J was safely returned to his holding compartment, the tech holding the dart gun lowered the weapon.

"What we've found with animal-human hybrids," the Doc explained, "is that they tend toward impulsiveness. They never really lose their animalistic itch. They follow orders if they feel like it, but if they don't, they can be quite aggressive and very unpredictable. We've also found that altering the skeletal structure of the host is much easier than altering the intelligence of the host. As of yet, only specimen Y, who recently passed away, could understand and articulate back certain words in

English. This is why the primary and secondary chimera we use in the field, for the General's operations, are humans containing animal enhancements. Here on the third, we test the theories exhaustively, and when we are certain that the science is understood and the recipe is right, we implant full-grown human operatives, much the same way Spencer got the serpent jaw."

"What was specimen Y, if I may ask," the Hand wondered out loud.

"Y was a chimpanzee. He was altered in vitro, born to his mamma a healthy little guy, and remained healthy until his fourth year when his body began to deteriorate quickly. His face had some human characteristics, most notably in the oral cavity, and he had a genetically altered vocal cord. Our mission with Y was to stimulate what's called Broca's Area of the frontal lobe to enable coherent speech. It worked to a certain extent. He could comprehend and correctly respond to simple questions, such as when a tech would hold up a red apple and ask, 'What color is this apple', Y would answer 'red.' And so forth. But he never did learn how to respond with a question or critically analyze and verbally respond to his own analysis."

The fiercest looking chimera in the Large Specimen room was what the techs called 'the Devil.' He was an animal-human hybrid that stood erect on two legs and was almost 8-feet-tall. The only human looking appendages were his legs and arms, hands and feet. He had the face of a ram, but a mutation made it more rounded (his nose did not protrude like a ram's). This mutation gave him a more human-like jawline as well. He had two huge, curved horns – like a bighorn sheep – that wrapped up and out from his forehead. He spent most of his time shaking and ramming the bars of his holding cell, which was down the other hallway, toward the morgue.

The Devil was in the Large Specimen Room on this particular day because he was being given his weekly checkup. He was clearly not happy about it. In fact, because the Devil was so obnoxious, their time in the LSR was cut short and the guests ventured back into the hallway to get away from the Devil's growls and barky howls.

Back in the hallway, the Doc asked, "Would you like to see the 4th?"

"Absolutely."

"Okay then, follow me. There are two separate areas that comprise the 4th ward. One is the maximum security lab, which we'll see first. The other is the OLS, which is our observation and monitoring side. The OLS is very comfortable and well appointed. We'll see that second..."

CHAPTER 14
The Drake

Rooter kept his promise and had a hot breakfast of fried eggs, bacon, and toast waiting for Sully and Anny. They were up and ready to go at just past 4 am. Con showed great restraint and slept through the sendoff, even as the aromas of bacon, eggs, and coffee permeated the safe house.

Rooter poured himself a cup of coffee and talked as they ate. They were like family. They bantered like family, argued like family, and defended one another against outsiders like family.

Normally, Rooter's shtick was to poke fun at Anny, dishing jazz for anything he could. She gave as well as she got. They both enjoyed the banter, and seemed to find an odd pleasure in the tension. But on this morning, Rooter was attentive and concerned for her wellbeing. He was even sweet toward her, like a protective brother making sure she knew exactly what to do if she got caught in a difficult situation. She reciprocated by being open to his advice and counsel, and working through his contingency plans.

Sully ate his food quietly and watched their exchange. He loved his crew, but on mornings such as this, his feelings for them were amplified. The banter could be fun, but it got overwhelming at times for he and Con. Their pace during breakfast was a nice change, and it reinforced the true undercurrent of love and admiration they had for one another.

In observing their mutual kindness and care, it wasn't long before Sully's mind began to drift back. Soon, he returned to a hazy place full of confusion, anger, and doubt.

She was so small, so frail and sweet and vulnerable. Did she hurt? Did it hurt when the bullet went into her chest? Did she cry for me? Did she hope that I'd come in and save her? And that look on her face – the look of shock – like she couldn't believe it was actually over. Her life ended so abruptly, so suddenly, so awfully. Why wasn't I there? How come I didn't see it coming…?

Although he spent nearly a decade with his beautiful one-and-only, it was difficult to recall her many expressions from life. Only one expression was evocable, and it came in vivid detail. It was that haunting look, that wide-eyed, gape-mouthed, emotionless expression of shock on the floor of the tub. Hot tears welled up in his eyes as he thought about the wedding dress she never put on, the children she'd never raise, and the places she'd never see. He held the tears back for a moment, but the hurt began to throb and he couldn't help it. With his left thumb, he wiped under an eye, and that's when he felt a hand on his forearm. It was Anny's, and her eyes were also moist.

Sully took a deep breath and forced a wry smile. She held onto his forearm, so Sully dropped his fork and tucked her hand in his. Rooter sipped his coffee and gazed to nowhere. After a second forced deep breath, the attorney said, "I'm okay. We're okay. We should probably get going."

He asked to drive and she was eager to let him. Within ten minutes they each stowed a suitcase in the trunk and were heading north on the aptly named, Solomon's Island Road. They would look veer northwest and merge onto the 301 to the Baltimore beltway.

Anny had her beautiful, multi-highlighted blond hair up in a ponytail and wore a casual t-shirt, shorts, and flip-flops. Though the assaulting sun was still hidden, she was ready for it, with a pair of sunglasses staged high on her head. Sully was also dressed casually, sporting the male-version of the same attire. In place of stylish sunglasses, he wore an old ball cap.

They made small talk to pass the time. He asked about KU and her life as an Alpha Chi Omega. He asked about her childhood and where she grew up. He dug a bit for some of her fond memories. She was good at carrying a conversation and talked, laughed, and giggled freely. He was thankful for her skill at levity. His heart was heavy and listening to her was the perfect elixir. She was always gregarious, but during their drive he realized just how fun and funny she really was. There was an ease about her, a facile nature in everything she did and said. He found it refreshing that she could so easily poke fun at herself and her past decisions.

"Hey, where did you book us?" she asked, somewhere around the Pennsylvania – Ohio border.

He smiled, "I booked the Drake. Where else?"

"No," she said in a manner that means *yes*, "That's rad."

"That's *rad?*"

"What?" she laughed. "Did I just date myself in a non-romantic way?"

"Yes you did."

Anny was not a high-maintenance gal by any stretch, but she loved to be spoiled if the opportunity presented itself. The Drake Hotel was one of those iconic places that she hoped to visit. He leaned forward, turned up the radio, and made a comment about her affinity for the '90's just as an old *Guns 'n Roses* song came on.

As the music took front-and-center, she watched the world pass by, and got lost in her thoughts.

I wonder how the sleeping situation is going to unfold? She bit her lip. That wasn't something she wondered about yet. Feeling a bit vulnerable, she glanced over her sunglasses at Sully, who paid no attention. *The Drake is expensive, so he probably got a single room. Good God, what if there is only one bed?*

She considered asking him outright, but decided against it to avoid the potential awkwardness. Nevertheless, she considered what to do in the event he only reserved one room.

She took a second glance at him, but this time for some reason her eyes settled on his defined forearm and drifted toward the strong hand that gripped the steering wheel. He had strong hands. A silly, erotic thought flashed across her mind as she reflexively looked to see if he had noticed her. He hadn't. She shook her head and laughed at herself, but then got realistic. *If this man comes onto me sober, I'll have a helluva time saying 'no.' If he does after a drink, there's no way I could say 'no.'*

She swallowed hard. That was a moment of honesty that scared her. She wasn't weak-minded with regard to sexual tension, but Sully was a trustworthy, good-looking guy, who made her feel safe and comfortable. She just knew she wouldn't say 'no' if he asked or pursued. *With that being the case, I'll not drink,* she decided abruptly. But her heart fluttered, nonetheless.

For the next few hours, she obsessed about the sleeping arrangements, all based on a set of assumptions. Oddly though, the more she obsessed about the travel particulars, the more she craved something that would propel them into a deeper relationship.

Where is this coming from? She wondered, frustrated. And then it dawned on her. She never considered him an option because for as long as she knew him, he was with Leola. *Leola. What a betrayal that I'm even thinking about this. Poor girl hasn't had time enough to settle in peace and I'm already plotting to bed her boyfriend? What sort of a sick person am I?*

By the time Sully pulled up to the Drake's valet, she was tied in emotional knots and not looking forward to checking in.

He too had noticed a marked change in her temperament hours earlier. At times, he casually wondered what she was thinking, and supposed it had to do with the upheaval of recent life. He considered asking her if everything was okay, but decided against it.

"Welcome to the Drake. Last name, please?" said a flamboyant front desk clerk.

"Keys," Sully smiled casually.

"Ah yes, it looks like you have two rooms booked with us today, and we have put you across the hallway from one another on the 14ᵗʰ floor. Will that be acceptable?"

"That's fine," Sully pulled out an American Express card.

Anny exhaled in relief louder than she expected. In fact, she was so demonstrative with her sigh that Sully immediately realized why she was so removed for the last few hours. The front desk clerk flimflammed his way through the check-in particulars as he did a thousand times per week, but Anny didn't hear any of it. She looked at Solomon and tried to use her eyes to say she was sorry for her absurd behavior, and silently whipped herself for letting cynicism ruin the last half of their drive. *What a great guy,* she thought. *Of course he wasn't going to take advantage of me. I'm so stupid.*

They got to the 14ᵗʰ floor and he followed Anny into her room to check it out before heading to his own to unpack. She was back to being herself, light-hearted and easy-breezy.

"Nice place, huh?" he said.

"It's beautiful. You're the man for booking us here."

"Look here, complimentary chocolate bites," he said, perusing a gold-leafed ornamental bowl full of goodies on the counter.

"Doubt it's free."

"True," he took one anyway and unwrapped it, "nothing's ever really free in life. You want one anyway?"

"Nah. So, what's the plan, friend?"

Sully called down to the front desk and asked the concierge for advice on a casual restaurant for dinner. She suggested and they agreed on Giordano's Pizza, just a few blocks over on Rush Street.

"Meet you at six in the lobby then?" she confirmed.

"I'll be there," he waved as he exited her room to find his own.

Anny decided to take a shower. As she went through the motions, she couldn't stop thinking about how proud she was of Solomon. She realized that one of the reasons she liked him so much, not just as a boss but as a friend, was because he always did the right thing. He wasn't a manipulative guy, the type that takes advantage of women or circumstances. He was a genuine man who didn't like game playing when it came to people and emotions.

She knew he was grieving, and moving into a new relationship was obviously far from his mind. But she wondered if, in time, there was a chance that they might build something together. Her heart skipped a beat at the thought. She stopped undressing and looked at her image in the bathroom mirror. *I'm almost 27. What is he? Mid-30's maybe? We'd be a cute couple...*

Her eyes settled on the clothes she picked out for the evening, a cute tank top and jeans.

I always do a tank top and jeans. Predictable people don't get noticed. She bit her lip and crossed her arms. *Screw it, if it's ever going to happen, he needs to start noticing me and that's not gonna happen unless I change it up from time to time.*

Turning, she grabbed the Egyptian cotton bathrobe, compliments of the Drake, and tossed it over her shoulders. Marching back to her bedroom, she consulted her suitcase a second time in search of something with a little more pizazz. She settled on a black tunic-style sleeved top, meant to drape over just one shoulder, and a black miniskirt with white trim along the bottom hem. She accessorized the outfit with black shoes and a generic black and white handbag. It was one of her many go-to outfits when making a first impression on a new mark.

Checking the time, she hurried into the shower. Some quality effort was needed for her hair and makeup to ensure the whole ensemble popped the way she wanted.

CHAPTER 15
A Shook Up Betty

Monday, August 22, 2011

Betty was waiting for Father Abelemy at the *Sweet Leaf Café* in McLean, a few miles south of CIA Headquarters. He was late, but she figured typical Monday traffic was the reason for the delay. To pass the time, she grabbed a booth, ordered a Coke, and perused her Facebook page on her cell.

When attending to an empty residence, she was only required to participate in two oversight review meetings per year. Normally, these took place at the Central Intelligence compound. However, because she was now attending to what CIA referred to as a *guesthouse* (occupied) instead of *safe house (unoccupied)*, her title and function were upgraded from *housekeeper* to *information liaison*. As an "IL," her pay increased, but so did her responsibilities. She was now required to attend one ORM per week with Father Abelemy.

Her weekly meetings with Father Abelemy – or a designee he might send – were scheduled to take place at public venues now. Due to once-a-week frequency, it was much easier for them to meet and exchange information off CIA grounds, as the security clearance and check-in process can be overbearing for outsiders. The *Sweet Leaf Café* was their spot, for now, and the ORM was scheduled for 2:30 pm every Monday.

Betty was seated at a window. At one point, she looked out and saw the Father pull up and park. She glanced at her wristwatch, which read 2:56 pm. She grunted something under her breath and summoned her best demeanor of indifference. A minute or so later, she looked up from her cell phone a second time and noticed, oddly, he was still sitting in his car. That's when she realized that her vantage point looked north, which meant he was not even parked in the café's lot. He was actually parked in Rocco's next door. She watched as he sat in his car slouched in the front seat until 3:02 pm, at which point he got out and walked briskly toward the front door of the café. Once inside, he suspiciously eyeballed the patrons one by one as he made his way toward her.

"Ever-thing Okay?" Betty asked as he sat and adjusted his ball cap, tugging it low on his aging brow. "You seem, I don't know, stressed out."

"Betty, I am," he took off his sunglasses and put them on the brim of his hat for safekeeping. "I keep seeing this black Toyota Tacoma with dark tinted windows. I can't help but wonder about it."

"This car followin' you?"

"I can't be sure. A few days ago I went to the crime scene," he paused, realizing she had no operational knowledge of anything, "The crime that landed your guests. Anyway, I went there to take a look around and think I saw a Tacoma parked in a public lot across the street. I can't be sure. The observation didn't matter at the time, so I never stopped to take a second glance."

"So you seen a random car twice and now you're all hopped up on jigglies? Sir, you don't mind me sayin' so, I recommend a nap 'n a cold shower." She gave him a big smile and it actually helped put him at ease.

Betty had a simple outlook on life and that's what was great about her. She just did her job, did it loyally, and never got involved with politics or drama. She was quick to tell a person off if it suited her, but quick to forgive and forget as well. She paid no mind to meddlers and busybodies, and expected others to do her the same courtesy.

The aproned server arrived just as Betty shoved her cell phone deep into her purse. The Father ordered a Raspberry Iced Tea.

A cold shower might have been the answer, had he merely seen the Tacoma twice. Betty would never know, but it was a tad more complicated than that.

After his case officer tipped him to the NSA Satellite intel, Dotty quickly pulled off the highway and into a roadside gas station. No sooner had he pulled the keys form the ignition, a black Tacoma went whizzing past him on the highway. The Tacoma caught his attention because it was moving well above the posted speed limit, and something *felt* odd about it. Next was in the middle of the night. Dotty woke to use the restroom, and on his way back to bed he saw headlights assaulting the slits in his horizontal blinds. He looked out just in time to see a dark colored pickup truck creep by the home; again, the whole thing felt odd. If that wasn't enough, he was certain a black pickup, which might have been a Tacoma, had tailed him on his drive from HQ to the café, that very afternoon. The Father was not late because of Monday traffic, he was late because he had to lose the tail; if indeed one actually existed.

With one eye out the window and one on the front door, he resolved to keep the meeting as brief as possible. "So, Betty, you make the drop?"

"Yessir I did."

"They give you anything?" He asked, not paying attention to the letter that she already pulled from her purse.

"Got somethin' right here," she said, slightly miffed by his distraction.

He took the envelope and opened it on the spot. She saw him frown momentarily when he realized that Sully had not answered his question about the cat. He reread the brief description of their plan and decided it was a good start. From his own briefcase, he pulled out paper and pen and scribbled a note acknowledging the plan and asked again, *did you and Leola own a cat??*

As he stuffed the note into a manila envelope, he saw, or thought he saw out of the corner of his eye, someone duck behind the back wall of Rocco's Italian Restaurant. He couldn't be sure. Did he see a shadow? He turned his attention out the window and watched with cold patience for a minute, then two. Betty began to fidget. A thick, cold air settled about their booth as nerves began to jump. A Rocco's kitchen employee then suddenly emerged, rounding the corner with a bag of garbage slung over his shoulder. The bag was tossed into a dumpster. *Was that what I saw? Something doesn't feel right.*

Abelemy glanced around at the other windows in the café, stretching and straining to see if he could spy the Tacoma somewhere. Betty mumbled something to herself but the Father ignored her. After a half-minute of working through the options in his mind, he asked Betty to get up and go to the restroom. Sternly, he told her to stay there until he came to get her. She obeyed without question and departed the booth, mumbling, "Lord have mercy, this man is a walkin' Crisco heart-attack, he is..."

Dotty left a $10 bill on the table to pay for the Coke and tea as he advanced to the front of the café, keeping his eyes on Rocco's back side. Once outside, he checked his sidearm to assure its live-fire status and hustled towards Rocco's at a hastened but calculated pace. Discreetly, he pulled his weapon and took careful steps along the concrete sidewalk that marked the edge of the café's property line. He scanned the parking lots and side streets for the Tacoma, but did not see it.

Behind Rocco's, he found two employees smoking pot on the back door stoop. They were startled initially, but Dotty held up a hand and told them to be at ease. He asked if they saw anyone hanging out behind the building.

"No sir, I see no-ting," one said while the other shrugged, signaling he did not understand English.

"Go on then," Dotty barked, frustratingly waving his gun hand at them, "Get out of here. Your boss doesn't pay you to sit outside and smoke dope."

They got the hint and ran back inside, slamming the door behind them. The old spook peered into a small parking lot behind some shrubbery, which was directly behind the Italian restaurant. No Tacoma. He holstered his gun and looked back at the café. From that vantage point, he could see into the restaurant and table where he and Betty had been sitting. He pulled his sunglasses off the brim and put them on. The polarized lenses actually deadened the glare further, making it even easier to see inside the eatery's windows. Had someone spied them from this vantage point, Betty's identity was no longer secure. He took one more lap around the café in search of the Tacoma, but found no sign of it.

In the world of espionage, circumstantial evidence and gut-feelings are quite often one and the same. Dotty was seasoned enough to know something was wrong and humble enough to know he was dealing with a professional. It was a stressful game of cat-and-mouse, a game he played a handful of times in his career and always detested. This game tended to end with someone dying.

"Betty?" he said, lightly knocking on the door to the women's room. "Betty, you can come out now."

"Everthin' okay sir?" she emerged cautiously.

"I think so. Come on out, hun."

Dotty took her by the elbow and gently walked her to the front of the café, "Look, Betty, I want you to drive slow and keep a tight eye on your rearview mirror on the way back to Edgewater. I did not see anything suspicious out there, but you can never be too safe. If you see a black Tacoma, or anything that gives you the, what did you call it earlier, the *jigglies*? You call me, hear?"

She nodded and chuckled, half from nerves and half from witnessing the old Greek use the word *jigglies*. "Yessir, I hear ya. Just one question tho. What's a Tacoma?"

Dotty smiled. He did not want her in harm's way, but more importantly, he didn't want her to unwittingly lead the Phantoms to his guests in Edgewater. She was a sweet, naïve, Southern lady, and totally out of her element. She really had no business being in the middle of this, but there was nothing he could do about it right then.

"Betty, hun, a Tacoma is a pickup truck made by Toyota. The one I'm nervous about is painted black and has dark tinted windows. Makes it hard to see who's inside."

"Yep, okay, I musta known it," she assured. "I'm fine, sir. I'll call ya if I see a black Tacoma or anythin' that looks queer-like and gives me the jigglies. No problem, sir."

Dotty held her gaze for a minute, then lightly squeezed her arm and smiled. "Okay, hun. I'll keep an eye on you from behind for awhile." She nodded again.

"You do have that letter I just scribbled?"

"Yessir, right in my luggage here," she patted her oversized purse.

"Okay then, on your way now. I'm going to follow you at a distance. At least until Mitchellville. I'll call your cell and give you the all-clear, so be sure to answer when I call, okay?"

"Yessir, I will." Betty looked rattled. Her eyes darted around suspiciously, and she fidgeted with her hands when nervous.

The Father knew her nerves were genuine, and that she was in over her head. He decided to consult his case officer as soon as possible about sending Sully's team someone for protection. There was no sense in being cavalier.

Dotty climbed into his car and circled into the café's parking lot so he could follow Betty. Were the Phantoms truly after him? It didn't make any sense. They surely could have killed him well before this point, just based on the evidence of their work at Alpha Kilo. The Father was beginning to get the distinct impression that he was not being targeted for assassination as much as he was being watched, studied somehow. What was their play? What was their operational goal? He simply did not know, and that was what really disturbed him.

Betty's driving signaled the world that she was a tentative and nervous vehicle operator. At least she was on this day. For 30 minutes, she was unable to relax and mumbled to herself as she drove. That was a nervous habit. She calmed down significantly after the Father called to say he saw nothing out of the ordinary, and that he was heading back to his office. Clicking off the phone, she said a little prayer of thanks out loud, inhaled a deep breath, and stretched her stiff neck. Frequent meetings aside, this level of stress was hardly worth the pay increase.

She kept an eye on the rearview as instructed, but was starting to think the Father might just be paranoid. Abelemy had managed to stress her out in a way she hadn't experienced since having a teenage daughter running around the house. As she neared her own home in Edgewater, she thought, *if I had that man's job I'd put a bullet in my head and say 'te hell wit it.' How's he live with his self? Cranky, stressed-out old man; I am quite happy to not see him any more than once per week. And if every meeting is going to be like this, he can go find a new housekeeper, or info lassy, or whatever the heck I am now! No sir...*

Her run-on thoughts lasted well into the night. She had a hard time falling asleep and kept going to her front window to peer into the sleepy neighborhood street. She thought about the black Tacoma continuously. During spats of bad sleep, she even dreamed about it. Eventually, after she sipped down a cup of nighttime tea with a pinch of Southern Comfort, she fell into a restless sleep that lasted the night.

CHAPTER 16
Marduk

Saturday August 27, 2011

It was after 2 pm when Con finally stumbled out of his room for the first time that day. He looked terrible; his short hair was flat on one side and poufy on the other and he wore a t-shirt that he'd not changed in 48 hours. Rooter looked up from his magazine, "There he is. Long time no see, bud. How's the research going?"

"Honestly you don't wanna know." Con stretched and yawned.

"The hell I don't. I've reread this issue of *Sports Illustrated* three times this morning alone and I'm bored stiff," Rooter tossed the magazine on the coffee table, stood up, and gestured to the sofa, "Here, sit down and I'll whip up a little lunch. Just do me a solid and spit a few cliff notes my way. I'm dying here."

"I won't say no to lunch," Con fell heavily into a seat. "Got any coffee?"

"I had some. I drank the whole pot this morning. I'll make some more, just give me a sec." The PI banged a few pots together as he reached for a cutting board, "So tell me what's going on already. You want me to beg or somethin'?"

"Alright. Where to begin?" Con scratched his fizzy head and thought about it for a second. "I had Father Abelemy send me whatever he could on Operation Iraqi Freedom and was able to identify the general area of intrigue as it relates to Sully's dad."

"His uncle, right?"

"That's right, his uncle Malcolm. Anyway, he could not get me the specific coordinates of the location where Malcolm died because I guess it's classified. So I've been trying to cross-reference what he's given me with the markings in the journal to try and narrow it down and that's how I landed where I did, but it's opened up a whole new can of worms."

"So where did he die, first off."

"Babylon." Con was leaning forward on the sofa, elbows to knees and rubbing his temples.

"Babylon? What, the city from the Bible?"

"Yeah, the historical site. Where Saddam Husain was rebuilding directly over the ruins."

"Saddam was rebuilding Babylon?"

"That's a matter of public record, dude. He was putting bricks directly over the ancient ruins of Babylon, inscribing them the exact same way King Nebuchadnezzar had, even."

"Huh," Rooter grunted, pretending to care.

"Anyway, there is an image that surfaces throughout Malcolm's journal. It's a picture is of a creature called a Mušḫuššu. I found the name for this thing after scanning it through my imagery software. Evidently, the Mušḫuššu was a Babylonian mythological creature that had the head and body of a dragon, hind legs resembling Eagle's talons, and the forelegs of a feline animal. It doesn't appear to have wings and ancient texts indicate it walked on all fours. That name, Mušḫuššu actually means 'reddish snake'."

"What's interesting about the Mušḫuššu is that artifacts recovered from ancient Babylonia consistently depict this beast from as early as 2500 Before-Common-Era, all the way through the Hellenistic period in the 330's BC-era. Some literature I've read actually makes a strong case that this red-snake was not so much mythological, but real, roaming the streets of the ancient city of Babylon. So that's how I figured out where Malcolm likely died; the Mušḫuššu markings found in Malcolm's book point to the ruins of ancient Babylon, and the military docs the Father sent also reference a region between the Tigris and Euphrates around 50-clicks south of current day Baghdad. Both docs point to the same place. An ex-Marine wrote a blog about his time in Iraq and referred to the ruins of Babylon as 'Alpha Kilo', so that's what I'm calling it from now on."

"Alpha-Kilo," Rooter repeated as he stuffed a couple hoagies with condiments, "equals ancient city of Babylon. Got it."

Con chuckled at the idea of trying to explain the rest of his findings. "This is where it gets pretty weird. It looks like Malcolm Bernard made a few wax paper rubbings of an image he found, wherever he was, and I think he considered these images very important."

"Why is that?" Rooter looked up and paused, "Wait, wax paper rubbings? What are you talking about?"

"I didn't tell you?" Con was grinning, "Yeah, I found wax paper rubbings embedded in the hardcover of Malcolm Bernard's journal."

"You fucking serious? Sully know about this?"

"Doubt it. The seal wasn't broken until I broke it yesterday and pulled them out."

"You mean to tell me you discovered secret wax paper rubbings in a secret compartment hidden in a secret book and didn't think to venture out of your room to let me know?" Rooter thought about it for a second before his vocal octave took an upward turn, "And you didn't think to bring it up at dinner last night?"

"Sorry, I guess not." Con said, slightly ashamed. He hadn't kept it from Rooter on purpose, it just had not occurred to him to talk about it.

Rooter shook his head in disbelief and went back to his sandwiches. "You're an asshole."

"So anyway," Con ignored the insult, "one of the wax papers holds the image of a person floating with a Mušḫuššu creature, and below them is another person who is huge in stature and mighty as indicated by the people below him that are small in comparison. The person next to the Mušḫuššu is dropping a crown onto the head of the one who is large and mighty, and this is happening in front of a huge phallic Tower or spear or something; I've since figured out it's the Tower of Babel. This did not make a lot of sense until I found a translated copy of the *Kitab al-Magall* online; in it, there's a story of an early king by the name of Nimrod who was given a crown from heaven as a result of his work on the Tower of Babel. This is the tower that angered God…"

"Yeah bud," Rooter interrupted, still agitated about the wax paper, "I know the story of the Tower of Babel. Keep going."

"No way, you've never heard the story told this way before. Look, there are ancient Jewish texts called the Apocrypha. These refer to a body of work that has either been referenced by the Bible, or found in conjunction with the Bible during discoveries; like when we found the Dead Sea Scrolls. The Bible doesn't say much about the Tower of Babel, except to note how much it displeased God, right? Well, many titles among the Jewish Apocrypha and Islamic Kitab al-Magall, also known as the Book of Rolls, discuss the Tower of Babel in great detail. They tell a story of a man named Nimrod who happened to be the great-grandson of Noah from the Bible. So this Nimrod was mighty and powerful, and all the ancient texts agree that he was the one who commissioned the Tower of Babel."

"So how does this relate to the wax paper I found? Because the Book of Rolls tells the story of how Nimrod was given a black piece of cloth, or some form of matter, out of heaven. This black matter was then forged into a crown. This story aligns with the wax paper, so it led me to research Nimrod and the time period just after the Great Deluge – also called Noah's Flood."

"You're losing me bro."

"Okay, Nimrod is all over antique books; he was the primary world-wide leader after the flood. Nimrod is definitely the primary character that Malcolm is referring to in his book, he's clearly a person of great importance to whatever Malcolm was doing in Iraq."

Rooter didn't say anything so Con continued, "So jumping straight into my thesis I'll tell you that I believe the person giving Nimrod his crown is a god referred to in Babylonian Mythology as Marduk. Now I found tons and tons of literature on Marduk because he is a key deity in that region. But when I started combining mythological stories with ancient Jewish-religious texts, including the Masoretic writings, something crazy begins to emerge. Ready for this?"

"Sure, but let me use the restroom first." Con rolled his eyes as his friend jogged to the can. After finishing he brought the sandwiches and coffee to the living room just as Con returned to the sofa with his notepad and tablet. They ate as Con continued.

"Okay, so start with Iraq. In the book of Genesis chapter 2, the location of the Garden of Eden is described as being between four rivers that converge, two of which have either dried up or have been renamed, and two of which clearly exist today; the Tigris and the Euphrates. Genesis further references an area north of Elam in Iran, which would put the Garden somewhere directly over, or to the immediate east of the ruins of ancient Babylon. If you believe Genesis, this puts the mythical garden housing the immortal first humans and extra-dimensional gods that walked with them on or near the agreed upon location of the Tower of Babel.

"Why is that significant? Because it's said, in many of the books when doing word-studies, that the Tower of Babel was some sort of an extra-dimensional portal that, 'stretched to the heavenly places'. This also marks the district of Ur from which Abraham and Nimrod both came according to historical texts as well as Islamic and Judeo-Christian tradition. This is also where the ancient city of Babylon existed, and where the Mušḫuššu were said to have 'walked the paths of the hanging gardens' with king Nebuchadnezzar. This is also the exact location where the recent dictator of Iraq was memorializing all of this history, and coincidently, it's also exactly where Alpha Kilo was, not to mention its relevance as a hotbed of government-level intrigue and secrecy today."

Rooter blinked and chewed, not knowing where Con was going with it all so the young researcher continued. "So we agree this area between the Tigris and the Euphrates, about fifty miles south of Baghdad is important, but all of this doesn't make a lot of sense or really matter until we consider the possibility that this Marduk, the Babylonian God of water, vegetation, judgment and magic – historical text, not my words - was or is real."

"You lost me," Rooter said, mouth full of sandwich. "You mean to say myths are real?"

"Bingo. By themselves, mythologies don't make any sense and seem to defy the natural laws that govern our cosmos, right? They are all stories of gods fighting for supremacy in some form or fashion. For this Alpha Kilo thing to make any sense at all, we have to consider for a second that mythology is not myth, but real. Say Marduk was or is real. If we read Jewish lore though texts like the books of Enoch or Jubilee, we see stories of extra-dimensional beings regularly coming and going from this earth between the time that the Garden of Eden supposedly existed and the time of the great deluge. What's more, if we read the Epic of Gilgamesh, we read about the same happenings during the same time. Homer's Iliad tells the same thing under the banner of Greek Mythology. See where I'm going?"

"Wait a sec," Rooter held up a hand, "You mean in order to make sense of nonsensical coincidences about southern Iraq you are pointing to nonsensical myth as the key that unlocks it all? You're a freak dude, I love it!" Rooter slapped his knee and laughed.

This is why I didn't tell you about the wax paper, moron. Con waited for Rooter to get it all out.

"No really, this is rich," he was mocking now and picked up the SI magazine, "You got to keep talking, this is better than the swimsuit edition bro. I got to know where you're going with this."

Con poked at the inside of his cheek with his tongue, "You finished?"

"Yeah," Rooter got a grip. "Sorry. Please, continue."

"I don't have to," Con retorted, "If this is too much for you."

"Take a joke dude. Keep talkin'."

"For starters," Con glanced at his notes, "The Great Flood isn't considered a goofy myth among many popular scientists. Evidence supporting a plausible thesis for the Flood has been building considerable momentum in recent years. One guy, a National Geographic explorer by the name of Robert Ballard has found mounds of physical evidence that point to the Black Sea as being a fresh-water lake at one point way back when. I'm not going to get into it because it doesn't really matter, but sufficed it to say, the flood is real."

"No kidding huh?" Rooter snorted.

"No, not kidding at all. So back to the point. I've been reading a whole slew of texts that go into great detail about what the Books of Enoch refer to as 'the rise of Nephilim' and the crossbreeding that took place between an alien species and humans before this Great Flood. Nephilim were the offspring of extra-terrestrial or extra-dimensional deities and human women, according to Enoch. But get this, in Aramaic culture the term *niyphelah* refers to the Constellation of Orion while

119

Nephilim refers to the offspring of Orion the Hunter in mythology. See how it all ties together?"

"Frankly, I don't."

"Ok, here it is. Take what you think you know, and throw it out. Just roll with my stream of consciousness for a minute... you got humans and aliens both living on earth. They get together and procreate, and the offspring are called Nephilim. These Aliens were transcendent beings with powers and abilities and technologies far beyond that which humans possessed, and so in our mythologies and religions, we've deified the aliens - we've made them into gods. Maybe they are, who knows? Anyway, these stories were audibly passed down the generations and eventually became legends. Then they were written down in various Sanskrit and Cuneiform all over the world, and those legends eventually became myths and religions. The stories became the fodder used to express faith in something or someone other than the self. We now call these myths *Christianity, Judaism, Islam, Greek Mythology, Babylonian Mythology, Hinduism, Taoism, Shintoism*, and whatever else. They are all based on the same story to one extent or another. A story where a celestial alien civilization comingled and cohabitated with our human species, engaged in a war for power, and eventually the alien and Nephilim factions departed earth. Presumably, when the Tower of Babel portal was destroyed somehow in the years after the great flood."

Con could tell Rooter was starting to catch up and gave him a minute to let that sink in.

"Think about it, Jewish tradition goes into great detail about the race of Nephilim coming forth from the cohabitation of celestial angels and human women. Well, Greek mythology says the same thing using different words. They say that human women had sexual intercourse with the gods, and the offspring were called Demigods. Like Hercules."

Con took a big bite and said with a mouthful, "Dude, Google the word *Anunnaki* if you want to see some of this freak-show stuff for yourself. These Anunnaki were the ancient super-freaks according to Babylonian mythology." He swallowed and continued.

"So why were the Aliens bedding down with our women? Who knows? Maybe for the purpose of multiplying demigod offspring, as is theorized in the book of Enoch. Or maybe to anger a singular truth, some sort of capital-G GOD? We don't know, but the behavior that turned nefarious begot a conflict of some sort that eventually closed down the portal sometime in the years just after the Great Flood."

"Hang on here," Rooter was shaking his head in disbelief, although slightly more sober this time. "Aliens bedding down with chicks? Seriously? This stuff is actually in the Bible even?"

"Yep. Take your pick of storyline. This narrative is everywhere. For whatever reason, everybody in the world, just a couple thousand years ago, believed that it was commonplace for Aliens to come and go from earth, and bed down with our women, and live among us."

"Yeah, okay," Rooter looked disturbed, "Say it's all true. Why is it a foreign concept to us now? If it's all real, how come I think you're a freak-show who's lost his mind?"

"I don't know. But that's why you got to wonder about the Tower of Babel."

"How do you mean?"

"I'm looking at the Tower of Babel as a superhighway. UFO's, unexplainable phenomenon, supernatural activities; these things still appear to happen in irregular fashion on earth. But it's so sporadic now that we don't credit it as authentic in a mass-populace sense. Back then, when the superhighway was open, the Aliens came and went with regularity and it was just a part of life."

"So why us? Why bed down with our chicks?"

"I don't know," Con shrugged, "because the Aliens are horny, maybe? Because our babes are hot and theirs are green? Who cares, you're getting off subject."

Rooter's mind was churning the info. It was oddly compelling how the dots seemed to align.

"A hundred different commentaries on Biblical and Qur'anical scriptures claim that this flood was a manifest judgment, perpetrated by a single, capital-G God, and was the result of cross-breeding and genetic abnormalities in that day. Other theories point to a decree issued by a counsel of deities that suspended celestial access to Earth for a time being for other reasons, also around the time of the Great Flood. We don't know for sure, we can only theorize. Point is, myth and religion both point to bad behavior and some sort of judgment or decree that closed down the portal, and limited manifest access by the Aliens to earth, some thousands of years ago."

"Fair enough," Rooter sipped his coffee.

"Now let me show you the wax paper. Remember, look at these with your myth and religion glasses on; pretend that religion and mythology are all real. This is the first piece." Con pulled the slips out and put them in order and began running them down for Rooter one by one.

"It shows this powerful winged Alien creature with a horde of women around him. This to me signifies the cross-breeding that was going on with our species. The next one here shows an Alien, who I believe is the one called Marduk, among other things, and his Mušḫuššu – an animal-hybrid – coming out of the waters. I believe this is the Great Deluge. I think that them coming out of the water signifies his escape from this judgment somehow. For some reason, this particular dude avoided punishment somehow. The next one shows Marduk crowning a king in front of the Tower of Babel and the king ruling over the people below, this king of course has to be Nimrod. The last one shows Marduk, missing an eye and reigning with a scepter over all the earth. At least that's how I'm interpreting these, but getting an expert to look at them would be good."

"Now, Noah's great-grandson was this guy Nimrod," Con continued, picking up his notes and referencing them as he talked, "And Nimrod was king over the entire post-Flood world; all the texts agree about that. Something made this guy a huge and powerful ruler, as depicted in the wax paper and ancient tablets. Nimrod was also known by other names, but I'll get into that later."

Con searched his notes then found what he was looking for. "Okay, here it is. Nimrod emerges a few generations after the flood, a direct descendent of Noah, but is miraculously crowned by the Alien named Marduk around the time that the Tower of Babel was commissioned and the portal opened. Nimrod's construction of the Tower of Babel appears to have upset the Judeo-Christian and Islamic, capital-G God, but the question is, why? What was the big deal with this Tower of Babel and why did it upset the monotheistic Deity of the three main faiths?"

Rooter shrugged.

"I think it's because Marduk was trying to reopen the portal, in direct defiance of the authority figure who had shut down celestial access to earth by bringing the Great Flood. You see, if you take anything from the ancient texts, the flood was an act of Judgment; it effectuated punishment against the Aliens, humans, and Nephilim race of hero-demigods. But for some reason not everybody died. Christians, Jews and Muslims all agree that this guy Noah and his family lived. Supposedly, everyone else who could die, died under the rising waters while the immortal Aliens were bound in chains."

Rooter sat up straight. "I don't know bud. That's a bit far-fetched to me."

"Maybe," Con was searching his notes. "Oh, check this out. Remember I told you that the Alien Marduk was the Babylonian God of water, vegetation, judgment and magic?"

"Yeah," Rooter said cautiously.

"Well, if it was a judgment that closed earth's access, interesting that this Alien Marduk was the one to reverse judgment unilaterally and succeed in reopening that ancient gateway by using Nimrod and the Tower of Babel, no? It would have been magic that was reckoned to cross-species genetic mutations in that day; now we call it science and genetic engineering. But back then this Alien would have been defined as the god of judgment and magic for these two reasons alone. What else?" He flipped a page and kept looking.

"He was called the God of water and vegetation. Think about the Hanging Gardens of Babylon. It was essentially more magic with water and vegetation that created the Hanging Gardens during the time of King Nebuchadnezzar the second. And want to know what else?"

"What?"

"The name Nebuchadnezzar means *O god Nabu, defender of...*" Con paused to find the exact words in his notes. "Here, *Nabu* means the son of the god Marduk. The exact translation of Nebuchadnezzar is 'O god Nabu, defender of my deed of property'. So what we have here is a lineage passed on, but not a lineage of human genetics, it's a lineage of Alien genetics that passed from generation to generation. I see the crown of Nimrod as a symbolic representation of that genetic line. These guys, Nimrod and Nebuchadnezzar are examples of Enoch's Nephilim or the Pantheon's demigods; offspring of a cross breeding between Alien and human genetics."

"Okay, let me see if I am following you," Rooter adjusted his posture nervously, "Aliens and humans are cross breeding and this upsets an authority of some sort."

"Actually," Con interrupted, "Aliens, humans and animals. Don't forget about the animal hybrid action going on."

"Right, so aliens, humans and animals are cross-breeding. This upsets some sort of an authority figure, or some high-echelon counsel of Aliens and a judgment was ordered. This came in the form of a great Flood that killed life on earth except for at least one person, Noah, and whatever he had in his boat."

"The ark, is what they call it," Con sniffed.

Rooter smiled sarcastically. "Somehow, this corrupted gene-line escaped the judgment of the deluge in the form of an Alien named Marduk, who then found a way to indwell this guy, Nimrod. Nimrod then began constructing the Babel Tower, opened a portal, got a crown, ruled, had sex, and passed the genetics down the line?"

"That's what I'm getting at."

"Okay, so how did Marduk escape the judgment?"

"Don't know."

"If the genetics were passed down the line back then, how come we don't see evidence of super-human genetics in people now?"

"Not sure."

They both sat there for a minute, Rooter absorbing the info as Con kept perusing his notes and looking things up on his Tablet.

"After all this, Malcolm's journal shifts to Egypt and I don't know what happens because I haven't got that far. But it seems clear that the Alien Marduk was able to indwell a certain many rulers throughout the course of history by way of the genetic line of descendants. But Babylonian king Nebuchadnezzar was definitely a part of that genetic line by virtue of his name, right? Not only that, but Nebuchadnezzar was able to cross-breed animals and somehow genetically engineer the Hanging Gardens of Babylon, so whatever Alien power that indwelled this Nimrod guy also indwelled king Nebuchadnezzar too, one would have to assume."

"So what's the link with current day Iraq and Malcolm?"

"Besides the geographical one," Con put his notepad down, "Saddam Hussein believed he was the reincarnated Nebuchadnezzar. That's why he was rebuilding Babylon directly over the ruins of the ancient city. Here, take a look." Con handed Rooter a number of aerial photographs of the site that had come with the packet provided by Father Abelemy.

"He was ascribing his own seal to the bricks just as Nebuchadnezzar had. Saddam's belief that he was the reincarnated Nebuchadnezzar was obvious by the commissioning of royal thrones and murals with the two of them in it, and the juxtaposition of the two on their coinage. If that's not enough, he openly said as much to the media and it's now a matter of public record."

"Dude, this is some crazy shit."

"It's all just a theory at this point," Con said soberly, "I'm just telling you what the research is telling me. None of this may be true. I know that I've only scratched the surface of the iconography in the journal though, so there is more to the story that needs to be unveiled. It'll just take tons of time and a lot of reading."

"What's this thing about Egypt?" Rooter asked as a sudden knock came at the front door. Con got up to answer it and Rooter's heart sunk when the door swung open; it was Betty. He instinctively started buttoning his shirt while Con exchanged pleasantries with her in the foyer.

"Ey, chocolate cake wit whip," She hollered in Rooter's direction, "You gonna come say hi or what?"

"Nope," he decided it was time to step onto the back porch and have a cigarette.

Rooter chain-smoked half a pack before he returning to find that Betty was gone and Con, presumably, had retreated back into his room for further study. He was glad to have missed the hurled insults and abuse. *What does this cougar have against me, anyway?*

He had a headache. Was the throb a result of too much nicotine or the conspiracy theories? He didn't know. But one thing was certain, Rooter needed some aspirin. He ventured into the shared bathroom and found a bottle of Motrin. After popping two pills in his mouth he went to the kitchen for a glass of water to help swallow them down.

Through the horizontal slits of the window blinds, he noticed a slow moving Toyota Tacoma ease past their driveway. He could not be sure but it appeared as though the driver was looking at their house; as if trying to spy the address. The truck came to almost a full and complete stop before it lunged into gear again and sped off.

Not thinking too much of it, Rooter grabbed the manila envelope left by Betty and retreated to his room for a little rest. Tossing the envelope on his nightstand he laid back into his squeaky bed. There was a lot to think about. Deep down in his gut somewhere he dreaded the feelings that were creeping up. *What if this freak-show stuff is true? What if the world is nearing a reopening, or some sort of a reengaging of a crazy past interplay between a powerful alien race and our own? Could this possibly be true? Is a part of it true?*

He wondered about Malcolm and considered knocking on Con's door to ask exactly how Malcolm had died, and what exactly had happened at Alpha Kilo, but decided against it. He needed to let his brain simmer down. Like drinking from a fire hydrant, talking to Con could get overwhelming.

Next he thought about Sully and Anny. He wondered how they were doing and when they'd come home. He wondered if they were getting anywhere with the TB Optics guy.

When he opened his eyes, it was dark outside. Somehow, he'd managed to sleep the afternoon away.

CHAPTER 17
The 4th Ward

Tuesday, September 20, 2011

The concrete holding box just outside the elevator on the 4th looked identical to the one on the 3rd. A moment passed, then a voice beckoned the group to enter, and the iron door in front of them clicked open. In the next room the company found four identical looking doors, each leading to a housing center. On the far left was the door and hallway that led to the maximum-security wing. Next to it were the doors to the medium-security housing and the hotel-like, minimum-security housing unit. On the far right was the door that led straight to the private residence that Abdullah Kahn owned on the southwest side of the hill.

Before going further, Doctor Monroe explained who resided where.

"Everybody who lives in this ward is either full-human or a human-hybrid, where the host was a human being. We have no animal-host chimera here on the 4th. The max security wing was established to house the behaviorally volatile; where our experimentation might have gone wrong, but we identified an intrigue within the specimen that prompted us to keep it rather than destroy it. The max security wing has only iron, soundproof cells, and the subjects are never allowed to leave except for medical reasons. Unfortunately, the nickname that stuck for this place is Hell Hall."

"The medium security wing houses our two new 'Life Essence' laboratories. This is where Professor Mikel Maldaceto is working on what he calls the 'Anima Imperium Component.' Currently, all the life-essence research that you've heard about is done right here. Also housed in this wing are the subjects with new genetic enhancements that present in a sophisticated and rational manner. Basically, if they show impulse control and display a high degree of intelligence, they live here, but still under close observation."

"Please elaborate further," Kahn interjected. "I'm curious, is this where you house our mercenaries, our so-called *super soldiers*?"

"No sir. The hybrid combat force no longer lives here at BSA. After testing-out successfully, they spend four months in boot camp at the combat training facility, and then go to the field. Once released, they go dark and we never see them here at BSA again. They're all chipped for suggestive and direct mind control. This is how we deliver orders. If they ever have issues in the field, we use the same chip for self-termination. The General can comment more on the Phantom protocols in a minute. The only subjects that live here are test subjects. In the medium security wing we house our recently enhanced or recently born human hybrids."

The Doc continued, pointing to the next door, "In the minimum security wing we house those subjects that have been brought here for the purpose of enhancement."

"You mean the men, women, and teenagers you've purchased for experimentation?"

"Yes sir, along with any volunteer test subjects. We also house employees who need a place to stay. It's arranged like a hotel and controlled with state-of-the-art surveillance monitoring of every person. From the security bunker, we can see into every corner of the facility."

"Really?" the Hand mused, "you watch the boys and girls take showers too?"

"We watch them do everything they do on this ward." Doctor Michael Monroe then walked over to the maximum security door and touched it while saying, "And we are being watched now."

At that moment, the maximum security door opened without a sound. The Hand looked around to see where the camera was, but couldn't locate it.

"How many cells are in here?" asked Kahn as they advanced down the hallway.

"We have seventy-five. About half of them are occupied at this time."

The hall wrapped around in an oval shape, with the cells protruding outward along the circumference. In the center was a room incased in glass where security watched and monitored the wing with an array of high-tech gadgetry. As the men advanced, Kahn peered into each cell.

He stopped at the cell marked, Number 13. Inside was a little boy, no more than 6 or 7-years-old. He looked at the Doc and said, "Surely this boy can be housed in the medium wing, no?"

When Kahn looked back into the cell, he saw that the little boy was now on all fours, his neck stretched, with spikes pushing against his skin along his spinal column. He was screaming, although no sound could be heard. The Doctor then looked at the security desk and nodded, and suddenly they could hear the scream from inside cell 13. It sent chills down Kahn's neck and back. The sound was nothing like what he expected from a young boy. It was a deep throated howl, loud and menacing.

Splice

The Hand put his hands over his ears and the Doc gave the security desk a second nod, which cut the audio. The boy was now running on all-fours back and forth, ramming his side into the walls of the cell. Kahn watched, amused.

"Still think this one's fit for the medium wing?" the General asked, smiling with fascination as the small, naked boy slammed into the walls with maniacal intensity.

"I suppose you all know what you're doing," Kahn replied.

In Number 21 there was a huge 525-pound woman with open sores and tumors all over her body. She, like most of the occupants in this wing, was completely nude. She was bleeding from many of the wounds, especially on her neck and upper back. It was a horrible sight. Even the Hand could only muster a brief glance. The Doctor explained that she had a mutant gene in the long arm of Chromosome 17, which encodes the neurofibromin protein. This protein plays a vital role in cell signaling and development. The story with Number 21 is that something went wrong with the protein encoding when they tried to transplant some nocturnal enhancements from an owl's genetics.

The Doc looked at the poor woman, "A genetic disorder known as NF type I and NF type 2 has been a major drag on medical research for decades. But the disorder is hereditary. This woman has what we call, NF-X, a sad ailment that could shed light on the damage we keep seeing in Chromosome 17. Anyway, that's why we're keeping her alive, even in her suffering. The information is just too valuable for us." The visitors were uncomfortable, and glazed over on the science.

"You know," Monroe continued, "she was only 14-years-old when we implanted the owl genetics. Want to know when that was?"

Abdullah nodded.

"That was eighteen months ago." The Doc raised his eyebrows to accentuate his point. "When we implanted her, she was 14-years-old, weighed 96 pounds, and stood 5-5. Eighteen months later, she stands nearly 6'7", weighs over 500 pounds, and is rapidly dying. She'll be dead by her eighteenth birthday, unless we terminate sooner."

Number 66 housed another little boy named Carlos. He was only 4-years-old, but was the size of an infant. He was a primary chimera, spliced en vitro, and born to a perfectly healthy mother. However, the genetic code they engineered and intermixed reacted to his host stem cells in a very peculiar and awful way. He'd been fighting through regenerating cycles of life ever since.

"In layman terms," Monroe explained, "his body is going through a perpetual cycle of rebuilding its organ and skeletal structure up to the point of birth. So every nine months, he essentially changes from being a human to being a wolf, and back again. His body has become the uterus for this phenomenon. Carlos is truly a medical miracle. For some reason, there is a reset of his entire genetic makeup on or around the nine-month mark, and his body simultaneously attacks the developed structure to break it down and begin anew. He's on pain killers now, which we gave him after we learned that they would not upset the cycle. Unfortunately, for the first year of little Carlos' life, he experienced pain that's only described in fiction."

"Why are you keeping him alive?" asked the Hand.

"Because he may be eternally perpetual."

"What does that mean?" asked Kahn.

"It means he is restarting at the point of fertilization every nine months. This could conceivably go on for eternity because we've found no loss of genetic information."

"So you may have found the fountain of youth in here somewhere?" clarified the Hand.

"Precisely."

Soon, they exited the maximum-security wing by the same door they came in. There were all kinds of unmentionable 'people' in those cells, and each had a unique story. Most of them were hard to look at, and most of the stories were hard to fathom. By the time they left, Kahn and his Hand were more than ready to leave "Hell Hall."

The group skipped the medium door and went straight to the minimum security wing. This area was quite nice and well appointed. The lighting was soft, the halls were carpeted, and the rooms featured beds and furnishings on par with a high-end hotel. There was a large cafeteria, game room, swimming pool, and workout facility.

"Everyone you see in here, except those wearing the blue BSA polo shirts, are residents," said the General. "It's quite the contrast from the max wing, huh?"

The halls and corridors were bustling with men and women, laughing and carrying on like tourists at a resort.

"It's remarkable," noted Kahn, "how do you keep them all so happy?"

"They're all high," snickered the General, picking up a tray with some mashed potatoes and gravy. "Here, compliments of the second ward. Go ahead, try some of this food and see how you feel."

"I'll pass. That's ingenious though."

"Yes," the Doc smiled. "We like to say, 'the Prozac is in the food' here, and we mean it. There is a downside, however."

"What's that?"

"The residents are compulsive about sex. They are happy, horny, and impulsively attempt to gratify the sexual urges regularly. It's due to an enzyme that metastasizes when the chemicals we put in the food; the 'Prozac' we use, enters their frontal lobe. It causes a very mild form of dementia, similarly symptomatic of Alzheimer's, that makes the subject forget what's going on. These effects wear off immediately when we pull the happy pill though. That's why we watch them everywhere, in bed, in the showers, in the closets. You name the place, we're watching it. Our staff separates the residents attempting to engage with one another hundreds of times per day. It's quite annoying, actually."

"What's the big deal? Why not just add a birth control pill to the food?" asked the Hand.

"Because, if we wanted them mixing genes on their own, we wouldn't pay top dollar for them. Here at BSA, the gene-mixing is our job, not theirs." The scientist winked.

A young man wearing a polo approached and handed the General an envelope. He walked away without a word as The General stuck a fat finger in the corner seam and tore it opened.

"What's that?" asked Kahn.

"Security report. Give me a sec," he replied without looking up.

"Our turnaround is 100% every 90 days," the Doc continued, taking little notice of the General's preoccupation. "This means every 90-days, every horny resident you see here will be selected and used in a specially-designed experiment or previously-formulated recipe. Based on initial testing, they will be transferred to max-security, mid-security, or terminated for malfunction."

"Damn it!" barked the General.

"What is it already?" demanded the Hand, echoing his boss's question.

The General ignored the Hand, but looked at Doctor Monroe, "BM didn't check in, third straight week. We may have a problem here."

"Indeed. That's not good…" the Doctor mused.

"What the fuck are you saying, exactly?" Kahn asked, agitated he was being left out of the loop.

The General snapped back, "I'm saying that one of the Phantoms hasn't checked-in, three weeks in a row. He missed the 5th, 12th, and apparently, yesterday as well."

The codename was originally, 'Specialized Para-Military Chimera Operative,' but since the moles in the U.S. and French agencies started referring to their mercenaries as "the Phantoms," the name stuck at BSA as well. The General looked back at the report and reread its contents.

"What's his protocol?"

"Every week, unless on mission-point."

"Why wouldn't he check in?" asked the Hand.

"I don't know," the General scratched his left shoulder with his right hand nervously. "Can we talk about this in private?"

The men turned down a few hallways and came to a private conference room. There was a flat TV on the wall, and the room's lighting was on a dimmer knob. Monroe radioed the bunker and asked for privacy, at which point a small red light on a security panel blinked a few times, then went off, indicating the audio and video feed had been cut. The black table was made of composite material, and they each took a chair.

Kahn asked the General to take it from the top, and explain what was upsetting him.

"Okay, Bast Molorek is one of our operatives in the U.S. He's stationed in the DC area. We call him BM. He's on a weekly check-in protocol, but he's missed his last three. We're finding that the longer we keep these operatives in the field, the less they seem to regard the rules. We can't tell if this is symptomatic of their genetic enhancements, if our control chips lose suggestive power over time, or if they're just a bunch of cocky pricks."

"It's none of the above," the Doctor interjected. "It's what I call the LE residue force. What we've found is when we take genetic information from one subject and use it to engineer another, there is a residue that carries over from the Life Essence of the donor specimen. This is a recent finding based on a bunch of research coming out of the mid-sec wing."

"Whatever," the General grunted.

"So, what's happening exactly?" Kahn asked.

"In the case of BM," Monroe explained, "he was engineered with DNA from a cougar, a breed of mountain lion. When they latch onto a target, they seem to hear, see, and sense nothing else until taking down their prey. They become so focused on the target, they sometimes go days without eating."

"Who is the target?" asked the Hand.

"The Greek, just like you told me last month," the General replied.

"The Greek is still alive?" Kahn was genuinely surprised.

"I need to get down to DC and make contact," the General said to Monroe, ignoring Kahn's comment. "Something must be wrong. My CIA informant assures me the Greek is both alive and well, and now we're not hearing from BM? I need to get down there. I should have gone last week."

"He's hunting," Monroe thought out loud. "The question is, who? If it were the Greek, he'd be dead by now…"

"You told me the other loose ends had been tied down, right? The nephew was framed, the girl is dead…?" the Hand asked.

The General gave the Hand a dismissive glare and ignored his rhetorical question. After a moment of silence, he reasserted his intentions. "I need to get down to DC. I need to go now, figure out what the hell is going on."

"Agreed," said Kahn, "Call me directly and let me know what you find out."

CHAPTER 18
Recovery

Monday, August 29, 2011

Solomon looked up from his oatmeal breakfast and saw Annette "Anny" Boyle approaching from the elevator bank. She looked stunning. She walked like she was on a fashion show runway. She wore business attire, and had worked her hair, makeup, and accessories perfectly. The look commanded professional respect, but teased with undertones of fun and mystery. She was masterful at making herself look the part for whatever occasion. She sat down across from him, crossed her legs casually, and leaned back into the high-back leather chair. The public seating area of the Drake Hotel was magnificently outfitted with lots of wood, leather, and soft yellow lighting.

"Finally, today is the day, huh? You look ready."

"Indeed." He managed a forced smile. "Not that I haven't had a good time walking through museums, eating out, and crying into my pillow to fall asleep this past week."

"Still hurts?" Anny frowned.

"You know, losing Jasper was really surreal but somewhat impersonal. It happened and I had to get out quick. It was like a whirlwind of activity for me, but he could have just as easily died on the ski slopes." He took a minute to get the next sentence composed, "But seeing Leola's face in that tub. Her expression haunts me. Especially at night."

"You know, I didn't realize you were struggling so much. At least until we got on the road together, and then this past week." She raised her eyebrows and frowned, "You really held it together those first few days. I'm no shrink, but I bet what you're going through is pretty normal."

"Maybe. I don't know. There was so much at stake those first few days. It felt like I was just running for my life. But now," he sighed and looked away, "God, I miss her."

Kyle Rasmussen took over as TB Optic's CTO after Malcolm died. Anny researched as much as she could, but there was precious little to be found in the public domains about him. He was a 51-year-old divorcee, who lived on the north side of the city. He started with TB Optics in the late 80's, and was now a central figure in the mid-sized R&D firm.

Anny went through his main secretary to get the sit-down. She billed it as a quick and painless interview to discuss Malcolm Bernard's legacy as the CTO of TB Optics. She told him it was for a project that the Bernard family was working on, in his memory. She suggested lunch but Rasmussen countered with mid-morning coffee instead. His response indicated a blow-off was coming, so she prepped extra diligently leading up to the meeting. After agreeing to mid-morning coffee, she asked for a time slot during their first week in Chicago, but he countered with the following Monday... another blow-off indicator.

After realizing she was not going to get together with the CTO any earlier, she asked Sully if he wanted to transfer to a less expensive hotel. Being a frugal man, he thought about it, but decided to bill the CIA for their expenses and live large instead. He figured a little luxury after the prior week was not so much to ask. Anny chose not to argue with that logic.

The first week in Chicago was difficult in more ways than one. For Sully, the slowdown in life provided an unwelcome opportunity to think, dwell, and grieve the loss of his beloved Leola. His preoccupation with those feelings made interacting with Anny difficult. When they were together, he felt pressured to force conversation. He tried to play it off, but he couldn't fake the fact that it was forced, and that made for plenty of awkward moments.

She was able to intellectualize his pain and emotional hurt, but knew there was nothing she could do for him, and that was hard on her. She tried at times to grieve alongside him, even though she didn't know Leola well. So the left-footed dance dawned every morning with breakfast in the lobby of the Drake Hotel, and it retreated every night when they each retired to their rooms. It was a forgettable week for both of them.

"I'm gonna go get a bowl of cereal. Need anything, friend?" Sully shook his head distantly.

She returned carefully carrying a bowl, and took a seat. "Lucky Charms. Brings me back to my childhood."

"Where are you meeting him?"

"At a Caribou Coffee, down on West Madison. He said it's in the CitiBank building."

"So what's the plan? Should I just drive you and hang around?"

"Hell no, I'll take a cab," she frowned. "It's not worth the hassle of getting the car out of valet."

Solomon nodded. "So, here's the deal," he said abruptly. "I'm tired of feeling sorry for myself. This past week has been one to forget, and I've been such a louse that you may feel the same. I don't know why all this is happening to me, or us, I mean. No matter how much I work the events over in my mind, I can't make sense of Leola's death. Frankly, whatever I've been feeling is starting to give way to, I don't know, real anger. I'm pissed that my life is upside down, and I'm really frustrated that you and the others were dragged into this dark, dank hole."

She shoveled another spoonful of Charms into her mouth and listened. *This is different...*

"What am I trying to say?" He sat back and stretched before trying again. "What I'm trying to say is, Thank You. Thanks for letting me have a funky week. Thanks for giving me the time and space I needed to just deal with all of this. I woke up today and decided that I'm a deadweight in this crisis if I can't get my mind right. And it's not fair to you or the others."

She softly nodded in agreement. It was forward of her, but she felt that the crisis at hand was serious enough that he couldn't afford a long, drawn-out period of feeling sorry for himself. He needed to get his wits about him and get back in the game. She needed him back in the game.

"Look, I'm saying thank you, and I'm telling you that my mind is coming back, and I'm trying to climb out of the mud puddle. That's basically it."

"So what I hear you saying is," she said, after swallowing her mouthful, "you're ready to go hit the town with me one of these days. Have a little fun. Live again?"

Sully laughed and thought about it, "Yeah, I think so."

"Good. I'm glad you're feeling better, friend."

"So, what did you do the past few days? I know we hit the museums and had dinners, but I don't feel like I really remember much of what we talked about."

"Really? You can't remember?" She looked at him sarcastically, "Let's see, I treated myself to the movies, alone, on two occasions. Actually, on one of those occasions, I snuck into a second show because I hadn't wasted enough time."

He chuckled at her high-school antics. *When was the last time I double-dipped at the theater?*

"I went window shopping, but didn't buy anything because I didn't bring much money, and you weren't around to tell me it was okay to charge shoes to the government. That said, I did make the bold decision to charge a few spa treatments to the room. Thank you for that, by the way." He nodded as if to say, *you're welcome.*

"What else? I went to a really cool jazz bar on Rush Street, which would have been really great had I not been the only person sitting alone. Well, to clarify, I was only alone until a greasy old man came up, flirted a bit and tried to grab my ass. That's when I left. I think that was Thursday night. Haven't hit the bars since. I don't know, that's about it. When we did stuff together, I talked a lot, and I knew you didn't hear much of what I said. But that's okay, I know what you're going through."

"I'm really sorry Anny," he was now visibly ashamed of his behavior.

"No apology necessary, friend."

Why does she keep calling me that? I can't think of a day she ever called me 'friend'. It's always been 'boss,' or 'chief,' or 'sir,' or something. Is it because I've been a baby, and she's had to carry the emotional load for a week? Does she pity me? Feel sorry for me?

"I think we should go dancing or get drunk or something tonight." As soon as the words came out, she regretted them. That sounded scary-close to a date proposition, a clear violation of the employer-employee understanding. She tried to retract, "I mean, if you want. I mean, if you do that sort of thing, and, you know, if you want some company."

He grinned with amusement. *Is she flirting?*

She bit her lip nervously and tried to come up with another justification for her forwardness, "You know, how often do people have an opportunity to do a city on the government's dime? Not *do* the city… you know what I mean. There's got to be a cool comedy hall or ballgame or something, right?"

His grin became full-fledged laughter. A reddish glow overcame her. She bit her lip again and looked away before throwing her hands up, "You know what? I'm just gonna shut up."

"No don't, you're right. I'm sure I could use a night of fun, and you deserve one too. We'll figure something out."

He admired her gumption. It took guts to basically ask her boss out on a date, even if that's not what she intended. And her embarrassment was cute and endearing. It was one of maybe a half-dozen times he saw her get flustered and blush. He eased her out of the nervous spotlight by changing the subject.

They chatted for a while longer to pass the time. At 9:40 am, Anny walked to the bellhop station and ordered a cab. Michigan Avenue was a bustle of business activity on that bright, sunny morning. The air was clean and a light breeze tossed a few wayward strands of her hair. She was in a good mood. Sully's dismounting of the pity-horse put her in good spirits. She cautiously hoped for a better second week in Chicago, as she climbed into the back seat of a taxi.

Her appointment with Rasmussen was not until 10:30, but she preferred to arrive first so that she could observe his mannerisms before they met. Over the years, she learned that valuable information is often inferred by simple observation, especially when the mark doesn't think he's being watched. Sully wished her luck, closed the cab door, and trotted back into the hotel.

With that simple decision and declaration, Solomon Keys knew he had his mind back. His emotions were finally coming into alignment, and he marveled at the power of a simple choice. *I should have done this earlier. I wouldn't be embarrassed now if I'd done this sooner...*

Like Anny, he felt a new freshness in the day, as if a big cloud had just passed.

Truth is, he never actually woke up to a newfound resolve to stop pitying himself that morning. Rather, he woke up with the same dread and despondent attitude that greeted him every morning since Leola's death. Nothing was different. He started talking, while she ate Lucky Charms, with every intention of roping her into another monologue about how hard it was to have lost her. But something happened while he talked, and the poor-is-me train never arrived. Instead, he heard himself say, *my mind is back and I'm getting out of the mud puddle.*

It hadn't even been a conscious decision on his part, but then the words came out, and that was that.

The elevator *dinged* and opened to the 14th, as Sully wondered about the power of an incantation. There was something effective about verbally audibilizing a mindset. For a week, he'd been the victim of uncontrolled grief and self-loathing. Then suddenly, by the power of a decision and a verbal commitment to its effect, the sun was bright and the air was clean again. Just like that.

But once in his room, the thought of Leola's facial expression in the tub flashed across his consciousness, as if trying to fight back, and reclaim its glory-role of just moments earlier. It was a direct attack on his willful choice to stop the destructive thoughts. There was an unseen defiance tempting him, coaxing him, back into the dark. He fought the urge. In an instant, he nearly caved and went back to his depression, but this time, he met the temptation with resolve.

If I can't show some discipline alone in my room, I can't show it anywhere. He pushed the seductive offer aside and kept his wits and newfound attitude.

He went into the bathroom and saw the tub. It was next to the shower stall and was not concealed by a shower curtain. Again it came, this time in a flash of light that revealed Leola's body, lifeless and emotionless, slinking into her final resting posture. The strong hand of uncontrollable emotion lunged at him again, but it could not grab hold. Solomon forced himself to look at that empty tub until he no longer saw her lying in it.

I will not be governed by this torment any longer. I love you, but I have to let you go, find out what happened, and make sure to destroy the son-of-a-bitch that did this.

Turning to the sink, he was aghast at the image in the mirror. He hadn't shaved in days, and dark brown stubble was invading his face in a haphazard pattern. His hair was messy, but the wrong type of messy. Stylish messy was his look, but this was just a tangle of grease and webbing. *Disgusting.*

He needed a shower and a shave.

He ripped off his T-shirt and took inventory of his physique. He still looked solid. It wasn't the body of a college athlete by any means, but he was still in good shape, with toned muscles lining his arms, shoulders, and chest. He'd lost the bottom two blocks of his six-pack, but the waistline was still a 34, and that was okay by him.

How am I going to avenge her? I don't know how to fight in this black ops world. I really don't know how to shoot a gun. A couple toned muscles and a decent head on my shoulders aren't going to get me very far when it comes to dealing with Phantom killers...

Under the lather of shampoo, he decided it was time to make up for the past week. He'd ask the hotel concierge for some ideas about a show, or a special event, and surprise Anny with them. Not just that, he decided to see if she wanted to go back to that jazz bar she liked. This time she'd have a 'date' to ward off the booty-trolls.

He also decided it was time for him to order-up one of those in-room massages.

CHAPTER 19
An Unwelcome Guest

Tuesday, August 30, 2011

Rooter opened his eyes and saw the blue numbers of his bedside digital clock. 2:19 am. *That's weird...* He was having one of those sleepless nights. Not precisely sleepless, but disturbed. He retired to bed at 10:30, and after an initial two-hour bout of insomnia, he managed to doze off. However, he was only getting 20-30 minute bursts of sleep. His mind was too alert, too on-edge.

Something was troubling him. Something *felt* misaligned, but he couldn't put his finger on it. The line between daydream and night-dream was blurred. *I wonder if Con's up? Maybe he's having a night like this too...*

A bolt of lightning flashed. The intense light blanketed the walls and ceiling of his room. His heart began to pound harder and his nerves were at attention. He swallowed hard. *What's happening? ...Where's the thunder?*

The thunderclap failed to follow the flash. Lightning flashed again. Again, no thunder.

Wide-awake and uneasy, he suddenly felt the urge to turn onto his other side. He had a strong sense that if he did, someone would be there, standing over him. He was paralyzed. *What's the matter with you? Get a grip!* He tried to logic his way back to a regular heartbeat, but it didn't work. He swallowed again; the lump in his throat was enormous.

Jerking into a seated position, he rolled his body in one motion and stared at the other side of his room. He expected to come face-to-face with some sort of malevolent evil, but nothing was there. His bedroom door was slightly ajar. *Odd. Very odd. I know I closed that door when I went to bed... Did I get up to use the restroom?*

Another flash of lightning lit up the room. Rooter's breathing was heavier. He looked at the closet. *Is someone or something in the closet?* The closet door was closed. *Was someone or something under his bed?* He couldn't shake the feeling that evil was watching his every move.

He tried to focus on his breathing. He needed to get some control over the fear that was crippling his senses and mocking his intelligence. He was now oriented toward the door and the closet, his back to the nightstand and bedroom window. Then the sensation of being watched returned and he felt something standing there, behind him by the window. Not thinking twice, he whipped back to his original posture, but again found nothing but his own skitso-paranoia. *What's happening?!*

He slowly opened the drawer of his nightstand. He kept a handgun in there. He felt the cold hilt of his .38 special. He held his breath, straining his ears for a sound, anything that might cue him into what was happening. *Nothing.*

Next, he popped the cylinder of his revolver to confirm it was loaded. The lightning was coming more frequently.

Rooter jumped from his bed and moved to the bedroom door. He closed the door quietly and flicked on the light switch. With the gun secured in his sweaty palm, he checked under the bed. Nothing. He checked the closet. Nothing. He went to the window and peered into the backyard, using his hand to shield the light from the room. Even with the strobe-light effect from the lightning, he could not see much of anything outside. The flashes were coming more frequently now. *Why isn't there any thunder?* As he struggled for a rational thought, he heard a distant rumble, faint and far away. *Storm's comin'.*

Turning, he walked back to the door. Tightly gripping the revolver in one hand, the doorknob in the other, he cracked the door open and peered across the hallway into the living room.

Rooter's experience as a cop and bodyguard taught him to never downplay intuition or coincidence. If something seemed wrong, something was wrong. He was uncommonly restless, the lightning was eerie, he felt a presence, the door was ajar... *Something's wrong.*

He opened the door further. Light from his bedroom carried his shadow across the floor. A couch and table were slowly illuminated in the living room. Another flash of lightning lit up the entire house and in that instant, he saw it. There, unmistakably, someone stood in the far corner of the living room near Sully's bedroom. He was tall, very tall. His eyes seemed to reflect the light, gleaming like small light bulbs with a reddish hue. Rooter lifted his gun and aimed in the direction of the intruder.

The reflective eyes vanished momentarily. Then another bolt of lightning illuminated the house. Rooter saw the giant image again and fired twice toward Sully's unoccupied bedroom. His ears screamed and the smell of gunpowder filled his nostrils, "Con! Con, wake up!"

An unexpected crack of loud thunder rocked the house, and more light poured in. Rooter called to his companion again, screaming his name hysterically. *Was Con okay?* Con burst from his room and stood in the hallway, dazed, in just his boxer shorts. Con's room was down the hall, behind Rooter's, and away from the living room.

"Hit that hall light for me," Rooter commanded, refusing to take his eyes off the living room. Con complied and three overhead lights flooded the hallway and peaked into the living room and kitchen. Rooter scanned the square-footage, looking for potential hiding spots.

"You okay?" He shot a glance toward Con as the skinny computer nerd nodded in bewilderment.

Rooter fully exited his doorway and walked slowly toward the front door. Reaching the foyer, he flicked the three light switches that were there, illuminating the front porch, living room, and kitchen. He heard rain start to tap the roof outside. First he checked the front door – locked. Then he advanced through every corner of the house, but found nobody.

When he reached the small circular kitchen table near Sully's bedroom door, he found that the window there was unlocked and slightly ajar. *This was his point of egress, maybe his point of entry also. Did we close and lock this window…?*

Looking out of the window toward the front of the house, he saw nothing. It was now a downpour. Bright lightning and loud thunder were now regular.

Satisfied that nobody was in the house, Rooter turned and saw Con standing there, scared, his arms folded across his bare chest. "Wh-What was it? What happened?"

"I don't know," Rooter said, stretching his neck and rubbing it with his hand. "Something was in this house. I caught a glimpse of what looked like a giant man standing right here when the lightning lit up the room. I took two shots at him, but he was already gone, I guess."

This made no sense to Rooter. He looked at the wall that separated the kitchen from Sully's bedroom and found the two bullet holes. *No blood and no trace remains. How could this guy move out of the way of both my shots?*

He turned around and the two looked at one another. Rooter took a series of deep breaths. "I don't know bud. It doesn't make a lot of sense. I saw him, then it was like he vanished or something."

Rooter replayed the series of events in his mind as he swept through the house. After going into every room and opening every closet, he went outside for a cursory glance around the property. When he came back in, he found Con yawning at the dining room table.

"Go, head back to sleep. I'm not sleeping tonight. I'm going to make coffee and stay up."

Con nodded, "Okay, but do you want company?"

"No, it's fine," Rooter took another deep breath. He was still visibly shaken. "I'll wake you if something happens. Go get some rest."

Con retired reluctantly. Rooter put on a pot of coffee. He went back to his room and threw on some sweatpants and a t-shirt. He replaced two rounds and stuffed the .38 in his right pocket. After pouring a cup and spicing it up with a shot of Johnny Walker, he walked out back and lit a cigarette under the awning. The rain was beginning to let up. He sucked the cigarette down so fast that he had a second lit within 90-seconds. He was starting to feel better and decided to sit in one of the patio chairs. *What just happened? Whoever that was, he moved way too fast for his size. Clearly this place is no longer safe. We need to get word to Sully in the morning. Who was that? I wonder if Anny is okay…*

Rooter's mind was racing at breakneck speed and not working toward any solutions at this point. His inability to really think was compounded by the fact that he was really scared. The person he saw had a strange look. Rooter closed his eyes and conjured up the image he saw during that short burst of lightning.

He was tall, definitely over 6'6," maybe even close to 7-feet. Malevolent. Powerful. Smiling, maybe? Not smiling, but I saw his teeth for some reason. Those red eyes; they swallowed the white light and bounced red light back at me. Reminded me of the eyes of a cat behind a beam of light. Did he duck or did he jump out of the way of my bullets? Or was he already gone, out of the window, by the time I shot?

He shivered involuntarily, even though the moist air was upper 70's on the back porch. Taking another big swig of his makeshift Irish coffee, the PI lit a third smoke, and rehashed the whole thing in his mind once again.

CHAPTER 20
The Zoe Ginosko Laboratories

Tuesday, September 20, 2011

The General excused himself to go home and pack while Doctor Monroe, Abdullah Kahn, and the Hand proceeded to the medium security wing within the 4th ward. The Scientist, Professor Mikel Maldaceto, greeted them enthusiastically in his awkward, gangly manner. "Hello, hello, my very important guests. Please come. You are most welcome in the OLS."

They exchanged pleasantries as Monroe began a tour of the section known as 'Observation Level Security.' The labs were in a cluster to the right. He decided to take the group there last.

The OLS was much more than research laboratories. Everywhere they looked, exceedingly tall, dark and handsome men milled about, wearing white linen pants and long sleeve shirts. Their female counterparts were a smidge shorter, but similarly stunning, with skin so smooth and blemish-free that they looked airbrushed. The women wore teal linen pants and long sleeve shirts in the same loose-fitting style as the men.

"The residents wear linen clothing in the OLS," explained Monroe, "because they are constantly undergoing tests and observation. We picked it because this clothing, like a hospital gown, is easily slipped on and off. The residents you see here today have been given our standard genetic enhancement, which alters the production of Melanocortin at the molecular level inside the pituitary gland. We use this methodology to reduce the interchange with the active receptors."

"I see," the Hand mumbled to himself, sarcastically.

"A reduced Melanocortin level interacting with the G Protein-Coupled Receptor ultimately produces more Eumelanin, which gives them their brown complexion."

"Of course it does," the Hand was now having fun, mumbling to himself in mockery of the Scientist's inability to speak plain English.

"The reason for standardizing this enhancement is because our clients need men and woman operatives that can go in and out of multi-cultural theatres. Medium-brown skin is the easiest to deploy."

Mikel took a step back on the technical terms, "The science is like baking a cake. At some point, we figure out how to follow a recipe and the biology just follows. For example, we have another standard ingredient in our recipe for men. Basically, we break the dam on the amount of testosterone secreted from the testicles. Then, we 'bake' this extra hormone production into the subject's body, which produces a well-defined, muscular, large, mesomorph-type. They look good, do they not?"

The Scientist looked to admire a male talking to a female thirty feet down one hall. He nodded in their direction, and his guests also took notice. It was admirable, and even somewhat seductive. The man and woman were beautiful in just about every imaginable way.

Monroe reclaimed his role as explainer-in-chief, "Similarly, we've tweaked the estrogen receptor count in our female population. The three main estrogen compounds naturally produced -- Estrone, Estradiol, and Estriol -- are actually made by the body in abundance. In most women, much of it is wasted due to the limited capacities of the receptors. So, in our females, we alter the receptor compound, which assures the estrogen steroid compounds are working at their fullest capacity."

"That's what produces this incredible beauty in our woman, then?" asked Kahn.

"Yes. We think this is how many of our great ancestors looked, beautiful and powerful. The receptor dilution in the female is a hereditary distilment. Female genetics are on a multi-generational, downward trajectory, affecting everything from physical strength and stamina to beauty and intelligence. Anyway, when we maximize the estrogen produced *and* used by the body, we get beautiful skin, full breasts, and very shapely fat storage in and around the buttocks. However, because of the hormone levels these women are enjoying, they would face more than an 80 percent chance of developing hormone-sensitive cancers. To counteract this, we've synthesized a xenoestrogen injection that they get four times per year, which effectively offsets the cancer risk. In fact, our girls have a less than 12% chance of getting hormone-related cancer, such as breast cancer, as a result of these injections."

"So, the men get big-balls and the girls get good looks, and it all comes standard here at the lab, huh?" Kahn mused.

"These enhancements are now standard. Of course, the client picks from a menu of other mastered genotype infusions." The Scientist grinned, "Buy the wolf's sense of smell and get the big balls for free." They all chuckled, as disturbing as it was.

"I understand the purpose of the standard enhancement in men," observed the Hand, "they become larger, stronger, and faster. There are many useful applications for a more advanced physical being, especially when mixing those with some of our non-standard enhancements. But I'm not sure I understand why you put so much effort into the female population."

"My dear sir," said Monroe, patting the Hand's back superciliously, "you are woefully mistaken. Right now, we have orders for female product at a rate of three-to-one against the males. The last two purchases we made were all trafficked women, and the ages are coming way down too. We're finding that the earlier our enhancements interact with the test subject, the better the outcome. We now try to infuse before puberty, when the girls are eight to ten. For males, we will infuse up to the age of twenty-seven. We've found that the timing of infusion is of little consequence in the males. Come, we will demonstrate the power of the female prototype. You'll enjoy this."

Monroe led them down a few halls and up one flight of stairs as he continued, "The female prototype is not just physically beautiful. The structural changes go far beyond looks – they experience an increase in uterine growth, vaginal lubrication, a thickening of the vaginal walls, an accelerated metabolism, and a much more precise governing and maintenance of their vessels and skin. None of our subjects use skincare products. This is how they look, naturally. We've discovered that when estrogen is received at the rate and frequency that our girls experience, a pheromone secretion phenomenon actually takes place. It's crazy -- like the power of the queen in a honeybee colony! And we've recently started teaching the girls how to use this power as part of their operative advantage in the field."

They arrived in an upstairs loft that had a huge, floor-to-ceiling, one-way, angled mirror looking over a pub. "What you see below is the OLS watering hole known as 'The Tavern.' We do hundreds of social experiments here."

There were at least 30 people milling about The Tavern, laughing and carrying-on. The two bartenders were dressed as residents, but were actually BSA employees. Mikel touched an intercom button and entered a short code. Then one of the bartenders put a finger to his ear as the Scientist said, "Rick, we're about to conduct the Orbit Protocol as a demonstration. Be advised."

The bartender looked up at the reflective glass and nodded slightly, indicating he got the message. The Scientist then made a quick phone call, alerting some other person in some other area of the OLS.

"We only started putting these prototypes on the market two and a half years ago. At first, they didn't look like this. We've mastered the ability to make them look beautiful and strong, I'd say. Believe you me, in the beginning of all this, our *successful* human hybrids were actually rather hideous."

"What type of operatives do we have in the field, or is that a question for the General?" Kahn asked.

"The General can be more specific, but I believe the ratio is around 60% old school, 40% new, like these here. We're slowly turning over the force. Obviously, everyone involved in the Alpha Kilo operation was of the old variety."

"What about the Primary versus Secondary?" asked Kahn, "These are all still Secondary, right?"

"Not all of them," the Scientist replied, looking at the patrons in The Tavern intently. "There, look. See that boy talking to the girl on the sofas near the television?"

"Yes."

"Those two are Primary. They were engineered en vitro." The boy and girl were obviously a bit younger, but looked and acted older than their age.

"Primary subjects like those two are still young. The oldest is twelve now. But they mature so much faster than normal human kids. For example, those there, the boy is seven and the girl is eight. As you can see, she's almost fully developed. And what is he, maybe five-foot-eleven and about 180 pounds of pure muscle? Our Primary hybrids all start being sexually active at around six or seven. Fascinating, isn't it?"

"Fascinating. So are any of the six or seven-year-olds pregnant?" The Hand asked, hoping the answer was no.

The Doc smiled down at him, "Of course."

A woman wearing typical resident scrubs walked through the front door of The Tavern and drew the Doc's attention. "Okay, here we go. That's our subject, Julia. She has a com-piece in her ear. She doesn't know her target yet, so, Mr. Hand, why don't you do the honors and pick on for us?"

The Hand looked around the room and picked out an older (by comparison) looking man, in his mid to late 30's, sitting at the bar by himself. "Okay, now what do you want Julia to make him do?"

"I don't know. Get in a fight?" The Hand suggested, shrugging.

"That's too easy," interjected Kahn, "pick something else. Men fight in bars over pretty girls everywhere, the world over." The Hand nodded in agreement as the Scientist looked at Kahn, stupid-like, as if trying to figure out if that were true or not.

"That's true. How about if he is made to attack the bartender? That'd be unusual, right?" Kahn thought about it and nodded with approval.

The Doc pushed the intercom buttons in a series of numbers specific to Julia's communication unit. She put her finger up to her ear and he said, "Julia, your mark is the man at the far end of the bar. Make him attack the bartender."

The men watched as she cast a glance in their direction and winked at the mirror. They all felt an unmistakable sensation in their stomachs when she did. *That's strange,* thought the Hand as he watched intensely. It was as though their blood pressure was immediately pumping harder, but why? All she did was glance in their direction.

She advanced to the man and passed behind him, brushing her fingertips along his shoulders, from his right to his left. The observers overheard, through the intercom system, her ask, *"Mind if I have a seat?"*

"No." He then turned his back toward her and postured himself to look at the rest of the club, purposefully ignoring her.

"Shall we place any wagers?" the Hand offered with satisfaction as he rubbed his hands together, "Looks like I picked a stone-cold killer."

"Just watch," the doc said, flatly.

The bartender came over and took her drink order, then departed to make it. Suddenly, the disinterested man spun around for no apparent reason and said, *"What are you doing?"*

"Nothing, I didn't touch you," she said, then looked at him awkwardly and suggested, *"Maybe you need to take a nap or something. You seem like you're wound pretty tight."*

"I need to be left alone," he snorted and turned back around.

She then unbuttoned the top three buttons of her shirt and leaned back on her stool, crossed her legs and said, *"I like it here, don't you?"*

"I don't want to talk," he said, but then glanced in her direction and his tone started to change. He became less sharp, more rounded and easy-going. *"Why do you ask, anyway? Have we met?"*

She smiled, *"No, no reason, just making small talk."* She paused for a minute and stared into his eyes, then said, *"Tell you what, I'll leave you alone like you asked. I should respect that. Let's have a drink sometime, okay?"*

She then got up and left before he had a chance to say anything. From behind however, he now watched her intently. The loft-level observers watched him watch her for the next five minutes, scarcely touching his drink. As the time passed, he became more agitated, and started fidgeting at the bar. He then began biting his fingernails as she occasionally glanced in his direction and shot him a perfect smile. She mingled with another group of really good-looking OLS residents as the bartender finally delivered her drink. The intercom had a hard time picking up her voice from where she was sitting in The Tavern, but a faint, *"Thank you,"* could be heard as the barkeep dropped off her beverage.

She took a sip of the drink as the barkeep turned to walk away, then, made a sour face, spat the drink back into the glass, and looked over at the mark, as if horrified. The mark sat erect, watching her with intensity. She then flipped her middle finger at the bartender who was still walking away, and the game was on. The mark flew off his stool and grabbed the bartender by the throat, pile-driving him to the ground, and smashing a chair in the process.

"Haha, see?" laughed Monroe, "You'd have lost your money, little man."

Security rushed into The Tavern and broke it up. Kahn looked for Julia in the bar, but she was nowhere to be found. A minute later, she sauntered into the observatory level. The men stopped in their tracks. They were truly enamored, not just by her beauty, but her very essence. She shook each of their hands as Monroe gave her a squeeze around the shoulders, congratulating her on a job well done.

Kahn now realized the true power she had. It was unlike anything he ever witnessed, or *felt*. Monroe spoke like a school kid in her midst; he even giggled once or twice. *Is he actually talking like a retarded fifth-grader, or am I just hearing it that way?*

The Hand couldn't take his eyes off her. He just stood there, speechless and gape-mouthed, even when she talked directly to him. It was absurd. Indeed, even Abdullah, who fancied himself greater than the average man, had a hard time keeping his wits about him. *But there, a little cleavage is visible if I... what, what?* He looked away when he realized a question had been addressed to him directly. Maintaining nonchalance was impossible in the presence of Julia. His heart was beating fast and his knees felt weak.

A few minutes later Julia left and the room re-balanced. The men looked at one another, astonished and hard-pressed for the right words to describe what just happened.

"That, gents," Monroe chuckled, "is why we have two-times the orders for female product."

"Good grief," whispered the Hand. "Imagine her in a strip-club. She'd bankrupt anyone who walked in."

"Every government we do business with is ordering what we've code-named, 'Queen Bee.' A woman with the power that Julia wields can lord authority over an entire kingdom."

"How do your employees operate? How do your doctors inspect *them* and not fall to that power?" asked the Hand.

"Chemicals, believe it or not. The employees who evaluate the subjects, and those who are in the labs with them, have to take a pill we've developed that temporarily numbs areas of the brainstem, the animalistic responses. It's the only way they are able to keep their head and get the job done. Even with the chems, it's not always easy. Ask me how I know."

"What about the male subjects? How do they fend off the smell of sex?" said Kahn.

"For them, it's different. It's a power struggle. They are all like demigods; the women simultaneously despise the male power, but also love having control over it if they can get it. The men simultaneously despise the lust, which can render them powerless, but they love breaking through the pheromones and making the females fall to their own sense of desire. When the female falls emotionally for the male, she foregoes her power and the male, from that point forward, always has his way with that individual. It's the truly fascinating story of our human race, unfolding on steroids, literally."

"Gentlemen," interjected the Scientist. "Shall we head to the Zoe Ginosko Labs?"

They meandered to a conference room near the laboratories. Once situated, the Scientist did most of the talking. He gave an account of how he began to process the intelligence obtained in Malcolm Bernard's journal, and who he enlisted to help him decode the various sections. He gave one disclaimer three separate times, noting emphatically that it had only been a couple weeks since he took possession of the book. Therefore, he was not close to concluding his investigation. It annoyed Kahn, but he let it slide. Doc Monroe spent most of this time looking at his phone, presumably checking his emails.

After the disclaimers and formalities, the Scientist got to the good stuff. Even the Doc put his phone down to listen.

"We are beginning to make real progress in identifying the true essence of the human – the character and conscience that transcend the chemicals. Indeed, we're talking about the soul. As we identify it, we seek to interact with it. As we interact with it, we find there is absolutely no doubt that extra-dimensional realities exist. Not only are we interacting with extra-dimensional realms, we see clear evidence for extra-dimensional beings within those realms. These past two weeks have given us insights into the myths of our ancestors in a way that will drive science like no other time in history. We're talking about harnessing the truth about trans-human supernaturalism, connecting the physical and metaphysical realities of the coming, *super human*." The Scientist leaned forward and said with emphasis, "We are on the doorstep."

"Take it from the top please, Mikel," Kahn said.

"Very well, let's start with the book. Section one, as I predicted in Rome, has to do with Malcolm's technology. We have translated the specs and are waiting on a number of components, most of which are available on the open market. Once we get the hardware, we fully anticipate being able to engineer, program, and rebuild his gizmo here at BSA. The specs are complicated, but in layman terms, Malcolm was able to use wavelength division multiplexing as a carrier vehicle for a series of isolated non-nuclear generated, electromagnetic pulses to neurological pointer feeds in the brain, along the visual cortex. You need a lot of dormant energy to accomplish it, but the pulse doesn't need to be strong, it just needs to oscillate."

"Laymen's terms, my ass," the Hand puffed.

The Scientist looked flustered by the comment, then grabbed two pens and pointed them towards his eyes, one pen to each eye. He continued, "Malcolm's technology works by interacting with the brain through the subject's eyes. Once the device is engaged, the subject's brain quickly believes that the body has died, and when this happens, the life essence begins to detach. The longer the life essence – or soul – is separated from the body, the less the life essence remembers about itself. It, for lack of a better descriptor, forgets what morals or ethics or conscience the person held sacred. It becomes more *childlike* throughout the process. When the device is turned off, the life essence returns immediately to the host, because it recognizes that the brain isn't really dead. The life essence then recalibrates with the memories retained in the brain, as well as the person's genetic information, and voila, the person is back, but less idealistic, less intense, less potent to the left or right side of behavior. He's more… childlike, in things like ideology and religion and politics."

"How do we know this component isn't just frying some area of the brain?" asked the Hand.

"According to Malcolm, neuroimaging of subjects after exposure to his device showed no loss of brain functionality at all, anywhere. The change in their core belief structure, or the numbing of their radical beliefs, must be derived outside the neurological makeup of the brain -- what some call, 'the mind.' Incidentally, Malcolm used this technique as an alternative to more invasive interrogation techniques in Iraq. It's likely the main reason he was there. His book indicates that patients took varying lengths of time to complete the cycle, anywhere from a few hours to a few days, but he had a 100% success rate as far as interrogation was concerned. Once the life essence was brought to what Bernard referred to as 'plus or minus 30 BAT alignment,' which was a scale he developed to measure the idealistic potency of enemy combatants, they sang like canaries. In their minds, or lack thereof, there was no longer a reason to really care. They were more childlike -- they cared about the food, the music, and what people thought about them. They could care less about protecting information related to a radical cleric or a military operation grounded in religious idealism."

The Hand was leaning into the table and Abdullah was nodding involuntarily as he considered all that was being said.

"Malcolm's journal further reports that after the Alpha Kilo site was discovered, the U.S. Military apparatus transferred him there to investigate what he calls 'the portal.' On numerous occasions, he used his device on enemy combatants at the portal location. When he did, their life essence returned with, how did he put it, 'wild and vivid descriptions of a world foreign to the human experience.' He also notes that among those who underwent the 'Life Essence Manipulation Cycle' at Alpha Kilo, not one came back 'childlike.' Rather, they came back 'uniquely different.' He claimed they were enlightened somehow, with deep insight and new information. He notes that the cuneiform inscriptions in and around the Alpha Kilo site were of great interest to the people who underwent the cycle there. These were simple, mission-driven, Arabic-speaking jihadists that now had an academic interest in archaeology, metaphysics, and a 4,000-year-old syllabic text."

"Did Malcolm ever use it on himself?" asked Kahn.

"I assume he did, based on the third section of his book and that strange Eteocypriot language." The Scientist shook his head, still looking at the book and his notes, "but if he did, he did not record it in any manner we yet understand."

Kahn stretched. "Okay, so what's the application here? When I was first ushered into our thing here, I was chiefly interested in renewable energy sources, revolutionary propulsion systems, and technologies like that. Biotech led us to the formulation of genetically engineered super-soldiers. Now, where are we heading with this life essence and extra-dimensional stuff? Are there viable applications here for our clients? Is this a course change for the group? I need your input, gentlemen."

The Doc cleared his throat, "Forgive me for interrupting, but how can we discuss potential commercial applications for something like this? We don't know what we don't know! Seriously, extra dimensional portals interacting with ancient celestial beings... And now we're intermingling, or at least communicating, with them again? Come on, this is a game-changer, no? This sounds like stuff from Homer or Dante or Hell Boy, and you want our strategic input on what we can commercialize for the underground clandestine markets?"

"Exactly, that's it -- *sounds like stuff from Homer*," the Scientist jumped-in. "The Greek demigods from yesterday are really no different than the trans-humanist half-breeds we're seeking today. In both cases, we're talking about a species that's part man, part 'other.' In the past, it was widely accepted that this 'other' was celestial, or god-like. Today, the 'other' is a product of science and technology. Based on Malcolm's account of what's happening at Alpha Kilo, I think we're about to experience a revolutionary intersection of both – the metaphysical and the technological!"

He paused and Kahn gestured for him to continue. "In the great myths and religions, we find no shortage of demigods, deities, super humans, extra-dimensional powers, animal-to-animal chimera, animal-to-human chimera, and the like. The eschatological views of these myths and religions also point to a day when the so-called 'gods' reengage with mankind, and all this crazy stuff starts up again.

Except this time, we have even more crazy science, technology, military, genetic engineering, etc. This is where we need to be when everything goes down. This is our core competence. There's no better organization in the world to act as gatekeeper between the science and the supernatural. Mr. Kahn, it's at this intersection that you will find your world-changing, commercial applications, I wager."

The Hand nodded and smiled. At least that was possible, even if hard to believe.

"Well said," Abdullah pondered it all for a minute. In truth, it was all conjecture at this point. They didn't know how anything was going to play out, so best course was to keep investigating and keep learning all they could.

"Let's steer in another direction for a moment," Abdullah said. "As I wrap my brain around all of this information, can we go back and discuss the concept and science behind 'Life Essence?' I could use a little more clarity there. This part could be huge for us as well. Are we referring to a so-called soul, like the one that floats away to heaven after mortal death?"

"I can try, but what we think we know is still theory at this point," Mikel said as he adjusted his glasses. "From a biological standpoint, a person's Life Essence seems to occupy a physical area, perhaps three to four feet in diameter, symmetrically centered between the heart and brain. The science is telling us that it is biomechanically connected to the brain. A particular Life Essence is identified to a particular brain by a ceaseless torsion connection to the photon resonance inside the hollow, crystal tubes of the brain's neuronal axons. This helps explain why each Life Essence has its own fingerprints, so-to-speak. It helps explain how the brain can inform the Life Essence, while also being directed by it."

The Scientist looked at the Hand who appeared to be keeping up, though from behind. He then glanced back at Kahn, and cautiously continued, "For most of us, our uninitiated brains limit data retrieval from the soul realm. Mostly, we upload data into our Life Essence for storage, and because the Life Essence is predominant, this function is natural. It's like your beating heart; you don't tell it to beat, it just knows to do it. That said, we're finding that humans can override this predominant upload link, and actually download data from the soul realm. Spiritualists, ritual séance or meditation enthusiasts, religious mystics – all these people learn to engage in ritual behavior that allows them to go in and out of communication with this extra 'soul' dimension. And the scientific proof is emerging too, most notably out of Cambridge, where they are using sophisticated instruments to run numerous tests on this same paranormal activity. What's really interesting is that the information one person downloads from the soul realm can be very different from the information someone else downloads. We call this phenomenon the Life Essence Filter Effect."

"What does that mean?" Abdullah asked.

"It means life on earth – our experiences, hurts, pains – these all seem to corrupt our ability to receive uniform and useful data from the extra-dimensional world. It means there is something corrosive about being human; something that corrupts, to one degree or another, our ability to collectively receive the technological and revelatory insights of the celestial. That's why mythology and religion, monotheism and polytheism, duality and nothingness, compete so violently for emphatic reign among our species. Are these beliefs and traditions equally relevant? What's the true nature of these supernatural entities? Is there one absolute truth? How can we know any of these answers without useful data? All we're prepared to state is, yes, humans can exchange information with the other side. However, the data is corrupted by our corrupt nature. I truly believe our science is the key that will bring uniformity to the expressions of this mystic interaction."

"So, what does that mean for us?" asked the Hand.

Kahn popped to attention with a personal epiphany, "Uniformity of data download from the other side equals timeless, tested, powerful information for us on this side! Harnessing that other-worldly information and experience equals ultimate power and control in all that we do!"

CHAPTER 21
Debauchery

Anny was sitting in the lobby and happened to be looking toward the elevator bank when a clean-shaved, handsome lawyer-type emerged and marched straight toward her; what's more, he had on a charming smile. He wore a blue suit with shiny brown shoes and had on his lucky court-day watch. His hair was messed, in a fashionable way, and he smelled of a shower and a splash of GIO by Giorgio Armani.

"Well, well, well," Anny grinned as he sat down across from her, "who are you and what did you do with the Solomon Keys I arrived in Chicago with?"

"Right?" he adjusted his collar, "thanks for the tip on the in-room massage. Life saver."

"U-huh, sure is."

"Let's get to it. How did it go?" Depressed Solomon was in and out of focus as it pertained to the whirlwind of life. Lawyer Solomon had eagle-eyes and often drove the 'paralegals' of K&A mad with his intensity. Clearly, he'd had a bellwether moment that afternoon and at least for the time being, was back to being his old self. Under the circumstances, it was a welcome change.

"Right," she straightened up, took a sip of a diet Coke and withdrew her phone from her purse. "Well, I recorded the whole thing, knowing it was going to be hard to re-tell the technological details. He didn't get into much tech though."

"Hang on, start at the beginning. Don't you normally observe first?" Solomon was on fire.

"You know me," she chortled admiringly. "And yes, that's how it started. I sat by a window and saw him on approach. He walked rigid. His phone rang when he was on the other side of the street but he rejected the call. Then when he got to the coffee shop it rang again, and again he rejected the call. Once inside he avoided looking around for me, which was a little odd. He sort of seemed like the guy who waited for the girl to ask him to the high school dance. Know the type?"

"Heard of the type. That wasn't me, sister."

"At that point I got in line behind him and listened as he barked orders to the poor little barista girl. He just seemed annoyed, put out, and really busy. After he ordered I tapped him on the shoulder and said, 'Mr. Rasmussen?' to which he did a double-take," she demonstrated the double-take for some reason, "and was sweet as pie from that point forward."

"Of course he was. There's worse things in life than having a cup of coffee with a good looking gal."

"Or spending a week with one, but I digress." she was quick; very quick on her feet. Solomon walked right into that one.

"Look," he chuckled, "I'm back to dressing better than you again, my head is back, and I'm ready to go figure this riddle out. I was off my game for a week. It's behind us now."

"Alright, just giving a little jazz, it's all good." She paused and became more serious, "unfortunately, when I asked about the component he said, 'sorry, classified'. When I asked why our boy was in Iraq, he said, 'sorry, classified'. When I asked if there was anything he could tell me about Malcolm that was not classified, he flirted and said, 'sure, but I'd have to kill you'. About then I started feeling like the whole thing was a bust so I put on the pouty face and resorted to cute begging. He asked me if I was used to getting my way, and I said I was. Then he was like, 'tell you what, there's no way I can give you everything you want to know, but if you want to meet me for dinner tomorrow night, I might could drop you a few nuggets of information'. I said 'what kind of information?' and he said, 'the kind that strongly blurs the classified boundary but won't get me fired'. I said 'sure' before I realized what he had in mind. He then handed me his card with the address to his personal residence on the back and told me to meet him at his place at eight tomorrow night."

"Okay, so how'd it end?" asked Sully.

"It ended with him assuring that I liked scallops, then leaving the coffee shop with a little more pep in his step than before. He looked like he'd just been asked to the prom, I guess."

"Tomorrow, huh?" Sully looked contemplative. "You know he's gonna want to get laid right?"

She rolled her eyes, "Of course he is, they all do. Only men in my life that don't want me to bed down with them are the guys I work with."

That was awkward. Sully didn't at all know how to respond to that. She could tell they were on the verge of having to deal with *atmosphere*, so she continued by reassuring him, with a wave of her hand, "But like every other time, I'll get the dirt and avoid that and everyone will be happy. Well, except the guy who got played."

Sully shook his head, "You're sick."

"No, I'm just good at what I do. You're sick for pimping me out."

That sent a twang of guilt up his intestines. There was enough truth to that statement that for a moment he contemplated calling it off. *Where is the boundary? Would I tolerate her coming back empty-handed? What if Anny was my daughter? ...* He decided right then that he needed to tell her something that was long overdue.

"It's important you know," he locked eyes with her and leaned forward, "that I have no expectation of you compromising your personal morals for the sake of my business. You go in, get put in a bind, can't get the info unless you 'do things' with the guy; you know I expect you to run away right?"

"I know," She said, flippantly gesturing for him to calm down, "I do this on my own free will and you are not held liable for anything that happens, etcetera, etcetera, may it please the court."

"It's not that, Anny," She slowed down to listen; this was new. Her heart rate picked up in anticipation. "It has nothing to do with liability. I don't want anything to happen to *you*; you are what matters to me."

"Re..." she coughed and swallowed and lowered her eyes, "Really? You've never said that. Thanks. It means a lot."

He shook his head in disgust, "If I've never said that, I don't deserve you."

She bit her lip and held back some rather unexpected emotions. Ever since joining the K&A team she'd learned to operate with her guard up. The guys were great but the environment could be coarse, even mean. *Well, not Con, mostly just Rooter...*

The environment was very fraternity-masculine at times and she'd rarely felt genuinely cared for by any of them. She'd taught herself to not expect that; told herself it wasn't professional to want to be cared for or cared about. Sure, before she headed out to meet a target for the first time Rooter would always give her the 101 on self-defense and good decision making, but by day two post her return, he'd be back to making fun of her for being a supposed slut. He didn't really care. None of them did.

What is this? She wondered as she fought to hold back a sudden desire to cry. *Why did his care and concern cause such a reaction in me?* She looked away and chewed at her lower lip, which was now beginning to quiver. She was taken aback by her own reaction. *What is this!*

"I'm sorry," she finally pushed the words out, realizing that the emotion was more powerful than her will. It was not as though she was fully crying, but her eyes were moist and her lip was quivering, and anyone in the lobby of the Drake could tell his words had powerfully affected her. In a whisper she ashamedly said, "I'm not sure where this is coming from."

"No, I'm sorry. When we get back, I'll rein him in." He was of course talking about Rooter's nonstop ridicule and coarse banter.

"No," she objected, "it's fine. I even like it most of the time. That's not fair to him. I know he doesn't mean anything by it."

"None of that matters." Solomon responded, flatly. "What matters is that you are allowed to be you, free of harassment and torment, whether it's in jest or not. We all haven't deserved you, Anny. I should have reined him in a long time ago."

"Good lord," She took a deep breath. "Crazy woman emotions huh?"

Sully grinned but refused the bait. Instead, he reached over and patted her hand, "Human emotions, and they are good, not crazy."

Anny's life had been exclusively dedicated to Keys & Associates for years. After she broke up with her only long-term relationship, the boy she'd followed to DC, she recoiled emotionally and purposed to avoid issues of the heart for a prolonged season. She had a few good friends but she rarely dated and she kept her personal life and feelings under lock and key. *It's easier that way*, she'd told herself.

Drama-free, she was eager and content to focus on her new career with Solomon's crew, and it was the perfect distraction that kept her far away from the complex world of emotion, expectation, relationship and most of all, sex. Then time simply got away from her. Weeks became months, months became years, and over that time she changed. *But have I changed for the better or the worse?*

Until that night in the Drake she'd have called her metamorphosis a 'toughening up', something she needed. But if she was honest with herself now, she knew she had simply changed, and not necessarily in a good way.

She excused herself to freshen up. They had dinner plans, Sully was finally back on track, and this unexpected assault of emotion was going to have to be dealt with at another time. She was determined to have a fun night. Sully watched as she marched with purpose toward the public restrooms.

God, I've lost the ability to let people love me! She thought, angrily. She dabbed the makeup with a paper towel as it all started to make more sense. *I'm afraid of deep relationships. Afraid to let anyone in. I've become the professional cat-woman, aging, single, and pathetic.* She was mad at letting the hurt of her breakup cripple her, emotionally.

For the first time she looked at herself in the mirror and saw not a successful, professional, gloriously single woman with no tie downs and freedoms-a-plenty.

Rather, she saw a beautiful lonely girl. There in the Drake, she decided she no longer wanted to be just a beautiful lonely girl. She took one last deep breath, adjusted her bra, dabbed on some lip gloss and marched back to the lobby where Solomon was waiting patiently. *I'm going to need to make a few changes when I get home. A few good changes are in order. But tonight… Tonight is a great night for a stiff drink.*

They had dinner at McCormick & Schmick's on Chestnut. He got a Filet and she ordered Chilean Sea Bass. They shared mushrooms, asparagus and mashed potatoes, as well as a bottle of 2009 Frog's Leap Merlot from Napa; though it was not at all a good pairing with her fish. She finished with a glass of Dows 30 Year aged Port and he, a simple cup of coffee. By the time they left the restaurant, she was on her wayward tipsiest and seemed intent on going all the way to stupid-drunk before the night was over. This was okay with him. He'd recognized her drinking intentions early on and resigned himself to making sure she'd get home safely.

They went from McCormick's to a little Irish Pub on Rush where she talked a lot about her parents. She said on numerous occasions how bad she missed them, and how bad her mother had wanted grandchildren. She also informed Solomon, to his surprise that she was in fact not an only child, but that she had a brother who passed away in a car accident while in high school.

"Tha's somfin we ne'er talk bou." She said, weaving back and forth, trying to look through the eye of the cocktail straw at him.

He had fun despite her inebriation. He learned a lot about his young accomplice that night; like when she told him about her brother; that was a bit of a shock. Or when she asked him if he ever thought about her; that question was out of the blue. Or when she talked about what an ass Rooter was and what a sweetheart Con was. Most insightful of all was a tell-all, slurred monologue that lasted about six minutes where she expressed in no uncertain terms how much she liked him and how willing she was to "prove it when we get back to the hotel". He knew it was the booze talking, but he'd never been around her when she was drunk, so he decided to have a little fun with it and played along. Though he played along, he'd have never taken advantage of her. He was much too principled for that.

After leaving the pub they found their way to the hotel's lobby bar just before last call. She tried to order one last round, but he managed to steer her toward the elevators instead. She leaned hard on him as they navigated the maze of lobby tables and chairs, and almost stumbled to the ground once. She giggled a lot; he found it quite amusing as well. When they finally got to the rooms she propped herself up against the wall and searched her purse for the room key while he steadied her, his arm around her midsection. She mumbled something about losing her key and he chuckled, offering to look through her purse for her.

"No," she said, drawing out the last letter, "A man never looks a purse's woman."

"ah huh? Okay then, you'll just have to come to my room."

"Really?" she said, "You're takin' advantage er me?"

"Come on little one." He helped her to the opposite side of the hallway and quickly inserted his own keycard; the green light lit and the door swung open. He got her to the bed and she fell like a sack of potatoes, perfectly sideways across it. He removed her shoes and pulled the sheets from under her, then swung her around, until she was oriented in the right direction. She muttered something about the room spinning, so he went and found a double-dose of pain killer and a glass of water and brought it to her.

After some coaxing she took it, lay back down, and passed out almost immediately. He pulled the sheets and blanket to her chin, then dialed the thermostat a few degrees lower than normal. After taking a quick shower, he flopped down in the chase lounge next to the bed and closed his eyes. It had been an enjoyable night, even though he had played the babysitter role.

At exactly 7:50 the next morning, Tuesday the 30th, the in-room phone rang and jolted Solomon out of a deep sleep. He scurried from his lounge chair to the bedside table nearest the window and answered the obnoxious thing. The sound didn't appear to faze Anny at all, who was half in and half outside of the sheets, still passed out in what looked like a dreadfully uncomfortable position on the bed. It was Rooter on the other end. He was wide awake, talking fast, and hard to understand.

"Hang on," Solomon said, glancing at Anny a second time. He didn't want to wake her so he decided to take the call in the bathroom where he had noticed a phone hanging on the wall. "Okay, start over."

Rooter told him about the intruder, how he woke up scared, saw someone in a flash of lightning, and how he fired off two rounds in the safe house the night prior. He still sounded upset. It didn't help when Sully asked unanswerable questions like, "what was the intruder looking for?" or "was it just a burglar or was the guy connected to everything else that's happened?"

"I don't know, I'm just telling you what happened bro-han! Now how do I get a hold of that Greek prick? I think we got a fight comin' our way."

"We can't, we just gotta wait for Betty's next visit, right?" Solomon said, trying to think of a way they might get word to Dotty.

"This is a terrible system boss," Sully heard his pal inhale a cigarette puff, "we should leave this place."

"Look, I think we'll only be here another day or two," Sully said, "Can you run security shifts with Con until we get back? Figure by then Betty will swing by and we'll get word to Dotty and devise a better plan."

"Well, you're goddamned right I'm gonna run shifts," he spat back, his voice strained and irritated, "but I ain't puttin' a spit-pistol in Con's hand while I sleep; you fuckin' kidding me? What's that kid gonna do with a gun? I may not sleep again. Ever!"

Sully chuckled at his friend's intensity. "If it's any consolation, I'm doing better."

"That's good." Sully heard him inhale another puff.

"Look, if she can't get what we need today, I'll just plan on renting a car and coming back to help you with the security watch. One way or another, I'll head back tomorrow morning at the latest."

There was a pause and then Rooter said, "I'd appreciate that. I'm actually geekin' out here boss. It's hard to explain. It feels like we're being hunted and Con ain't exactly the delta force that was maimed at Alpha Kilo, know what I mean?"

He did, but to be real honest, neither was Rooter, or Sully for that matter. "Hunted?"

"Yeah boss. I knew this person; or thing, was in the house before I saw it. It's weird. I could sense it looking at me. Still gives me the willies."

Solomon's mind drifted back to his own experiences in Alton. The image of the Phantom assassin peering out of the window, looking at him behind the hedge where he crouched, rendering him stone-cold petrified... "I know what you mean. That's how I felt in Alton."

"It's all connected," Rooter whispered, exhaling another puff. "This thing could have killed me and Con in our sleep last night, but it didn't. I bet you hams to gold dimes though, it's comin' back sooner or later, and we're gonna need some serious artillery or a new place to hide, and quick."

"How's Con?"

"Con? He's fine." Rooter took another puff. His deliberate pull on the cigarette was evidence of his unnerved state. "Damn near slept through the whole ordeal had I not screamed for him to wake the fuck up! I didn't tell him everything. I'm tryin' to make him think it was a neighborhood kid; a burglar or somethin'. I'm gonna need to bring him in though, I can't stay up all night every night."

"Just stay up until tomorrow afternoon, I'll be there," Sully assured, "I'll see ya tomorrow."

"Tomorrow then," and with that Rooter disconnected the call.

As Solomon went to hang up his end, he heard a second *click*. Walking back into the bedroom he found Anny awake and nervously biting her lip. She'd listened in on the conversation, and she looked worried.

CHAPTER 22
Braxton Hill

Tuesday, August 30, 2011

Con came out of his room at 6:55 am to the sounds of Rooter talking on the phone. The PI was on the back porch and pacing back and forth. Just as Con was wondering what was being talked about, Rooter stomped out his cigarette and came inside.

"Hey, how'd you sleep?"

"Is that a joke?" Con replied, searching the fruit bowl for a mango. "Who was that?"

"Sully. I asked him to finish his business and get back here."

Con's demeanor elevated, "Is he coming back?"

"Yes, tomorrow."

"Thank God," he said, almost to himself. The scent of tobacco clung to Rooter's Hawaiian shirt and invaded Con's nostrils. The PI smelled like an ashtray. They both sat at the kitchen table as Con inspected the bullet holes in the wall. "Maybe you should teach me how to fire a gun today."

"That's a good idea," Rooter was rubbing his forehead with the palms of his hands, his elbows to the table. "Pass me an apple, will ya? At say, 2 pm today, I want to get a couple hours of sleep. Before I retire, I'll teach you how to use a handgun. While I'm asleep, you'll need to stay off your computer and keep an eye open for anything suspicious."

"Okay. What about tonight?"

"That's why I'm going to get a few z's today. I'll stay up tonight. Won't have it any other way."

"Do you have any idea who it was?" The left side of Con's fro was matted down and his undershirt hung loosely on his skinny frame. Chin-stubble was trying to invade his face; this in itself was remarkable because Con struggled mightily to grow facial hair.

162

"I don't." Rooter took a bite of the apple and peered into the distance, blankly. They said very little to one another for the rest of the morning. The tension was palpable. Both men's nerves were pushing the red line. There was no sense in asking the questions they each so desperately wanted to ask because at this point, there were no answers. *Who was it? Was it a government operative? Was the person connected to Alton and Leola? Was the person still looking for something they possessed? Was the person even a person? Was the person meaning to slit their throats in the middle of the night, some other night? Was the person still out there, watching them that very moment?*

As Rooter got up to brew another pot of coffee, Con said, "You didn't see a Toyota Tacoma last night, did you?"

Rooter looked at him hard, "No, why?"

Con shrugged, "Nothing, just Betty said that the Father Dotty had mentioned being tailed by someone in a Tacoma, possibly."

"Wait," Rooter suddenly remembered the slow moving truck he saw from the kitchen window. "I did see a Tacoma, actually. Con, you should have told me."

Rooter now stared at the computer nerd with an angry look. Uncomfortable, Con stuttered his next, "Yo, you should have stayed to talk to Betty with me."

"First the wax paper, now this." Rooter shook his head and forced a grin to try and ease the tension. "You really need to learn to communicate better, bud. I'm no computer genius hacker, but right now, I'm all that stands between you and your little book, and some monster looking to turn you into coco-pebbles. What else did she say?"

"She said that Father Dotty felt like a Toyota Tacoma was tracking him from time to time. At their last meeting, the Father cut it short because he didn't know if it was safe, and he told Betty to be on the lookout for a Tacoma. A black one."

Damn it, he thought.

"The envelope." He went to his bedroom to retrieve the last drop from Betty. It was still on his end table, still unopened. He scolded himself and wondered whether he was losing his edge for this stuff. Back at the kitchen table, he opened the envelope and read its contents out loud.

"Dear team, your plan for research sounds fine. I have identified a possible tail, driver unknown, driving a black colored Toyota Tacoma pickup truck. This may be nothing, but better safe than sorry. I need an answer to the question posed previously: Did Sully and Leola own a cat?"

"Well," Rooter sighed, "It's right here. I should have looked at this."

For the rest of the morning, every ten to fifteen minutes, Rooter got up and walked the interior of the house, pausing to peer out of every window, looking for anything that might seem suspicious, especially that Tacoma. At 1:30 pm, just after lunch, Con offered to take the watch for a few hours, and though Rooter was still feeling fine, he knew he needed a few hours of sleep so he wouldn't be vulnerable from midnight onward. After showing Con the patrol route and giving him a brief explanation of the safety switch, as well as how to aim and fire his S&W SD 9mm, Rooter retired for a few hours of restless sleep.

Sleep was too generous a description. Rather, he went in and out of being conscious of a terrible, haunting nightmare. Over and over, he saw the red glow of the intruder's eyes. He felt the fear in his chest. He felt those eyes watching him. Without help, Rooter knew that he and Con were sitting ducks.

He looked at the clock showing 2:18. He was sweating and his heart was racing. He couldn't shake the dread. *Screw it. I need a smoke.*

The first thing he did was reclaim his gun. Sleeping was a futile endeavor. The PI suspected he'd be able to get through the night on adrenaline alone, if nothing else. It likely didn't matter anyway. *What am I thinking...? This freak-show intruder can kick my ass, whether I'm groggy or not.*

Across the bridge, in the neighboring city of Crofton, Father Abelemy was having lunch with a Brit named Braxton Hill. He met Braxton once previously, but this was their first real meeting.

Braxton Hill, called 'Bax' by his friends, was a 34-year-old ex-SBS operative with combat experience in Iraq and Afghanistan. He was 5'9", athletic, and 'always in fighting shape,' as he liked to say. He was clean-shaven with short brown hair, and rather ordinary looking, except for his bright, attentive, blue eyes. His eyes flashed about in his head, as if taking hundreds of pictures per second. His eyes were always moving. There was a liveliness and keen sparkle to them that the ladies found especially attractive.

Bax never married. He fancied himself a career spy, and knew that relationships and espionage went together like oil and water. He was a patriotic man, but what drove him to the job was his boyish need for adventure and an insatiable addiction to the spy's coveted endorphin rush. He liked pushing his mind and body to the outer limits. He found great joy in the pursuit and honing of his tactical and on-spot analytic skills. This job was something he was born to do, and he never regretted it. That is, until he became ensnared in the labyrinth of U.S. politics.

In 2007, he was recruited by MI-6, and quickly put in charge of the British investigation into the disappearance of Gill Spates, the British scientist who was working at Alpha Kilo with Malcolm Bernard. At the time he took the assignment, the Spates matter was converted from a missing person's case handled by a separate division of British Intelligence, to a murder case the British clandestine apparatus called a 'significantly disturbing matter of intrigue and suspicion.'

Bax took the assignment, even though there were no leads, suspects, or motives. Gill Spates was dead over a year before his remains were positively identified in 2007. In fact, it was a needle-in-a-haystack DNA match after the Brits determined that he died in the United States months after the Alpha Kilo slaughter.

"Surprisingly," Bax explained over his Caesar salad, "Spates' DNA records were added to a US database by a lab in St. Louis, Missouri. Did Spates actually escape the assault at Alpha Kilo? If so, how did he do it? How did he exit Iraq and enter the United States undetected? How did he ultimately die? After we positively identified our man, your country handed over the autopsy results. We hoped for some answers, but it only served to raise more questions. How did he break his arm? Why were there high levels of arsenic in his system, suggesting he was poisoned? Where did he die? Why was he in the US? Because the questions and answers were significant to British intelligence, I was recruited."

Bax recently received orders to return to London and was scheduled to depart the United States on the first of September. He had nothing to lose and rather liked the Greek, so he withheld nothing and told the rest of his story.

"So, how did it begin for me? In 2007, I started my investigation at the Army Special Operations Command Center at Fort Bragg. Specifically, I was interested in information out of the Joint Special Operations Command. You know the place?" The Father nodded and chewed.

"For nine months I was in the most maddening cycle of bureaucratic red tape. My superiors request info, the U.S. reviews the request, then assigns a committee, and tell me to piss off when I ask for a status update. I went around so many times I got dizzy. Once, a wanker literally dragged me around the cold-water flat like a sightseer after I went cross on him." He paused and chuckled as a memory of one such experience crossed his mind.

"Every time mate, every time. They ultimately denied every request on the basis of 'National Security.' I swear to ya brov, you wouldn't know our two countries were allies." The Brit shook his head, disgusted with the run-you-around machinery of the U.S. Federal Government.

"I suppose that by the summer of 2008, my insistent requests to the JSOC were such an annoyance to the ponce bowlers there, that they issued me temporary, conditional, diplomatic security clearance status and sent me to the Pentagon to meet with an FBI information attaché by the name of Miller."

"Miller," Abelemy grunted, "Now there's a real piece of work, huh?"

"You can say that again," Bax agreed. "For a long time I believed that Miller was a plonker; some mindless bureaucratic dummy. Then I began wondering what type of player he actually was. I soon realized my conditional security clearance was rubbish – a symbolic gesture at best – and this Mr. Miller was brazen, arrogant; an untouchable type and I wondered about him all the more. He kept me in the dark on everything that really mattered. He presents like he's following orders, but I half wonder…"

"I know it," the Father was chewing again.

"Anyway, this was my life all the way up until the afternoon of Friday August 19th when I found myself in that meeting with Miller, that wanker from the FBI, your higher-ups from Central Intelligence, and you."

Bax smiled widely, "Your very agitated manner got some things moving. I never did thank you for that. Miller kept telling me, 'You'll meet the Greek -- he's in on everything we know.' Clearly though, you are not as 'in' as Miller said you are."

"Clearly."

"So who is Miller?"

"I don't know," the Father thought about how much he wanted to disclose. *He seems trustworthy enough…*

"Ah well," Bax waved off the question, "It doesn't matter now. I knew I had to reach out. I could tell you were as discomfited as I, and that was good enough for me. Thanks for connecting on this level."

Dotty nodded contemplatively. "Sorry it took so long. It wasn't immediately obvious how we might help one another."

"That's true."

"So, what's your status now?"

"I'm heading over the pond on the first. Case closed, I suppose." Bax sucked down a mouthful of salad.

"I know you said you've been out of the game a while, but do you still feel combat-ready?"

Bax smiled, swallowed and said, "I've done nothing but exercise for four years. You never lose the tactics. Honestly, I could use a good scrape. Nothing oils the gears like politics mate. Bloody vexing time here in your country."

Dotty grinned at his good fortunes. "Tell you what, you do something for me and I'll give you everything I know."

"Yeah? What's that?"

"I want your government to lend you to me for the time being. I'm on a unique operation that could really use someone like you. I want the record to show you were pulled home, took your flight back to London, everything on the record, but quietly, I want you to stay here and post up with a team I have working off the books."

"Absolutely. Yes, absolutely," he repeated excitedly. He had been out of real action since arriving in the U.S.

"Will your ups be okay with it?"

"Of course." Bax thought for a moment and then said what the Greek had been thinking for a week, "It's very disturbing that we are relegated to keeping this investigation away from the eyes of the chiefs above though, no?"

"Indeed it is." Father Abelemy leaned in and spoke more quietly now. He relayed everything he knew, starting with Spates. He told Bax about Alpha Kilo and how the Phantoms killed the Delta personnel. He detailed their methods, their weaponry, and every fact he could conjure up about that event. Bax already had operational intelligence about the Alpha Kilo assault, but let the Greek retell it all, just to be sure they were on the same page.

"Believe it or not, what you just told me about Spates is actually recent news for me. It wasn't until last year that I even made that connection, about him being in the U.S. and dying here." That statement surprised Bax, who figured the U.S. had been behind the cover-up of Spates' death.

So who's pulling the strings here? He thought.

After briefly talking about the surveillance campaign he set up to watch Keys & Associates, the Greek jumped forward and told the tale of Jasper's death and Solomon's escape in Alton. He shared all the details about Solomon and his experience over that 24-hour period. After answering a few technical questions about the Phantoms and their tactics, the Father shared how Solomon's girlfriend, Leola, was gunned down. He summed it all up with a brief explanation of the K&A team hiding in Edgewater.

Bax took all the information in stride, but was visibly disturbed when the Father told him about the NSA satellite, the black Toyota Tacoma, and the possible assassin on their tail. That was when the Brit fully understood why his services were needed.

"Your mates need protection then?" he asked.

"Yes, but you are only the second person I've discussed this operation with. The other is my case officer, a trustworthy guy."

"How do you know you can trust him?"

"I don't, but it's a little late for that. He took the guesthouse off line and he is very careful about how and when we talk. I think he's clean." Dotty glanced around the room, as he often did.

"A Tacoma, huh? That's a pickup truck, yeah?"

Dotty nodded. "I haven't seen it in a few days. There is an intermediary named Betty who carries correspondence from me to the guesthouse. She's a civilian. I'm concerned she might lead this tail to the honey jar, unwittingly."

"Then we do away with the intermediary," Bax suggested, his mind in tactical evasion mode.

"If you're there, I'd support that," Dotty leaned forward again, "Look, Mr. Hill…"

"Call me Bax," he interjected.

"Okay, Bax. I'm calling the shots for as long as we're in this together. But if I get taken out, I'm asking you to get those kids out of the country. Head back to the U.K."

Braxton Hill's eyebrows rose with sobriety, "Really?"

"Really," Dotty chuckled, "God, I never imagined saying those words to an operator from another country before. But this world is changing fast and I'm no longer sure who's right and who's wrong, if there even is a right and wrong."

Dotty took a swig of his iced tea, "All I know for sure, I want my friend Solomon and his associates protected. At my core, that's maybe the only thing I feel right about. These are good people with purpose. They are the type of people that guys like us got into the business to protect. That is, if guys like us can remember that far back…"

"I understand," Bax said, "and I'll do my best."

"It's settled then," Dotty looked up and waved to the waitress. "How much time do you need to make your preparations?"

Bax looked at his watch and calculated the time difference to London, "I could be prepped in eight hours. Six if I hump it."

Dotty looked at his watch and said, "Take eight then. Be sure to cross your t's. I'll get a hold of the handler and have her meet you at your apartment tonight, say, eleven?"

"Great," Bax passed Dotty a slip of paper with his address on it. "She'll drive?"

"She'll drive." The check arrived and Dotty dropped some cash on the table. The smell of ground beef and cheese was thick by the front door, closer to the kitchen. They were thanked by a college-aged hostess as they departed the restaurant and Dotty offered to give his new British friend a ride home.

"Nah, I'll take the Metro."

"Fair enough. Until next time…"

"Dotty?" Bax asked, cutting the Father off. "I know you can't be sure, but who are these Phantoms, according to your gut?"

Father Abelemy picked at a piece of lettuce in his teeth with his pinky nail, "If I had to guess, I'd say these are the guys that got next.'"

"How's that?"

"Playground basketball jargon. The guys waiting for the court will often call out, 'we got next'; it's a signal that means they get to play the winner."

Bax nodded and slipped his sunglasses on, though it was obvious he didn't understand the analogy.

"These Phantoms are well funded, well-connected, covert, and scientifically advanced. This much is undisputable. It's not a government, or I'd know. That means it's a paramilitary operation, but who runs it? My gut, if you're asking, is that they are somehow either affiliated with, or an offshoot of, the Club of Rome."

"What's that?"

"In the 1960's, members of the Morgenthau Group came together at an invite-only gala at Rockefeller's private residence in Bellagio, Italy. There, this group of elites from the world of banking, business and politics founded what's known as the Club of Rome. The meeting was organized by a radical industrialist by the name of Aurelio Peccei, an Italian business tycoon. He convinced the charter that only through a *One World Order* and system of central governance, could the socioeconomic fabric of civilization continue long into the future. He must have been convincing because they adopted and ratified his beliefs as the Club's founding principles."

"We're dealing with the so-called Illuminati, then?"

"In a way, maybe, but these guys aren't shadowy. They are hiding in plain sight. I'll give you an example. The Club of Rome was first established in the '60's with 75 charter members from 25 separate countries. Then, their membership exploded in numbers just before NATO split into its two groups – the political faction and its military counterpart. After the split, NATO adopted the policies of its incestuous little think-tank, the Club of Rome."

Bax nodded, making a note to do a little research of his own on the Club of Rome when he got home.

"Not just that," the Father continued, "but in 1973 these guys published an audacious book that read like an evil mission statement, *Regionalized and Adoptive Model of the Global World System*. However, since the late '70's, they've been pretty quiet – less overt, more cunning. Based on my role at the Agency, I've collected little bits of circumstantial evidence over the years that tie the Phantoms to these few hundred globalist whack jobs."

"Can you share some of this evidence?"

"The main recurring evidence are these special filters within CIA systems, which inhibit me from following Club member's money. As you probably know, following the flow of money through the international system is one of our primary tools, right? It's like these guys were taken off the grid in a very special way. These filters were developed privately, and installed in a compartmentalized manner. The money flow filters also roll over into other areas, like communications, logistics, arms trafficking... Someone purposely blocked our favorite snoop techniques with respect to a few large players, all of which are members of the Club of Rome. Recently, I've uncovered some new ties between our boy Miller and a few 'suspected' new members of the Club. Not just Miller either. Similar ties can be found all over the Federal apparatus."

"How high does it go?"

Dotty glanced around and smiled rather dejectedly, "If I'm right, it's as high up as it gets. It's everywhere."

"The White House?"

Dotty nodded slightly.

"What's the goal? Do you know?"

"No, everything I have is circumstantial at best. You're not the only one who's been given the Federal run-around, my friend." Dotty touched the button on his keychain that unlocked his car with a subdued *beep*. "Best guess, their end goal is what they've published openly for years -- centralized governance over a ten-kingdom economic reallocation of the entire world. It's like a bad episode of the Twilight Zone, huh?"

"No such thing as a bad episode of the Twilight Zone," Bax quipped.

Dotty chuckled and turned toward his car. Leaning back toward his British pal, he said, "There's not much we can do about the big picture schemes of the global elite, but we can sure as hell do our part on the piece we've been sliced. Truly, thanks for your help. Keep your eyes open, Bax. From this point forward, live life very awake and very aware."

CHAPTER 23
Rain Check

Tuesday, August 30, 2011

"I'm so sorry," Anny said, stringing out the middle word.

"It's fine. You have every right to know what's going on. I just took the call in the bathroom because I didn't want it to wake you."

"Not that," she looked down, sheepishly. "I'm sorry for last night."

"Oh," he grinned. Sully was going to enjoy this. He plopped down in the chase lounge and reclined, crossing his legs at the ankles. "Right, about that."

She winced, "Was it bad?"

"If you can't remember, could it have possibly been good?" He blurted out, laughing.

"Oh no, what happened?" Before he could answer, she shook her head and looked away, "Nope, never mind. I don't even want to know."

"Oh yes you do," he teased. "It ended with me trying hard to get you to go to bed in your own room, but you just weren't having it."

"Dear God," she whispered, "did I seduce you? Stop. Why are you laughing?"

"Because you're adorable. You don't remember anything?"

She shook her head slowly and shrugged her shoulders, "Red wine that paired poorly with my fish dinner. That's about it."

"Okay. Well, imagine a really drunk girl going on about this and that, making totally inappropriate comments about her boss's anatomy, refusing to go to her own hotel room, and ending up in my bed. That about sums it up."

"Dear God, what a lush. I'm so sorry." She feigned disgust, but didn't actually feel that bad. Next she braced for his answer to a question she mightily despised having to ask, "Did we, um…?"

"You're still wearing your clothing from last night, aren't you?" He pointed out the obvious as she shot a glance at her attire. Anny failed to hide her relief, as he mumbled, "No good deed goes unpunished, if you're me."

That made her blush. *Did he mean that?* She couldn't tell.

Pointing at the door, she swung her legs off the bed and onto the sturdy floor. "I'm just gonna head across the hall there and take a shower. I am really sorry. Not sure what got into me."

"Go on," he chuckled, "I'll do the same. It was a fun night, all things considered. No need to apologize."

When she bent down to grab her shoes, she stumbled slightly, still under the effects of the prior night. Grabbing at her head, she moaned in agony and ambled toward the door. He watched her with amusement. *It's going to be a long day for you.*

Twenty minutes later, he went to her room and knocked on the door. She answered, wearing only the hotel bathrobe. "How long does it take to shower and get dressed?" he asked.

"I don't know. What's up?" She got out of the way and he walked in like he owned the joint. He sat down in the office chair near a built-in desk and flipped open the room service menu. "Let's talk about this phone call from Rooter while you're getting ready. I think we need to devise a plan. How much of that did you hear?"

"Pretty much all of it," she passed into the bathroom and kept the door cracked so they could hear one another. "He sounded pretty freaked out. What are you thinking?"

"I think I need to get back there. Sooner rather than later."

"We, you mean?"

"What?" he looked up from the menu, not understanding what she meant.

"We need to get back there. I'm not staying here alone."

"Why not?" He could hear noises coming from the bathroom, the sounds of her going from item to item as she worked on her makeup and hair. *She's acted as a solo-operator before. Why was this different?*

"Because, I'm not going to sit in Chicago, while my friends are getting stalked in their sleep back at some creepy safe house. Rooter's a tough guy, and if his voice was any indication, he fears for his life."

"I agree, but that's all the more reason you should stay here," argued Sully. "You should stay out of harm's way."

"Screw you," she said, suddenly appearing in the doorway. "Look, I liked you showing care and concern yesterday, and it even touched a nice nerve, but there is no way I'm staying here thinking about some pending attack from some super-creep stalker-assassin. I'm part of this team too, you know. I'm a girl, but I can shoot a gun, probably better then Con by the way."

She has a point.

Disappearing again, she continued, "It's just not gonna happen. I'll tell Rasmussen that my Auntie got sick and I have to go. I'll tell him I'll be back to take him up on dinner another time. In fact…"

"You could see if he'll give you the donut this morning on the basis of this family emergency," Sully interrupted, "and maybe we hit the road sooner rather than later?"

"That's what I was gonna say," she said, "He seemed like a pretty good guy, really. If I promise to come and have a dinner date in the future, he'll do it."

"Worth a try." Sully looked at his fingernails. Nervous chomping had done a number on them over the last couple weeks. A hairdryer turned on in the bathroom and remained on for a few minutes.

"Hey," she said as the dryer shut off, "There's a brown handbag on my suitcase. Mind bringing it to me? Don't come in."

He passed the bag through the opening and she took it, saying thanks as if she had something between her teeth. He sat back down and decided on a few breakfast items, "Hey, I'm going back to my room. Let's call Rasmussen from there. I'll order room service for breakfast and if all goes well we'll get out of here in a couple hours."

"Roger-dodger," she sounded preoccupied.

"What do you want for breakfast?"

"Aspirin."

"No, really."

"Aspirin, really."

From his room he called up two omelets, hash browns, toast, coffee, a liter of OJ, and six aspirin. Twenty-five minutes later, she came over wearing a tank top,

174

shorts, and flip-flops. The food arrived a minute later. By 9:15, Sully was done eating. Anny stuck with aspirin and a few bites of toast. He nodded toward the in-room phone, "Ready to call Mr. CTO?"

"Yeah," she belched internally. "I feel like I may get sick."

"You look pale. Maybe you should try and throw up before we leave. That car ride's gonna be murder on your gut." He moved the makeshift dining table out of her way so she could get to the phone without having to climb over the bed.

"Yeah, maybe. I hate doing that."

She dialed the number on Rasmussen's card and waited a few seconds before a cheerful voice answered, "TB Optics. How may I direct your call?"

"Hi, calling for Mr. Rasmussen?"

"Your name please?"

"Annette Boyle."

"One minute please."

A minute or so later, a very happy sounding Kyle Rasmussen came on, "Hi Annette, it's Kyle. To what do I owe the pleasure?"

"Hi Kyle. I, um, have some sad news," she said, forcing a remarkably believable tone of lamentation. "It's my Auntie Beth."

"Everything okay?" he sounded concerned.

"I'm not sure. She fell and got herself admitted to the hospital back home. I'm going to have to take a rain check on our date."

"I'm so sorry. Is she okay?"

"I really don't know. The hospital won't tell me anything over the phone. They just asked me to come." She was putting on a world-class performance.

"I understand, it's perfectly fine if we reschedule," he assured her.

"Thank you. There's just one thing though," she said, leading him on. "If she's in real bad shape, I'd love to tell her something about her nephew. This whole project was her idea after all, and if she's…" Anny paused and choked back some emotion before continuing. "If she's getting ready to pass…"

"Yes, of course," he said, assuredly. "I haven't had the chance to write anything down, but I could give you the verbal version and a few quick notes if you'd like. Are you able to come by my office on your way out of town? I'd love to see you again."

"That'd be wonderful, Kyle. Thank you so much."

"It's my pleasure," he paused, as if considering whether or not to go where he went next, "really, it's just because you called our dinner, a *date.*"

Anny rolled her eyes as Solomon gave her the thumbs up. "That's what it was, and that's what it will be when I make this up to you."

"Perfect, I'll hold you to it," he said, sounding more desperate than he hoped.

"Okay then," she graciously let him off the hook, "I can be there in a half-hour or so."

Rasmussen gave her the address to his office. He all too eagerly told her he was pushing his 10 am meeting to 11:30 to make time for her. She thanked him and hung up.

"Nice job," Sully said. "You're quite the pro at this."

"Think I should go dressed like this?" she asked.

"Yeah, why not? It looks like you're gearing up for a long drive home. It's perfect."

"I feel bad," she said, mostly to herself.

"Why, for lying? Do you like him?"

"Not any more or less than anyone else. I don't know. He didn't do anything to deserve being manipulated. I just feel bad."

"Do you always feel bad? With all the professional targets, I mean?"

"No. If the target is a sleaze-ball, I rather like it. This guy is nice though. Almost innocent-like."

"Well, don't lie about making it up to him and I'm sure he'll forgive you," Sully winked. "Will you be ready to go in 20?"

"Yeah, I'll meet'cha in the lobby." She retreated back to her room.

Solomon drove her to the TB Optics offices situated along the famed Chicago Loop. After dropping her in front, he parked in a nearby public garage. He walked to a bagel shop across the street from TB Optics, where they agreed to meet when she was finished. Not 40 minutes later, Anny walked into the bagel place, carrying a file. She ordered a large coffee to go, and by 11:30 they were on the road again, heading back to Edgewater.

It didn't take long for Anny to fall asleep, her bare feet resting on the dash, her knees against her door, and her seatback at extreme tilt. Her body was still trying to dispel the remaining alcohol. Sully found a 1990's rock station and turned it up just a little. Anny wouldn't mind.

The cityscape disappeared in their rear-view mirror as the surroundings were overtaken by suburbia. Eventually, suburbia turned into a sparsely populated roadway. Anny slept. Her Civic hummed along the smooth pavement and handled well. The traffic was minimal. Truthfully, Solomon enjoyed the peaceful drive and used the time to let his mind wander all over the place.

He learned a lot about his young accomplice in Chicago. Their relationship had changed too. Two weeks prior, Anny would have never passed out in the passenger seat with her bare feet and legs up against the dash. She had relaxed around him. She was now comfortable in a new way. While she slept, it was his turn to wonder about her and the new feelings that were percolating between them. He realized he was protective of her in a way he was not with anyone else. Even with Leola, it was different.

Friend. He smiled and looked at a gal whom he now called *a friend.*

When he thought about the intruder at the guesthouse, he felt a palpable rage boil in his gut. The idea of something happening to his team, especially Anny, hurt. *She feels safe with me*, he thought, glancing at her again. *They all trust me...*

The idea of getting into a conflict with an assassin made him nervous, and he started to bite at his raw thumbnail. *How did my little legal team get into this crazy spy crap? How do we fend off a professional attack? Based on what I experienced with Jasper and Leola, these guys are ruthless. I hope Rooter has some kind of plan...*

Still sleeping, Anny adjusted her posture toward Sully in her seat, tucking her left leg under her right. A few strands of hair fell into her face. Without thinking, he gently moved them away from her eyes, and hooked them behind her right ear. She made a small sound and nestled into the seat, and he felt it then, the butterflies of attraction, fluttering inside his chest.

He was determined to not let anything happen to her. He owed it to her. He owed it to Jasper and Leola too. He'd sacrifice his life before another one of his friends had to die.

CHAPTER 24
Bast Molorek

Tuesday, August 30, 2011

At the back edge of the property, beyond the privacy fence, a few sand dunes and a narrow, empty stretch of rocky beach marked the boundary of Glebe Bay. It was a picturesque scene, and during his many patrols around the property, Rooter became fond of stopping there to have a cigarette and admire the southeasterly view.

From that vantage point, he could watch a variety of watercraft pass by in both directions. Further down, he could see the mouth of the bay opening to the expansive Atlantic Ocean, and the occasional navy vessel motor past. The Naval Academy at Annapolis was just a few miles northeast. Rooter looked up into the blotchy clouds above and breathed deeply. The sticky salt in the air, the seagulls soaring high above – *this safe house is the type of place where I could easily retire.*

Until aroused by the intruder, Rooter hardly ever ventured past the property line. The only neighbors in close proximity lived to the northeast, about 250 yards away. The guesthouse was somewhat isolated, with only the front road as the clear escape route.

Earlier in the day, he ventured toward the neighbor's house, but turned back when it was clear to him that nobody lived there. There was a 'For Sale' sign in the disheveled front yard, and crumbling plywood nailed to the windows. By the look of things, the place had been vacant for over a year.

The undergrowth was thick, and poisonous plants were abundant, so he was eager to turn around and get back to his primary patrol. But turning back was a tactical mistake. If he trudged forward just a bit, he might have discovered a black Toyota Tacoma partially hidden under a tarp on the far northeast side of the property. Indeed, at that very instant, Bast Molorek, a chimera conceived at the Bio-Systems Academy of Brazil, was watching his every move from inside the neighbor's house. He was watching, and waiting, and calculating.

Rooter dropped his cigarette butt and mashed it into the gritty sand. The air was typically muggy, but a nice breeze was coming off the bay, keeping him from perspiring too heavily. He checked his watch, *just past 5:00. I should get something figured out for dinner...*

After one last long look toward the ocean, he turned his back on the epic view and continued his security sweep. He now knew all the critical spots along the inner perimeter by memory. He understood where windows or doorways offered a point of entry, or where the house or garage gave partial, or even full, cover. Once inside the privacy fence, he checked each point of vulnerability again. *All clear.*

The wind off the bay was hardly noticeable inside the fence, so he was now perspiring heavily. Using his right wrist, he wiped a river of sweat off his forehead and hustled back into the comfort of climate control.

In the kitchen, Con was doing something Rooter had never seen him do before; he was cooking dinner. "Smells good, bud. What is it?"

"It's a chicken casserole my mom taught me how to make before I left for college," he said. "Figured if we're gonna die tonight, I wanted to have it one last time."

Rooter was going to respond with something smart, but decided to join his nervous friend and be serious for a moment. "We'll be fine. We get through this night together, and Sully will be back tomorrow. Any luck, we get word to that Spook and he finds us a new place to stay by week's end."

"I hate it here. It's too empty. I'd prefer doing this in a city where we can blend into the population. This place is a horror movie waiting to happen."

"If it is, you're in luck, because in most horror movies I see, the black nerd gets away. It's the overweight white guy that usually gets done in."

"Hope so," Con mused, not realizing how rude that sounded. His back was to the PI, who cocked his head and dropped into a seat at the circular kitchen table. Con was scared, and Rooter didn't quite know how to respond to him. His behavior was oddly off-base, and frankly, Rooter didn't need it. However, after thinking about it, he decided straight reassurance was the best course of action.

"Hey."

"Yeah," Con answered but didn't turn around.

"Hey, look at me, bud."

With a deep breath he turned, revealing his tense face. "Yeah?"

"We're going to deal with whatever, together, and live to laugh about it tomorrow. Understand?"

"Sure," he didn't look convinced.

"No ghoul, demon, or deranged non-ape is going to get the better of us. We're fortified, and all things considered, this is not a bad place, as far as defensive layout. We don't know if anybody is going to come back, but even if they do, we'll be fine.

I got this under control." Rooter didn't believe the words he spoke, but put on a good show anyway. Con appreciated the confidence and nodded.

During dinner; which was remarkably good, they realized that Sully could, theoretically, get back at some point that night, as early as two or three in the morning. That also brought Con some comfort. Not that Sully was any kind of better 'commando' than Rooter, but at least there was strength in numbers.

At 8:50, the sun dipped below the horizon and twilight was on. Rooter decided to do one final outer perimeter check before buttoning down inside the fence for the evening.

He started on the northeast side and walked around the outside of the fence, clockwise. He heard and saw nothing, but stopped for his typical smoke along the back. He marveled at the fish jumping out of the still water in search of an after-dinner snack. The lights were beginning to twinkle across the waterway on the northern shoreline. The wind had dipped, but so had the temperature. Mosquitoes, hundreds of them, were the only characters in this picturesque scene Rooter could do without. After stomping his cig out in the rocks, he continued onward.

When he reached the detached garage, he turned the side-door knob and found, strangely, that it was unlocked. He swallowed hard. *Damn it.* That could only mean one thing. He immediately regretted his cigarette break along the shoreline. The light was now fading fast and he didn't have a flashlight. Peering through the dirty window on the garage door, all he could see was the driver-side of his parked vehicle. Nothing else was discernible.

His heart started pounding like a drum as he considered his options. The hilt of his Ruger felt slippery in his sweat-soaked palm. He tapped the doorknob with his free hand, and then looked back at the house. He was frozen with indecision about what to do next. *Someone has got to be in the garage, hiding. Maybe? Or, maybe Con came out here for some reason? No way.*

There was 25 feet between the garage door and the side door of the house leading into the hallway with the bedrooms. Rooter made the short walk and checked the knob of the house door. It was still locked. He took a deep breath and decided on a course of action.

He went back to the garage and slowly put his ear close to the door. He listened for any kind of sound coming from inside the garage. He heard nothing strange. However, it was hard to discern much over the ruckus created by thousands of bugs and crickets getting ready for a rowdy night. The chirping seemed, in that moment, to be louder than usual.

He swallowed hard and turned the knob harder. The door swung outward as he slowly extended the gun out in front of him, and stepped inside. The garage was hot and musty. He thought he smelled the scent of a wet dog. *Weird.* It was as though rot hung in the air. He decided not to turn on the light for fear of spooking whoever, or whatever, was inside.

Above him, Bast Molorek crouched motionless behind some boxes in the rafters of the garage. He watched the PI with morbid curiosity. He flicked his lips, his tongue moving from the left corner of his mouth to the right in sporadic succession. It was a nervous twitch he developed sometime after being spliced with the genetic enhancements that made him such an efficient killer. He would easily bring death to the Italian PI if he dared look up. It would be Molorek's pleasure. Silently, he waited and watched from the shadows.

Rooter eased along the driver's side of his vehicle as silently as he could. When he reached the back of his car, he peered around its corner, toward the other empty parking spots. *Nobody.* A drop of sweat lost its grip and fell helplessly from his nose. His hands started to tremble, so he gripped the gun with both hands and tried to steady his breathing. Something felt strange. *What is that?*

He could not shake it. It was definitely the sensation of being watched. Another droplet fell from his nose and salty sweat assaulted the corners of his eyes. He wiped at his face with his palm. Right then, he recognized the feeling. It was the same sensation he had during the lightning storm. That's when the world slowed back down and a sense of calm overtook him. Somehow, he knew for certain, that he was not alone in that garage.

Slowly, his eyes skimmed upward and he saw the rafters above. But as soon as he glanced, he recoiled and decided not to look. He had no idea how, but he knew *something* was up there. He could feel the essence of a malevolent pair of eyes watching him from the shadows. Whatever it was, it had the upper hand. If it came down on him, he'd be dead before he got a shot off. He tried swallowing. He tried again. He had no spit.

Forcing a more casual demeanor, he purposefully lowered his gun and began moving toward the door with as much nonchalance as he could muster. He knew he had walked into a compromising position, and just needed to get out of the garage.

Why doesn't this creep just jump me and be done with it? No matter… Just live to fight another day.

He was surprised when he was allowed to reach the door. He was shocked when he was allowed to slip outside the garage and lock the door behind him. Once he was safely outside, he quickly moved along the side of the house, around the bend, and in the back sliding door. Con immediately knew something was wrong and stood up with a look of terror.

"Wh, what? What is it?"

"Water," Rooter whispered, pointing to the kitchen. Con ran over and poured him a glass. When he turned back around Rooter was gone. Con walked back to the living room and saw his companion at the end of the hallway between their bedrooms, looking out the window that was set into the locked side door. The window looked directly at the garage door. Con approached with the water and handed it to the PI.

"What?" Con repeated.

"I ain't gonna bullshit you bud. We're under attack." Rooter took the whole glass down in one gulp. He heard Con's breathing, which was remarkable because his own breathing was loud and elevated. "I don't think we're dealing with a human. I've never felt this before; this feeling like I can sense him when he's near."

"Where. Where i-is he?" Con asked.

"In the garage," Rooter said, not taking his eyes off the window and tapping the pane with the barrel of his gun. "I'm not moving until I see this prick's red eyeballs in that window there, and when I do, I'm putting a bullet in both. Go get me a chair kid."

Con fetched a living room chair and pushed it down the hall toward his friend. Rooter turned to get out of the way as the chair slid into position. It was an overstuffed chair that worked better when he sat on the back support. Getting comfortable, he resumed his watch. Time passed, Con fidgeted, but Rooter kept his sights on the garage door, scarcely blinking. He was determined to sit there all night if he had to. This *thing* was not going to get the drop on him.

Con had disappeared in the house somewhere when Rooter called out to him. "Hey Con, come here a sec."

He appeared, "What?"

"I need to stand up and stretch. Keep an eye on this garage door for me? I'm not going anywhere, just my back is cramping up and I need to stretch it out."

Con looked out the window and saw the side of the garage. The window in the garage door was black, as if looking into a bottomless pit. Rooter was stretching in the hallway when he said, "It's almost 11. We're like a quarter of the way there already."

"Uh huh," Con was unenthusiastic. "Almost 11. We only have like eight more hours of this."

"Better than ten more hours." Rooter finished stretching for the ground, "Mind if I have a quick smoke?"

"Only if you have it in the hall. I'm not sitting here alone. If I see those two eyes you talk about, my luck, I'd miss."

"If you miss from here, you deserve to get got." *That was mean, and poorly timed too.*

Rooter lit a smoke. "Alright, so long as I'm smokin' in the house, I'll just reestablish my position. Hop out of the way."

Rooter kept an eye on the garage door as Con slithered back and over the chair. Having resumed his position, Con was about to walk away when he said, "Hey, hang on. Take this."

Rooter reached for a Smith & Wesson that was lodged in the small of his back and accidently dropped it in the chair cushion. He looked down to locate it and handed it to his sidekick. As he was about to give some instructions, his words evaporated into thin air. He turned and realized that the garage door was open.

"Fuck me!" he grunted, scrambling off the chair and falling to the floor. *What is this!? How did he move so fast?*

Con mumbled something. Rooter looked up at him and saw shear terror in his eyes. His mouth was wide open as he stared back at the window. Rooter whipped around and gasped when he saw, standing in the window, the upper torso of a man, but not just a man, a beast with wild red eyes. These were the eyes of a predator, with vertical slits for pupils, just like some kind of cat. His face popped close to the windowpane. He looked down the hallway directly at them. Rooter instinctively aimed and shot his gun as Con screamed and cupped his ears. But before they knew what happened, the *thing* was gone. Rooter struggled to a crouched position and grabbed Con's arm. That's when Con opened his eyes and stopped screaming.

"Come with me," Rooter said, and led the way back into the living room. He spied the landline phone on the coffee table, grabbed it, and shoved it into Con's skinny chest. "Call 911, we'll have to just deal with the Greek's fallout."

"H-Hello?" Con was clicking the connect button furiously and putting the headset up to his ear. His hands were trembling violently. He then suddenly became still and looked at the PI, "No dial tone."

"Figures, typical B-rate horror movie," he mumbled in return. Rooter was surprisingly alert and calm. "Come on kid, help me out here."

They tipped the sofa onto its side and crouched behind it, their backs up against the wall leading to Sully's bathroom. "Maybe we should turn the lights off," Rooter suggested.

"N-n-no," Con stuttered, "That th-thing has vertical pupils. That m-means he s-sees better in the d-dark then we do."

"Oh yeah?" Rooter glanced at a light switch bank on the wall across the room. "Maybe we should turn all the lights on then."

"Yes. That's a g-good idea."

"Keep that pee-shooter aimed at the back door and cover me. You see anything, pull the trigger. Understand?"

"Yes."

Rooter made a quick dash to the opposite wall and flipped the light switches. "Damn it," Rooter said through clinched teeth. "He's hit the breaker. We're sitting ducks."

A few minutes passed and Con's rapid breathing was about all Rooter could hear. Their eyes started to adjust to the dark. They were lucky; a bright moon cast shadows across the backyard. Con was pressed up against Rooter so hard that Rooter had to adjust. A few more minutes passed and Con's breathing started to regulate. *What's he doing?* They waited.

Then Con's breathing elevated again, "What? What do you see?" Rooter whispered. He didn't need a response, not that he was going to get an intelligible one anyway. He saw it too.

In the backyard there stood a large being, hunched at the waist in front of the gazebo. All that was visible was his silhouette frame and a set of reflective, reddish eyes. Slowly, he took a step toward them, then another. He moved like a lion, hunting down a gazelle. Rooter unloaded a few rounds through the sliding back door as Con reflexively followed suit. At first the glass splintered like a spider web, then came crashing down in a thousand splinters.

They stopped shooting, and thorough the pale whiff of gun smoke Rooter saw, as his heart sank, that the monster was undeterred.

The shots had merely prompted him to crouch down and get into what looked like three-point lineman's stance. Then, from all four limbs, he lunged forward with huge strides toward the house, juking left and right as he bounded towards the shattered back door.

Though he had half a mag, Con dropped his gun, closed his eyes, and ducked behind the sofa in the fetal position. Rooter tried to follow Molorek's movements, but the beast was too quick. He tried to anticipate the next juke or lunge and shot the gun in an attempt at luck. It was futile. The creature moved so fast that it was hard to follow him with the naked eye. Rooter shot again, and again, but he was more likely to win the lotto than hit his attacker. Rooter knew it was pointless, but decided to unload his rounds with a spray of bangs and flashes anyway. He hoped beyond reason that a bullet would land, or graze him.

When his eyes adjusted, he saw the beast draw to its full height and stand erect, just behind the glass door. He could see its eyes, now large and red. The pupils pulsated from thin to wide as he searched to locate his prey. Rooter shot again, *click*. He was out. He tried to swallow, but couldn't. Con was shaking beside him on the ground.

Rooter knew Con still had bullets, but where was the gun? He wanted to look for it but couldn't. He tried to move, but couldn't. The petrifying eye-lock of the beast incapacitated him. *What sort of demon is this?*

Molorek seemed to want to grin as he raised one hand slowly and thrust it through the pane. The glass splintered into a thousand pieces as Con screamed something unintelligible. In what seemed like a nanosecond, the beast burst into the house and crossed the living room, landing on the upturned sofa. He rammed his might into the solid piece of furniture, thrusting the couch and two men behind it back into the wall with a thud.

A huge hand grabbed Rooter around the side of the head, whipping him around in an awkward manner. The PI heard a snap in his neck, followed by excruciating pain that shot down his right side. The beast's other hand found Con's slender shoulder, and tore him out from behind the sofa, tossing him across the room like an obstinate toy. Con bounced off the far wall, immediately knocked unconscious.

The beast ripped and tore at Rooter, who was now lying as low to the ground as possible. One hand found Rooter's leg, the other his forearm. He was violently yanked from behind the couch, sending pain down his back as he heard another pop, this time in his left arm.

He hit the ground somewhere between the sofa and the shattered back door. His eyes were blurry, but he managed to pull a nine-inch blade from his shin holster, just as the beast lunged on top of him. Rooter blindly swung the knife and it landed in the fleshy shoulder of the powerful monster. The beast hissed and curled its upper lip, recoiling momentarily before raising a huge fist high into the air.

Rooter closed his eyes and braced for impact. It came in the form of a downward, gorilla-thrust. It landed right-center torso, and seemed to crush his insides. The PI's eyes rolled back in his head. He couldn't breath. He couldn't see. He couldn't move. He was certain death was seconds away. Deep inside, he begged the next blow would end his life. But the next blow never came.

Instead, hot sticky liquid poured down on him from above as the beast made a slushing sound and tried in vain to gasp some air. With senses racing back to the present, Rooter opened his eyes as a red river of blood gushed from an ear-to-ear laceration of Molorek's throat. Rooter tried to move as the beast fought for life, but he couldn't.

When the red gleam of its eyes dimmed, the beast could not help but fall, deadweight, next to Rooter's broken body. The attacker gave two more reflexive muscular convulsions before going still. Rooter was covered in blood, but through the sticky haze, he glimpsed what looked like an average man. The man was holding the bloodstained knife that he'd, just seconds earlier, lodged in the beast's shoulder.

From somewhere, a flood of emotion welled to the surface just as he regained his breath. Rooter didn't try to stop it. He was hyperventilating and it hurt like hell, but at least he was breathing. He couldn't move any limb except for his left leg. This brought him some comfort – *at least I'm not paralyzed*. But Rooter was in bad shape and he knew it.

From what seemed like quite a distance, he heard an unfamiliar British accent lean over and say, "Steady on, mate. You beat Mr. Grim Death, and I need a bloody ale, so don't die on me now."

Through gasped utterances, Rooter forced himself to ask, "Who-who a-are you?"

"Bax is the name. We have a common friend, Father Abelemy."

Rooter closed his eyes and tried to ask about Con, but couldn't get the words to form. Knowing what he was trying to say, Bax answered, "Shhh. Don't talk. I'll get to him next brov. He's better off than you, so just let me work."

Bax was using the bloody knife to cut Rooter's clothing. The obvious diagnosis was an untold number of broken bones and mild to severe internal damage. Bax couldn't immediately identify the extent of his injuries.

A sudden resurgence of pain sent Rooter into a dark, numb, oasis of nothingness, and that's where he remained as Braxton Hill worked to save his teetering life.

CHAPTER 25
Cleanup

Wednesday, August 31, 2011

It was 1:45 am when Sully pulled the Civic into the second bay of the garage and turned off the engine. With suitcases in tote, he and Anny meandered to the front door and saw the split doorjamb. Sully put a hand up to Anny, gesturing for her to stay back, as he swallowed hard and put down his suitcase. Quietly, he tapped the door and it opened without a sound.

He could see Rooter, sitting in a living room chair near the shattered sliding glass door. His eyes and face were swollen. He had a bandaged head and his left arm was in a sling. The corpse of an enormous, muscular man was in the center of the living room, facedown in a sticky brown splotch on the carpet. Anny moved into view and gasped when she saw the scene. She put her hands to her mouth just before she buried her face in Sully's shoulder. It was an involuntary reaction of shock and sorrow.

"My God," Sully managed, "Rooter?"

"Welcome to the party," Rooter forced a smile and looked in their direction, mostly with his eyes. "You two jerk-offs enjoy the Drake Hotel?" Any movements he made were slow and painful.

Sully took a few steps toward him, careful to not step in the random splatters of blood and debris all over the floor. A man appeared from the hallway leading to the bedrooms. He had just moved Con to his room and attended to his injuries. Bax was wearing a bloodstained undershirt and cargo pants. His presence seemed odd. There was pep to his step and a casualness to his demeanor that didn't fit the heavy circumstances.

"Who are you?" Sully asked.

"Who am I?" he paused briefly to look at Sully and Anny with pretend distrust, then continued past them to attend to Rooter, "Who the hell are you two?"

Solomon looked puzzled so Rooter coughed and said, "This is Bax. He saved our lives."

"Oh my God, Con?" Anny burst out, her hands still in front of her mouth.

Bax held his hand up and answered before she could get too hysterical. "He's okay, got a concussion and a few bumps and bruises but he'll be fine. He's in his room if you want to see him."

"I'm sorry, who are you?" Sully repeated, this time expecting to be answered.

Bax took a step toward him and they shook hands over Molorek's lifeless corpse. "Braxton Hill is the name. I was recruited by the Greek for your protection. I showed up right as this thing was getting ready to sit for supper, if you catch my meaning. I got the drop on him while he attacked your friends here."

Solomon was looking down at Molorek, trying to see his face. The beast's mouth was open and stained brownish red from the blood. The gash along his neckline was now blackish. His eyes were open and displayed those vertical-slit pupils. "Who is this?"

"I'm sorry, you are?" Bax asked.

"Oh, forgive me," Solomon said, realizing he was being rude. "Solomon Keys. I'm um. I guess I'm at the center of all of this. That there is Annette Boyle. Do you work with Father Abelemy?"

"Not exactly," Bax said as he went back to checking on Rooter's wounds. "I'm British, as you might have guessed by the accent. I'm ex-British Special Forces and have been working on the Alpha Kilo investigation for a few years. I came in from the vantage point of my government and the disappearance of one of our military scientists, Dr. Spates. Heard of him?"

Sully thought about it for a second and nodded, "Indeed, I have. He was Malcolm's partner, right? In a strange way we all owe our involvement in this thing to him, don't we?"

"Yes sir, apparently." Bax looked at Molorek, "This here was a hard-nut, quick enough to get out of the way of bullets, even. Had I arrived a few minutes earlier and not been able to sneak up on him, he'd have us all by the proverbials, and we wouldn't be havin' this conversation."

"How bad are you hurt?" Sully asked in Rooter's direction.

Bax answered for him, "He's got a dislocated shoulder on this side, and may have some ligament damage. Broken elbow on this other side. He's got lots of scrapes, and a rather deep laceration on the back of his neck. He was hit with some mighty wicked whiplash, which is why he's not moving his neck much. At least three broken ribs and possible internal damage, but we're not sure yet. If I see signs of it, we'll rush him to a clinic. All things considered, he's lucky, and he should eventually recover."

"Did you drive? I didn't see a car out front."

"No, Betty drove me. She'll no longer be making calls, by the by. I'll be networking with the Greek from this point forward. I didn't let her see what had happened in here. When I pulled up, the lights were off and so we saw the gunshot flashes. I told her to wait in the car. After doing him in, I went back to her, collected my things and told her to leave. She didn't argue."

Bax scratched his forehead as Anny headed off to check on Con. "Mr. Keys…"

"Please, call me Sully."

"Sully then," Bax was looking at Rooter, who was fumbling with a cigarette. "We need to move him to his room so he can rest, but there is a lot to do out here."

"Okay, what do you have in mind?"

"It's going to be muggy in this house until we can get that door fixed. This boy's gonna start rotting, so we need to get him outside. Also, the carpet there is ruined. The blood saturated it there and again over there. As I was looking about, I noticed we have hardwood under it so my thought was to rip it out and wrap him in it, then put it all out back. We need some supplies though."

"Good deal. Let me check on Con and I'll send Anny to the market with a list."

Even in the middle of the night, the central A/C had a hard time keeping up with the infiltration of muggy air. They knew it would be unbearable the next day if something was not done about the door, but for the time being, more pressing concerns meant they needed to grin and bear it. Solomon and Bax moved any unsullied or unbroken furniture to the kitchen and started tearing up the carpet in the living room. They were each drenched in sweat when Anny returned with a number of cleaning supplies.

After the carpet was loose they stretched it out next to Molorek. For the sake of proper intelligence gathering, Bax used a tape measure he found in the garage to take a few measurements. The beast was six foot, nine inches. He was also muscular and had very little body fat. They decided to inspect his anatomy, and that's when Anny left to check on her hurt companions.

His body looked just like that of a man's, except for his sunken stomach region. It was as though he was missing some vital organs, as if his stomach cavity was hollow. His hair had an odd feel to it, and not just the hair on his head either. His body was covered in thin hairs that had more of a prickly feel than normal human body hair. His eyes were just like those of a cat's and his teeth were small and razor-sharp at the tips. Bax took samples of his hair, skin and blood, and put them in separately marked zip-lock bags. They snapped a number of pictures to catalog the creature for future analysis.

His fingernails were strange. They could actually extend and contract, and were either filed to a point or grew that way. When Bax tried to snip one, he found they were dense like bone. He actually chipped the cheap metal on the fingernail clippers.

Bax stood and crossed his arms. "What? What is this bugger?"

"If I didn't think it was a ridiculous thing to suggest, I'd say he's been somehow spliced with the genetic attributes of a lion or something. Over and over, there are feline characteristics, but I'm no vet. What's your take?"

"Yeah mate, that's what I was just thinking."

After they finished inspecting him, they spread a large section of painter's plastic over the carpet and rolled Molorek onto the plastic, wrapping him tightly in it using duct tape. After that, they rolled him up in the carpet like a burrito. It took all three – Sully, Bax and Anny – to muscle him out on the back porch. By that time, the sun was almost at the horizon and the birds were singing loudly.

Cleaning up was grueling work. Both Bax and Sully desperately needed showers. Anny started mopping the floor with a cocktail of detergents, while Bax opted to take a well-earned breather and enjoy a cold beer. Sully joined him.

Bax put his feet up on the chimera burrito and leaned back in a patio chair. He lifted his bottle toward Sully and said, "Here's to the twit that sent this thing to kill us. May he burn in hell."

Sully smiled and tipped his bottle. After a large gulp he asked, "Do we stay here?"

"I'm not sure. We should defer to your man at the Central Intelligence Agency on that. Tell you what though, it would be my pleasure to off another of these unnatural bastards, if I ever get the chance."

There was a cocky air about Bax. He wasn't overt, but he definitely thought he was the toughest guy around. Sully sipped his Heineken and wondered about him. *Is it dumb luck that brought you to us, right in that instant? Or was it something more? The timing was just so miraculous! And who are you, a British National working in America answering to a rogue CIA agent…?*

While they inspected the dead body, Sully excused himself twice due to nausea. However, the whole thing didn't faze Bax at all. It was impressive, actually.

Nodding at the burrito, Sully said, "So we agree, he was some sort of a genetic mutant?"

"That's a good question."

"You ever see anything like him before? You know, in the field?"

"No brov. Never."

Sully waited, but he didn't say anything else about it. The Brit seemed to be lost in a memory or deep thought. Sully finished his beer and stretched. Before going inside, he extended his hand once more to Bax and said, "Thank you for saving our lives Bax. I'm very thankful you've decided to join us."

Bax nodded and smiled. By 7:15, all three of them had showered. By 7:45, everyone besides Bax was resting peacefully in their rooms. Bax remained on the back porch for some time, thinking, processing what happened. *If this monster is an Alpha Kilo Phantom, and he's not owned by the U.S., the French, or the Brits, then who controls this hybrid militia? The Club of Rome? Do they have the technology to actually create human hybrid super soldiers?*

CHAPTER 26
A Holiday

Thursday, November 24, 2011

October started with high tension, as the crew braced for what they assumed would be an inevitable second assault on the guesthouse. It was inconceivable that the beast acted alone. However, as days became weeks, no evidence of a second attacker ever appeared. Tactically, the houseguests were on their heels and in disarray in the days after the first attack, so a second attack, if there was going to be one, should have come quickly. But it never did. It was as though only Molorek knew where they were hiding, and for some reason, he never shared that information with anyone else.

In the months following Molorek's attack, they each settled into a role and routine. Braxton made it his personal mission to renovate the facilities from top to bottom, installing upgrades such as high-tech surveillance and an ironclad panic room. Though the safe house was well equipped in the virtual sense, its physical defense was sub-par.

Con was laid up initially, but back to researching Malcolm's journal within a few days. Rooter's injuries were much more severe. His neck and back got worse before they started to heal, so he spent a few months on his bed, and in a foul mood. During the recovery, he was an angry, bitter guy. Not because of physical pain, but because of the anguish of being an invalid. The feeling of uselessness gnawed at his pride like termites on wood, eroding his sense of identity and purpose. With coarse language, he mocked and belittled the others, especially Anny. To the best of their ability, the others tried to give him a pass. However, on more than one occasion, Bax nearly set his recovery back; way back.

Anny dealt with Rooter remarkably well. In spite of the endless insults and ridicule, she remained supportive and empathetic throughout. Both Bax and Sully were not just impressed by her tolerance level, but deeply thankful she took on the task of caring for him. On many occasions, the others in the home wondered what they might have done to Rooter had she not been there to assume the heavy lifting. Con was sure Bax would have killed him, had it not been for her.

For Solomon, his routine involved following Bax around and learning the nuances of defensive strategies. When not with Bax, he helped Con research. They developed an efficient working relationship for sharing the reading load and comparing notes. As they dug deeper, they unearthed more. In time, the saying 'truth is stranger than fiction' became their mantra.

The others were eager to know what the research was uncovering, so at dinnertime each evening Con gave a report. He'd tell them how Roman, Greek, Sumerian, Babylonian, and Egyptian mythology were all essentially telling the same story – the story of a powerful, pre-human, celestial civilization of gods and goddesses, all jockeying for power and control. He'd support the mythological findings with Jewish stories from sources like the Books of Genesis, Enoch, Jasher, Jubilees and others. Over a few months, a picture came into focus involving powerful ancient beings in possession of both selfish and selfless tendencies. They fought with one another, supported one another, and ultimately comingled with the human race. When viewed as partial history, rather than sheer myth, it was all rather mind-boggling.

Malcolm's journal was a coveted item. The Phantoms went to great lengths to recover it, but why? How did ancient myth relate to the present or future? Malcolm's journal cued more to the past than it did the future, but the iconography, pictographs, and cuneiform all hinted at the direction the human race was headed. And if these sources were even somewhat correct, humanity wasn't destined to sail into a free-and-easy sunset.

Each day passed much the same as the one before, but on this particular Thursday, all normal activity was suspended. It was a special day, and no work was to be done. It was Sully's idea. They all needed a break.

Solomon and Anny began the day in the kitchen. They labored all morning. There was much to be thankful for and the team intended to celebrate Thanksgiving in epic fashion. The plan was to feast and drink, and do as much of that as humanly possible.

By 1 pm, the aroma of turkey, green bean casserole, potatoes au gratin, stuffing, corn on the cob, and sautéed mushrooms filled the safe house they now called home. Bax, being of British decent, had no real background with the holiday, but decided it was a great opportunity to introduce everyone to the Snake Bite. It was a favorite beverage of his kinfolk, a 50-50 blend of stout beer and cider.

Rooter limped out of his room just before 2 pm. He wore the typical Hawaiian shirt, unbuttoned, with shorts. "That smells pretty damn good, family."

"There he is," Solomon said as Anny washed her hands before attending to him.

After he was situated at the table she asked, "You want somethin' to drink? Bax is out getting his Snake Bite ingredients, but we have light beer, juice or wine."

"Yeah, water would be nice." She filled a glass while Rooter changed the subject, "So, how's the weather out there today?"

"50's. They say it'll rain later," the attorney responded.

"How's the back feeling?" Anny handed him the glass of water.

"I don't know. Day to day, it's hard to tell, but this week is better than last week." Rooter managed a weak smile. Anny gently touched his shoulder and went back to cooking.

"He seems like he's in a better mood," Sully whispered to his co-chef.

"Yeah right? Maybe we've turned a corner."

Rooter was not used to being hurt, and always fancied himself a tough guy. Molorek had bested him physically, but his pain ran deeper than any physical malady. He detested the fact that others had to empty his catheter those first few weeks after the incident. He hated having to wear a diaper even longer. When his arms were both immobilized, he had to be fed. It was all so humiliating.

Worst of all, every time Anny came into his room to help him, it felt like an excruciating gut-shot. She literally spent her time giving him sponge baths, changing his soiled clothing, or dressing his wounds. *Why hadn't one of the guys drawn the short straw? They probably laugh about the stories she tells...*

Rooter's mind told him that the others were all getting a kick out of his torment, but it was actually Anny who had *volunteered* to serve him in this manner. She volunteered so that in the long run, Rooter's dignity would be in-tact with the other men. She actually knew something about the pride of a self-avowed tough guy; something that Rooter didn't even realize about himself. In the long run, dignity with the guys was more – much more – important than temporary embarrassment with Anny.

By Thanksgiving, the stubborn PI began figuring this out. He realized that nobody was morbidly joyous over his suffering. Nobody joked about his pain behind closed doors. These were his friends. When he finally realized that Anny had actually volunteered to be his nurse and not drawn a short stick, his bruised pride was exchanged for an overwhelming sense of guilt.

In time, he accepted her role in his life and became thankful that Bax never saw him covered in his own feces. Thankful that Sully never witnessed him fall down at the toilet with his pants around his knees. It was always Anny. She was the only one who ever dealt with those things. Eventually, he realized she never told stories to the others about his travails. She never gossiped about his indignity, and no matter how horribly he treated her, she never retaliated. Lord knows she could have.

"This isn't perfect, but it will do." Bax was carrying an ample supply of Strongbow cider and Harp lager. "Blackcurrant cordial is exiled from this country, but this brew should catch your nod."

Sully carved the turkey about the time Con meandered from his room to join the others at the table. Bax poured the drinks. Once everyone was plated and seated, there came an awkward silence. Someone needed to say something, so Sully decided that someone was rightfully him. Awkwardly, he stood up, holding his glass.

"Four months ago, I never thought I'd be celebrating Thanksgiving dinner in a safe house operated by a clandestine element of the U.S. government, with my work buddies and a new friend from across the pond. I never thought I'd witness a murder, much less two. I never guessed that my time with Leola was so nearly over. I never imagined coming home to find two of my best friends beat up, one to within inches of his life. But it all happened." Solomon raised his glass higher, and the others joined him.

"But it all happened, and today I'm thankful for good friendships. I'm thankful for each of you. I'm thankful for Dotty. I'm thankful to whatever unseen forces have brought us to this place where peace is once again reigning. So, here's to the memory of the loved ones we've lost, and to the day we avenge them. But most of all, here's to being thankful in the moment for the abundance of what's before us."

They touched glasses, burst into cheer, and the feasting began. Their camaraderie ran deep and filled the air around the table. Even Rooter was beaming.

They told jokes, they shared laughs, and eventually they slid into a tipsy haze. It was a Snake Bite induced state of careless bliss. The Brit's drink definitely snuck up on them.

Bax held his liquor like a fraternity champ. Though he refilled his glass time and again, his speech remained sharp and his wit stayed fast. Anny, fearing a repeat of Chicago, kept a close eye on her intake and stopped at the point where her skin flushed and her teeth buzzed. Con was wasted after a single pint, and couldn't help it. He never drank alcohol, and he only weighed a buck-thirty. He was a lightweight and didn't mind being called one. From the first toast, Rooter shamelessly dove off the cliff of inebriety. He lost count of how many pints he drank, and it really didn't matter anyway. He was happy to let his hair down and get lost in the haze of that amber-colored holiday potion. Sully felt good, but kept his wits. Such was his nature.

After dinner, Bax shagged the dishes, while everyone else retreated to the living room. Inspired by Rooter's challenge that he could "wax the floor with them in a game of poker," a deck of cards hit the table. It was a futile endeavor. The only thing Rooter was going to wax was his pillow with his drunken face. By 5:30 pm, Con disappeared for the night and Rooter was deposited in his bed.

With Rooter passed out for the night, Anny felt the liberty to have a little more. So when Bax offered to pour a fresh round, they all partook together.

Bax retired next, just before 8. He might have had the most to drink, but his motor skills were still intact. His resistance to the Bite was remarkable.

Just before retiring for the night, Bax said, "So, I take it you two are a thing?"

Anny tensed at the question. Sully felt her do it because somehow, at some point, she reclined against him on the sofa. Somehow, at some point, he also draped his arm across her shoulders. Nervously, she sat up and picked at her earlobe with the hand that didn't hold a Snake Bite.

Bax smiled, "None-a my business, really. But as we Brits say, before Chinese whispers make a banana skin, you might pin 'er and be done with it, mate."

"That's totally inappropriate," Sully gasped, assuming he knew what Bax was trying to convey. He actually didn't.

"Nah it's not. The translation in American is, make your intentions known to the rest of us before a gossip-chain starts, and makes life in this little cabin uncomfortable for everyone. That's all."

Turning toward his room, he put up a two-fingered peace sign and disappeared through the door. It was actually good advice, but the awkward air between them on that sofa didn't just disappear. It lingered.

Anny scooted to the far end of the couch and tucked one leg under the other. She didn't know what to say. She sipped her drink and hoped he'd talk about it with her, but Solomon wasn't thinking about her at that moment. His mind had wandered to Leola.

Eventually, he glanced up at her as she raised her eyebrows, beckoning him to start a conversation. She tried every non-verbal cue in her toolkit. He knew what she wanted. He knew she wanted to talk about it, consider it, and maybe even put the option of *them* on the table.

He slid toward her and took her free hand in his. He touched the smooth skin of her cheek with the back of his index finger. Her heart fluttered and she longed for him. She closed her eyes and savored the moment. Would he kiss her? The booze was an aphrodisiac.

She felt a light squeeze on her hand, and opened her eyes as he leaned in and kissed her on the forehead. She bit her lip and tried to hold back a smile. Without a word, he stood up. They were still holding hands. She tightened her grip and hoped he might decide to stay a little longer. She felt him squeeze her hand in his strong grip once more, just before the connection was lost, "Happy Thanksgiving, Anny." Without looking back, he retired to his room and closed the door.

Schnackenberg

CHAPTER 27
Ancient Riddles

Sunday, January 29, 2012

Abdullah Kahn and his Hand accompanied the Cardinal, General, and Scientist to the mansion's formal dining room. The centerpiece was an eight-seat table made of a very unique single slab of reclaimed Acacia wood from an old tobacco plantation in Nicaragua. It was being sold at auction some years ago in NYC and Abdullah had to have it. He remodeled the dining room around the table, with raised paneling and beautifully hand-carved crown molding around the ceiling. There was a stunning Schonbek chandelier made of brass and Swarovski crystal that hung above the centerpiece, casting what Abdullah referred to as "ice-light" throughout the room. It was breathtaking.

The estate's chef, who simply went by the name Claude, prepped a four-course meal that began with crab cakes dripped in Granny Smith apple chutney and a glass of Pinot Gris Vendange Tardive from Alsace, France. The sweet, late harvest wine came from the best year in a decade, 2001.

The second course was Mediterranean-style tomato bisque served with lemon and fresh mint, bordered by salt crackers. The main course was orgasmic. Stuffed flank steak rolled in spinach pesto, prosciutto, and roasted red peppers in a balsamic demi-glaze. The course came with Asiago potato mash, béarnaise asparagus, and homemade butter rolls. It was accompanied with an ample supply of 2002 Beringer Merlot, an inexpensive red from Napa, but one of Abdullah's favorites. For dessert, a raspberry almond flan served with after-dinner cocktails in the Great Room.

During the meal, they engaged in casual conversation about the state of the world, the politics of the elite, and the women of Italian films. At one point, a lively debate about European soccer (the Hand refused to call it futbol) erupted between the General, Viktor Dultsev, and the Cardinal, Mahmood Salah. *Wars have been waged on the basis of less passionate debate,* thought Kahn.

Once they were situated in the Great Room and had their cigars and cocktails in hand, a discussion of a more serious nature ensued.

"Gentlemen, we're here to review our findings, to discuss the meaning and impact of those findings, and to consider what comes next. I have a strong hunch that some of what is said here tonight may not sit well with some or all of us. It may confront our politics, ideologies, and religious beliefs, but it all must be said and considered nonetheless."

After a moment of silence, the Scientist, Professor Mikel Maldaceto, leaned forward, "May I begin?" Abdullah gestured for him to take the floor.

"In section one of Malcolm Bernard's journal we found technical specifications for his device, the machine he used to interact with a being's 'Life Essence,' or what some refer to as the 'Soul.'"

The Cardinal adjusted his posture, already uncomfortable with where this was going.

"We have now recreated this machine, the *Anima Imperium* – Latin for 'command of the breath of life.' This device works exactly how Dr. Bernard claimed it would."

Though he already explained the science to Kahn and the Hand during their visit to BSA, the Cardinal looked confused, even distraught, so the Scientist gave a broad-stroke overview.

"The science is complicated, but the device essentially interacts with a person's visual cortex by sending signals through the eyes. What we've found is that the technology does not work unless signals are sent through both eyes, thereby blanketing the entire visual cortex and effectively tricking the brain into believing the body has died. When this happens, the brain is no longer able to maintain the torsion connection it has to the Life Essence. Because the Life Essence is bound to an individual person, when we turn the device off, the brain reengages, and the LE reestablishes that personal connection."

The Cardinal coughed nervously, "So when the connection is released, where does the soul go?"

"We don't know. We can't see it."

"But we do know," the Hand led, "that something happens, right?"

"Yes," the Scientist nodded. "We know that prolonged detachment from the host causes the Life Essence to revert back to a baseline form. Beliefs, ideologies, and faith structures are largely wiped away."

"Give the analogy, Mikel." Kahn Interrupted.

"Yes, okay then. Pretend that each Life Essence – or soul, as you call it – is represented by a blank canvas. Our experiences as a whole, including childhood, what we learn, what we see, hear, taste and touch; our life events and internal thoughts, as we experience them, become the paint on that canvas. Each experience is represented by a new brush stroke, a new color. Those strokes paint a picture. They write our unique human signature on our unique Life Essence. When the *Anima Imperium* is used, the LE detaches from the brain, and if away from the brain for a prolonged period of time, when it returns, it does so in its original form.

The markings of our life's experience are erased and the canvas is largely reset to blank. This has nothing to do with the skills, memories, and instincts in our brain. Those stay in tact. It's the deeper stuff – the things of ideology, faith and emotion – that disappear at one level or another."

"I'm not sure I follow," said the Cardinal. "Does the subject have to re-learn how to walk and talk and things like that?"

"No, as I just indicated, the brain controls things like motor skills. The brain is generally unaffected by the *Anima Imperium*. The Life Essence seems to be the hub on which unique signatures associated with loyalty, honor, values, morality, faith, and abstract belief are all written and stored. When hooked up to the *Anima*, the only things affected are those somehow housed and processed with the LE."

The others sat blankly, so the Scientist continued, "Malcolm Bernard quantified the potency of an individual's Life Essence on a scale he developed called the BAT-rating grid. A detached Life Essence under the influence of the *Anima Imperium* will eventually reach what Malcolm called 'plus or minus 30 BAT alignment.' At plus-or-minus 30 BAT, the LE is considered neutral and can no longer be affected by the *Anima Imperium*. The canvas is not actually blank – it's just wiped, erased in a way. A residue can still be seen... as if erasing thick pencil markings with a coarse eraser."

"So using this man's BAT scale, you're saying that once the subject reaches plus or minus 30, the image on the canvas can't be erased any further?"

"Precisely," the Scientist nodded.

"And though value, morality, character has been reset, the residue of the person's former belief still exists, making him, what?" the Cardinal looked at the Scientist inquisitively. "How does that work?"

"Basically yes," the Scientist said. "After the *Anima* experience at plus or minus 30 BAT alignment, if he was extremist jihadist Muslim before, he'll be partial to those beliefs when he reengages the world. He experiences life, and a natural filter uses those experiences to inform Muslim thought and belief. However, the extremist jihadist part is gone, at least for a time. It's quite remarkable, actually."

The Cardinal stared off into the distance, contemplating the effect this technology would have on his beloved Catholicism. In a daze, he popped another question, "How quickly do they recover their sense of militant-ness or extreme religiosity?"

"That seems to depend on the person. In our experiments, when the subject has a strong memory bank in the brain, he can conjure up dramatic, emotional experiences from his past that ultimately contributed to the formation of his belief structure, and reconnect those to his Life Essence. At least to some extent we've found the stronger the memories, the quicker the LE can return to its previous potency. Some of these militant ideologues return to a form of militancy within a couple weeks. If memories cannot be recalled and reconnected, we've found that the subject has to re-learn his ideological faith though new human experience and revelation. In this case, they will naturally tend toward becoming what they were, but new experiences bring new revelations. The interaction between the brain and Life Essence is all very mysterious."

"So, what exactly is the 'big picture' significance of the *Anima Imperium*?" Kahn asked, wanting to get to the point.

"The significance is this," the Scientist cleared his throat and adjusted his posture. "Every human and possibly every animal on Earth has an identifiable, perfectly unique, Life Essence that is theirs and theirs alone. The Life Essence is not a material subsystem of the human body though. We do not understand how it works because it does not behave according to the laws of biology and physics. It transcends our known natural laws. It comes from beyond our physical world and undeniably proves the existence of an original designer, a creator or creators that developed our species for a reason, a purpose. The extra-dimensional properties strongly lend proof to an afterlife of some sort. In a nutshell, the LE represents information that transcends the organic body. Like computer code, it exists invisible and apart from the storage medium and can be transferred from device to device. The Life Essence is very similar, and therefore exists beyond the life of its host. It appears to be immortal.

The Hand looked at Kahn, "Well, you wanted 'big picture' significance – This is utterly fantastic!"

The Scientist paused for Kahn to reflect, and then continued, "When the human body dies, the LE seems to transcend to another place or state of being, or something. Frankly, it's hard to measure what we can't see. Could it be that the human Life Essence is a vehicle of transport that carries information from here to *there*? Is it more personal than that? We don't know. We're seeking answers to questions like, 'why does the LE purge and return to what we consider a baseline state?' Or 'does the LE deposit its information somewhere else, like a dump truck deposits sand?' We don't know. We have no real answers, but we know the LE behaves extra-dimensionally in some form or fashion, and our *Anima Imperium* proves this."

"Very well." Abdullah took a long drag on his 60-gage La Gloria Cubana and exhaled the blue-gray smoke. "Cardinal Salah. Would you please enlighten us as to what you've found in the second section of Mr. Bernard's book?"

"I can," he said, pondering where to begin. "But first, maybe I can ask you, General. Where was Alpha Kilo, specifically?"

"The location is known in the annals of history as Etemenanki, located north of Hillah, just inside the ruins of ancient Babylon."

"That's correct," the Cardinal said, matter-of-factly, "and Etemenanki is Sumerian for 'Temple of the foundation of heaven and earth.' It is the name of the ziggurat dedicated to lord Marduk in the city of Babylon, circa 600 BC. At its prime, it measured 91 meters square at the base. That's almost exactly the full length of an American football field on all four sides. It stood nearly 300 feet high. It was a remarkable structure in its day."

"I began my research by looking into the origins of Mr. Bernard's copied iconography, cuneiform, and other scribbles and notations. It was not difficult to pinpoint the location of Alpha Kilo, and once I did, I realized the significance of that site. It is located on the Plains of Shinar, the exact place the Hebrew Bible places the Tower of Babel after the Great Flood. However, the Jewish Scriptures never use the exact phrase, *Tower of Babel*. It is always noted in the Hebrew as 'the city and its tower' or simply, 'the city.' The word Babel comes from the Akkadian and means, 'the gate of god.' Within the walls of the Vatican, we have long held to the belief that the Tower of Babel was less a large temple structure and much more of a metaphysical portal to the world of angels and beyond."

"The god to whom this structure was dedicated is known by the name Marduk. Within the Babylonian Pantheon, Marduk was the chief deity and protector of the city. In ancient Mesopotamia, the New Year celebration was known as Zagmuk. This festival of Zagmuk lasted 12 days, every year, and celebrated the battle between Marduk and the forces of Chaos. Now, Chaos refers to the formless void that existed when God first separated the heavens and the earth. So during Zagmuk, a reenactment of Marduk's triumph over Chaos is performed by the king of Babylon using sacrifice, death, and sexual intercourse."

"Based on the clues, I needed to know more about Marduk so I went searching in our own archives and was granted access to a section of the vault that is strictly off-limits to non-clergymen. There, I found something rather interesting. You may or may now know that in 1498, an official who worked under Pope Alexander VI, a guy named Annius of Viterbo, announced the discovery of the lost books of Berosus. The Vatican squashed it as a hoax, but in the vault, I found that it was not. Indeed, the lost books of Berosus do exist. Berosus was a Hellenitic-era Babylonian writer, and a priest of Bel Marduk. Among the lost books, I found a series of tablets and scrolls that were in various states of translation by our Vatican experts. One of the most complete translations was a compilation of the Marduk prophesies, including a script detailing the genealogy of Marduk's bloodline from before the Great Deluge."

"Are you all keeping up?" They nodded and so the Cardinal continued his history lesson. "Sargon of Akkad, also known as Sargon the Great, was the ruler of the Mesopotamian region in and around 2800 BCE. Sargon is also referred to as Gilgamesh in certain texts – I'm sure you've heard that name. Anyway, although we don't know the exact years of his reign, we do know that his empire encompassed an area from current-day Iran to Syria in the years before the Flood. Berosus claims that Sargon was the human offspring of Marduk and a Nephilim ruler of Babylon. Through Sargon, Marduk was therefore undeniably linked to that ancient city and the kings who ruled there after the Flood."

"Now, according to Berosus, the first celebration of Zagmuk was commissioned by Sargon himself. During the rite of Zagmuk, it was customary for the king to have sexual intercourse with a high priestess chosen from among the *naditum*, a special class of priestesses who take a vow to never bear children. The high priestess chosen for the rite was known as the *Entu*. Her ritual act of intercourse with the king during Zagmuk was thought to regenerate the cosmos through a reenactment of the primordial coupling of the pantheon's cosmic parents, blah, blah, blah. Sorry guys, too much detail. I guess these facts really don't matter."

The Cardinal sipped his beverage before continuing, "What does matter is that one year the *Entu* got pregnant with Sargon's child. According to the ruler's directive, the *Entu* carried the child to term and gave birth to a daughter. Once Sargon realized it was a girl, he instructed the *Entu* to secretly discard the child, thus avoiding violation of her oath and escaping the wrath of the god Marduk. This baby was found and raised by a working class family, and became the mother of a girl by the name of Ne'elatama'uk, who as you may know is listed in the Hebrew Bible as the wife of Ham, son of Noah. Do we all see the connection?"

"No," Abdullah said plainly.

The Cardinal smiled and explained slowly, "The human offspring of an extra-dimensional being known as Marduk, impregnated the high priestess during the ritual rite of Zagmuk, and a baby girl was born. Thus, this little girl was born with altered genetic-makeup. She was spliced with the genetic makeup of the extra-dimensional species. In fact, Gilgamesh is said to be more god than human – four parts god to one part human, to be exact. The mutant little girl then grew up and eventually gave birth to the wife of Noah's son, Ham. The mutant wife gained access to the Ark during the Flood, thereby continuing the altered genetic line of the Nephilim long after the Great Deluge. Ham's wife was essentially an alien-human hybrid. By marrying the genetically-pure son of Noah, she survived the Flood and altered the bloodline of Ham's descendants, from which came a great hunter and king named Nimrod, and later, King Nebuchadnezzar of Babylon."

"Now, this gets important. Nimrod was the great grandson of Noah, and his name is interchangeable with Osiris. Nimrod was not a king of a city or empire, Nimrod was the king of the whole earth. He was the human embodiment of Marduk. He was the one that commissioned the construction of the Tower of Babel. Are you starting to see any significance for our analysis of Alpha Kilo?"

"Contained in the Book of Rolls is a description of what happened when the tower portal was opened by Nimrod long ago. According to the Kitab al-Magall, from heaven came a black matter which was later fashioned into a crown. Nimrod AKA

Osiris wore this crown and is credited as the first king to ever wear a crown on earth." The Cardinal shook his head.

"I know this is a lot of historical jibberish, but you'll see why this is hugely important to our investigation of Alpha Kilo. I subscribe to the theory originally coined by English historian and scholar, George Rawlinson. He believed that Nimrod and Belus were one in the same, and I rather agree. Belus or Belos refers to the Babylonian god, Bel Marduk, and he is identified with the Greek Zeus and the Latin Jupiter throughout history – Zeus Belo, Jupiter Belus – get it? In other cases, Belus is euhemerized as an ancient lord who built the ziggurat in Babylon, which I believe was the Tower of Babel. He is recognized and worshipped as the god of war across mythological lines and I believe Marduk, or at least his essence through genetics, may have been the only surviving celestial remnant on earth from the time of the flood to the time of the portal in Babel."

"Cardinal, let me please interject," said the Scientist. "Am I understanding correctly that you are ascribing evidential value to mythological legend?"

"Look, the older I get, the more I see. The more I research the ancient texts buried within the Vatican, the more I see recurring themes that bridge truth and legend. Yes, I find it increasingly plausible that the historical, mythological, and religious texts actually agree on many of the 'big stories' of antiquity. Sure, we see cultural embelishments and inacurracies creep in over the centuries, but the basics are intact. General, tell me. What did your assault team at Alpha Kilo recover, in terms of artifacts?"

"A few tablets and bones."

"Yes, and the bones belonged to who?"

"They are said to be bones recovered at the tomb of Gilgamesh. I understand they were discovered and claimed by the allied forces in 2003."

"That's right," the Cardinal said. "The bones of Gilgamesh-Nimrod-Osiris-Appolo-Zeus-Jupiter, all are names for the human personification of an alien-lord by the name of Marduk. These men are all one man, the descendant of Sargon, the Nephilim ruler of ancient, pre-flood Babylon. On the tablets you recovered, there are written instructions on how to carry out the rite of Zagmuk, correct?"

"Ceremonial instructions, yes…"

"And these tablets," the Cardinal cut him off, "were taken by the U.S. military from an exhibit at the Baghdad Museum in 2003. Zagmuk had to happen during the equinox. Maybe you could tell me, on what day did the vernal equinox fall in 2006?"

The Hand looked it up on his phone and said, "The 20th of March."

"On March 20, 2006, under the direction of some agency of the U.S. Government, the ancient Tower of Babel was opened again for the first time in 4,000 years. It was opened with trans-human DNA from the material remains of Nimrod, which contained the genetic essence of Marduk, the proof of which has been found in the lost books of Berosus. With those bones present, the ritual celebration of Zagmuk commenced, thereby opening the portal to another world. In a nutshell, Malcolm's journal is the only known record of this entire crazy episode."

"I knew it," Kahn slapped his knee with excitement.

"We knew it!" the Hand corrected.

"The portal closed before our arrival," the General said, leaning into the conversation now. "We took what we could, but Dr. Bernard blew himself up before we could take his, what-da-ya-call-it, Anim…"

"*Anima Imperium*," the Scientist interjected with a finger pointing up.

"Yes, that's it!" Kahn interrupted excitedly. "Whatever interaction he had with the open portal must be chronicled in that third section of his journal. Any idea about that language script used in the final section, Mr. Salah?"

"No. Plainly, we need a cypher, and to my knowledge, one does not exist."

"No cypher exists," repeated the Hand contemplatively.

The General rolled his eyes with irritation at the Hand's presence, and took a deep swig of his drink.

"We may yet find it," the Cardinal said, smiling. The others waited for him to continue. "My part of the story is not yet complete. There are many references to the tomb of Osiris in Malcolm's journal. Remember, Nimrod is Gilgamesh, and Gilgamesh's tomb helped unlock the portal. Nimrod is also Osiris to the Egyptians, and I believe strongly that something in Osiris' tomb will help us unlock the next step."

"I'm sure," Abdullah grunted cynically. "But Cardinal, I have friends in very high places, and since 2003 the Egyptian government has disallowed any access whatsoever to the location of the Osiris Sarcophagus. We have been working on the problem of access for nearly a decade. But frankly, I doubt we will be able to have a look inside until we petition the new regime, and that won't happen until after Egypt's upcoming elections."

"Be that as it may," Cardinal Salah continued, "the book referenced a heavenly gift, something that would help to usher in a new world. I don't know exactly what it is, but if, at some point, we can get into Egypt and have a look inside that Osiris tomb, we may find the cypher that unlocks the Eteocypriot writing in Malcolm's book. That's what I'm hoping for, at least."

"Is that what you think is buried down there? What's to say the Egyptians haven't recovered it?"

"I can't say one way or another, but the writing in the third section seems important. It may contain information vital to the formulation of peace on this earth, which as you all know, is the cornerstone of my mission at the Vatican. Cypher or not, there's got to be something of value to our mission in that tomb."

"Good. General, without getting too specific," Kahn nodded gently, hoping the General caught his meaning, "please tell us what you found out about operator Bast Molorek."

The General leaned forward and cast a glance at the Cardinal. He knew exactly what Kahn meant. "Yes, operator BM was one of our assault team at Alpha Kilo and he's been on assignment in DC, keeping an eye on a CIA operative who recently stumbled very close, and possibly into, our pond of information. After this operator failed to check in per his protocol, I went to DC and had a look around. It is clear to me that BM was terminated. The concern here is that BM had, um, something on his person, that if looked at closely, might point a very astute individual to us."

"I'm not following," said the Cardinal.

"Cardinal," Kahn took over and chose his words carefully. "This operator had something that subtly points to us as the perpetrators behind the assault at Alpha Kilo. This something was genetic in nature, if you catch my meaning."

The Cardinal leaned back in his chair as a flood of memories came to him. Specifically, he recalled a pointed discussion with Kahn a few years ago about the ethical appropriateness of pursuing genetically engineered mutations in humans. *Has Kahn created a chimera?*

"The clues are not obvious," Kahn continued, "and I'm sorry I can't be more specific, but you understand. It's confidential. So General, what are we doing about it?"

"Right now we have our operators within the U.S. government keeping an ear to the wall and reporting in every 72 hours. I watched the Greek myself while I was there, and I've put two new pair of eyes on him since. But there's not much we can do. Just wait and see what happens, and respond with gusto when it does."

"What's your assessment?" The Hand asked, patronizingly.

"My assessment is that the Greek doesn't have the book, and the Greek has not made us yet. If he ID's any one of us, he could ID the double agents around him at the Agency, and it doesn't appear he has. We're okay so far, but the situation is fluid."

"Why not take out the Greek?" asked the Hand.

"Because," Kahn replied for the General, "we don't know what he knows, who he's told, or how he's getting his information. We know he had people working for him, but we don't know who. He's taking whatever he's doing off official CIA channels. Originally, BM's orders were to take him out, but BM never did, and evidently never even tried. This means that BM caught a sniff for something he thought was more important, and there, something went wrong. If we took out the Greek now, we miss the opportunity for information, and things could unravel fast. Fact is, we're just waiting and watching until we have better intel."

With the update portion of the meeting complete, the men began brainstorming potential contacts that could lead to more access in Egypt. They needed to get a team into the tomb of Osiris on the Giza Plateau. They didn't know if anything was there, but the Osiris shaft location was the clear next step.

As the brandy flowed, the discussion deteriorated. Eventually, each of the men retired to a separate wing of the home. They'd finalize the discussion over breakfast and pursue a plan of action.

CHAPTER 28
A Visitor

Wednesday, February 22, 2012

The winter was unseasonably moderate, although forecasters called for rain by the weekend. Braxton Hill sat in the living room, cinching the laces on his boots, gearing up for his customary morning walk of the premises. Since his arrival six months prior, he'd done the same thing each and every morning – come rain, sleet, wind or sunshine. Meticulous security was not a job to him. It was a pursuit of passion.

He wore light cargo pants and a plain white t-shirt under a green pullover hoodie. Most mornings, the moist air swooping down off the North Atlantic Ocean had a chilly bite, so Bax wore a solid black beanie on his head. It was rare to see him not wearing it, whether he was indoors or out. Nothing he wore was overly baggy. He learned long ago that sacrificing a little comfort for uninhibited range of motion could mean the difference between his and someone else's life.

The morning survey always happened between sun-up and 9 am. He changed-up his routines constantly, and even logged his own behavior in a notebook that he kept for personal assessment and review. The security walk normally took him about 90 minutes. If he rushed, he could do it in 45, but again, his was a pursuit of passion. Like a world-class tracker/survivalist on cable TV, he took care to note fresh animal tracks in the ground, disturbed undergrowth, and any other clues he might find. Any evidence – animal, human, or *both* – was always investigated. If they learned anything from Bast Molorek's assault, it was that conventional tips and tracks could not be trusted.

His second survey came in early afternoon, and the final check always took place between 5:00 and sundown. He walked the first and last, but preferred to jog the second to keep his wind from "going Yankee" on him.

Stepping into the clear crisp morning air, he breathed deep and held the chill in his lungs. Bax loved the security detail. As he advanced toward what he called "Stage I," someone grabbed his attention from behind.

"Hey Bax, mind if I tag along?"

Turning, he saw Sully at the front door wearing jeans, sneakers, and a light windbreaker. "Nah, come on then."

After chopping up the chimera attacker and sinking its remains in the Bay, Bax fixed the broken doors and replaced the broken furniture. After those immediate needs were addressed, he got to work on the physical layout, and began modifying and improving the team's security.

First, he added a very sharp fiberglass resin to the top of the existing perimeter fence. Over time, he made it all the way around the property. An intruder wearing thick gloves could break through it, but it was effective at keeping squirrels and other little animals from running along the fence and tripping the motion detectors. Much time was then spent on mitigation work with the shrubbery and trees just outside the fence. By beating back a 15-meter barrier between the woodland and the perimeter, Bax enjoyed a controlled zone where new tracks and evidence were easy to identify.

The area that gave Bax the most heartburn was not the perimeter fence, but the front of the property along the street. There, the driveway was only obstructed by a wire cord. It was laughable. The rest of the front property line was obstructed by a series of shrubs, which acted more like cover for intruders than movement inhibitors. Additionally, the lighting was poor and the garage was a perfect second cover point, located halfway between the street and the front door. Therefore, lots of modifications were made, thanks to Dotty and the petty cash fund of a clandestine element within the U.S. government.

First, he dug out the shrubbery in front and replaced it with a reinforced concrete wall. He ran power throughout the block and then covered it in smooth stucco. In the end, it stood 10-feet, with a nice topper of tasteful razor wire. The cord was replaced with an iron gate that only opened or closed by thumb sensor. There were sensor panels on the entry and exit sides of the gate, the kitchen, Con's room, and the back porch.

Other upgrades included iron-casements on windows and doors, bulletproof glass, automatic locks, exterior lighting, and a series of integrated cameras. Bax installed the main monitoring system in the living room and gave each person a comprehensive lesson on how to use the new technology.

"Can I ask you a question?" Sully finally said as they trudged along the inner perimeter. Bax's eyes were on the ground, carefully searching for any sign of disturbance.

"Sure, have at it."

"Have you ever lost somebody close to you?"

"Of course mate. You don't do this business without experiencing that, pretty sure."

"Not, you know, a fellow soldier. More like a loved one. Have you ever lost a girlfriend, or wife, or child?"

Bax paused to give him a look of admonishment, "I never did get spliced. I don't have children. But losing a bro who wore the same boots as me was, I assure you, every bit as devastating as what happened with your girlfriend, if that's what you're getting at."

"Of course," Sully was embarrassed. "Sorry."

The Brit turned back to what he was doing, "Why? Why do you ask?"

"I don't know. I guess I figured you'd been down this road before and I was wondering how you coped. How you moved on."

Bax didn't initially answer him, so he continued, "Every night, right before I fall asleep, I get this feeling in my gut. Like nerves. I see her staring up at me from the tub. The feeling of butterflies comes. Then I can't get her image, her expression, out of my head. I feel like I had this kicked for a while, but it's been harder recently. I guess what I'm asking is, does that image ever go away?"

Bax knelt down and moved some dirt with his index finger. Without looking up at Sully, he said, "A buddy in the SBS once told me, 'grief is a fight, a bloody war that rages between the memory of love and the reality of loss. A war that will never see a winner, it only ends when one side gives up.' Does that make any sense to you?"

"Yes, I suppose." Sully shivered and blew into his hands.

"I find the only way to move on is to choose either the memory of love or the reality of loss. So long as they are allowed to compete, grief becomes the silent thief that steals our joy. Grief feeds on our morbid need to know, and to understand *why*. So I believe it's strengthened by our need to hold onto the past, if that makes any sense."

Bax stood and looked at his friend. "So, for us soldiers, we normally forego the memory of love and choose to accept the reality of loss. For us, the reality of loss overwhelms the memory of love. It's not even a fair fight mate. It's why we come home withdrawn. It's why we have post-traumatic-whatever-whatever. I think it's why most of us live the rest of our lives detached, often with superficial relationships."

He then pointed at his heart and said, "In here, I know it's better for me if I hold to the memory of love, and let go of the reality of loss. But it's much harder to do that, brov."

"How?"

"Pardon?"

"How do you keep the memory of love and let go of the loss?"

"Not sure mate," Bax shook his head, "but I suspect it has to do with choosing to love again when the fear of loss tries to choke you. Has to do with things like choosing to dream, choosing to forgive, choosing to look forward, not back."

"Your SBS brother seems like a smart guy," Sully finally said, after walking some distance in silence. "He say anything else?"

"Yeah, once he said, 'choosing love is hard, but courageous – choosing loss is a little easier, but cowardly.' He wasn't one for mincing words. I suppose I've always taken the cowardly out."

When he glanced up, Solomon saw something in his eyes. For a nanosecond it was evident. He saw and realized what becomes of a man who chooses the reality of loss over the memory of love. It was sobering.

Sully spent a few more minutes with Bax before excusing himself to walk and think alone. He wanted to process it all, try to rework the Rubik's Cube of emotional pain, once again. Some moments felt like breakthrough, others felt like despair. He ventured outside the compound and walked up the street to where Bax found the Toyota Tacoma half a year before. From there, he veered toward the water and found the beach, where he walked until his feet ached.

The walks became his therapy. In solitude along the shoreline, he routinely went through the gamut of the emotional war Bax so eloquently described. The cycle was pretty simple – hope replaced by guilt replaced by pain, cycling to hope again. Over and over, he bobbed along the unforgiving, unrelenting cycle of loss. There was no reprieve. Sometimes he'd scream. Sometimes he'd curse. Sometimes he'd fall to his knees and fist the rocky sand. *Will this never end?*

On return from his walks, he visited *his* sprawling beech tree that stood on a mound of earth above the beach, about 75 yards from the safe house. He spent hundreds of hours there, his back against its thick trunk, gazing out over the bay. It became his favorite think-spot. Sometimes he forced his mind to dream about the future. Other times his mind forced him to live in the past. Over the weeks, his tree witnessed his greatest highs, his worst lows, and the nothingness in between. The tree never judged him. It just stood there and let Sully be Sully.

"Mind if I join you?" Anny startled him on her approach.

Her arms were folded across her chest, her hands tucked inside the sleeves of her sweatshirt. The cutting wind coming off Glebe Bay was pulling at the strands of hair not tucked into a hair tie. The winter had paled her skin, but the afternoon sunshine lit her up and made her look vibrant.

"Of course," he scooted over to give her some room. She noticed his red, slightly puffy cheeks. She'd come to know them well. It was clearly an emotional walk. "So what's up? What time is it?"

"It's after 3. You've been out a long time so I figured I'd try and find you."

He didn't respond. His eyes settled on a little motorboat bobbing through the choppy surf. It was headed east. He could hear its motor faintly. *It turned into a beautiful day. The wind is still cold, but the temperature, especially in the sun, has to be upper fifties. Maybe even low sixties.* He thought, quietly hoping she'd not do too much talking.

"You doin' okay, friend?" She drew close and looped her left arm through his right elbow.

"Yeah," he took a deep breath, "You know, day-by-day."

He looked at her and knew she wanted more. *Does she really want me to blabber on about this? Is she just being polite?*

He decided to test the waters and give her a little more meat, "I find that when I start thinking about the future, you know, having a new relationship with someone or one day having a family, I get confronted by guilt. This isn't just guilt though. It's like this overpowering wave of hatred for myself. It tells me, 'your soul mate was supposed to be Leola. You blew her off, then let her die, and now you're betraying her memory.' So I feel like I'm betraying her by even thinking about moving on, you know?"

"I don't," she said, almost in a whisper.

He glanced at her before continuing "Then, those thoughts lead me to think about the good and bad times, the ups and downs. This leads to heartache and more anger, and an all-encompassing sense of aloneness in the present. Know what I'm saying?"

She shrugged

"You ever lose someone close?"

"No. The only person I ever had an intimate relationship with was Mike, that guy I followed out here. Believe it or not, he was actually my first. We met my freshman year in college." She paused, wondering if she ever told him that. "Anyway, you remember I broke up with him, not the other way around. For some reason, that was enough to make me shut out the possibility of future relationships for like two years. So I can't imagine what you're going through."

The wind ruffled up the scent she was wearing. He could identify hints of fruit and lavender. It wasn't overpowering, but fit her well. "What are you wearing?" he asked.

"It's called Princess, by Vera Wang. You like it?" She put the inside of her wrist up to her nose and smelled.

"I do." He adjusted his posture and returned to the subject, "So then, when did you decide you were ready to date again?"

When I went to Chicago, she thought, but verbalized something else entirely. "You know, sometime later. At some point I realized I was missing out. You know, on the special stuff. I never really dated though..."

"That was my fault," he blamed himself before she could.

"No. No it wasn't," she patted his arm reassuringly. "Sure, work was busy there for a while, but honestly, I never missed an episode of Law and Order. Not like I couldn't have forced the issue, you know? Law and Order... God rest its soul."

He didn't say anything, so she continued, "Even though I'm done isolating, the occasion hasn't really come. So I haven't really dated, I guess."

"And?" It seemed to him that Anny was purposefully being vague, so he pushed. "And now?"

"And what?" she nudged him and bit her lip. Then with barely a whisper she said, "And now... I guess I'm waiting for him to show up and ask me out."

He slid his right hand down the inside of her left arm, tickling her sweatshirt sleeve as he went. When he reached the end, he pulled the sleeve up and exposed her hand. He interlocked his fingers with hers as she looked away, smiling, unable to contain it. A gesture like this was enough to keep her going for another month.

At some point between Chicago and their simple life since the attack, she had fallen in love with him. She knew it beyond any doubt. He became everything to her, but it took everything she had to pretend otherwise. On rare occasions over the last few months, a moment came that captivated her, rejuvenated her, and excited her like nothing else in the world. *How I love the simple gesture of him holding my hand.* This was one of those moments, and she hoped it would last a lifetime.

But it didn't. It only lasted a couple minutes before they heard the sound of an approaching vehicle. She instinctively let go of his hand, silently cursing whoever drew near. They both looked and saw it was a cab. It stopped in front of the gate and someone got out. A minute later, the gate opened and Bax met the person in the courtyard and shook his hand.

Sully was too far away to see the person definitively, but he rightly guessed who it was and said, "That's gotta be Dotty. Let's go see what's going on."

"Fine," she moaned, over-exaggerating her disappointment.

He got up first and turned to help her up. She put her hands in his and he pulled her to her feet. He didn't immediately let go however, so she looked up at him as he searched her eyes. She was lost in that gaze, so much so that she didn't feel his fingers exploring her hands, and she almost didn't hear him say, "I'd like you to walk with me tomorrow. I want you to be a part of what I'm going through. Will you do that for me?"

She bit her lip again and tried to hold back the smile, but didn't do a very good job.

"Yes." Simple, sweet, it was all she could manage as she nodded, staring back into his clear green eyes.

The redness in his cheeks was now gone, the puffiness too. He looked like his old self. Her mind wondered, even as her heart hoped, *maybe he's finally going to start letting me in?*

CHAPTER 29
A Reunion

Wednesday, February 22, 2012

"To what do we owe this pleasure?" Solomon said, as he held the door for Anny. They found Dotty chatting good-humoredly in the living room, while the others clamored about him.

"Sully!" The CIA agent stood to embrace his old friend. "I just decided it was time for a visit. It's been much too long."

"It sure has."

"And you, my dear. You look wonderful, as always." Dotty embraced Anny then gestured for them to join the others.

"I was beginning to wonder if you were even alive."

"I know it. I'm really sorry I've been out of contact…"

Before sitting, Anny noticed that their guest had nothing to drink, so she gave the others a disapproving look and offered one. He asked for water, no ice.

"Truth is," he continued, "I've had a pretty serious tail ever since you guys were attacked last year. In the beginning I thought it was just a matter of time before I was attacked myself, but they've kept their distance. Just been surveying me; watching me day and night."

"Any idea who?" Bax asked.

"Not precisely, but they're connected to the Phantoms, just as sure as your assailant was. Can't be sure, but I think they're waiting for me to make a mistake and lead them to you. That's why I was out of contact for so long."

"What changed?" Rooter asked nervously. "They didn't follow you here did they?"

"No way," Dotty shook his head emphatically. "I went out of my way to ensure nobody followed me here. Two days and half a world out of my way, to be exact."

Solomon noticed something between he and Bax. It was a look. They had a moment, as if Braxton now knew something the rest of them didn't. Nobody else seemed to notice it, but Sully thought, *Wonder what that's about?*

"Fact is," the Father continued, "everything has taken a long time, but this was by my own design. When you sent me those DNA samples, I had to sit on them for months. Eventually, I found an obscure, off-shore lab that seemed far enough away from prying eyes."

He then looked at Bax and said, "And I'll tell you right now, the Phantom infiltration into our government is way above any group or division. We're talking the Department of State, DHS, DOD – you name it. Not just that, but my case officer at the Agency, that guy I trusted, he was transferred five months ago. I can't tell you if he's alive or dead at this point. He just dropped off the map.

Dotty shook his head and exhaled in frustration. "The guy I report to now, let's just say he makes everything I do ten-times harder than it was, and I can tell he's got an itch about me. I'd bet the only reason this guy hasn't killed me himself is because nobody can figure out what I know, who I've told, and who I'm involved with. But beyond a doubt, what we've stumbled onto here is huge, global. This Phantom group is involved in international banking, business, commerce, technology, military, and just about any relevant, first world government you can name. They are massive, secretive, run a hell of a militia, and have cash to burn in pursuit of whatever they're after."

Dotty's hair was longer and grayer than before. He looked tired in the face, as though he'd aged more than he should in the past six months. He had dark bags under his keen, bright eyes. There was a droop to his look, as if his face was tired of pretending. Anny delivered the glass of water and he took a large gulp.

"So, at long last, you're here and you bring tidings of joy," Rooter said. "Sure can't wait to hear what that thing was last year."

"Yes, well actually," Dotty replied, "it would help me if you guys could start by bringing me up to speed on what you've uncovered about that book, if anything. That way, we'll all be on the same page and I can overlay it with the stuff I've discovered."

"Sure. Con, you want to present the broad strokes?" Sully gestured toward his associate.

Con jumped right in about section two of Malcolm's journal. Clearly, he was well rehearsed. He told the story of the human race, as portrayed in the journal's pictographs, hieroglyphics, and cuneiform text. He eloquently bridged the monotheistic religions with Mesopotamian, Egyptian, Greek and Eastern mythologies. He explained how the Tower of Babel was not a temple, but some kind of portal, a gateway to an unseen celestial world. He translated Malcolm's description of the portal dimensions at Alpha Kilo, and connected Alpha Kilo to two possible locations.

"It was either at a ziggurat structure called Etemenanki inside the ancient city of Babylon, or it was at a place called Eridu, which is arguably the oldest city in the world. I'm pretty sure Alpha Kilo was at Etemenanki, because the patron deity of Babylon is Marduk, and that lines up with everything else in the journal…"

"You nailed it! You're actually right," the Greek interrupted as he slapped his own knee in surprise. "Alpha Kilo was right underneath the excavation site at ancient Babylon. That's really impressive."

With pride, Con went on to give a detailed narrative of celestial-human contact and cohabitation prior to the Great Flood, and cited evidence found in mythical, religious, and historical texts. Some of this was new to everyone, not just the Greek.

"On one side, you have a quasi-monotheistic perspective that's best articulated in the old Ge'ez language texts, such as the Books of Enoch, Zohar, and Jubilees. These were strongly confirmed and clarified with the discovery of the Dead Sea Scrolls in the late 40's, early 50's. Anyway, these texts claim that celestial beings called 'Watchers' were assigned by a powerful deity named Samyaza at the point of creation." Con paused for a moment, and hit a quick side-bar, "Incidentally, based on all this research, if the story of Adam and the Garden of Eden is true, that came about not as the inception of creation, but as the inception of the human race. Outside the garden, there were definitely other intelligent beings living about, but more on that later." His voice tailed off as he tried to recapture his original stream of thought.

"Right, so this Samyaza ordered the Watchers to come to earth for the purpose of keeping an eye on all of creation – to protect it. From what? I don't know. Supposedly, in the beginning, this assignment was even approved at the top alien/celestial level, the so-called *God of Light*."

As if immersed in Kindergarten story time, the others listened intently. "Translations vary a little, but there were between 200 and 300 of these Watchers assigned to earth. They were granted full access to the creation, and later to humans by that powerful deity named Samyaza. At one point, at the behest of Samyaza, these Watchers started behaving poorly. They started dabbling in cross-species genetic engineering. Gold was a big deal, even back then, so a few obscure references I found seem to indicate that they took primates and engineered them to be miners, mining for gold and other precious metals. Once the human race came around, they taught the human race a myriad of evils, and eventually fell to uncontrollable urges of lust."

Rooter shook his head as if mocking himself for entertaining this crazy story again. Con saw it and continued, "I know, crazy freak-show stuff. Anyway, they even started having sexual relations with human women. Thus, a race of hybrid-offspring called the 'Nephilim' was born into the world. These Nephilim are referenced, in depth, in the ancient apocryphal books, and even talked about a few times in the Bible. This was a trans-human race acknowledged by a broad section of the ancient world. They were beings of incredible size, power, and supernatural ability. Genetically speaking, they were part-man and part-god. They were the offspring of these Watcher-aliens and human women."

"Hang on," the Father interjected, "my knowledge of mythology is limited, but I've always been familiar with the concept of the Nephilim because they are part of our orthodoxy. In our tradition, evil, fallen angels have relations with humans and the race of the Nephilim is produced. They occupy so much of the earth, that God sends the Flood as a judgment against them, in order to wipe them out. Are you saying that Greek, Egyptian, Babylonian, even Roman, mythology echoes that story?"

"Basically, yes. Think of it this way. The Nephilim are the offspring of alien-human parents. The Heroes of Greek mythology are the offspring of alien-human parents. Essentially, everyone is telling the same story. There is a deification of these things in Mythological language. The Heroes were portrayed as being greater than human. But in most monotheistic orthodoxies, these things are not deified so much as they are depicted as accursed and fallen. Beings less than human. Though the depictions are different, both religion and mythology agree, first, that they existed, and second, where they came from."

"That's stunning." The father mused mostly to himself.

"Right," Anny chimed. "So ancient Jewish and Greek traditions tell similar stories, but Con, you also said something about Babylonian mythology."

"In Babylonian mythology, characters like Sargon, Nimrod, Gilgamesh, and Nebuchadnezzar are all referred to as *demigods* – part man, part god. Same thing as *Hero*, or *Nephilim*, but they call the frisky angels 'Annanuki' in their texts and traditions.

"The Anunnaki?" Rooter said. "You've mentioned them before, right?"

"Yes, the aliens of old. In Babylonian mythology, some say they seeded the race of man, and at this point, I rather agree. Look, let me break it down this way. On one side, you have Watchers, Gods, and Anunnaki. They are the aliens according to the Jewish, Greek, and Babylonian traditions respectively. Then, on the other side, you have Nephilim, Heroes, and Demigods. They are the offspring of aliens and humans according to the same Jewish, Greek and, Babylonian traditions, respectively. Don't you see? The ancient myths and fables all tell the exact same pre-human, or early-human story, broadly speaking."

There was a pause for Dotty to take another long gulp, then Con continued. "It is also said that the Watchers taught secrets to the humans, including astronomy, cosmetics, weaponry, ritual worship, the arts of deception, writing, and others. And all this seems to align pretty well with a few Biblical references in Genesis about the Nephilim. They became rulers because they were so advanced. They ruled with an iron fist. They were great and terrible, all at the same time…"

"So, what was Malcolm trying to say in his book?" Solomon interrupted. "I get that he's telling a story of his view of early human history, but why?"

Con stopped, looked around, and sipped his soda. They all looked back at him, so he asked, "What? Is that directed at me? Because I'd be speculating at this point."

"Then speculate," Rooter said. "Just help fill in some of these blanks."

"Alright," Con leaned onto his elbows. "Regardless of the historical text, the story goes something like this: The world – Earth – is created and it is given to the alien race to inhabit. It is somehow corrupted by this celestial occupation, and Humans are created by the whim or thought of a singular truth, or a single powerful celestial alien. Our ancestors are then put here and given some sort of safe haven to live and grow in. Maybe it's the mythological Garden of Eden. Maybe it's a remote corner of an unpopulated area of the world. Who knows."

"The new creation is cared for by a group of aliens known as various things in various ancient languages. We'll call them Watchers. These aliens care for our ancestors. They teach us how to live, cook food, make fire, make pigment-died paste, write, read, talk, you name it. In time, these Watchers begin to push the boundaries of what's acceptable. Personally, I believe they do this at the behest of a malicious evil god-king within the celestial race. Before long, the offspring are born into the world and take control of it, lording over our human ancestors. The creator god-alien grieves for what's happened to mankind, and somehow delivers judgment on the earth in the form of a great flood. Who knows, maybe he had a technology that caused our early earth atmosphere to dump its water vapor in one fell swoop. Anyway, the flood, which is recorded in numerous texts, wiped out everything – the race of Nephilim and the race of man – of course, with the exception of those who were spared on a big boat. Actually, some believe that the "ark" was a large spacecraft. Again, the story differs slightly, depending on the tradition."

"Yeah brodin, we got this much. What does it mean to us?"

"I'm getting there," Con put a hand up to Rooter. "So, after the flood, the stories all converge on one guy. In the Bible, he's called Nimrod, the great grandson of Noah. In Babylonian myth, he's known as Gilgamesh. In Egypt, he's known as Osiris. In Grecian tradition, he's Apollo. I have come to believe that all the traditions are telling the story of the same person. Now, sticking with Jewish lore, Nimrod is referenced as Noah's great-grandson. The apocryphal texts speak of him as *the* one, great, worldwide leader of his generation. He is reckoned to have been the one to commission the Tower of Babel – what I believe was an ancient portal to the celestial alien race – and evoked the anger and wrath of the powerful celestial God when he did so. From there, the tribes are split and languages are confused. New spoken and written languages spread around the ancient world, nations develop, and we get different names and historical nuances -- Nimrod, Gilgamesh, Osiris, Apollo. Get it? This is one person, one historical truth. He was the prime ruler over the post-flood world."

Con paused for a quick drink of soda to re-wet his mouth. "So, here's my thinking. Here's the relevance for us. The Tower of Babel is what connects the past, present, and future. It has to be. When I read Malcolm's journal in historical context, this whole thing at Alpha Kilo had something to do with recapturing lordship or kingship or power over the world. See, the Book of Rolls tells of a crown that was given to Nimrod after the Babel portal was opened. Stories claim that this Nimrod was the first human to ever wear a crown. This all has to do with the rise of a one-world king, and the power to go with it. Since you asked, I guess this is my best theory right now."

"Wait, what allows you to jump to that conclusion?" asked the Father.

"Lots of stuff, but nothing's all that obvious. Example, in Greek mythology the word used for Babylon was from the original Akkadian, *Bāb-ilim*, which means the 'Gate of the Gods.' The word studies alone lead me to believe this was an ancient portal, even without the evidence of what happened to Malcolm at Alpha Kilo. This extra-dimensional gateway is the only clear and obvious linkage between ancient history and the here-and-now."

Con paused as if he expected other questions but nobody said anything. He flipped open his notes and started reading from them.

"So here are some of the names attributed to the personification of this mighty ruler named Nimrod. You have Ba'al, a rather generic name assigned to the god of thunder, rain, agriculture and other things, worshiped from current-day Spain to Central Asia. You have Melqart, venerated deity of vegetation in Phoenician and Punic cultures. Then there is the Syrian Adonis and the Semitic Baal Hadad, both akin to the Egyptian Osiris in the various spellings and iconography. And, you guessed it, all of these dudes are considered deities of rebirth and vegetation. Next there's Ninurta, Mesopotamian deity who, in some translations is called by the name Ninib, Ninip, or Nimrud. In Zoroastrianism, you have Mithra, the goddess of the garden, the harvest, and the waters. Nimrod was a great and powerful hunter before God, according to Genesis. Orion was the same to Egyptology. Seventy nations and seventy languages were born out of whatever happened at the Tower of Babel. The portal was shut, and the truths about it were concealed until a later day and time. I believe that day and time was in 2006. I believe a guy named Malcolm Bernard discovered a cypher and unlocked it again."

Con paused to clear his throat. He internalized a debate about whether to go to the Bible, and finally went with, *Why not?* "In the Bible's book of Matthew, chapter 24, verse 37, Jesus is being asked about what the end of human civilization will look like. Jesus answers his people and tells them that only God knows when it will happen, but that – and I quote here – 'as it was in the days of Noah, so it will be at the coming of the son of man.'"

Con glanced up and looked at the group before continuing, "This is scary because whatever attacked us was clearly not human. Back in the days of Noah, Nephilim existed alongside animal chimera – that's a word used for *genetically engineered animal cross-species* – and there was a great and sudden rise in technology back then as well, as Watchers taught all sorts of things to humans. Today, we are in the middle of an unexplainable rise in tech, even right now."

The Father was nodding with emphatic agreement, as he knew the passages well.

"So here's the connection to the here-and-now, and it involves Egypt," Con said. "Nimrod reigned from Babylonia, but he regularly made trips to other parts of his kingdom. Apparently, one of his favorite spots was Egypt, the land from which he would eventually rule the ancient world, even after his death. Chapter 14 of the Book of Jasher introduces a very intriguing character named Rikayon, an Egyptian man who would eventually become the first Pharaoh, a governing prefect under Osiris, which is actually spelled O-s-w-i-r-i-s in Jasher. Essentially, Rikayon achieved his status by taking it upon himself to extract a tax from the people before they were allowed to bury their dead. In exchange for this tax, Rikayon performed mummification rituals, and became known as a master of this art. The people felt that Rikayon took advantage of them, so when Nimrod, the crown-wearing king known to the Egyptians as *Oswiris*, came to Egypt during his annual pilgrimage, the people presented their grievances. But, as the story goes, Rikayon made so much money from the death ritual tax that he came to King Osiris with lavish gifts, thus earning Osiris' favor."

"Now, I'm quoting from the book of Jasher 14, starting in verse 27. Listen to this: *And the king answered and said to Rikayon, 'Thy name shall no more be called Rikayon, but Pharaoh, since thou exacted a tax from the dead; and he called his name Pharaoh. …And they made Rikayon Pharaoh the prefect under Oswiris king of Egypt, and Rikayon Pharaoh governed over Egypt, daily administering justice to the whole city, but Oswiris the king would judge the people of the land one day in the year, when he went out to make his appearance…. And all the inhabitants of Egypt greatly loved Rikayon Pharaoh, and they made a decree to call every king that should reign over them and their seed in Egypt, Pharaoh.*"

Con glanced up excitedly, "So Osiris ordained the first Pharaoh of Egypt. This is huge, if you overlay this information with Judaism. It was the pharaoh who enslaved the Israelites, remember? A picture of good versus evil begins to emerge, even as these stories lay atop one another."

"I'm following you," Rooter said, as the others nodded.

"Okay then, the future? I believe it has to do with Egypt, because the rest of this section in Malcolm's book speaks to the Tomb of Osiris. The Tomb of Osiris is located between the Sphinx and Great Pyramid in Giza, Egypt. The way I read it, Malcolm is indicating that something will be found there that will set off a chain of events that will bring about a major thing. Something huge."

"A major thing?" Rooter asked with a tone meant to scold Con for such an ambiguous description. "What the hell is that?"

"Exactly," Con said, "maybe hell. I have no idea, but I believe it has something to do with this epic story I've been revealing. It may bring about some cosmic shift having to do with our species and these ancient celestials that used to walk among us. Is it a war? Will it be an extinction event? Are we talking about the end of our civilization and the beginning of a new one? This is the crazy conclusion of the book, at least how I read it, anyway."

"You can't be serious," Anny said.

"Look, I'm not a religious person," Con put his hands up defensively. "I knew nothing about any of this six months ago, and there are plenty of days I wish I had my head buried in the sand somewhere. But I'm inclined to agree with Dotty here – something is happening, and it's global. Even bigger than global."

"And the next part of the story, the next clue, comes out of Egypt?" Sully asked.

"In my opinion, yes..."

Con paused, and leaned back in his chair, "In Malcolm's book there is as much documented about Osiris, and whatever comes after what will be found at his tomb, as there is about Marduk and Nimrod and the location that ended up being Alpha Kilo. I think Malcolm was an IT specialist who fell into *the* story of the human race. I think his journal is essentially the cypher that ties together ancient myth, present-day reality, and future prophetic events. With this book, the dots just connect. All of it makes sense. At this point we only know half the story and I can't tell you what's coming, only that it has something to do with the Osiris tomb in Giza."

"If that's the case, you can bet the Phantom's are already involved in Egypt too," Anny noted.

"That's right," Rooter agreed.

"Fair enough. Let's move on then. Anny, let's bring him up to speed on what we got in Chicago, shall we?"

Anny's information was straight forward compared to what Con shared. She did not know the technical details, but gave a wealth of information about Malcolm's device and why he was ordered to bring it to Iraq. She told them that Malcolm blew up the device when he killed himself with a grenade. This was actually new information to Dotty, but not Bax. She explained that Rasmussen got that intel from a friend of his in the Department of Defense. On condition of anonymity, the secret had been disclosed. Supposedly, Rasmussen never told anyone. But even as she finished, Bax piped in and told the Greek that his operational knowledge of the situation agreed, that Malcolm had blown himself up. Dotty had a hard time getting past the fact that he was unaware of how Malcolm died. The Greek always assumed that he was slaughtered by the Phantoms, no different than the others, one to the head and two to the chest.

During Anny's time to talk, Con made an interesting observation, "So, if the device pretty much neutralizes one's ideology, how was Malcolm able to blow himself up for his 'cause'?"

"What are you asking?" Rooter chided, frustrated again by the intelligence gap between he and Con. "Bring it with an English-tint, will ya?"

"I am speaking English, retard," but before Rooter could reload, he reworked his question. "I'm saying Malcolm obviously interacted with the open portal, right? We know this by the contents of his journal. To do that, he must have used the device on himself, thereby allowing his Life Essence to experience the other side of the portal, right? If that was the case, how come, upon his soul returning to his body, did he have the wherewithal to kill himself and destroy the device in such a selfless act? Shouldn't he have been, what ya say, 'brain neutral' at that point? The behavior doesn't make sense to me, that's all."

It was an interesting observation and nobody had an answer. Clearly, Malcolm interacted with the portal by virtue of the undefined third section of his journal. But how? The dimensions of the portal were described in the journal as *one foot by six inches, with the appearance of a rip in the air.* As Con pointed out, these dimensions were not large enough to physically climb through.

They moved on without an answer, and a few minutes later Anny wrapped up and they took a break. Rooter went outside for a smoke. It was getting late so Anny started looking though the kitchen for some dinner options.

From his seated vantage point, Sully watched as Bax and Father Abelemy went to the Gazebo together. Something about their interactions worried him. They were definitely secretive. *What was that look they shot each other earlier?*

He felt Anny's fingers on the back of his neck and turned around. "Hey, how are you holding up?" she asked.

"Okay, you?"

"Fine. It's a lot of info, right?"

"It is. Con amazes me with his processing power."

"Hey, what do you think I should make for dinner? It's getting late." He stood and followed her to the kitchen.

"Spaghetti is easy," he suggested.

"Think we should have a side salad or something?"

"Why? Just put something greenish in the sauce."

She rolled her eyes and smiled as he ventured back to the living room to stare at the gazebo. The two government workers spoke quietly for some time. It was unnerving, but Sully noticed that the rest of his team appeared oblivious to the covert interaction. After 20 minutes, Sully went back to the kitchen and suggested they go ahead and start dinner, as it appeared the Father and Bax had a lot to talk about.

She caught something in his tone. "You worried about them?"

"A little. Why be secretive? We're all risking our lives here, right?" She shrugged and filled a pot of water.

"So, about earlier, why did you ask me to join you on your walks?"

He laughed and pinched her side playfully, "It's *walks* now huh? I thought I just invited you to walk with me tomorrow?"

"You can't blame a girl for trying," she giggled.

She put the pot on the stovetop and lit the fire. He approached her from behind and put his hands on her shoulders, kneading gently. He whiffed that scent of hers as she closed her eyes and enjoyed the feel of his hands. He draped her shoulder length hair to one side to expose more of her neck. She especially liked it when his fingers crept up and down, just under the straps of her bra.

Suddenly, Con walked into the kitchen and they separated, awkwardly. The skinny third wheel grabbed a handful of peanuts from the counter and popped a few in his mouth. At first, it looked as if he was going to say something. But as he smacked on the peanuts, he simply smiled, winked at Sully, and walked away.

Anny bit her lip to hide the amusement, and glanced at her mortified boss. She tried to help him out of the embarrassing moment by saying, "What, can't a girl who works all day get a neck massage?"

It didn't work. Con's reply from another area of the house was, "Sure, just get a room next time."

She looked back at Sully and shrugged, "I tried. Maybe next time you should just own it and keep going. That way it won't be as awkward."

And awkward it was. He stood there trying to think of something to say, but couldn't. Finally, he grunted something totally off-point and left to see what was going on in the gazebo.

She started on the sauce and beamed with inner excitement. Things between them, she thought, were beginning to change for the better. Over boiling spaghetti noodles and bubbling marinara sauce, she thought about their planned walk-date, and hoped the relationship would progress. That led her to dream about what it would be like to share her life with his. She thought about traveling, planning a wedding, making a family. She blushed at the thought of a shared bubble bath, and romance by candlelight, then pushed the fantasy away for fear that someone might read her face and peek in on her dreams. *One way or another, things seem to be moving the right direction though!*

Solomon didn't learn anything from the duo at the gazebo. They told him they were chitchatting about old stuff they discussed back when they first met. He didn't buy that. They asked how he was doing and turned the conversation around to him. This annoyed Sully, but rather than try to pry into what was really going on, he decided to play ball. *I won't get anything out of these guys anyway.*

Even though the temperature was dropping, the team decided to eat in the gazebo. It was a nice afternoon, and everyone was tired of being cooped up in the house.

Splice

After dinner they reconvened in the living room with coffee and an assortment of chocolate-covered cookies. It was finally Father Abelemy's turn to tell what he uncovered the past 6 months.

"Well, I suppose I can start by announcing something that you've already figured out. Human-hybrids are not just strange entries in the ancient texts or theoretical science journals. They are living among us. Ironclad proof was found in the DNA samples you sent me, which conclude that your assailant was part man, part feline - - mountain lion, to be exact."

"I knew it," Rooter shouted, slamming his hand down on the arm of the chair. "That's why that thing moved so fast. I could-a beat its ass had it not cheated with special super powers!"

"I did beat its ass," Bax grinned at the PI.

"Now wait ju…"

"I'm sure you would have," Solomon interrupted, "because you're a tough guy and we all know it, but rather than show us your balls right now, let's let Dotty keep the floor."

Rooter put up his hands in a show of submission, and gestured for the Greek to continue. Anny and Con both chuckled quietly.

"If it's any consolation, they did wipe out a Delta squadron at Alpha Kilo. There's no shame in you surviving the attack."

Rooter nodded his appreciation of Dotty's support, as the Father then launched from the beginning. "Six months ago, Bax used Betty one final time to get me the DNA evidence you took off the assailant. She wasn't able to tell me what happened. She couldn't even tell me if any of you died, and that was the hardest part for me. Then, in late September, I got a comprehensive report on everything that happened to you guys that night from a liaison Bax set up through the SBS. That liaison asked me to unlock $65,000 for facility upgrades. This was pretty hard to hide, but we managed the transaction by going through the Bank of Baroda, as you guys may know. That was the last thing my case officer did for me before getting shipped to a field office overseas somewhere. In fact, if you were a week later with that request, I couldn't have pulled it off."

"While this was all happening, the surveillance on me was growing. For a couple weeks in late September, a black bearded, barrel chested fellow followed me everywhere. This guy was arrogant beyond belief and clearly didn't care that I saw him. He watched me in a manner that conveyed his authority. I managed a few pictures and had a friend of mine at Abbot Tech run them thorough facial recognition. The man was positively identified as Viktor Dultsev, a Polish national with U.S. citizenship. Crazy enough, a job he held in the early 2000's put him in Iraq at the time of Alpha Kilo. More to the point, he suddenly resigned a rather lofty post with NATO and disappeared just after the Alpha Kilo assault."

Dotty pulled out a file and handed it to Bax. "That's everything I have on Dultsev. He's a player. I'd bet the farm on it. But during his visit to the DC area, my case officer was transferred and I was no longer able to use Agency resources to do much digging on him. So, I've not been able to figure out who he works for or how high up the chain he actually goes."

"Was this guy one of those cat-dudes?" Rooter asked.

"No indication of that. Bax mentioned in the SBS report that your guy had vertical pupils. If you look at that picture you can see his eyes. Dultsev seems to be all human in the eyes."

"Were you ever able to run our Lion-O's pictures through facial recognition?" Rooter followed.

"I did, but the program returned no 100-percenters. There were a few plausible matches. The most interesting was an ex-KGB operative by the name of Velocros. Anyway, he was booted for bad behavior of some sort and given a dishonorable discharge. From the KGB, he presumably took up residence in a town called Kovalevka, about four hours west of Moscow. I guess he had a young wife and infant child back in '94. That's all my friend could find on him. My best working theory at this point is that the Phantoms, under the guidance of some well-funded and well-connected individuals, pick up highly trained riffraff who bottom out of military service by offering a life of redemption somehow. That's my theory, anyway."

"These kids agree to enlist," Bax continued. "They get a few genetic enhancements, and coupled with their training, become super solders. Makes some sense to me. The bigger question has to be, what other *weapons* are these Phantoms brewing up in their lab?"

"That's right," the Greek took over, "and be assured, these solders are being created in some far-away and off-the-grid lab somewhere. It would be impossible to hide this type of activity here. All WHO compliant, first-world governments have layers of accountability set up to oversee genetic laboratories. You can't move a stem cell without a government agency breathing down your neck. If that's not enough, we also have non-governmental organizations that monitor, whistle-blow, and report any perceived negligence or abuse."

"Tax-money can't be used to openly fund this type of R&D either," Rooter offered up. "You're right bro, no way this happened in the homeland."

"So," asked Sully, in the Father's general direction, "where you figure this thing came from? Any ideas?"

"I looked into it. The *stans,* and other areas of far-east Europe, are distinct possibilities. Uzbekistan. Kazakhstan, Georgia, Armenia, the Ukraine. The list goes on over there. But, based on access to R&D universities and infrastructure, I think South America, or even Mexico, is more likely. You could bury something with a few large bribes, but 'official' trade relations are cleaner. It's easier to move money through banking channels too. All that said, the best possible matches came down to a lab in Mexico City, one in Rio de Janeiro, and one outside of Caracas in Venezuela. Each lab is cozy with a university, but owned by some kind of shell-company. I also uncovered layers of incorporated entities birthed in places where the laws favor secrecy. So far, that's all I've got through my contacts."

"If you don't mind me asking, who are these guys at *Abbot Tech*?" Con jumped in.

"They are a private firm and DOD contractor. These guys are cozy with the Feds and contracted to build tech systems that support the U.S. military industrial complex."

"Are they like TB Optics?" asked Anny.

"No. TB's platform is laser development for research purposes. Abbot is all about nano-system engineering, advanced ballistics technologies, and virtual reality related applications. They were only founded in the 90's. You go figure how they got to where they are now? Like twelve different lab complexes scattered across the U.S. and a multi-billion dollar budget. They recruit and hire the best talent in the world."

"Forgive me, but I don't see any connections," Solomon noted, attempting to bring the conversation back. "Con's research leads us to look at the Middle East, Egypt in particular. Does anything you've uncovered happen to intersect with what Con's found?"

Dotty smiled, "Egypt. Not just Egypt, but specifically the Osiris shaft that Con was talking about. Let me explain. After your attacker's DNA analysis came back indicating he was a human-animal hybrid, I realized that our attempts to forensically investigate the other assumed Phantom cases were making a false assumption about the assailants. We were looking for human DNA. We were trying to extract human DNA from the evidence collected. When these fragments came back as likely matches to various animals, we figured the crime scene had been contaminated by carnivores and rodents."

Looking at Sully he said, "The reason I asked you if you had a cat is because we found traces of cat dander around the tub and throughout the apartment. But we found no cat food or litter box. It didn't make any sense until you guys sent me the DNA sample from the attacker."

"Anyway, I had an awful time maneuvering around prying eyes, but I went after the forensic evidence gathered at other assumed Phantom crime locations. I managed to acquire two samples from the Alpha Kilo scene and four from an assumed Phantom attack that happened in Egypt awhile back. The Alpha Kilo analysis came back as an exact match to…" He pointed at Rooter who said, "Lion-O! By the way, that's a Thunder Cats reference, for those of you who missed your Saturday cartoons."

"Exactly. And of the four samples from Egypt, one came back as a 98% probable match to your cat-man hybrid, while the others came back as variations of other animal DNA offshoots. But it was enough for me to investigate what happened in Egypt, and there I unearthed a wealth of interesting information."

Anny, Con, and Sully all repositioned to more comfortable positions. *This was getting good.*

"The Great Pyramid is connected to the Sphinx by a causeway cut directly into the earth between the two monuments. The causeway was first reported in the *London Daily Telegraph* on March 4, 1935. The article reports that an archeologist, Professor Selim Hassan, found not only the subway connecting the two monuments, but also the opening to a shaft that descended at an angle, about 33 feet to another landing point. According to the article, from this point, a vertical shaft descends straight down into the earth about 50 feet. This shaft opens to a large tomb area, with seven burial chambers, some of which still have sarcophagi in them."

"I think I've seen this on the Discovery Channel." Con said.

"Likely so," the Father assured, "it's been on TV many times. Anyway, interesting point of note, some of the sarcophagi in that tomb are said to be large enough to hold the body of a full-grown bull. Makes you think. The article goes on to describe the back of that tomb, where another vertical shaft connects and descends another 40 feet to what we now believe is the Tomb of Osiris. However, back in the 30's, they probed no further, because the final shaft was full of water."

"Water?" asked Sully.

"That's right," Con piped up. "The shaft was used as a well, and even a hidden swimming hole for adventurous local kids, until the mid-90's. This is when the Egyptian Government got interested and officially closed all access. Enter filmmaker, Boris Said."

Con stopped and gestured for the Father to continue, though it was perfectly clear that Con could tell the story, which he learned during his own research.

"Right, Boris Said. He was surveying Giza for a location to film a documentary in 1992, when one of the guards patrolling the area took him to the shaft and presented the well. The shaft was so intriguing, that in 1995, he partnered with Dr.

Joseph Shor, famous for conducting acoustic and radar surveys of subterranean passages below the Giza plateau. Together, they launched an investigation into this shaft. By 1995, they both had full permits issued by the Egyptian Government to conduct their survey."

"Together, they returned to the shaft in November of 1996. Upon descending into it, they found that a new water pump was set up and actively pumping water out of the shaft. At this point, the intermediate level and final vertical shaft had been revealed as a result. Since they couldn't get to the bottom of the second vertical shaft yet, they decided to suspend the inquiry and return a few months later, hoping that the water would continue to recede. This is where the story gets strange."

"They returned to the tomb in February of 1997, and as Con will tell you, this is all public record stuff here. When they returned, the water was gone and they found easy access to the lowest level. They go down with ropes and survey equipment. While Boris Said was brushing the dirt to make a level spot for his tripod, he comes across the smooth basalt lid of a sarcophagus. It turns out this was later identified as the sarcophagus belonging to the ancient god, Osiris."

"The two men and their team uncover the sarcophagus, and Mr. Said then tells his partner, Dr. Schor, to inform Egypt's Director General of the Giza Plateau, Dr. Hawass, about their discovery. But Schor informs Said that he could not, due to his permit being revoked just a week prior. When Said asked Schor why they revoked his permit, Schor explains that no reason was given. It was unexpectedly revoked after he informed the Egyptian authorities of his intent to return to the shaft."

"So, the men decide to set up their instrumentation anyway and conduct a radar survey of the ground under the Osiris sarcophagus. According to both researchers, radar imaging revealed a tunnel that started about 24 feet below that huge sarcophagus lid. The tunnel is said to have an arched ceiling, extending at a 10% angle in the direction of the Sphinx. It's at least 825 feet in length. Ultimately, they used a pulley system to move the multi-ton sarcophagus lid and start digging to unearth the hidden tunnel. However, they were found out and deported by the authorities before successfully unearthing the next tunnel. Neither of these men has been allowed to return."

"That's nuts," Rooter said.

"Crazier still," Con piped in, "after the men were deported and the national staff members thrown in jail, the United States military showed up and assumed containment responsibilities around the site of the shaft. That's never been done before, except during active war, like in the case of Alpha Kilo."

"Com'on, really?"

"That's actually true," the Father confirmed. "All of a sudden, in the months and years after the two men were deported, the Director General of the Giza plateau, Dr. Hawass, was given lucrative contracts from U.S. government and business interests, and promoted to a cabinet position within the Egyptian government."

"Why?" Sully asked the obvious question.

"Exactly. Why indeed? Dr. Hawass then embarked on a global information tour, stopping at every western University with an archeology department, and opening every seminar with the words, 'I'm here to disprove to you the notion that, deep within the Osiris shaft, there exists a hidden tunnel, or evidence of an ancient, celestial civilization.'"

Anny grabbed at her neck, as the hairs suddenly stood on-end. It was all so hard to believe.

"The evidence of Said's find," the Father continued, "was never allowed to be published because it was collected without permit. Said, for years, tried to publish it legally, but was unsuccessful. Then, in January of 2002, he decided to publish his evidence on his website without permission or accreditation. The evidence consisted of pictures and video of his crew going in and out of the hole they were digging under the sarcophagus lid, as well as the radar proof of the tunnel below."

The Father paused and then said, "Within 24 hours of his publication, everything disappeared. Scarier still, Said was found dead, not one month later, on the 24th of March, 2002. Officially, cause of death was liver cancer, but I couldn't find a single shred of evidence to support that claim, not in medical records or otherwise. Don't believe me? Google it."

"How do you know his proof was published?"

"Because a friend at the NSA sent me the date stamp entry for the exact moment the evidence was seized and classified."

"Christ almighty," Rooter sat back and stretched. "So where do we stand with regard to the shaft now?"

"Good question. After Schor and Said's '97 survey and subsequent deportation, Dr. Hawass personally took over the site, which was under U.S. military control for about six months. Hawass brought in his own experts to dispel the theory of a second tunnel, did the media dance, etc. From 1998 to 2003, the Osiris shaft was protected by Egyptian military, and in 2003, Egypt let the water back in. Egypt, to my knowledge, has not issued a permit to look at the shaft to anyone since 1997. This shaft may be the most inaccessible, locked-down place on the planet at this point."

"It's funny how much of this is actually a matter of public record," Con mused. "On the internet you'll see the videos where Dr. Hawass, back in the late '90's, brought attention to the shaft with camera crews from National Geographic. The Father's right though, in the early 2000's, his tune changes and he goes on that information tour, affirmatively telling the world that no tunnel or evidence exists regarding an ancient civilization. It's pretty wild."

"All this history brings us to the here and now," Dotty said. "On January 25, 2011, a revolution started in Egypt. Known as the Arab Spring, it dispelled longtime Egyptian President Hosni Mubarak. January 28, 2011 was called 'The Friday of Rage' in Egypt, as Mubarak brought his top officials from all over the country to Cairo for a meeting to plan how they might dispel the protestors and demonstrators. There, in a conference room inside the *Mugamma* -- which is an enormous government complex in the heart of Cairo -- eight top Mubarak lieutenants were shot dead, assassinated. The incident was never publicized. The party line was that the men were sent into protective hiding due to the riots. You'll be interested to know, each man caught one to the head and two to the chest."

"Mubarak was not there when it happened. The reason I know what happened is because Mubarak asked the U.S. to investigate the murders. Mubarak no longer trusted the military apparatus in Egypt. He supposed they might be planning a coup d'état. As history would later prove, his suspicions were spot on."

"So, that was a Phantom operation in Egypt?" asked Anny.

"Yes, evidence I got from FBI, code-named *cabinet murders,* is what I sent to my lab contact. In a nutshell, we have smoking gun evidence that shows the Phantoms were not only a party to the events at Alpha Kilo, but were participants in some Arab Spring revolutions, including Egypt. Hawass is now on thin ice and may be thrown out of office. The current acting head of State, Husain Tantawi, is coming under heavy pressure to throw him in jail for his alleged crimes."

"What's with the vitriol toward Hawass?" asked Sully. "It makes no sense, he's just the country's head archeologist, right?"

"True. Only way it makes sense is that the people are merely puppets being controlled by a puppet master somewhere." The Father sipped on a lukewarm cup of coffee and continued, "In any event, the fact that Tantawi has resisted pressure from the mob, and kept Hawass in play thus far, indicates strongly that Tantawi shares Mubarak's feelings about foreign eyes on the Osiris shaft. You can bet whoever is in control of the Phantoms is all over this upcoming election."

"I have a question," Con said, to which Dotty nodded. "Do we think there's a chance someone has already found whatever is referenced in Malcolm's journal?"

"That's a good question," Dotty answered. "I honestly don't know, but if I had to guess, I'd say no. If they found and removed whatever Malcolm was talking about, why keep the shaft so locked down? In that case, what would be the big deal? What we do know is that an entity with considerable influence has gone to the trouble of sparking a regional revolution, which has ousted President Mubarak, has Dr. Hawass on the ropes, and as soon as Egypt's elections conclude in June, will usher in the next regime. A regime that I suspect might be more sympathetic to the Phantom's agenda. Maybe even a member of their order. Who knows?"

"This is why you decided now was a good time for a visit?" Solomon asked.

"That's right. Something's happening in Egypt and I needed to know if any of your research pointed to Giza. I suspected that it might. In light of all this information, I need to impose on you all once again, and ask for a favor."

The Greek frowned and looked at Rooter. "At first, I was going to ask you to go to Egypt, Rooter. Your background makes you a suitable candidate for surveillance work. I was going to ask you to take up residence there and keep an eye on that shaft in Giza. But your back is still pretty bad. In spite of the painkillers, you're obviously still wincing and squirming. So you're out. Con needs to stay here and run the analysis."

He then looked at Sully and Anny, who were sitting next to one another on the sofa. "You two will need to go. It would work pretty well if you went as a married couple. Say, on a honeymoon visit to the ruins in Egypt."

Everyone looked at them. Anny could feel the blood rushing to blush her complexion. Solomon leaned forward and gestured toward Anny, "You want us to pretend to be married huh? Why?"

"Because the cover is perfect. Anyone looking for you is looking for a single guy named Solomon Keys. We'll get you new papers, a new name and identity. I have a contact at the U.S. Passport Agency in DC. We'll work the back story and get you on your way as soon as possible. That is, if you're up for it."

Anny made it clear that she was up for it. Solomon put up a negative front at first, but his anxiety had more to do with the fake-marriage cover story than it did going to Egypt to conduct a spy mission.

Truthfully, they were both tired of being cooped up in the safe house, so the idea of traveling under the freedom of an alias was appealing. By the time everyone retired for the night, Sully had come around to the idea and signed off. As soon as he did, his mind became a blitz of prep and contingency planning, and the aching heart that had burdened him so horribly the past few months was suddenly replaced by a new agenda. It was a welcome change.

CHAPTER 30
Toronto

Friday, May 18, 2012

They left the guesthouse before the first gleam of sunlight, heading for Toronto, Canada. Bax drove, while Solomon stared out the window of the passenger side. Anny was fast asleep in the back.

One of the Greek's contacts was going to meet them in Buffalo, NY. His job was to drive them through border customs and deliver them to Toronto Pearson International Airport.

The logistics came together in two months. The first challenge was getting the Social Security Administration to go along with issuing new numbers without proper paperwork from the CIA. Predictably, it was a tall order. Father Abelemy tried to call in a few favors, but struck out. After exhausting his resources, Rooter took a stab at it and got a hold of an old contact. The contact personally called the Director of the SSA on behalf of the crew, and asked that non-registered, temporary SSN's be issued for Roger and Ruth Madison. Just like that, they had their new numbers. Rooter was hailed as a genius. The Director put his job, and even incarceration, on the line to comply with the request, which begged the question, what did Rooter's contact have on him? They'd never know.

Once the request was accepted, the turnaround was double time because the order had come from the top of the SSA. On March 8th, Bax drove Solomon and Anny to a locally owned stationery store in Edgewater where they got new passport photos. After that errand, he picked up the newly minted social security cards.

On the 9th of March, with passport photos and social security cards in hand, Bax delivered packets to Dotty's contact at the U.S. Passport Agency. By the 19th, they had a fake marriage certificate, fake passports, Maryland-issued fake driver licenses, and fake social security numbers all corresponding to Mr. Roger and Mrs. Ruth Madison.

After securing their papers, they applied for multi-entry visas for Egypt. They didn't know if or when the Phantoms would appear, but the odds favored them showing up at the Osiris Tomb during, or just after, the Egyptian presidential elections in June. They applied for the visas on March 21st, but because the Egyptian consulate was in such disarray, this part took time. They all knew it would.

They applied for their visas through a travel agency attached to a religious non-profit organization that Keys & Associates represented years ago. There were no *official* links between the travel agency and the organization. It was merely a partnership of convenience. Missionaries had an easier time getting into certain countries when traveling under the banner of vacation, rather than proselytization. The travel agency could charge a hefty fee for this service. The "Madisons" needed visas quickly and quietly.

The visas were granted on Thursday, May 10th, after which the travel agency booked them on a May 18th flight out of Toronto.

Anny found a Starwood Hotel, located a mile from the pyramid complex on the Giza Plateau. It was called *Le Méridien*, and seemed like the type of place honeymooners might stay. Solomon strongly advocated for a suite, with a separate seating area. He campaigned for it on the basis of honeymooners going all-out, but privately knew that having an extra room would ease the tensions around their sleeping arrangement, which he tried not to think about.

Anny spent a lot of time online getting a handle on the Egyptian customs and culture in the weeks leading up to their departure. She'd never traveled to a Muslim part of the world, so she had no idea what type of clothing to pack. After reading the reports on Tripadvisor.com, she felt comfortable packing anything for time spent around the resort, but decided to go with a layered top and pants or long skirt for when they ventured out. At one point Solomon asked her what he should pack and she answered, with some amount of jealousy, "Guys can wear whatever the hell they want."

Bax only stopped when he needed to gas up the car or let his passengers stretch their legs. They drove through fast-food places when they got hungry, but did not stop to eat. They hit morning traffic outside Baltimore and were delayed slightly due to a bad accident just south of Sunbury, Pennsylvania. The rest of their trip was smooth, and at just before 1 pm, Bax pulled off the highway at the Niagara Street exit in Buffalo, New York. It was the last exit before the Peace Bridge Plaza into Canada. He parked at an industrial building on the corner of Niagara and Carolina. Dotty's contact, Lee, waited patiently in his blue Chevy Suburban.

Bax gave Solomon a man's handshake and Anny got a peck on the cheek before he tossed their suitcases into Lee's Chevy. Lee asked that they both sit in the back until they were on Canadian soil, at which time he'd welcome a passenger up front with him if they wanted. He said it was a surveillance and protocol thing.

Lee maneuvered his vehicle onto the bridge that spanned the northernmost tip of Lake Erie. On the Canadian side, he entered Customs Lane 3, which was not the shortest line available. They chugged forward until finally reaching the booth. Lee presented a card and paid the fee. A young border agent looked inside the vehicle, and then casually waved them through without a word.

"That was easy," Solomon said. "I could have sworn he saw us in here."

"We do it for VIPs all the time. Those guys in the booth know what's going on. They take a cursory look inside the vehicle as a show for the cameras watching them, but that's all. Some of us have authorization to cargo people through without harassment. We do the same for the Canucks on our end."

"Great," Solomon looked at his traveling companion. "Well, Mrs. Madison, soon we'll be on a jet plane, huh?"

She made an exaggerated face, grabbed his hand reflexively, and cupped it. As soon as she did it, she felt child-like and self-conscious, but rather than pull-away, he reciprocated by interlocking his fingers with hers. She bit her lip, trying to hold back that persistent smile. He had come to know that expression of hers, the bite-lip-and-look-away-in-attempt-to-hide-my-true-joy expression. It was a cute little thing she did, perfect and unique to her, a mannerism he grew to like a lot.

Past customs, Lee asked if they wanted to stop for lunch. They declined, so he sped right along. Anny was delighted to have Solomon in the back of the Suburban holding her hand. *God, I'm 27-years-old and look at me, acting like a love-struck schoolgirl.*

CHAPTER 31
Spy Games

Monday, May 21, 2012

Bax pulled Anny's Civic onto the street and glanced at Father Abelemy. The Greek was fidgeting nervously in the passenger seat. The Brit thought about offering a word of encouragement, but there was really nothing he could say to ease the old Spook's tension. The next 24 hours were going to be interesting, that much was certain.

Unknown to the others, Braxton knew how much Dotty compromised in coming to the guesthouse three months ago. It was a decision that bordered on reckless, and one that might come back to haunt them all.

From Braxton's point of view, established intermediaries should have been used to pass information, as opposed to Dotty bringing it personally. If nobody else, the Greek could have used Bax's SBS link. Intermediaries, though time consuming and inconvenient, would have kept Dotty under Phantom surveillance. Now, it was assumed that the Phantoms felt the pressure – they were pushed into a corner.

"As it is," Bax argued, "what's now stopping them from a rip-and-beat until they get the intel you possess? The only thing that kept them at bay before was concern for who you might talk to and what you might know. By slipping out of their net, they now realize you're in communication with *someone* and they'll want to get you off the street, pronto. We've lost our tactical edge."

"I was running out of time, Bax. It would have taken a month to get your guy vetted and I knew we were going to have to spend months organizing fake papers for whoever we sent down there. It would have taken too long and we might have missed our narrow window of opportunity. We needed our own eyes down there on that Osiris shaft. I'll just have to live with the consequences."

This, of course, was what they were debating in the gazebo the night Dotty arrived. Though they disagreed about his decision to come, they both agreed on two distinct points. First, Solomon had the makings of a great spy. Second, this operation to try and reinsert Dotty back under the Phantoms' surveillance net would be kept from the others, just in case things went terribly wrong. That day had finally come, the day they hoped to drop Dotty back into regular life in and around Washington, DC.

North of DC, in the city of Greenbelt, they exited the highway and pulled into the parking lot of a Hilton Garden Inn. There, they ditched Anny's car and called a cab. The dispatcher let them know that it would be 45 minutes, so they grabbed some lunch at a nearby KFC. About an hour later, the cab arrived and they both got into the back seat.

"I live west of North Portal Estates, know the neighborhood?" Dotty asked the cabbie.

"Yeah, on which side of Beach?"

"Just west, literally off the 410."

"You bet."

The cabbie blasted some Elvis-era oldies as he sped west. The radio was a few ticks louder than the considerable noise of road and wind that assaulted them from the open windows. Dotty took a deep breath and moved his fingers though his shaggy hair.

Bax wore a dark brown newsboy cap, sunglasses, dark jeans, and a checkered blazer. He carried a dark green Timbuk2 canvas bag, which contained a few spy-man essentials. He concealed a firearm in a shoulder harness and a wad of cash in his pocket. He carried no identification. He dropped his entire phone's memory onto a SIM card before they left, and installed a blank one. Now, only a few generic apps remained on his phone. Any contact numbers of importance were committed to memory.

The cab zigzagged in and out of traffic as though they were in a hurry, which frankly, they weren't. They approached Dotty's neighborhood in record time. He instructed the driver to turn north on Curtis, then east onto Kerry Lane. His house was on the right, but he let the driver pass right by so he could get a good look. Pretending he wasn't paying attention, he asked the driver to loop back around using Glendale. By looping around Glendale, Bax was able to have a look at the other houses in the neighborhood, and find a suitable staging location of his own.

The neighborhood was thick with springtime vegetation, which Bax knew may or may not work to their advantage. Father Abelemy revealed that the Phantoms normally sat in a generic, burgundy colored, Dodge minivan when they staked his house.

Since the New Year, the Phantoms seemed to care very little about whether Dotty saw them watching from their minivan. Their style had become brazen, cocky even. When Dotty slithered out from under their net, their pride was undoubtedly wounded. The question was, how wounded? Once they realized the Greek was back, their opportunity for revenge was at hand. How would they choose to play that hand?

Once the driver pulled to a stop, Dotty exited the vehicle, gathered his belongings, and walked to the front door, alone. Braxton remained in the cab with his hat low on his brow, just in case someone was watching the house. Once his companion disappeared through the front door, Bax instructed the cabbie to drop him off at the Columbia Country Club, which was less than a mile to the west.

The million dollar question: *How would the Phantoms deal with the return of the Greek?* They might just kill him quickly and quietly. However, that was less likely than abduction and interrogation. They probably had no idea how much the Greek knew or who he told, and that would be considered valuable intel. They may just put him back under close surveillance, although tactically speaking, that made the least sense. Therefore, Bax and Dotty planned for one of the first two likely scenarios.

The plan was for Dotty to give Bax about 45 minutes to get into position, then call into his office and give a quick and casual report of his activities the past three months. If their suspicions about the appointed case officer were correct, the Phantoms would arrive at his house within an hour after the call.

The clubhouse was on the northwest corner of Connecticut Ave and the 410, known locally as the East-West Highway. Bax paid the cab driver and threw on his shoulder bag. He walked at a brisk pace north on Connecticut, the golf course on his left and Dotty's neighborhood extending east on his right. A quarter- mile up Connecticut, he came to Dunlop Street. When light traffic offered him an opportunity, he ran across the avenue and jogged east on Dunlop toward Dotty's house. He knew, as a result of the planning portion of this operation, that Dunlop turned into Kerry Lane just before the residence. The jog was less than a mile. Bax got more cautious as he drew near the home.

He stopped running when he got close to Dotty's place. For the most part, the Father's house fit into the neighborhood well, except for the brown and weedy front yard. The subdivision was solid middle-class, but compared to other manicured fronts, his was an eyesore. It indicated that nobody lived there, at least for some time. Dotty's house was split-level, with the front door on the half-landing and the garage to the lower-left. Bax now stood directly across the street.

Bax pulled out his phone and pretended to check an email. He quickly glanced at the large window just to the right of Dotty's front door. The signal was for Dotty to appear in the window once every two minutes until Bax saw him, this was the sign that he was okay and everything was progressing according to plan. A minute passed. Then two. Then three. Something was wrong. Braxton closed his phone and dropped it in his inside chest pocket and was about to cross the street when the curtain moved and Dotty appeared.

Bax turned and began walking up the street as they planned, but something was off.

Was it just a sense, or did he actually see something? In his peripheral vision he thought he saw something to the left of the front door. Glancing, he saw horizontal blinds in a second floor window above the garage. Did they move ever so slightly just as the Greek appeared in the window? He didn't know for sure, but his spy-gut was churning. Something was askew.

It wasn't just the blinds. Father Abelemy had a strange countenance in the window. Bax couldn't put his finger on it, but years of training told him to never write off circumstantial evidence as coincidence. *Coincidences do not exist.*

The curtain was flipped open too quickly. *That's not how Dotty would open the curtain for a reveal.* His posture in the window was too rigid. *Was Dotty being supported from behind?* Dotty was late. *Dotty is never late when executing a planned schedule.*

Bax walked with casual indifference as he analyzed the data. Quickly, he was 90% certain that the Phantoms were already on top of his friend. *Now, what to do about it?*

The Brit rounded a corner and was out of sight of Dotty's house when he heard, in the distance behind him, the faint sound of a garage door opening. Instinct told him to hide. He was now on Glendale, but ducked behind some tall shrubbery that adorned the neighbor's front yard. Just as he suspected, a maroon minivan drove by. He saw two individuals in the front, but the tint on the windows blocked his view of the back.

As soon as the van passed, Bax cut through the properties to get back to the house across the street from Dotty's. Crouching low in the cover of some bushes along the driveway, he hoped to God that anyone home would not see him and come out. He watched Dotty's house across the street with an unblinking eye. He was trying to ascertain whether anyone was dropped off when the van came crawling up Dunlop from the west. The garage door across the street opened once again and the van entered. *That answers that,* he thought.

In an effort to gain better understanding about the layout of Dotty's home, he circled the property in a wide sweep. He found a better staging location behind Dotty's home and repositioned there. The new hiding spot was between three properties and lots of trees, and had an unobstructed view into Dotty's backyard. Once settled, he decided he was going to need some help if he wanted to get right up to the house in the middle of the afternoon.

Using his cell phone, he opened the Domino's website and submitted an online order for two large pizzas. He sent them to the Greek's address. He used a pre-paid debit card to complete the order. It wasn't a great distraction, but hopefully enough to serve his purpose.

He pulled compact binoculars from his shoulder pack and took a visual inventory of the house. Everything matched the details provided by the Greek during the planning phase of this risky op.

While surveying, Bax consistently saw a muscular, African American, standing about 6'6". *This must be a third Phantom. The first two in the minivan were both Caucasian.* After fifteen minutes of watching the windows, he made the calculated guess that there were only three bad guys. Strangely, the men inside did not appear to pay much attention to the back of the house. Bax only saw the black guy peer out the rear sliding glass door on one occasion.

Putting down the binoculars, he grabbed a small plastic case containing nanotech communications equipment. This technology was a bit outdated in the spy world, but it would do just fine. He put one skin-toned device in his right ear canal and took two other components out of the case. They were small, about the circumference of a pen and only a half-inch long. On one end was a tiny suction cup with miniscule, barely visible wires protruding out of the center. The other end was like a twist-top. Bax turned the twist-top one click. That activated the tiny transmitters, and assured him that everything worked.

Even though it was now outdated, the tech associated with his *Comm Unit* was state-of-the-art when issued. The components could transmit audio on a much higher frequency than older base-band communications solutions used by militaries. The earpiece housed a very powerful digital processing chip that transposed the signals down to the audible domain. The nano-chip was built to carry out other complex tasks, such as automatic gain control, loudness limitation, and soft squelch neutralization. By transmitting on such a high frequency, Bax's communication system was also immune to electromagnetic interference.

He glanced at the clock on his phone and knew that the delivery person would be driving up any minute. He took one final look through the binoculars and then got in position. There were two partial obstructions on his way to the back wall of the house. He would use both for cover along the way. The first was a thick tree trunk and the other was a hedge that protruded into Dotty's yard from the neighbor's fence area.

After a few more minutes, Bax heard a car pull into the driveway on the other side of the house. The Black Phantom stood up abruptly from his seated vantage point in the living room. Bax noted the geometry of the shadows cast by the sun and decided on his path.

He made it to the first obstruction with no problem. He dipped his head slightly to the left and saw nobody at the window next to the back door. He was about to run to the next obstruction when he decided to wait another five seconds. It was good intuition, as another Phantom conducted a quick security sweep, moving from left to right in the house toward the garage. It seemed amateurish to Bax that he stopped to look out of every window as he went, clearly telegraphing his path. When the coast was clear, Bax ran to the second obstruction, but just before he got there, he decided to make the entire run straight to the house.

When he got to the rear wall, he heard the doorbell ring two consecutive times and a muffled voice say, "Just go answer the door and tell him to get the hell out of here."

Bax was crouched just outside a bathroom window. He could tell by the frame's thin, rectangular shape. If he was running the show, his prisoner would be staged in the lower level of the house, probably in the room next the door that leads to the garage. It was clearly the most isolated room. As he looked along the length of the house, he saw a window built into a well depression. He needed to get there, but couldn't risk jogging past the back door, so he scanned for another route. The roof overhang was about seven feet above him. There was a rain gutter and downspout coming off at the corner. He used the drainage pipe to quickly climb onto the roof. Once on the roof, he softly scampered to the other side of the house.

There were fewer windows on this side, but the drop was considerably more treacherous, 15 feet, at least. Bax took note of the large tree in front of him. There was a less-than-substantial branch stretching in his direction. He thought about it for a minute and then looked for another way down. The branch seemed to be his only option. He winced and jumped towards the center of the trunk. He grasped for the branch and it started to give way. He expected the branch wouldn't support his weight, so he just used the grip to propel himself further into the tree, eventually falling into the trunk with a series of cracks and a thud.

He felt the sting of a few scratches and bruises, but didn't stop to assess the damage. He swooped down the tree and jumped the last six feet before taking cover behind the corner of the house. Next he heard the delivery boy mumble a string of obscenities as he climbed into his car and drove away. One Phantom came to the back door and stepped outside briefly, then someone must have said something because he turned and went back inside saying, "Hang on, I'll show you."

When the coast was clear, Bax crawled to the window well and peered down into the first-floor family room. He saw Dotty tied to a chair. He didn't look good. Not like he was terribly beat up, but he looked drugged. He was sweating profusely and had a queer look on his face – half smile, half frown. He glanced to his left and saw the Brit outside the window. His facial expression changed, suddenly more serious. The Greek nodded his head back and forth, as if saying, *No*

The Greek's countenance was disturbing. Braxton frowned as he stuck one of his transmitters to the top corner of the window. He gave Dotty the thumbs up and was gone, returning to the back corner of the house. He needed his second transmitter to get audio from the more central part of the house, the living room by the front door, but that's where the bad guys were congregating. The Greek must have had an idea what Braxton was trying to do, because as clear as day, Bax could hear him yell, "Yey, I need-e du use-a de potty. Yey, I need-e du use-a der protty!"

The slurred speech was not good. Bax correctly assumed that they gave him some sort of a hypnotic medication, which begged the question, *how much had the Greek already disclosed?* The commotion downstairs led the Phantoms to see what was going on. Through his earpiece, Bax could tell that at least two of them had approached Dotty and were making fun of him. Bax used the opportunity to circle around to the front of the house and stick a second transmitter on the window next to the front door. From there, he abandoned his position and retreated back to his staging spot in the woods. He decided to listen and wait.

CHAPTER 32
Dust Bowl

Monday, May 21, 2012

Spaghetti-minded is how Anny defined her state of consciousness upon arriving in Cairo. Their flight out of Amsterdam was delayed six hours, which made a long trip even longer. Solomon knew the feeling of jetlag, but the *spaghetti-minded* phenomenon was a whole new thing for the girl from Kansas.

It was 3 am. Both of them were dopey in the head, but wide-awake. Anny skimmed the pictures of a magazine in the bedroom, while Sully watched CNN in the suite's living room. He thought about ordering food, but decided against the risk of early morning ethnic fare. He opted for his last granola bar instead.

Earlier that day, they saw a portion of Cairo from inside the taxi cab. It was a blur. The buildings blitzed by as they traversed the late morning hubbub en route to the hotel. They passed nice neighborhoods and poor neighborhoods, but the city as a whole had an undeniable spirit. They both agreed it had an air of sophistication, almost as if Cairo considered itself exceptional among its Middle Eastern and North African neighbors. Sure, it lacked the sleek glass skyscrapers and master planned communities prevalent among the *Nuevas Ciudades* that dotted the oil-rich countries, but the aura of Cairo was socially progressive, academic, and cosmopolitan.

"Hey," Solomon called through the door. His thumb was clicking to a rhythm as the TV channels cycled through. He lost interest in CNN. He lost interest in TV altogether. He was ready to get up and do something.

"What's up baby-cakes?" She started calling him baby-cakes in Amsterdam, claiming that real honeymooners always called each other by pet names. Initially, Solomon refused to play the game. However, after a couple days of fun pressure from Mrs. Madison, he relented and told her she could call him whatever she wanted.

"Since we're both up, I think we should go ahead and consummate our marriage." Sully listened for anything through the thick silence. *What, no baby-cakes? No smart remark?* Chuckling to himself, he walked to the door and peeked in at her. She was biting her lip, go figure. She looked at him and realized it was a stupid joke, "Just kidding."

"You're hysterical," she turned back to her magazine.

"In all seriousness, I was trying to figure out if I was hungry. I'm not actually certain that I am, but I'm bored to death and was wondering if you'd like to accompany me as I troll for something to eat in the main building."

"Sure," she slipped some sweatpants over her shorts and slid into her sandals.

They found a 24-hour restaurant called 'Latest Recipe' and asked for a table. The employee frowned on sweatpants, but ushered them in, saying, "It's fine, it's late."

The menu was eclectic, offering everything from Chinese favorites to French delicacies. Solomon settled on a bowl of French onion soup and a sandwich, while Anny ordered a salad. They both got Heinekens. They managed to kill so much time gabbing back and forth, that at around 5:45 am, their server asked them to leave so they could set up the breakfast buffet.

By the time they got back to their room, both of them were one-half drunk, other-half jetlagged, and ready to sleep. Knowing that it would be easy to sleep the day away, Solomon scheduled a wake-up call for 10 am. The strategy was to push through one more day until a more appropriate bedtime and get the jetlag under control.

"So," Anny said, gesturing to the bedroom, "how do we do this?"

"You take the bed," he offered. "I'll take the sofa out here. We need to have a longer discussion about us, but I'm a zombie. I'd rather have it when we're more alert."

"Okay."

"That work for you?"

"Sure, but it's not really fair that I get the bed. Want to change it up every other night or something?"

"Nope. Sofa works great," he said as he adjusted the cushions.

"Hey Solomon?" her tone was more serious, so he looked back at her. "I do want to have that talk with you. Would you be willing to commit to a time?"

He frowned sheepishly. His intentions were never to blow her off, but in essence, that's exactly what he was doing. If he was honest with himself, he had blown her off for nearly half a year.

"Of course. How about over dinner tonight?"

"That's great. Thanks, baby-cakes." She smiled and disappeared into the bedroom.

During plenty of dead time from Toronto to Cairo, Sully thought long and hard about how to engage the *talk*. Admittedly, he was not good at this type of thing. The fact that he now committed to an actual time to start *talking* did nothing for his attempt at sleep. But eventually he managed to drift off.

And then, the loud shrieking chime of the phone – *How could it be 10 am already?*

Sully jolted awake, but there was no movement from the bedroom. He waited a couple minutes until he knocked on the door and softly called to his traveling companion. Still nothing. He cracked the door and found strewn across the bed a single beam of bright light coming through the center crack of a heavy curtain hanging over the window. Anny was still sound asleep, one leg out of the covers and everything else underneath. The insufferable ring of the telephone had not fazed her in the slightest. He called her name, a little louder this time. Nothing. Awkwardly, he came to her bedside and put his hand on her shoulder. Only then did she open an eye.

"It can't be 10 am already," she growled.

"It's not. It's like 10:20. You want a few more minutes or you want me to open those curtains?"

"You better open the curtains. I'll never get up otherwise."

The flood of white light jarred their senses, but served its purpose.

By noon, the couple ventured outside the hotel for the first time. The sun was hot and the air was dry and dusty. There was a crisp rot heavy in the air. It was the smell of millions of people doing life together in the desert. The locals were generally kind and courteous, but here and there, a young showoff would catcall or say something they didn't understand. Anny read that it was wise to wear sunglasses because making eye contact with a member of the opposite sex was considered flirtatious in the Middle East. Under her glasses, she noticed that just about everywhere she looked, men were trying to make eye contact with her. She grabbed Solomon's hand and interlocked her fingers with his. As soon as she did, the wandering eyes looked elsewhere for unclaimed domain.

The hotel concierge told them that if they walked along Alexandria Desert Road, then west on Al Ahram until it dead-ended, a guard would accept $20 and let them into the Necropolis from that northern entry point. This was supposedly a much shorter walk than going all the way around to the main entry, where the Great Sphinx sits on the easternmost edge of the Giza plateau.

They decided to give it a whirl. It was less than a half-mile to the junction, but by the time they got there, both of them were perspiring heavily under the heat. Specs of dust clung noticeably to the sweat on their brows. Just as the concierge said, the guard took the $20 bribe (*official fee, who knows*) and let them walk down the less obvious continuation of Al Ahram Street that led all the way up to the north face of the Great Pyramid.

The heat radiating off the ground was remarkable. It was as if the ground itself was a heat source. The slight breeze only served to move the hot air around, and brought very little relief. Although they brought waters from the hotel minibar, they were each dry by the time they reached the southern side of the Great Pyramid. It was smoldering and they considered turning around, but saw in the distance their version of a desert oasis, the main gate. There, it was obvious that venders were selling all sorts of touristy-stuff, including bottled water.

The Giza Plateau is home to three large pyramids and a number of smaller structures and ruins. It is also home to the Great Sphinx. A sense of awe is heightened by the fact that all the ancient structures are elevated, extending upward from the base plateau. As the compass turns, a visitor sees two starkly different views at Giza. If oriented to the south or west, the scene features ruins and a barren desert backdrop for as far as the eyes can see. However, if a visitor is oriented to the north or east, the scene features a modern city skyline and the yellow haze generated by a massive population. It's like passing between ancient and modern worlds in a matter of a few steps.

Sully and Anny noticed a healthy number of 'Antiquities Police' dressed in cheese-ball white uniforms with gold tassels, armed with ragtag automatic weapons. They chuckled at the number of AK-47's with noticeable duct tape holding something together. The political climate in Egypt was still tense, and having suffered a number of raids at the local museums and historical sites during the protests, the security apparatus was at attention. In addition to the Antiquities Police, there were more serious guards lurking in the corners. These guys looked a bit more menacing. Solomon decided to keep a low profile and steer clear of these obvious professionals.

At the main gate, they found a hullabaloo of activity. There were tourists and tour guides going every direction. There were rows of hollering merchants trying to peddle their wares. Anny immediately noticed the alarming number of western tourists that disregarded Egyptian decorum. Many women were wearing short-shorts and tank tops. She felt mildly ashamed of the arrogant bravado of a few, and lamented the message it sent. *Of course, the vendors and security guards didn't seem to mind.* Among an array of languages, the primary two were Arabic and English. French was a close third.

They approached a shopkeeper who looked about fifteen. He was manning an ice chest full of sodas and water. The Coca-Colas were enticing, but they each settled on a liter of ice-cold, bottled water. Solomon popped the lid and splashed some on his hands and face. It felt great, but like iron powder to a magnet, the dust clung to his skin all the more. He tried to wipe himself down, but soon realized the cleanliness war was lost, at least until he got back to the hotel.

Anny ventured to a nearby clothing rack. Sully took a few chugs of water. Suddenly, the boy shopkeeper jumped in Sully's face, trying to tell him something in broken English.

"I'm sorry, I don't understand…"

"No, no, look, see," the boy shouted and pointed past his shoulder.

Solomon turned around and saw a man looking at him from across the street. He was tall, maybe six and a half feet. He wore a cream-colored, full-length cloak, and his face was hidden in the shadow under a long hood. He appeared to be staring straight at the attorney, evoking a sense of immediate unease, even fear. Sully's heart rate quickened.

Turning back to the young merchant, and in a desperate voice that was louder than the ruckus around him, Solomon said, "Who is that?" The boy shrugged in return and looked baffled himself.

Sully turned back around to take another look, but now a tour bus obstructed his view across the street. When the bus passed, the man was gone. A chill went up his spine as his eyes darted back and forth, searching the area for the cream-colored cloak. *He was the height of an NBA player; surely, I can find him…*

"Hey, what do-ya think?" Anny called to him from the next stall over, holding up a silver and purple scarf.

Solomon didn't answer. All he gave was a hastened smile and nod before resuming his search for the cloaked intrigue. He could not locate him. *How odd.* He then realized the boy who had been manning the ice chest was suddenly gone, now replaced by an older gent, whom Solomon assumed was his father. *What's going on?* Sully shook his head as if trying to rid it of fog.

Anny bought the scarf, wrapped it around her sleeved shoulders, and struck a pose, "You like?"

"Yeah, it's nice."

"Hey, earth to Sully. You okay? You look pale."

"Yeah," he looked confused. "Sorry, I'm just feeling a bit nauseous. I'll be fine."

She walked up to him and gently removed his sunglasses. "Good Lord, you look like you saw a ghost."

He managed an ironic smile and thought, *yeah, I think I did,* all the while assuring her he was fine and merely adjusting to the dust bowl climate. After he sat and took a few sips of water, he started coming around.

As tourists, they decided to have a look at the causeway that connected the Sphinx and the Great Pyramid. Strolling nonchalantly and snapping occasional pictures, they tried to figure out where the Osiris shaft might connect. *No clue.*

Though Anny had on modest clothing, a security guard sitting on the wooden decking surrounding the Sphinx obviously admired her from afar. He looked nice enough, so disregarding Solomon's objection, she decided to ask him for help.

"Oh yes, Idris the Prophet." Surprisingly, the guard spoke rather eloquent English. He pointed down the causeway and said, "Over there."

"No, not Idris, Osiris," Anny clarified.

"They are one and the same. Idris was a Prophet, the Lord of Egypt in our Book, the Holy Quran."

"You gotta be kidding me," Solomon said, as he joined the conversation. "You mean to tell me the Egyptian God of the Underworld is referenced as a Prophet in the Quran?"

"Yes," the guard nodded knowingly, while keeping his eyes on Anny. "Yes indeed."

"Can you show us his tomb?" Anny asked, enticing him with a million dollar smile.

"Yes, sure," the guard agreed willingly. He introduced himself as he led the way, "I'm Adofo. Pleased to meet you."

"I'm Anny, this here is my husband, Solomon." *That sounds weird to say out loud...*

"Thanks for showing us Adofo. We're here on our honeymoon and became fascinated with Egyptian history when we started planning this trip." Solomon's attempt at small talk was received awkwardly. Clearly, Adofo would have been happier if Anny came alone.

"He's nice, huh?" Anny whispered. "Aren't you glad I asked?"

Solomon nodded to cede her point, and a minute later, they approached the entrance. It was so unremarkable that Solomon was skeptical. He then realized that his expectations were aligned with the enormity of whatever was going on. He didn't consider that a low-roofed hole in the rock would mark the entrance to the tomb of Osiris, God of the Underworld.

"Can we go in?" he asked, looking into the tunnel.

"No, sorry."

"Can I pay you and we go in?"

"Yes, of course," Adofo shrugged shamelessly. "Twenty US."

Sully whipped out a $20 and Adofo gave a quick look in both directions before leading the way. The passage descended at a slight angle and flattened out where an iron ladder disappeared down into the darkness. As he looked into the shaft, Sully was hit by a wave of anxiety. It was followed by a thick case of *deja vu*. He felt like the world around him was trying to warn of an impending cosmic doom. Then it hit him. This was the feeling he had in the cab on approach to his mother's house, the night Jasper was killed.

"I have a light, you want to go down?" Adofo held out a small flashlight for Sully.

"N-no," Solomon shivered. "No thanks, not today."

"Common!" Anny couldn't believe her ears. "We came here for this, didn't we?"

"We need to go, Anny." Solomon grasped her elbow and squeezed hard enough to show her he was serious.

"Yeah, okay," she looked at him with a puzzled look. "Adofo, do you work here all week?"

"Yes, sure."

"Can we impose on you later in the week, maybe?"

"Yes, sure," he nodded and gestured to himself. "You just find me. Sure."

"You're sweet," she smiled at him and turned to follow Solomon who was already on his way out.

When Solomon exited the shaft, he happened to look up at the second largest pyramid in the Giza complex, the Pyramid of Khafre. There, on the top, he saw (or thought he saw) someone standing with a cream-colored, hooded cloak. He blinked hard in the bright light and fumbled with his sunglasses. Ramming them into his forehead, he took another look at the pyramid. His heart pounded like a fist into his chest. *Nothing. What's happening? Am I hallucinating?*

"Nice view isn't it?" Anny exited the shaft and stared up at the pyramid with him.

"Yeah, beautiful. I'm sorry; I need to get back to the hotel. I'm not feeling well."

"Okay," she looked at him with concern. This behavior was not like him. Sully was not one to let a little nausea bring him down like this. "We'll go. Let's get a cab, so we don't have to walk all the way back."

CHAPTER 33
Where Were We?

Monday, May 21, 2012

"Guess who just showed up?" a muffled voice asked on the other end of the phone.

"The Greek?"

"The Greek. This guy's insane. I lost the pool over here. I was certain he fell off a cliff."

A silent half-minute passed as the General considered what the Greek's sudden appearance might mean. He slipped out of their surveillance net three months earlier, in a manner that baffled the Phantoms. Even the General had to admit it was a nice piece of incognito and deception on the part of the old spook.

After he disappeared, the Phantoms took up residence in the Greek's house. They figured that if and when he surfaced, he'd come home. After three long months, some in the organization began to wonder if he was ever coming back. Speculation and side bets followed.

"What's his status?" the General finally asked.

"Controlled and happy," that was code for *tied-up and drugged*. "He's wondering about the plan," code for *we need orders*.

"Give him whatever he wants. I'll talk to you after lunch." The phone disconnected and the one they called Tom, the on-site leader of the company, looked at the phone receiver before tossing it on the dining room table.

"What'd he say?" asked the Black Phantom with bright blue eyes, the one they called Franklin.

"He said to keep him drugged and wait for a callback." Tom slinked into his seat and sipped from a wide neck bottle of Budweiser. He was less than an arm's length from the main front window. He gently pushed the edge of the curtain with his index finger and gazed out front as he muttered, "So, that's what we'll do."

"He say when he'd call back?"

"Within the next few hours." Tom looked up at the operative standing over him and nodded toward the back door, "Franklin, keep your eyes on the property and stay alert. Sure as toilets clog, that loner wasn't no neighbor. I ain't seen him around here in the three months we've been squattin.' He's connected to the prisoner down there somehow. You eyeball him prowling around again, you take him out, understand?"

"Yes sir."

Franklin retreated to his post near the back door, but did a rather poor job keeping his eyes on the yard. Franklin had a fidgety disposition that made him a lousy watchdog. His short attention span was not a product of a physical disorder, but rather, a byproduct of a psychological tweak. His genetic enhancement included a specialized auditory modality. He could hear so well and so clearly that sounds were constantly pulling at his assiduity. From the scamper of a mouse in the wall to the sounds of birds outside, Franklin was able to hear and isolate them all, as needed. It was a remarkable genetic modification that paid great dividends during combat ops or when tracking someone or something in a barren landscape. The drawback was that when he wasn't engaged in an operation, he made a teenage boy with ADHD look like a meditating monk.

* * * * *

On the other side of the globe, General Viktor Dultsev hung up the phone and returned to his dinner. He was meeting with one of Amir Mussa's campaign officials, attempting to negotiate access to specific archeological sites in the event that the former Egyptian Foreign Minister should win the election.

Voting was scheduled to start later that week, and the race was going to be a photo finish. Baseera, an independent survey center, went on the record earlier that day, claiming that the combined support for the top four leading candidates was still quite a bit lower than the 'still undecided' vote. Therefore, Dultsev was having an awful time trying to forecast the winner, and was in the middle of a mad dash to meet with anyone who had a legitimate shot. He was squeezing contact with a dozen different campaigns into less than a week.

As the vote drew near, the Phantoms flexed their persuasive muscle. Dultsev and his crew had successfully infiltrated enough of the so-called 'neutral military' and 'election oversight' apparatus that they were sure to swing the final tally in the direction that best suited their agenda.

Election tampering was a mindless routine in the developing world. Any individual with influence or money could corrupt the system. It was harder to do in established democratic nations, but not impossible. The first time they swung the vote in the United States was 2004, effectuating the outcome of the ultra-close race between Bush and Kerry. Since that time, the Phantom infrastructure managed to successfully carry *its* candidate to victory, and probably always would.

Splice

In 2012 Egypt, the question was still *who?* Who best served the Phantom's interests among the leading candidates? Candidate assessment was the General's job that week. Learning of the Greek's sudden re-emergence was a distraction he didn't need.

Political manipulation was challenging. Divulging too much about what the Phantom cabal could provide a candidate was dangerous, especially if a candidate lost. Not revealing enough about the Phantom's level of influence and aid was risky too, because that's where the power was grounded. This type of geo-political jockeying was an art, a delicate dance -- a Terpsichore of wit. Viktor liked the challenge of it all, and fancied himself a master... *but that didn't mean he needed distractions.*

The food server asked him if he cared for more wine. The General accepted, pleasantly.

"Everything okay sir?" asked the campaign aid.

"Yes, just business unrelated to this fine country," the General tipped his glass in the direction of his companion. "Now, where were we?"

* * * * *

In east Bethesda, Maryland, Braxton sat in the shadow of a Burr Oak along the outer perimeter of Dotty's backyard. He listened intently to the murmurs of random conversation inside the Greek's home. The conversation turned to dinner, with one operative making a fuss about not taking the pizzas when they had the chance.

We should have kept those pizzas, the disgruntled one said. *The Greek had every opportunity to order them before getting here, and we could have checked 'em for bugs, anyhow.*

I don't believe it, another chimed in. *Food doesn't just show up. And why did he order two large pies for just himself? Sure, he could have ordered them online from the cab, but I just don't believe it. Something doesn't sit right.* The sound of the ringing land-line cut into the debate.

Hello... Yes sir... Agreed... I doubt it; he's in the biz... Understood...

Bax could only hear one side of the conversation and wondered who the operative was talking to. However, he knew the language of espionage, and deduced that whoever called was likely their commanding officer.

I doubt it, he's in the biz could have been a response to a number of questions. It might have been, "will he crack under conventional interrogation techniques?" or, "will he cooperate in exchange for a deal?" The phrase noting that the prisoner is 'in the biz' indicated to Bax that they were probably questioning Dotty's psychological strength under heavy duress, but he couldn't be sure.

What did he say, Tom? one of the Phantom's demanded.

He said we're setting up the circus, on-site. He'll advise later as to disposal. Bax knew exactly what that meant. The Phantoms had been ordered to interrogate the prisoner on-site and kill him. He was going to have to intervene. He cast a glance into the sky above and guessed that at least two, maybe three, hours of daylight still remained. The time on his cellphone glimmered: 6:19 pm.

Bax considered his options. Dotty's drug-induced state confounded the idea of a clean getaway. Bax listened closely as the operatives yakked about nothing important, hoping they would use the pharmaceutical name of whatever substance they gave their prisoner. That information would help planning in a couple different ways.

Bax imagined ten different rescue options, leading to a hundred possible intermediate realities, all converging to a few likely ultimate scenarios. In the end, some would die and some would live. The challenge was figuring out which set of procedures offered the lowest degree of difficulty and the highest likelihood of success. His mind defaulted to training basics, and he worked the options systematically. Each avenue was quickly analyzed for pros and cons. Suddenly, Dotty's voice snatched his full attention.

"What are you doing? Wh-what's that?" He sounded terrified, but more alert. Bax popped the binoculars to his eyes and looked for any movement.

"What's the matter, Greek? Are you afraid?" said the third solder. Bax knew it was the third one because he rarely said anything. His voice was raspy, as if an obstruction clogged his breathing passage. "This is my genetic enhancement. You like it? It's the abdomen cavity and stinger of the Pepsis wasp. Have you ever heard of the Tarantula Hawk, Greek?"

"Roe, what are you doing down there?" shouted Tom's voice. "You're not messing with the Greek are you?"

Bax heard a sinister chuckle, followed by the response, "No Tom, just showing him the goods."

"Is he alert enough to get started?"

"I don't know, are you?" Roe asked Dotty before raising his voice and answering Tom, "Within the hour, I'd guess."

"Good, then put your shirt back on and leave him alone until then."

"Tom saved you this time, Greek," Roe taunted in a low voice. "But in an hour, I'll show you the meaning of pain, and I'll do it in the name of Bast Molarek."

Bax flicked on his phone and queried the web. It landed on a type of spider wasp known as the tarantula hawk for its spider-hunting behavior, size, and incapacitating sting. The sting of the tarantula hawk was said to be the second most painful insect sting on the planet, just behind the bullet ant. It had the power to completely debilitate a full-grown human for between two and four minutes, per sting. He swallowed hard and shook his head in disgust at the thought of how, or more precisely, *where,* the wasp's abdomen and stinger might be attached to this human hybrid named Roe.

As he looked through the binoculars once again, he heard a twig snap beneath him. He paid little attention to it until the one they called Franklin suddenly appeared in the back door, peering out in the direction Bax was hiding. He searched the landscape slowly and intensely. In his earpiece Bax heard Tom ask, "What is it? You hear something?"

"I did. It was out of place." Franklin leaned back into the house and grabbed his MAC-11 subcompact machine pistol and began searching the backyard.

Bugger-me! Bax thought, *how'd this oaf hear that?* His rescue operation was about to go down in flames as he slowly inched out of view and withdrew his weapon. Tom appeared next and followed his comrade into the backyard. "Where'd you hear it coming from?"

"Not sure. Back here somewhere."

Franklin walked to within feet of the Brit's hiding spot when something happened. It was either Divine Providence or dumb luck, Bax might never know, but a fat red squirrel scampered down a nearby tree and ran across the yard in the direction of the house.

"That what you heard?" Tom asked, unenthusiastically.

"I heard a twig snap. Sure, that little fat ass might have caused it."

"Must have, I don't see anyone back here."

Braxton took a deep quiet sigh of relief as the operatives disappeared back into the house. When he turned, he noticed that his shoulder bag was beside him. It would have been in plain view of Franklin. *How did he not see this?*

Franklin's inability to recognize the foreign object on the ground, Bax's bag, was yet another of the negative side effects of his mutation. He relied so heavily on his sense of hearing that other sensory perceptions had diminished, and were diminishing the older he got.

Franklin was past due for his annual health screening at the BSA facility. He was already well under the minimum cognitive levels acceptable for combat duty. The next time he stepped into a BSA testing lab, he would never see the outside world again. They would test him, analyze his genomics, make tweaks to the recipe, and then discard him as a 'positive-failure.'

Now that Bax realized how well Franklin could hear, he moved very slowly and with deliberate movements. He needed to call for a vehicle, but dare not try and whisper into the phone this close to Franklin's ears. He started to move, inch by inch, back into the trees behind him.

The further he got, the more he quickened his pace, and eventually he was well into the property directly behind Dotty's house. Once it seemed safe to do so, he jogged to the 410, turned north briefly, then headed south on Rocton Avenue in search of a 'For Sale' sign. He found one rather quickly and noted the address.

Next, Bax looked up the number to a cab company and called the dispatcher. He ordered a cab, which the dispatcher said would be to him within fifteen minutes. Waiting, he paced the sidewalk and listened to those inside his friend's house. The audio was a little fuzzy at this distance, but still audible. It sounded like the company was getting ready to begin interrogation.

After 20-minutes, the cab was still a no-show. Bax considered calling the police. However, if he got the local cops to intervene at Dotty's residence, this would definitely complicate the operation and certainly compromise the likelihood of anonymity. It was the best option to temporarily suspend the torture and buy Bax a little more time. But if Bax were conducting the interrogation and a cop showed up, he'd just bind and gag him until the business was complete. From a tactical standpoint, it wouldn't matter unless the cops showed up in force, which meant that Bax would have to use hot button words like *bomb, explosives, bio-tech weapons* when describing the happenings at the house. If he said something like that, there's no way the cops wouldn't ID him as a matter of standard protocol, pulling cell phone records and using an array of surveillance options. *Com'on,* he looked at his phone to check the time again, *Com'on, let's go cabbie.*

A minute later, his earpiece lit-up with one of the most blood curdling screams imaginable. His friend was obviously in terrible agony. "Where have you been, Greek?" Tom asked again. "Where have you been these past three months?"

"V-vis." Dotty's words came between grunts and screams, "Visiting f-friends."

"Don't be cute, Greek," Tom responded. "I'll tell Roe to stick you in the urethra next if you're going to sass me. I'll ask again, where were you for three months?"

Dotty didn't answer; he just coughed, moaned, and sputtered unintelligible sounds of pain. A few minutes passed and the scene quieted. Then Tom's voice came back,

"Now, see? That's better right? The beauty of the wasp sting is that the mind-numbing pain only lasts a few minutes and then we can talk again. Let's start with something simpler, Greek. Who employs you?"

"The se-secret service. The US secret ser-service." He sounded exhausted.

"Good, see? That wasn't so hard…"

Finally, a yellow cab approached. Bax gave the driver two $100 bills as a retainer, took down his Cab ID Number, and instructing him to wait in the driveway of the 'For Sale' house with the meter running until he returned. "Hey man, I can't just wait here all night," the driver was a twenty-something wearing a backwards ball cap. He also had both forearms tattooed to the wrists. "When are you comin' back?"

"Within an hour, max two. I have to first see a man about a dog, you understand." The cabbie nodded, though it was clear he didn't understand much of anything. "There's an additional $200 in it for you, if you wait."

"Alright man," the cabbie said reluctantly, "but two hours from now is 8:42. At 8:42, I'm driving away, OK?"

"Thanks," Bax said, and jogged towards Dotty's home.

The terrible screaming pierced his ears again just as he left the cabbie. Above the shrieks, Tom yelled, "Give him a double dose, Roe!" That was followed by a short burst of unintelligible noise, which abruptly ended with dead silence.

"He passed out. Wake'im up." Tom mumbled in a low voice. A moment later, Dotty returned to his agonizing convulsing and sputtering. Then Tom said something so quietly that Bax couldn't make it out. He stopped running, pressed his finger to his earpiece, and tried to pick up the voice. Nothing.

A few minutes passed. Bax carefully and quietly found his way through the neighbor's yard en route to his hiding spot. But the next thing he heard froze him in place: "6240 W-Widows Mite R-Road." *That was the address to the safe house.* Bax dropped his head in frustration.

Amid a growing sense of despair and urgency, the Brit crawled onward, listening to the Phantoms along the way. They called one of their contacts, presumably at the CIA, who confirmed that the address they got from Dotty was an old safe house taken off-line about a year ago. Once the intel was vetted, Tom decided to take Franklin on a road trip to Edgewater. Without preparation or packing, they were gone.

Once Franklin's ears had left the scene, Bax moved faster and reached his staging spot within seconds. Since they likely called the CIA, Bax knew the safe house was now certainly being monitored. Therefore, he couldn't call Rooter and warn him about the approaching danger. He quickly calculated his alternatives. Within seconds, he dialed Betty. She answered on the third ring and Bax asked her where she was.

"I'm at home, why?"

"You're near Edgewater, aren't you?"

"Sure am. Just sat down to dinna. What-chu want?"

"Listen carefully. I need for you to drive to the place you first took me. Only two of our company are there, but you need to get them out of there right away. Danger is heading their direction."

"Oh my," he heard her gasp. Then he heard a sound like she dropped something, followed by an obscenity. "Dear Lord, I'm sorry for my mouth. Just dropped the casserole."

"Betty, never mind about that now. Are you listening to me?"

"Yes, oh my," he could hear her moving about, "I'm just lookin' for my keys, shuga."

"Okay, good. When you get there, you'll have fifteen minutes, maybe twenty. One of them needs to load as much equipment as possible into the cars. You and the other need to clean. Scrub as much DNA evidence as possible. You time them, Betty. Twenty minutes and you're on the road, driving. Now repeat it back to me."

She repeated the instructions with accuracy. Bax concluded by saying, "You guys go south on Highway 2 and keep driving until I tell you to stop. Call me back when you're on the road, understand?"

Fortunately, it was rush hour on Monday, and Bax knew the Beltway would be jammed. He checked his clock again and redid the calculation, confirming to himself, *they should have at least 20 minutes from the time she gets there.* He had to leave the rest to fate.

With Con and Rooter covered, he prepped his rescue plan and started thinking about the one remaining operative called Roe. He ditched his blazer and threw on a thin, long sleeved black shirt. He put on a tactical belt and holstered four extra magazines. He pulled a lock-pick kit from his gear and stuffed everything else in his shoulder bag, which he left in a bush at the base of a large tree. He advanced toward the house. In his ear, he could hear Roe taunting the Greek, which meant he was downstairs. The quickest point of entry was now the back door. Surprisingly, the door was unlocked. Easing into the house, he saw the staircase in the far corner, off to his left.

Gun tucked into his chest, Bax maneuvered with swift silence across the room and headed down the stairs. The third-from-the-bottom stair creaked and Roe stopped talking mid-sentence. Bax knew he was made, so he jumped the last two stairs and burst into the interrogation room. It was a shocking and unholy sight.

Dotty was being used as a shield. He looked lifeless and slumped over, but managed to look up and give an unenthusiastic nod to the Brit. Roe was shirtless and looked very muscular, powerful. A large growth of some sort extended from the base of his neck. It was patterned, like the scales of a snake, but smooth and almost translucent. Bax couldn't see his enemy fully, since his friend was being used as a shield. However, he correctly assumed that this crazy protrusion was the abdomen and stinger of a tarantula wasp.

Roe slowly moved back and to his right. He wrapped his left arm under Dotty's left armpit, propping him up as he retreated one careful step at a time. Bax stared down the barrel of his Beretta and contemplated taking a shot. He thought he could hit Roe between the eyes, but the Phantom quickly jerked, and better positioned himself behind the Greek.

Dotty's body was a mess. He had about a dozen huge growths on his torso, chest, neck and face. Some were the size of golf balls, while the largest was the size of a bowling ball on the right side of his torso. Most were bleeding. Some were also oozing a yellow puss. The sight was grotesque and Dotty was in obvious pain. Bax quickly deduced that Dotty's chances of making it were slim.

Roe held a handgun to Dotty's head, "You want your friend to die? Step back!"

"Let him go and I'll take it easy on you, freak."

It seemed like an eternity while both men stared and weighed their options. Eventually, Roe made the first move. In a singular motion, he extended his gun hand toward Bax and began firing. Dotty's chest jerked forward and the tip of the insect stinger burst out in a mess of blood and bone fragments. Instinctively, Bax lunged back and to his left, behind the stairs for cover, firing back at the hybrid creature as he did. He landed behind the staircase wall and knew he was still alive, although his arm hurt like hell. He heard a thud on the other end of the room. Then all was quiet. Bax peeked around the corner and saw Roe lying motionless, half under Dotty, who was gasping for air.

On cautious approach, Bax saw that Roe had caught two bullets, one in his stomach and one through the mouth, exiting the back of his neck. The one through the face was the kill shot. It severed the spinal column at the base of Roe's brain.

Confident that Roe was no longer a threat, Bax dropped his guard and attended to Dotty. As he looked at his fallen comrade struggling to hold onto life, a sense of grief and anger began to well up inside him. Dotty was cleaved straight through the chest by Roe's mutant stinger. He would be gone in a matter of seconds.

Bax knew the scene all too well.

Kneeling, he cupped Father Abelemy's head in his lap. Dotty looked up and choked out the words, "Con, Rooter."

Bax assured him that help was on the way to the safe house. Then, Dotty said slowly, summoning every ounce of remnant energy, "Safe, under m-my bed. 22. 25. 8. Ro-Roger Weaverly."

With those words, the muscles in his body relaxed, and he passed away. Bax closed his eyes and mumbled a few choice words. His hands were shaking with fury and frustration. He clenched his jaw and focused his rocketing emotions.

22-25-8, Roger Weaverly.

He couldn't afford to forget that combo, so he memorized a quick number association in his head before moving his friend's body off the hybrid Phantom. He carried the Father to the sofa across the room and gently laid him down. Too many of his friends and fellow soldiers had died in his arms. This part of the job only got harder each time.

He found a quilt and draped it over his friend. He pressed the palm of his hand against the Father's swollen forehead. Anger consumed him as he took a deep breath and shut his eyes tight. *Enough.* He knew he needed to stay on task.

CHAPTER 34
On the Road Again

Monday, May 21, 2012

Betty was in Solomon's bathroom scrubbing faucet handles and bleaching the toilet. Rooter threw his elbow grease into the kitchen. Con was loading the two vehicles with equipment and bags of personal belongings. They were moving as fast as they could, but weren't going to get the whole house scrubbed in just 20 minutes. It was impossible. Rooter was a trained investigator. *Something always got left behind.*

"Betty," Rooter said as he knocked on the bathroom door, "I put trash bags in these two bedrooms. After you're done, toss whatever you can in the bags, will ya?"

"Yep." She sounded nervous. Contrary to her normal joking manner, she arrived on this night with her hair up, ready to rock-n-roll. She scrubbed down the house like she was on speed. She was sweating, but made sure no droplets got left behind.

As Rooter turned to head back to the dining room, he heard her humming the old hymn, *Amazing Grace*, while she banged and clanged inside the bathroom. *Thank God this lady had the stones to come back and warn us. Guess we're even...*

"Con, you got bags?" Rooter was already onto his next chore and shouted across the house.

"Already using them," Con called back, "I need the bleach for the bathroom though."

"Okay. If you guys see any dishes, toss them in the dishwasher. I'll run it before we leave." Rooter was calling the shots. This was his natural role when Sully wasn't around. After finishing in the kitchen, he collected the trash, including his cigarette butts from the ashtray outside. He tossed two full bags of rubbish in his car.

At the 18-minute mark, Rooter started the dishwasher as Betty rubbed down the final light switch near the front door. They all wore latex gloves during the entire cleaning sprint. Remarkably, the place looked uninhabited by the time they finished. It helped that they never amassed much junk during their stay. It also helped that Sully and Anny took most of their stuff on the trip.

They had no time to discuss their next plan of action, so Betty led the way, with Con riding shotgun in her car. Rooter followed in his rig, close behind.

They never saw the Phantoms or their minivan. In fact, they were gone a half-hour before the Phantoms actually arrived and triggered Bax's flamboyant alarm system. It didn't take long to realize that nobody was there. After a crazy display of frustration, Tom oriented his vehicle west and slammed his foot into the acceleration pedal.

"The Greek is a dead man," he said as he slammed his hand on the steering wheel. "He's trying my patience with this cat-and-mouse bullshit."

"He had to know we'd come down hard on him as soon as we figured this out," said Franklin. "So, why did he send us on this Waldo hunt?"

"To get some relief from Roe's stick, what else?" Tom snarled.

"Or maybe he's playing us," Franklin mused quietly.

"How? What does he gain here?"

They sat in silence as Tom maneuvered the vehicle onto the northbound lane of Solomon's Island Road toward Annapolis. He then pulled out a cell phone and called his contact at the Agency. He verified that no calls came into the safe house. When he asked if a satellite uplink gave visual confirmation that the place was uninhabited, the contact informed him that older images would need to be found and analyzed by a higher up. It wasn't possible to assess satellite footage for a day or two, at least. Tom hung up without saying goodbye. The Phantom infiltration was remarkable, and they covertly operated all over the Federal apparatus, but it still wasn't easy to get access to classified or proprietary systems, especially when those systems were used on citizens within the borders of the United States.

"You gonna call the General?" asked Franklin.

"Hell no. We need to find out what's going on and call when we have some better news." Tom glanced at his watch and tried to justify his decision, "It's the middle of the night there anyway."

As Tom and Franklin merged onto the John Hanson Highway going west, Betty and Rooter were speeding southbound on Hwy 2, on the opposite end of DC, heading in the opposite direction. Betty phoned Bax when they were a few miles north of Lothian. The conversation was short. They were instructed to keep driving south, and wait for his callback.

Bax was busy going through the documents in Dotty's hidden floor-safe under the bed. Most of the contents were Agency-related papers and various procedural memorandums. There was also some cash and a few personal keepsakes.

He painstakingly searched every piece of paper for the name Roger Weaverly. Then, he came across Dotty's half-page will and found what he was looking for. The will listed a few bank accounts and named Roger Weaverly as the executor and beneficiary of Dotty's estate. At the bottom was a hand-scribbled telephone number and Atlanta address to a non-profit organization called the *Crossroads Foundation*.

He called the number. Weaverly's voice mail answered without a single ring. "Mr. Weaverly, Braxton Hill here. We've never met, but I have some sad news about Father Abelemy. I'd like you to ring me back as soon as you are able. The Father asked me to get ahold of you."

Bax hung up the phone and considered the situation again. *Why did the Greek reference this man in his dying breath?* Without any more hesitation, he decided this was his best option. Since the address was in Atlanta, he decided to direct the remaining K&A crew there. *I'll just trust that everything falls in place on the way.*

Bax knew the tracking and surveillance power held by the government. Between satellites and an array of traffic cameras, the government had an incredible ability to find people trying to move from city to city. He had to assume that the government's surveillance apparatus was not yet engaged in this scenario.

He checked the time and knew that the other two Phantoms, if not pursuing Betty, would be arriving back soon. Having stuffed the Greek's will and cash into his pocket, he returned to the family room to reconstruct the crime scene.

First, he adjusted Dotty's orientation by drooping his body over the couch, facing the opposite direction from the Phantom. He then cut an inconspicuous slit into the side of the sofa cushion, wiped off the prints, and slid one of his loaded magazines into it. He then wiped down his gun, and put it in the Greek's right hand.

This made it look like the Father attempted to reach a hidden gun in the sofa while his captor was distracted. It also explains why he might have sent the other two on a wild-goose chase. Bax stepped back and reviewed the plausible sequencing.

As he lunged for his weapon, the Phantom ran him through from behind with the stinger. Then, staggering to the sofa, he found the slit, grabbed the loaded gun, turned, and got off a couple rounds. *Then he would have fallen sort of here...* Bax played the sequencing once more and adjusted Dotty's posture slightly.

It wasn't perfect, and a crime scene investigator might even see through it, but it was enough to keep the Phantoms off their tail temporarily. *I just have to assume that Betty and the others made it out of Edgewater clean.* Satisfied, Bax grabbed his two transmitters and jogged to the staged taxi.

The last of the sun's afternoon glow was barely visible as Bax climbed in the back of the cab. He asked the driver to head to the 410. There, he found a turnoff that served nicely as a hiding spot, and told the driver to pull off the road and back the car into the overgrowth on Twin Forks Lane. The cabbie didn't ask any questions.

By doing so, they could see the southbound traffic clearly as it passed toward the Greek's neighborhood. From a hidden position, Bax looked at each passing vehicle, searching for the red minivan. If the minivan passed, he could be all but certain that the Phantom infrastructure was still playing catch-up. It took twenty-five minutes, but eventually he saw what he was waiting for -- *Tremendous.*

Relieved, Bax tapped the driver on the shoulder and asked to be taken to a picnic area just off the I-95. This was pretty close to the Hilton Garden Inn where they'd earlier ditched Anny's car.

The picnic area was part of a large wooded park just to the east of the hotel. Once there, Bax paid the promised $200 tip. He also gave the young man a cautionary pep talk.

"So, your name is Jose Salvatore?" Bax asked.

"Yep, dat's it."

"Ok. So Jose, are these taxi cabs electronically monitored?"

"Some are, not dis one." Jose had a slight Spanish accent, with a little Rastafarian tossed in.

"I see. Will your superiors want an accounting of this transaction?"

"If I give dem da meter, dey don't ask questions. Dey just want da meter, man."

"That's good, Jose." Bax leaned closer to him, with an intense stare, "It's very important to me that nobody knows where you dropped me off. Can I trust you to forget everything about me and drive away?"

Initially, Jose appeared to think his passenger was joking. However, his facial expression changed quickly when he realized Bax was serious. Things got awkward, so he looked away nervously, "Yes, yes, of course."

"Good." Bax let the moment linger for emphasis. When the driver started to squirm under the heavy gaze, Bax slapped him on the arm more lightheartedly and said, "Because you don't ever want to see me again."

Jose nodded and Bax got out. Quickly, the cab sped away and the Brit was left standing in a light haze of dust. Bax was a good psychological operator. He knew how to strike a slap-up balance between intimidation and reassurance. Jose was left mildly frightened, but reassured to know that if he upheld his end of the bargain, he'd be left alone.

Bax waited for the dust to settle and looked up in the trees. He had a lot of natural cover in the park. He found it easy to keep out of sight as he weaved his way towards Anny's car.

Armed with the knowledge that the Phantoms were not yet on their tail, he decided to call and give further instructions to Betty. He asked her to pull over so he could speak to Rooter. In that conversation they decided to transfer whatever they could to Rooter's car and let Betty return home. Based on initial intel, Betty wasn't ID'd and her returning home seemed safe enough. They decided to rendezvous in Richmond, Virginia.

Within a few minutes of hanging up the phone, the Navigator was re-packed and they said their goodbyes to Betty once again. This time, Rooter gave her a hug and thanked her with fondness. However, while he was being serious, she helped herself to a handful of his left butt-cheek and sarcastically thanked *him* instead.

Con laughed, Rooter winked, and they drove into the night with a final wave.

CHAPTER 35
If You're Referred, You're Family

Tuesday, May 22, 2012

They stayed the night at a Candlewood Suites on the north side of Richmond. The hotel was fine, but Con envied Bax's private room. Rooter's clarion snoring could wake the dead. Con was sure it kept him from any meaningful sleep.

They convened at a McDonald's across the street for breakfast. Con wasn't partial to coffee, but strongly considered adding a McCafe to his order of hotcakes and orange juice. They got their food and sat at a table along the window of the PlayPlace. Bax wasn't there yet.

"Just so you know, I'm not driving today. I'm sleeping the whole way." Con took a drink of his OJ. He decided one night of bad sleep wasn't enough to justify drinking 'black tar.' If he still needed a kick in an hour or two, he'd get a Red Bull.

"Oh, poor baby, didn't get good sleepy-sleep," Rooter mocked. "Please, as if I'd let you drive, anyway. Do your feet even reach the pedals?

"'Ello gents," Bax approached. "Sleep well?"

"Lumberjack over here did great," Con nodded toward his roommate. "I doubt anyone else on the second floor caught a single Z."

Bax chuckled and took a seat. Rooter laughed too.

"I slept great, thanks for asking," Rooter said with a smile.

"Me too," Bax winked at Con who had a mouthful of hotcakes. "I was on the third floor."

Bax hadn't told them what happened to Dotty yet. Initially, he decided that he wasn't going to say anything until Sully and Anny were back stateside. They could all hear the news and process it together. But as he thought about it late into the night, he decided otherwise. There was a solid chance they would find out despite his efforts to keep it from them, especially when they linked up with this Mr. Roger Weaverly. Finding out from a stranger would erode trust, so Bax took a deep breath and launched into the story, right then and there.

Con took the news hard. At times, he was quite emotional.

Splice

Bax tried to spare them the specifics, but Rooter would have none of that. His presentation was more stoic and composed, but Bax could tell that below it all, he too teetered on the emotional plank. Regardless, Rooter negotiated for the details. He had to know it all.

After everything was thrown on the table, Con excused himself and went to the washroom to take some space and regain his composure. Rooter stepped outside for some air, which he quickly polluted when he lit a cig. Bax finished his breakfast and marveled at how much of a family they had become over the past year. He thought about how deeply they cared for one another. He realized how deeply he cared for them.

The sense of loss they felt was heightened by the undignified and painful way that the Father passed. They wanted to see him, say goodbye, properly eulogize and honor him for the friend and brother he'd been, but they'd never get that chance. The suddenness and absoluteness of this news was devastating.

It was a 9-hour drive to Atlanta. Con slept some, but mostly stared out his window with dead eyes. Rooter was in a foul mood, one that only got worse when his back started giving him fits, about two hours into the drive. By the time they got to Archdale, North Carolina, he couldn't continue and was forced to ask Con to take a turn behind the wheel. In the passenger seat Rooter got some relief when he engaged full tilt, but it didn't improve his demeanor much.

Con was quiet and carried a sad deportment all day. He processed his grief in depressive isolation. He didn't want to talk about it, and preferred to be alone to work things out on his own terms whenever they stopped for food or to stretch. He wasn't angry, just sad and numb.

It was quite the contrast from Rooter's homicidal anger. He couldn't stop thinking about creative ways to disembowel the Phantoms responsible for Dotty's death. Whenever they stopped, he'd pound Bax with questions, clarifying and re-clarifying the gory details of the torture and rescue attempt. He openly questioned Bax' decision making, he mocked Con's sadness, and swore like a drunk with every sentence he uttered.

At one point he even declared that Bax should have "fisted the monster's eye socket" as a tangible act of contempt for the Phantom's carcass. To those suggestions, Bax uneasily and delicately changed the subject, and wondered how close Rooter was to a psychiatric breakdown. He'd seen such an episode before and it wasn't pretty. On more than one occasion, Bax witnessed his comrades in the field lose it upstairs, and behave in unspeakable ways with the dead remains of enemy combatants.

Rooter actually wasn't crazy or psychologically unstable. He just had his own process for dealing with grief. It was a gritty one, a dark devolution that eventually

268

balanced out and turned around. Bax didn't know him well enough to see it, so he kept his interactions tender and empathetic and tried his best to give both men the time and space they needed to work it all through. Time and space, after all, was still the world's best cure for grief.

They made it to the outskirts of Atlanta by 8:15 pm and Bax used a map he purchased at a gas station to navigate into the city. Though Bax had left numerous messages, he had not managed to reach Mr. Weaverly nor had he received a callback. This annoyed him, if he were being honest.

The address to Crossroads Foundation was 155 Mills Street, supposedly located just north of the downtown corridor between Centennial Olympic Park and Lovejoy Street. However, at the location corresponding to the address they found only a parking lot. It appeared to be an overflow lot serving the Salvation Army complex to the east. Directly across the street from the parking lot was the Atlanta Mission, on the south side of Mills, where a number of the destitute loitered about and watched them look for an address that didn't appear to exist.

After driving around the block a half-dozen times, Bax finally parked where Crossroads Foundation should have been. He consulted his map again under the soft glow of the dome light and mumbled to himself frustratingly. He had to be missing something obvious. Rooter also parked, and walked over to Bax's driver's side window to try and help decipher the address location. On cue, a small group of ragtag locals crossed the road and approached them from the Mission.

"You need somethin'?" one of them said. "Why you loiterin' about?"

Rooter rolled his eyes and turned to face the group. With no small measure of contempt, he shot back, "What's up gangsta? You claimin' the hood in front of the soup kitchen? Don't worry kid, we're the paying type and we'll buy our own grub elsewhere. Now beat it before this gets ugly."

"Take it easy," Bax said, as he nudged Rooter away from his door so he could get out. "Can you chaps help us find what we're looking for?"

"Not likely," Rooter answered for them. "These are what we Yanks call *illiterate bastards*. See, the problem is, they don't actually have brains, they just..."

Bax gave him a hard elbow straight to the ribcage, and Rooter turned away, wincing in pain. Bax hoped they hadn't heard the insults, but it appeared they had when two of the five men drew their firearms and smiled cockily.

Bax put his hands up and reasoned, "Gents, no need to be hostile. My friend is grieving the death of a loved one and doesn't mean what he's saying. We're just looking for an address to a dwelling that should be here, and hoping one of you might point us in the right direction."

A woman with dark, frizzy hair stepped forward from the back of the group. She was above-average height, and noticeably thick and strong in the caboose and legs. She appeared to be of either Latin or mixed-racial descent, but Bax couldn't tell in the dim light. She was not disheveled like the others. She wore jeans, a t-shirt, and nice shoes. Her skin and hair were clean. There was an unmistakable air of authority around her, evident by the way the others got out of her way as she advanced to the front.

"You from the Feds?" She asked, cautiously eyeing them.

Bax glanced at Rooter who looked as puzzled as he felt. They both found that question to be strange. Bax answered her but didn't know what to say, so he fumbled around. "The Fe... I mean. Did you say the Feds? I'm British, love."

"Yeah? Or maybe you're a Federal agent with a cute British accent?"

One of the men holding a gun adjusted his posture and scowled, "How would we know?"

"Okay, I'll put it another way. I'm not affiliated, we, rather," he gestured toward Rooter and Con who emerged from the passenger side of the other car. "We are not agents of the U.S. government, we're just three blokes looking for Crossroads Foundation."

"What are you doing here?" the woman asked.

"Like I said..." Bax started but was cut off by one of the guys with a gun.

"No white-boy, who sent you here?"

"Christ, take it easy," Rooter said as Bax raised a hand in his direction and answered the question.

"We're here to see a mister Roger Weaverly, sent by mister Abelemy."

The woman's look of distrust transformed into a grin as she gestured for the guys to lower their weapons, "There, he done slipped in right? Damn, why you didn't just say so fool?"

"Why I didn't..." Bax turned to Rooter for help. He didn't understand what she just said and was behind the growth-curve on American street vernacular. Rooter was no help at all. He just snickered, as if to say that not understating these people was typical. Bax finally looked back at her and said, "Sorry?"

"Nah, just come wit us. We'll take you to where you can wait for your peeps."

On the north end of the parking lot, there was a fenced-in vacant lot that shared a property boundary with the four-story Salvation Army building just to the west. A green park with big leafy trees and a couple picnic benches separated the parking lot from the vacant area beyond. There, between the picnic benches, was a tuff shed that looked like it might house lawn equipment. They advanced to its door. The woman withdrew a key that hung around her neck on a chain, unlocked it, and gestured for them to enter.

There were no lights. "You can't be serious," Rooter said. "They're gonna lock us in there and steal our shit, Bax. We'd be the world's dumbest jerk-offs to walk in."

"Now you need-a take it easy," the woman said as she gave Rooter a light shove. "I was jus bein' polite."

Passing him, she led the way, and her entourage followed. Suspiciously, Bax entered behind them, followed by Con and finally Rooter. Once everyone was in the shed, the woman shut the door and locked it from the inside. After the door was shut and locked, someone turned on a light. Once the light was on, they realized the structure had a concrete foundation and was disguised to look like a storage shed from the outside. In the middle of the room they saw what looked like a metal storm cellar door flush with the ground. It was rectangular, about 4' x 3', which the woman unlocked and opened with the same key around her neck. Behind that door was an iron ladder descending into a dark hole.

Rooter chuckled with disbelief and shook his head, "This is gettin' better and better. Where are we headed? The dining commons?"

"You're kind of an ass-hole," replied one of the men standing beside him. He pronounced the word 'hole' as 'hoe.' To Bax's great relief, Rooter showed some restraint and didn't verbalize what he was thinking, which involved the man's mother, a Waffle House bathroom, and a ten-dollar bill.

"Come'on," she said, leading the way down into the hole. "I'm not sure why your contact didn't say nothin' about all this."

I know why, because he DIED lady! Rooter thought, angrily choking back more of that raw emotion.

They followed her down the ladder. At the bottom, she entered a final door leading to a room that looked like a recreation hall. There was a pool table, dartboard, and a few tattered sofas and chairs scattered about. There was even an Xbox hooked up to a tube-style television set. Along one wall there was a sink, microwave, and small refrigerator.

She picked up the television remote control and handed it to Rooter, "Y'all can stay here the night. I'll let 'em know you're here and they'll get-chu in the mornin.' There's food in the fridge there, and bathroom's around the cornah."

The woman walked over to Bax and handed him a card with a telephone number on it. She pointed to a hardline phone on the wall by the sink. "Here, I'll be topside at my post. You need anythin,' just hollah usin' that phone."

"Okay, but what is this place?" he asked.

"What-a mean? We're the A.T.L. chaptah."

"The ATL Chapter of what? We don't even know what Crossroads Foundation is."

"We go by lots-a names, but if you know about us, means you're referred. If you're referred, you're family. That's all I can say. We're home-team doe right? Same side, know what I'm sayin?"

"I think so," Bax was looking at the card with her number. "What's your name?"

"You call me Sis for now. Y'all boys need anythin' else?"

"When will someone come get us?" asked Rooter, whose tone was much gentler now.

"I'll hollah at cha when I know, answer that there phone when I call."

"That happening tonight?" Rooter wanted to clarify the particulars. He was feeling better about the ordeal but was still leery about being locked in a hole in the middle of Atlanta.

"Yeah, gimme an hour to raise home-dude on the telly, and I'll let-cha know."

This was now most unexpected. Clearly, either Abelemy or the name Weaverly held some weight with these young people, as their attitude toward the three travelers changed for the better the minute Bax noted his contact. After Sis and her posse vanished 'top side,' the men had a look around their new digs.

The place was clean. Two of the sofas extended to full-length beds. There was a linen closet in the bathroom with extra blankets and pillows. Bax took one of the sofas and Con took the other. Rooter woefully opted for the hard surface of the floor to aid his aching back. Their belongings were still in the vehicles, but they decided to not worry about it until Sis called them with news of Weaverly.

The door they entered was along the east wall. There was a second door in the west wall that they guessed might lead in the direction of the Salvation Army's basement. They couldn't tell for sure because it was locked. Every other door and cupboard was accessible to them. They decided to make themselves at home and heated up a few TV dinners while watching cable news.

The suddenness of being approached by what initially appeared to be street thugs, followed by this most unexpected underground living situation, provided respite from the day's endless grief and sadness. Their visage was markedly elevated. It was as though their fears, apprehensions, grief and sadness had all been shut out and kept 'top side' while they enjoyed a welcome break from it all in the protective confines of this underground lair.

Con was mocked relentlessly when he suggested they play him in a first-person shooter on the Xbox. Bax joined the banter and challenged them to a wager in billiards. Nobody was tired, and cable news wasn't cutting it, so they acted like members of a youth group and took a stab at the gaming options around them.

Sis called after an hour or so to let them know that *Papa Roger* would be coming into town the following day or two, depending on flight availability. She told them it may be a couple days, and asked if they were okay with that. She insisted they stay put, as opposed to renting a hotel room. Bax agreed without consulting the others and arranged to get their belongings.

As they settled in to retire for the evening, a palpable peace came over the atmosphere of the "lair". Rooter's sharp demeanor and relentless picking about Dotty was gone, replaced by joy and a spirit of carefree. Con no longer wallowed in depressive isolation. Instead, he smiled, laughed and joked with the guys, as if Dotty was still alive. Bax no longer felt responsible for the Father's death, and for maybe the first time in his life, he let himself accept the loss of a brother without wearing the typical badge of self-condemnation.

They still missed Dotty, but an atypical essence strangely surrounded them, eradicating the dark cloud that had clung to them all day. It was nice. It was needed relief in the profoundest sense. So much so, that when Bax informed the others that their contact may not arrive for a few days, both Rooter and Con were happy to hear it, and eager to settle into the lair for as long as needed.

If you're referred, you're family. Rooter thought about those words as they drifted off. There was something very *family* about this place, and about Sis, and about her band of misfits. *What is Crossroads Foundation, anyway?*

That night they slept soundly. If Rooter snored, it didn't matter to the others.

CHAPTER 36
On Egypt Side

Sunday, May 27, 2012

"Again, just the broad strokes, please," Abdullah repeated, tersely. "You're giving me a history lesson in Egyptian politics, and it's irrelevant."

"Fine. Here are the broad strokes. The election runoff will be held between Muslim Brotherhood champion, Mohamed Morsi, and former Prime Minister, Ahmad Shafiq. Voting will take place on June 16th and 17th. It's either man's race to win."

"Yes, but I'm assuming Shafiq is not as good a candidate for us. Am I wrong?" Abdullah had the phone pressed to his head, as if that would improve the spotty connection.

"Technically, you are not wrong, but he is for sale."

"What's the price?"

"Huh? Come again?"

"The price. What's the price?"

"Mostly informational, but also some potential military-based crowd control. He may also want help with a new constitution, which I don't think we're in a position to help with, but I don't see it being ... breaker."

The political climate in Egypt was so volatile that many of the candidates were interested in concepts of groupthink and mind-control as a means to ratchet down the opposition's intensity. Phantom techs were actively working on an application for the Anima Imperium, seeking to create a machine that functioned like it, but on a mass scale. Conservatively, such a machine was still a few years away, but the candidates didn't need to know that.

In its current form, the Anima could be used on influential individuals with sway over the masses. Use of the Anima was something the General quietly suggested to a few of the campaigns. If effective, outspoken clerics on the Jihadi side, and humanitarian activists on the human rights side, could be manipulated to become more 'team-Egypt oriented.' This was music to the ears of some candidates.

"These idiots never think long-term," Kahn complained. "Tell him to look at his northern neighbor in Syria, and then ask him again, why he thinks militaristic crowd control serves a lasting purpose? All it does is enrage the talking heads at the UN and furnish the newswire with unhelpful talking points."

"Don't I know," the General either paused or the line cut out momentarily. Then Abdullah heard him take a long drag on his cigarette, "But at least we know a deal is to be made if this guy ends up winning."

"Right. It'll be a pain in the ass. We'll have to kidnap a dozen ulemas, put 'em under the light, douse their brains in cold water, then get them back into the public square without arousing suspicion. Fantastic option, if there ever was one."

Abdullah was right. He was speaking from experience. This wasn't their first go-around with election tampering. Almost every politician has a price for just about any favor. However, the time it takes to compromise the politician's desires can end up creating an investment price that's not worth the long-term return. With regard to the moderate, Ahmed Shafiq, they ran the risk of a 'deal' becoming too cumbersome. They needed another angle for him if he ended up winning the election.

Maybe we could find some dirt on him. If not, we could always create some dirt... There are always two ways to skin a cat. Abdullah's mind turned over the options.

"What about the other guy, Morsi?" he finally asked.

"This is our man," the General replied. "He's got the political prowess of a seasoned veteran. His price is targeted assassinations and covert ops relating to his anti-Israeli ideology. He's not interested in an immediate return either. He's the type that would rather carry a card and pull it out when he needs a serious favor. He's already asked, and I told him you'd meet with him to assure that what we say, we deliver."

"Yeah?"

"Yep. He's not concerned with reforming popular opinion. This guy's all about establishing his own version of revolution by quiet, covert politics. His exact words to me were, 'like the way Bush got the Patriot Act passed in the U.S. -- one piece of legislation for a seemingly righteous motive gave the American Government infinite power over its people.' If you think he loved Bush, he's gaga over Obama. This man doesn't appear to view politics in the narrow paradigm of party lines at all. He's about legacy and ego, and has a full-fledged hard-on over Israel. He's a true believer that the world is a better place without Jews. The world is a better place if everyone believes one truth – in his case, that's Islam. This is the only way for the world to thrive."

"I like him already. What's our play?"

"Everyone I'm talking to thinks it's going to be a photo-finish. I'm not comfortable with our SPEC access. I could use a little more help. A few bucks and a few more people."

"Remind me, what's SPEC?"

"Now he wants a history lesson," the General grunted. "SPEC – Egypt's Supreme Presidential Election Commission. These guys are the watchdogs here."

"Watchdogs my ass," snorted Kahn. "These are the great merchants."

"That's right, and they're being pulled in a million different directions right now. They're siding with the highest bidder and I'm not the only buyer in the game."

"You'll have what you need. I'll send you the Madoff brothers as well."

After the General hung up, he walked over to his floor-to-ceiling window and looked out over the Nile River. *This time next month we'll have a winner and I'm taking a vacation.*

He was staying in the Semiramis InterContinental Hotel on political, extended-stay status. He had been in Cairo since March and was ready to get back home to Rio where he had the comfort of his own bed, ready-access to promiscuous women, and food that didn't have to include dates and veggies.

* * * * * * * * *

The Shepherd Hotel had an old world, European feel to it, and blended the art and culture of Cairo with its own storied legacy. It was an iconic landmark in Cairo, and was widely believed to be the grandest hotel in the world between the 1880's and 1950's. It was the more modern InterContinental Hotel's southern neighbor, and just as the General was peering out over the Nile River from his hotel room, Sully and Anny stood at the front desk, waiting to check into their room.

Earlier in the morning they checked out of the Le Méridien per the counsel of Bax and Dotty. They were warned about getting too comfortable in one place. At a minimum, they planned to change hotels every six to eight days, so as to avoid routines and minimize the chance of detection by 'un-friendlies.'

Since their initial arrival, Sully and Anny spent most of their time at the Giza Plateau or other touristy spots. They checked out the museums, the various venders, and got a guided tour into one of the hallways leading into the Great Pyramid. They even rode camels and took pictures of themselves having fun. As serious as the mission was, it did not take long to realize there would be an inordinate amount of down-time.

They found the Osiris shaft to be a dirty hole that got little attention from the tourists. Once they were comfortable with the lay of the land, they reduced their presence on the Plateau and spent more time at the hotel's pool. They wanted to monitor activity at the shaft, but didn't want to be so visible that the guards and shopkeepers started recognizing them.

Solomon had not seen the cloaked figure since that first day at the pyramids. He was thankful for that. He also opted to keep this experience from Anny, at least for the time being. Privately, he couldn't decide if the cloaked person was imaginary or real. To Sully, the experience fell somewhere in between.

Anny, for the most part, was having the time of her life. Her stomach did a funky twist on Thursday and caused her to spend the better hours of that day upchucking in the bathroom. However, it was short lived, and she fully embraced the tourist thing otherwise. She got serious when they were doing the 'official business' of spying on the shaft, but other than that, she was there to have fun and experience Egypt.

Sully handed the clerk a pre-paid Visa to secure the incidentals, just as Anny leaned up on her tiptoes and gave him a kiss. That was new behavior, a result of the 'talk' they'd had a week earlier. It happened one evening over dinner at the Le Méridien grill …

Uncharacteristically for him, Sully found the 'talk' to be difficult and nerve racking. The 'talk' forced him to think about a few things that he had avoided. It forced him into a better realization of just how much he was falling for Anny. He stammered, drank lots of water, and awkwardly pushed the words out.

She hung on every sentence. Her time had finally come. His care and concern was deeper than she hoped, and her favorite part of the evening was when he talked about his long-term intentions.

"So, what I'm trying to say is I want to care for you, grow with you, and develop a life that intertwines with yours, but there's an issue that I'm not sure how to explain. But I'll try."

He took a long drink of water and took an even longer breath. This was the part that had the potential to get uncomfortable. She smiled with clear recognition of his anxiety and nodded, as if to say it was safe to tell her whatever he was thinking.

"I don't know how to start this. Basically, the one thing Leola ever wanted from me was a ring. She always wanted me to put a ring on her finger. The only thing she ever wanted was the one thing I never gave her. I decided I wanted to give her diamonds, but not a ring. I bought her a nice lifestyle, car, furniture, whatever, but never a ring. See, I've always felt like two lives coming together to create an interwoven strand was the same as two lives coming together to be one, but it's not. Do you understand?"

"I'm not sure I do," she said, searching him for answers. He swallowed hard, realizing he just needed to come out and say it.

"I don't want to date you or play house with you, or live in a make-believe world with you. Leola knew something that I never realized until it was too late, and that's that two strands woven together are still two strands. I..." He paused momentarily, "I'm saying, I want to marry you and become one with you, and if us doesn't lead to that, I'm not interested in taking a wait-and-see approach."

He looked at her with utter terror, having no idea how she'd take such a bold statement. He was relieved when he saw a gleaming tear at the corner of her eye. He took a deep breath and waited for her to say something. He asked again if she understood what he was saying, and she nodded. She didn't need for that moment to pass too quickly – it was, after all, the happiest moment of her life. The one she loved with everything in her being had just told her what every girl, at some level, hopes to hear from the time they start playing with dolls. *I want to marry you and become one with you.*

"So," she finally said, "What does that mean exactly? I'm guessing there are rules to the dating game for us then?"

He shrugged and turned a shade redder. "I'm not putting rules on us, but I'm telling you that before we get too serious about things like living together, I'd like to meet your parents and be able to look your dad in the eye and tell him what I'm all about. You deserve that."

"Really?" She smiled in a way that warmed his soul. She was not just appreciative, but shocked and enamored by this gesture of a gentleman.

"Really. I always avoided Leola's folks. I did so because at some level I think I was ashamed for how I treated their daughter. Not like I was bad to her, but she deserved a man who understood her desires and needs, someone who would choose to give her what she wanted rather than take for himself all the perks of a sexual relationship without the responsibilities of caring for her."

"I've never heard a man talk like this before. In fact, I've never even heard a man talk like this before in fiction books."

"I would never understand what I'm feeling had Leola not been murdered. Marriage was always a tired tradition to me, something that people did for the sake of ritual, something that lacked a logical purpose. I was so wrong."

Now it was his turn to be emotional. Leola's death had changed him in ways he never fathomed. He agonized over not giving her a ring more than any other thing since her death. It was the single greatest regret of his life, and not one that he intended to relive again.

They ate and drank and enjoyed one another's company at the restaurant. They laughed a lot. After dinner they found a piano bar in another hotel. It came highly recommended by a cab driver who spoke very little English. The Pianist was good. They danced like lovers to lounge classics, alongside drunken tourists and Egypt's swells alike. More than anything, they laughed.

Later, in the elevator, they shared their first kiss. It was sweet and passionate, and would not end for some time. He picked her up and she wrapped her legs around his waist, her sandals hanging loosely from her bare toes. He carried her to the room and fumbled with the keycard as it continued. Once inside the room, he laid her down on the bed and asked her if she'd share it with him. Her answer was implied when she cupped his cheeks and kissed him some more.

Deep into the night they enjoyed sensual explorations and passionate expressions of their feelings for one another, but in staying true to Solomon's stated desire, Anny pulled back on the reins before they got too close to the cliff. She was determined to join him in honoring Leola's memory and his strong desire to do things differently this time. So they talked and played, then did more of the same.

It was, as Anny put it, "The most fantastic night of my life."

Since that night, Solomon was a different guy. He too began finding enjoyment in being the tourist in love, and let his guard down about the intrigue of the Phantoms for the first time since August 15th of the prior year. It had been a long time, but he was beginning to revert back to the man he once was -- fun, charismatic, enthusiastic, and full of life.

Splice

They decided to stay a week at the Shepherd Hotel before hopping a flight to another country, maybe Turkey or the United Arab Emirates. They hadn't decided yet. They planned to stay out of the country until the Presidential Election concluded in mid-June, at which point they'd return and take another look at the Osiris shaft.

They planned to Skype Braxton on June 15th and give a full report. That meant Solomon and Anny had 20 full days to be tourists in love. *Not a bad gig. Not bad at all.*

CHAPTER 37
The Underground

Sunday, May 28, 2012

A full week passed since arriving in Atlanta, but there was still no sign of Roger Weaverly or any other *official* from the foundation. Sis and her band of what Rooter dubbed, "The Lost Boys," loitered around top-side near the entrance to the Atlanta Mission, but they were mum to questions about Crossroads. As hours turned into days, and days into a full week, the K&A Crew began feeling like freeloaders. Nobody could – or would – say when *Papa Roger* might show up. Nobody would discuss Crossroads Foundation. The guests felt trapped in limbo, between a past of significance and a future of intrigue. They just couldn't seem to get free of the present.

Sis turned out to be a true sweetheart who was both attentive and gracious, eagerly seeking to make time in the bunker as comfortable as possible. She had a special appeal about her. She commanded a strong degree of respect and admiration, while also being motherly and nurturing. Her undeniable leadership qualities were especially remarkable considering her age. Con rightly guessed and later confirmed that she was only nineteen-years-old. After the rough beginning, even her armed entourage went out of their way to make relational inroads with their guests.

The spirit of good cheer that initially supplanted their grief continued in the days that passed. It was as though a peaceful magic lived in the bunker with them, a magic that defied their best attempts to define. Rooter seemed legitimately happy. He was not just happy, but confident and secure in a way that Con never experienced. Con was jovial, funny, and outspoken in a way Rooter had never seen. Among the three, the feelings in that place came to be known as 'the spirit of the bunker.'

"This hole is like an oasis in a hot, smelly, corrupted world," Rooter mused. "The furniture is tattered, this bunker is stark, the lighting sucks, and the TV is ancient… but it's the most comfortable place I've been in ages. And them lost boys – who knew they'd turn out to be so great, right?"

"Like I said," Con responded, "the spirit of the bunker is life-giving. It's not like I don't miss Dotty, but here, all I think about are the good times. It's like I lost the ability to dwell on my inner pain."

"Right, we all feel it, but what is it?" Bax persisted.

"I'm tellin' you, it's the spirit of the bunker guys," Con reasserted. He sounded corny but he didn't care. "It compels us to see life in the context of joy, opportunity, hope and love. Not the usual stuff of pessimism, hurt, pain and such. That's what I think, anyway."

"I have a thought," Rooter said, licking the Cheetos grease off his fingers. "It has to do with Sis and her gangdom up there. I see them like guardian angels over this place. Not afraid to point a gun, and probably willing to kill someone on the one hand, but once they start calling you *family*, all of a sudden they get sensitive, gentle, hospitable. I mean, these people are the most unlikely, thuggish, dirty, unintelligent street-urchins you can imagine. But what if it's all an act, just their disguise?"

"What are you gettin' at?" asked Con.

"I don't know," he shrugged, stuffing another handful of Cheetos in his mouth. "I was just thinkin' about that portal at Alpha Kilo. Thinkin' about all of it actually. The whole interplay between open portals, ancient celestial civilizations, and the idea that good doesn't exist without evil, and war can't exist without peace, and so forth."

Bax and Con were listening intently, not wanting to miss something profound, as rare as it was from Rooter. The PI liked the captive audience, and milked it just a little longer before continuing.

"Everywhere you look there's a counter-balance to things, and there's so much evil everywhere. You got the Gilgamesh-slash-Nimrod thing, right? Then there's Lion-O and the Thundercats that keep hunting us. Outside of aliens and mythology, even in our own history books, it's all about mankind's endless attempt to control people and consolidate power, wage wars, what have you. Now high-tech is being used to basically create new species, build meat-suits without souls, or birth donkey-chick babies with six heads, and whatever the hell else. It's all evil. So, my point is, what if there's a counter-balance? Something less flashy? Less obvious? What if these people top-side are part of that counter-balance?"

"Well, that's rather thought provoking," Bax mused.

"Who are you and what did you do with my grease-ball, idiot friend?" Con asked, to which the PI winked and made a remark about how his supposed lack of intelligence was also a disguise. They had a laugh and dished a little jazz, but Bax brought them back on point.

"So you're suggesting these kids may somehow be involved in this saga we've been thrust into?"

"I'm saying," Rooter clearly enjoyed the moment of intellectual originality, "what's with the secret-speak? 'We go by many names.' 'If you're referred, you're family.' Then remember what Sis said yesterday, 'We're the true guardians of truth in a world hell bent on decay and ruin?' Com'on, that's some funky-bird talk from a chola, no? And then you have to wonder, what is this Crossroads Foundation thing, besides an address to nowhere? It may just be me, but it's strange we show up at a parking lot, get accosted by Wendy and the Lost Boys, get sent into a hole in the ground, then all of a sudden we're the ones who don't want to leave? It just makes you wonder, if a portal to somewhere bad can open by man's efforts, maybe a portal to somewhere good can too? Maybe that's what we're feeling in here, you're so-called 'spirit of the bunker.'"

Rooter's musings were thought provoking because of the certainty of that spirit. There was also an ingrained joy and confidence that clung to Sis and her group. These kids seemed to have some depth of understanding that defied regular folks; those members of the super majority, always hurrying this way and that in the rat race of life.

What's more, they were not street-kids at all. This was obvious within minutes of being top-side with them outside the Atlanta Mission. Sis lacked nothing she needed or wanted, and her crew didn't eat in the soup kitchen either. They always had their own food and drink. Hamburgers, sodas, and chips were abundantly available. They even had the good stuff on occasion.

On Friday, the bunker dwellers were invited top-side for some of what she called *home southern chow*.

They found out that Home Southern Chow night was Sis' phrase for two gas grills and a huge smoker packed full of pork ribs and beef brisket. She also served greens and all the fixings. The smells drew the crowds, and before the day was over, they fed over six hundred people loitering along the street. It went late into the night, too.

Home Southern Chow night was an event unique unto itself, but the rest of the week had its fair share of intrigue as well. As an example, Sis and her boys had such an abundance of general goods that they were continually giving things away. One after another, shipments full of all sorts of things showed up and unloaded just outside the Mission, or sometimes when traffic got congested, in the parking lot above the bunker.

At one point, an inconspicuous, unmarked, semi-truck drove up and unloaded a full container of clothing, shoes, and snacks. There were even electronics such as iPods, Beats headsets, and brand-named outdoor gear. The homeless milling around took the goods and departed. But then inevitably, a few hours later, they'd show up again and the cycle repeated itself.

When Bax asked what was going on, Sis wouldn't talk about it. She jokingly said, "I could tell you but I'd have to sic you wit my dog (pronounced dawg)."

It was obvious the homeless were not stashing the goods under a bridge somewhere, but what were they doing with all that merchandise? Was it stolen? Who was it being taken to? Sis assured her guests that they were welcome to ask any questions they liked to Papa Roger whenever he arrived, but indicated that she either could not, or would not, get into the details of how the network was put together. Not until "I gets the okay from dat boss man," she said.

Much of the commerce and happening top-side made little sense to the guests. Though they sought answers, their curiosity remained unsatisfied. For the time being, they knew for certain that the atmosphere was positive, and they didn't mind Roger Weaverly's delay. They knew that an uncommon joy and sense of peace hung around their new friends. And since Rooter's musings, a new question began to grow... *Do these kids somehow play a part in the story of ancient portals, current-day science, and whatever's poised to come?*

Their new question missed the mark slightly. Had they known better, the more appropriate question was, *within the unfolding saga, how big a part do these kids actually play?*

CHAPTER 38
Papa Roger

Friday, June 15, 2012

It was 9:30 a.m. in Houston, Texas, and 6:30 p.m. in Istanbul, Turkey. Solomon used Skype to check-in with his pals stateside. The connection was fuzzy because of the filters Con used, but such was the inconvenience of being new shadow-recruits playing spy-games.

At the behest of Papa Roger Weaverly, who made his appearance on the 3rd of June, the three bunker-dwellers relocated to a home owned by the Crossroads Foundation in a town called Manvel, just south of Houston. The house was unoccupied, and had been for some time. On arrival, they were greeted by the remains of thousands of fly carcasses and other unidentifiable critters on the hardwood floor and windowsills. Day one they fumigated, got the utilities running, and procured a few essentials such as air mattresses, window AC units, and some food.

The weeds around the house were overwhelming. The "yard" was a bosky thicket of plant life and creepy, crawly things. Out back, the gnarly vegetation was alive with activity. It looked like a scene out of *A Bug's Life*. There were huge spiders, cockroaches, ants and crickets everywhere.

There was no fence, which was fine by Bax because they were in a remote area of south Houston, on a road seldom used. The neighbors were spread out, and they all appeared to have a decent sized parcel of land. Most were tens of acres, and some were easily hundreds of acres in size.

Though southern hospitality was evident when they intermingled with the public in the marketplace, there was a certain code about interacting with neighbors. Namely, that you don't interact with your neighbors unless you had to, or unless it was an emergency. People in Manvel minded their own business and expected the world around them to adhere to that status quo. It was therefore a perfect hideout. It was in plain sight, surrounded by plenty of countryside, and the few neighbors that lived in the vicinity were of the armed-country-hick variety who kept to themselves unless galvanized by their mutual dislike and distrust of anyone with a badge.

"What have you been up to?" Bax asked, staring into the little webcam.

"We're honeymooners!" Sully said overenthusiastically. "We've been touring the Golden Horn of Istanbul for a couple weeks now. That's where we are. I'm calling from a rooftop garden-terrace at our little bed & breakfast. The view is amazing, overlooks the Bosphorus in one direction, and in the other, I see hundreds of minarets rising into the air. We're both doing great. How about you guys?"

"Brilliant, but we had to leg it double-time when our location was discovered. Look Solomon, I'm going to be vague because I'm not sure how secure this conversation is, but we're holed up in another state now."

"I see, everybody okay?"

Rooter shook his head off-camera, indicating it was neither the time nor the place to get into Father Abelemy's murder. Bax glanced at him and nodded slightly, "Yeah mate, we're good, our new friends are the dog's bollocks. Charming people, really. It doesn't feel like we're alone anymore. I'll fill you in more when we link."

"Okay. I'll keep it vague too then. Nothing was going on down there that we could tell, but we did find the spot and had a look around. The place is easy to navigate. We're thinking about heading back in a week or so."

"Right. I'm all set to join you, but let's push to as late in the month as possible. We may not know who tilts the runoff 'til July even, so coming in later will give us the biggest window."

Sully nodded at Anny and then said into the webcam, "Okay, agreed. Anny's just telling me now that she got transferrable flights so that's no problem."

"What hotel? Did you find a place?"

"We hadn't looked yet but we'll get on it and IM the name and address."

"Roger that," Bax was looking at another window on his laptop while he talked. It was an open calendar. "I'm coming in on the 1st then. I'll shoot you the flight details, but I'll find my own way to the hotel. You good on green?"

"What now?"

"Money, you still have enough money or do I need to bring extra?"

"We're good."

Solomon said a few things to Rooter and Con, then turned his side of the connection over to Anny who took a couple minutes to say hi as well. Their chat was brief but it hit the spot. Anny missed her friends. A few minutes later, the call was disconnected and Bax began working on his own travel itinerary.

Rooter called Papa Roger Weaverly a *trippy dude*, as he represented something the K&A crew had never really encountered in all their years of defending religious organizations.

For starters, Weaverly chose to drive with them to Texas, rather than take his return flight which he'd already paid for. Even after they were settled, the man seemed to genuinely like his new guests, and loyally stopped by their home every other day at 1:45 p.m. just to say hi, grab a Diet Coke out of the fridge, *Spark a Stick* – as he called it – and carry on about nothing important for an hour or more. Remarkably, he slid into the natural-feeling role of friend and confidant to each of them, though they only recently met.

Weaverly was a big, happy, loud, and borderline obnoxious old Texan. He used words like *y'all* (singular sense) or *all y'all* (plural sense), and did everything big. His laugh was loud, his mannerisms were overdone, his gestures were enlarged and passionate... he brought a persona that filled every corner of the room regardless of his own social intentions. Even Rooter and his bravado faded into the background when Weaverly came around. Perhaps the most peculiar of his affectation was his choice of words when delving into issues of depth and emotional significance.

He'd say things like, *"how's your heart?"* as a way of asking how they were doing with Dotty's death. He often noted, *"Papa loves us"* as a way to describe God's intimate feelings for humans. Bax, especially, found him to be fascinating, and eagerly launched into deep conversations with the papa about an array of topics. It was as though Weaverly was a shrink who was uniquely gifted in diving into, and swimming around in, the heavy things of life. He was easy to talk to. He seemed to care and understand, and he reserved judgment like no *Christian* Bax had ever known.

So Bax engaged often, and set his mind to try and understand his host better. He talked to the balding, round-faced Texan about politics, Weaverly's past and childhood, and his Crossroads network (though this was a topic the Texan rather avoided). They also talked a lot about religion, and Christianity in particular. Though Bax always intended to learn new things about the Texan, it was Weaverly who carefully and craftily maneuvered the conversations, inevitably coaxing more out of Bax than Bax thought possible.

That was part of the intrigue.

Of all the discussion topics, Weaverly's religiosity was the most interesting to the Brit. Weaverly's expression of faith circled around some of the more popular Christian viewpoints, but there was something distinctly odd about the distance he maintained from what he called *"the Industry of Faith,"* *"Christendom,"* or *"the nasty business of Christians peddling wares to Christians under a quasi-Christian set of marketplace rules."* Weaverly was always smooth and jovial, but when he got going about *"the Machinery of Christendom,"* Bax detected a bite of well-reasoned rage.

Though he had an undeniable religious bent, Weaverly didn't fit the bill of a Bible-thumper from Texas at all. He swore for emphasis and told dirty jokes whenever he thought of one. He drank whisky and had a special affinity for expensive Scotch. He absolutely loved his cigars, and on occasion even joined Rooter for a cigarette on the back porch - which was a concrete slab overrun by weeds and bugs. Weaverly was a fantastic host, and even Con ventured out of his room when he came calling every other day at 1:45 sharp.

The government well dried up when Dotty passed, so they kept a close eye on their expenses. Papa Roger knew this and lent a helping hand by procuring a ton of stuff, most of it used, including desks, chairs, a dining room table, sofas, and the like. He also went above and beyond by setting them up with all their utilities and charged them nothing to stay in the home. He even made it clear that they could stay as long as they needed. The house had an attached two-car garage, in which they permanently parked Rooter and Anny's vehicles, and used a loaner car for local transport instead. The loaner was a brand-sparkling new F-150, "compliments of the family," as Weaverly put it.

Though Bax hadn't managed to get much info at all about Crossroads Foundation, one day he decided to divulge everything pertaining to Dotty. It was obvious that Weaverly knew Dotty, and from a friendship standpoint, deserved to know what happened.

He told how Dotty recruited him to safeguard the K&A crew living in witness protection. He explained that they were dealing with human-hybrids, to which Weaverly barely batted an eye... *odd*. Papa Roger asked precious few questions, which Bax found a little strange as well. For being a group so hell-bent on secrecy and procedure, Bax expected more prodding and vetting, but it never came.

The team came to understand that they were welcome to be guests of the network for as long as they needed help, but for the time being, that was it. Bax was unable to learn how Papa Roger knew Dotty, why the Greek willed his property and assets to the network, or what greater purpose the network actually served. There were no answers about how far the network extended either. Was it confined to a few southern states or was it bigger? Was it international? Bax assumed it was bigger, but he didn't know for sure.

Because there were so many conversational no-fly zones, their interactions during Weaverly's visits to the house always danced around bizarre topics like their physical health, cigars, booze, their hearts and how their hearts were feeling (in the Papa's verbiage), their families, loved ones, and so forth. As awkward as these tête-à-têtes could sometimes get, the guests liked his visits and always looked forward to them.

Those visits were a nice spice, a welcome change of routine. To the guys, Weaverly was the embodiment of *real* and *substantive* in a world so overrun by shallow and vain.

CHAPTER 39
Rising Tide

Sunday, July 1, 2012

"Folks, this area is off limits."

Solomon looked up to see the palm of a man's hand about a foot from his face. He was cradling an assault weapon in his other arm. He stood about six-six; a beefy six-six. He had an odd accent, *maybe Russian?* Solomon and Anny were caught off-guard and completely by surprised.

"Move on," the man said, and waved them toward the pyramids in the distance. Sully quickly turned and grabbed Anny by the elbow, and without saying anything, did as instructed. He was mortified.

Had he really not bothered to recon the Osiris shaft from a distance, in order to assure nobody was standing guard? Had he really just walked up to the front door and come face to face with a mercenary?

Once situated a healthy distance from the shaft, Sully was able to assess the situation. The mercenaries looked like they belonged. They all dressed in boots, jeans, dark undershirts, tan vests, straw hats and had on dark sunglasses. Were it not for the unconcealed cache of guns, ammunition and explosive ordinances stacked neatly near the mouth of the tunnel, they might have even passed for tourists.

The appearance of the mercenaries was unsettling, but his jitters really flared up when he spotted the cloaked figure in the distance. While spying on the Osiris shaft, he noticed that the cloaked man was also watching the mercenaries from across the plateau. He was standing atop a sandy perch near the smaller, G1A pyramid which sits at the foot of the Great Pyramid. This time, Solomon called Anny's attention to the figure, and she saw him too.

Their stint as tourists was short lived, but had been engrossing. For a month, their life consisted of late wakeups, coffee and beignets, lazily sampling local fare in the afternoons, having a nice dinner, wine, and rich desserts in the evenings, and enjoying the local nightlife thereafter. Their slaphappy time in Istanbul had clearly numbed their awareness and attention.

"I'm a fool," Solomon said as he sipped a cup of tea in the lobby of the Mercure Cairo, their newfound hotel which was located just a block north of the Le Méridien. "I was carrying on about Edgewater and Rooter when that guy came up on us. For God's sake, how could I be so careless?"

"I don't know." Anny was sitting across from him, leaning forward with her elbows on her now dark-tanned knees. She bit a fingernail as they tensely waited for Bax, who was due any minute. "I guess we should be thankful for the time we had to relax, but now that we've been shoved back into this chimera-hell, all I want to do is disappear."

"And that cloaked guy... What'd you think of that? Crazy, right?"

"It was crazy when you told me about him in Istanbul. Now that I've seen him, it's not crazy at all. It's terrifying. You never saw his face before?"

"No. Before, it was just like that. His face was disguised in shadow. You gotta figure he's not a Phantom though, right? I mean, he wasn't guarding the shaft. If anything, he was spying on the people guarding the shaft, just like us."

"Maybe I should go hit on him and see if I can get some info," She winked at him and smiled.

"Your days of hitting on men to get info are over, babe."

Solomon took another sip of his tea and cupped the mug at his chest. As if lost in thought, he slumped back into his chair. He felt sure they were embarking on another period of stress and turmoil, and was remembering the hell he'd already gone through. Whether he wanted it, or whether he felt up to it or not, life seemed primed to pick up speed and intensity. *I suppose she's right. We should be thankful for the time we had to live and love. Now back to whatever is next...*

Slowly, their gaze locked and he noticed the light in her eyes. Her spirit was full and happy and content, even amid the stress of their morning. He hated the idea of something happening to her. All of a sudden, thoughts of Leola's lifeless body flashed in his psyche. He quickly jumped out of that awful place and refocused on Anny's eyes.

Maybe we could leave, he thought, *disappear, just like she said. Bax isn't here, we'll just go with the money we have and start a new life.*

The thought dissipated as quickly as it metastasized. He couldn't do such a thing to Rooter and Con, who were now both fugitives of an unseen power and running for their lives. Disappearing was what he wanted, but disappearing was the one thing he could not do.

* * * * * * * * * *

Official texts and pictures published by the Egyptian Office of Antiquities showed that, at one point, there was a moat of water surrounding a rectangular 'island,' with four pillars rising up from the four corners of the island as a sort of shrine to Osiris. In the center of those pillars lay the sarcophagus. However, when Abdullah's team arrived on the third level, they found no evidence of the water moat or the ornamental pillars. There was no sarcophagus either. The only visible artifact was the sarcophagus lid, peacefully lying in the dirt amid an array of garbage and debris. At first glance, the shaft was nothing more than a dry, hot hole in the ground pilfered by grave robbers centuries ago.

After rigging a pulley system and heaving the nine-foot by four-foot, 2000-pound, basalt lid on its end, they found the sarcophagus box buried in the debris below. Somehow, it was still full of foul water. This made no sense to the team. Where did the water come from after all these years?

Day one was spent removing the lid and flushing out the water from inside the box. The national team given to Abdullah by the Morsi government used shovels and pails, and an assortment of scraping tools to get the grime off the inner walls of the sarcophagus.

The next day, to their astonishment, the stone box was full of stale water again. The team was baffled. This time, absent the sludge, the smelly water went all the way to the brim of the sarcophagus box.

Where did the water come from? It wasn't dripping down from above. The shaft's walls and ceiling were completely dry. It wasn't seeping in through the solid basalt from below. The box was a solid piece of lava rock. That much had been verified the prior night. They suspected foul play, as it was the only plausible option, but this too was difficult to accept because the entrance to the shaft was under 24-hour guard. The foul play explanation was completely disproven when the team arrived on day three to find the box, once again, full of water.

On day three, they used a jackhammer to cut through the bottom of the sarcophagus. This turned out to be a monumental task. The jackhammer would not initially make a dent. This meant that the sarcophagus was not pure basalt, but some sort of other material. In order to get the jackhammer going, they had to cut breaks in the smooth finish with a rotary tool, but this too failed until a set of diamond bits and blades arrived. Once they got the stone to crack, the jackhammer did the rest. What was expected to take a few hours, took the better part of a full day. After breaking the sarcophagus apart, it took the rest of the night to hoist the heavy chunks of stone out of the box.

Once the basalt was removed from the newly constructed hole, they used shovels and spades, pails and ropes, to lift the dirt and mud out of the shaft. This process required a great many man-hours, so Abdullah paid for two teams, each working 12-hour shifts, to assure there was no break in the action. It was grueling work. The shaft was hot, normally around 110 degrees where the work was progressing. It was only marginally cooler the higher up the buckets climbed.

Abdullah stayed away from the shaft during this process. Once they broke the water-plane, the air was not just hot, but thick and muggy. The aromas of body odor and stinky water made things nearly unbearable. The air was so rotten, that a few of the national staff became ill and were dismissed from the job site.

At the fifteen-foot mark, the muddy texture diminished and the team began hoisting only clear water out of the hole. At that point they connected a pumping mechanism and made things more efficient. However, to their surprise, the water level failed to diminish, even after hours of pumping thousands of gallons. According to Dr. Schor's radar imaging work, they were looking for the mouth of a new tunnel at around the 26-foot mark. Since the water was now clear, a diver was sent down to survey.

At the 27-foot mark, the diver found what they were looking for. It was a second basalt-looking doorway. As promised, it had an arched ceiling, and looked to descend at a 30-degree angle to the southeast. Though Dr. Schor would never know, his research was now vindicated in a significant way.

They decided that the walls of the vertical hole below the Osiris tomb would need to be encased in tubing. This way, they could manage the seepage that relentlessly refilled the shaft. The plastic tubing gave them a diameter of four feet, and came in piece-together slats, three to a four-foot section. It was easy to assemble, and only took the Egyptian nationals a half-day to build. This tactic worked. The pumps cleared the next section of the shaft.

Once the hole was dry and they had a working surface on the new door, the same diamond-based tools and jackhammers were used to crack a seam in the dense material.

To their surprise, at the first breakthrough cut of the jackhammer, a powerful stream of water burst through the opening. More water, but this time it was under tremendous pressure. So much, that it knocked the tool operator down and caused the jackhammer to take a meaty bite out of his thigh.

Though it was only a small crack in the basalt-looking material, the water came forth with such force that the hole encased, and again the tubing began to fill with water. The pumps tried to keep up, but to no avail. They quickly calculated that the water was coming in so fast that the levels were creeping up at a rate of six inches per hour, despite the pumps operating at full-tilt.

"This is a disaster!" shouted Kahn, who scampered up the ladder ahead of his Hand. "Did that lunatic know there was this sort of pressure down there?" He was talking about the former Antiquities chief, Dr. Hawass. His question was rhetorical, so the Hand didn't answer. Once they stepped outside the shaft, the Hand decided to offer his thoughts.

"The way I see it, we have a matter of hours before water is pouring out of this hole here. If we want to know what's down there, we need to go now."

"Yeah?" Kahn smiled sadistically and got to within inches of the Hand's face and screamed, "How do you propose we run a jackhammer underwater, ace?"

This upset the Hand. His nose flared, his fists clenched, and his jaw got stiff. He looked like a fifth-grader on the verge of throwing a temper tantrum. It was an odd sight to see. Odder still was how Kahn responded to his demeanor, quickly saying, "I'm sorry Jonesey, I'm just frustrated. I didn't mean to yell at you."

"But you did," the Hand replied flatly, squinting up at his boss. "I won't tolerate it."

"I know, please forgive me." Kahn said this with a jaw-dropping amount of mortal shame.

"It's fine. I'll procure the needed marine-tools. We'll send divers down and they'll have to cut through that rock with handhelds. We need as many water pumps as we can get, and if we don't want the plateau flooding, I suggest we get some water tankers here too. And you'll need to tell Morsi."

The Hand then nodded, having made the decision as to how they'd proceed, and without another word or permission, departed from Kahn's presence. Abdullah nervously looked around to ascertain whether or not that exchange had been witnessed by anyone within his company. He didn't see anyone paying any attention to him. *Thank God.*

Their relationship was an odd one at best, and incidents like these needed to be kept... private.

CHAPTER 40
Lux et Veritas

Monday, July 2, 2012

Braxton got the Dotty matter out of the way fast. They hardly shared hellos and hugs before he launched straight in and told them how Father Abelemy died at the hands of the Phantoms. It was abrupt, but effective.

Anny cried and Solomon internalized. Bax decided to disclose the tragedy quickly for two reasons. One, he was tired of carrying it around with him, and did not want to be burdened with trying to identify a good time to talk about it while they were on mission together. Two, and more importantly, he wanted to give Solomon and Anny as much time as possible to process the information and grieve the loss before returning to the saga at hand. From experience, Bax knew there was never a good time to talk about the death of a loved one. It was often easier to get it out of the way fast, like ripping off a Band-Aid with one swift motion.

Bax also explained why the crew was forced to abandon the safe house in Edgewater. He told the general story surrounding Atlanta, Sis, the bunker, and their new home in Manvel, Texas, before wrapping up with, "That's about it, really. What's been going on with you two?"

His ending drew a needed chuckle from Sully and Anny. Clearly, the team State-side had been under more strain than they had these past few weeks.

The next morning they met for breakfast in the hotel's rather unattractive café. When Anny stepped away to use the restroom, Bax leaned over, slapped Sully on the shoulder and said, "Bloody well fit, isn't she?"

"Huh?" Solomon was chewing on a mediocre egg omelet, cooked to order at the grille.

"She's smokin' hot bruv; she's got some sort of radiance about her. You two together, I'm assuming?"

"Oh, yeah, we are. It's been fun. I won't lie to you, we almost decided to disappear and punt this mess."

"Rooter might-a had somethin' to say 'bout that."

Solomon nodded, as if to say, *that's why we're still here.*

Splice

When Anny returned she looked at Bax and point-blank asked if he wanted to know if they were together. She exaggerated her annoyance that he hadn't brought it up sooner. He told her about his suspicions and congratulated her on persevering until the dimwit – Sully – finally caught the clue. A little jazz was dished back and forth, they all had a laugh, and then they returned to business.

"What do you plan on doing? There's something going on over there, but we're not getting close to that hole without some conflict."

"Let's go after breakfast and have a look around," Bax said. "We're just going to play a wait-and-see game for now, alright? Take it as it comes, as they say."

After breakfast they ventured to the northeast entrance of the Giza Plateau, but were surprised to find that the Antiquities Police who normally occupied that post were replaced with Egyptian military. These guys were not at all interested in taking $20 in exchange for granting access to the rear-side of the pyramids. Instead, they were told to walk around to the main tourist entrance.

Once through the main entrance, they kept to the crowded areas so as to avoid detection. From various vantage points, they counted three large water hoses protruding from the mouth of the shaft. The hoses followed the base of the causeway toward the Great Pyramid, then at around the half-way point, the hoses turned due-north for about 300 feet, until disappearing underneath large, portable, industrial barriers that said in English – and presumably in Arabic and French - "Please excuse our mess."

From the north entrance to the plateau, water tankers drove in and out of the area behind the construction barriers. They were splashing water everywhere as they exited the Pyramid complex.

"They're pumping water out of the shaft," Solomon was first to verbalize the obvious. "That's why we couldn't get in from over there."

"Did you see any water in that hole before?"

"No," Anny fielded the question, "we only got as far as the first vertical shaft and it seemed dry as a bone."

Bax was trained to notice the nuances that normal folks generally miss. Though he pretended to gawk at one of the three pyramids like any British tourist, from behind his sunglasses, he kept his eyes on the commotion surrounding the shaft. As he watched, an older gent emerged from the hole. He was bearded, likely of Middle Eastern descent. Something about this guy piqued the Brit's interest. There was something out of the ordinary about him…

For starters, he was being followed by a pale-skinned half-link of a man who wore a suit in the blazing hot sun. The short fellow held a clipboard that seemed awkward and out-of-place. Not just that, when these two came out, the guards went from slouched and relaxed to rigid and tense. Bax smiled. This was the man in charge, or at least the man in charge of this operation. *And he's giving us an appearance in the plain light of day. There's a score...*

Bax needed to get a picture.

His camera only had a 4x zoom, so they were going to have to get within 150 feet of the man in order for the image to render any quality worth sending back to Con for analysis. Adjusting his position, he stood between the shaft and the others and said, "Ey, look over my shoulder. See that Carpet Jockey with the beard, standing at the entrance? He's the boss."

"How do you know?"

"I just know. Anny, take the camera. You guys approach from the south. I'll meet you along the causeway just in front of the shaft there." Bax slowly started to move away from them, but he kept instructing as he did. "Say 'hi again' when we see one another. Ask me to take your picture. I'll position you for the shot. Any luck, I snap this fig-eater and we make hay while the sun shines, right?"

The plan worked perfectly, but the bearded man was a natural incognito and instinctively kept his back toward the camera while they snapped their pictures. The little man with skin the color of cream cheese was less aware, and gawked with a stupid, open-mouthed *I'm the village idiot* face for a perfect high definition full-frontal.

Bax wanted a photo of the boss, but he knew they couldn't linger.

Both Anny and Solomon wore full-brim straw hats and sunglasses, so Bax was sure their identity was secure, but to be safe, he instructed them to meet back at the entrance to the plateau and to keep their backs to the men of intrigue. They complied and maneuvered northward as Braxton followed the causeway in the other direction, toward the Sphinx.

The short man was still gawking with a droopy-eyed countenance as he passed, so Bax gave a casual wave, as if to say 'hi,' and that brought him out of his sag. As if being jolted out of a memory from long ago, he came to attention, gave a half-smile to Bax in return, and nervously turned his attention back to the boss-man. As he did, the older gent glanced over his shoulder, presumably making sure the tourists had moved on before turning around and reengaging his right-hand man.

Braxton felt as if they stumbled on a pot of gold. There was something authoritative about the older man in particular. He stood tall, in a way, and moved with a sense of supreme confidence. The Brit wondered how high up the chain of

Splice

command he went. After a few minutes of waiting, Bax began looking around for the others. His pulse elevated when he finally spotted them in the crowd among the cart merchants.

"Everything okay?" he asked as they approached.

Solomon looked at Anny before responding, "There's this guy we've seen off and on since we arrived the first time." Anny was looking back into the crowd, nervously.

"Who is he?"

"Don't know. He's tall, wears a cloak and a hood, and we've never seen his face. He just stands off in the distance and stares, and then disappears when the timing suits him. There's something about him that gives me the willies."

"It's true," Anny turned around and looked at Bax. "Sully told me about him in Istanbul, but the day we got back he appeared again. He's connected to all this, somehow."

"You guys just see him?"

"Yeah, over there," Solomon nodded toward the cart venders. "This guy can move, even though he's tall. Crazy, one minute he's there, the next he's gone without a trace. Never seen anything like it."

Though the cloaked figure was an intrigue, Bax was most critically interested in getting his digital images to Con for an amateur workup. The chance they'd be able to ID the short man without access to a large-scale database was slim but worth a shot. If Con's efforts failed to ID the man, Braxton knew he had a shot to call in a favor with MI6.

They maneuvered back through the venders toward Al Mansoureya Road, the main thoroughfare that cut north-south through the shantytown along the eastern boarder of the plateau. This road led back toward the hotel.

The hot, arid temperatures were not nearly as bothersome to Solomon or Anny now, as their bodies had somewhat acclimated. Bax, who spent years in desert-type theaters of war, was also unaffected by the heat. They decided to walk, rather than hail a cab. Along the way, they talked about the activity at the shaft and openly wondered about the water being pumped out. Bax was convinced that they were moving a large quantity of water, as evidenced by the industrial pipes and hoses and the large tanker trucks filled one after another in rapid succession. He wondered if the water-pumping was a 24-hour endeavor, and resolved to return later that night to find out.

When they reached the hotel elevators, Braxton told them that he was unable to log onto the Internet through the hotel's network the night prior. Anny suggested that he use one of their computers for now and try again with the front office later. He agreed, so skipped the sixth floor and followed them to their room on the 8th. Solomon used his keycard to unlock the door and stepped out of the way for Anny, showcasing some old-fashioned chivalry. But as soon as she entered, she stopped short and startlingly gasped, "Oh my God!"

Bax moved before thinking and pushed passed Sully with a defensive posture. There was a bathroom on the right and the hall opened to the bedroom a few steps further. Upon entering, he found Anny shivering uncontrollably with her hands around her mouth and staring down at the floor. On the other side of the room he saw an enormous person, broad shouldered and tall, cloaked and hooded, standing and staring at them. Though under the cloak, his arms looked as if they were crossed across his chest. His face was hidden in the shadow of his hood. Solomon was right -- this person's presence conjured awful feelings of terror.

Solomon burst into the room a second after Bax and stopped short when he saw the being. He muttered something under his breath before stepping behind Bax and over to Anny. He put an arm around her and tried to bring comfort, but she shivered and kept her eyes downcast. He could hear her whispering a prayer, "please God, make it go away, please…"

The door slammed behind them with uncommon force, *BANG,* they all jumped involuntarily. Bax attempted to step forward and engage the intruder, but all he could manage was a partial, half step and a quivering voice, "wh-what do you want with us?"

Then they all heard, somewhere inside their souls, the bass-deep boom of a bellowing voice say, "Do not be afraid. I'm Abele from a distant place, and you have been chosen."

Anny fainted. She literally lost consciousness and fell to the floor at the sound of Abele's voice in her head. Solomon grabbed at his temples and fell to one knee in discomfort. It wasn't physical pain, but a jarring sensation that came as a result of suddenly lacking all sense of privacy. The scrutiny he was under was too much. It made him want to get low, crawl into a hole and hide. He looked at Anny and touched her cheek, envying her for checking out of this awful reality.

Bax held his ground, but it took every ounce of his trained will to stay on his feet and keep his eyes up. The Brit was feeling the same sensations. The sense of internal scrutiny was so powerful that it was impossible to stand with shoulders high. He hunched slightly and gaped from a contorted face.

His discomfort was the result of the nakedness and transparency he felt under the piercing presence of this clearly non-human life form. He too wanted to hide from what he felt were the eyes of millions of onlookers, studying and analyzing the totality of his life and actions. The sensation was unlike anything he'd ever experienced. In the midst of it all, Braxton watched with a petrified gaze as the being opened his cloak and tossed off his hood. He was not human, but he appeared human-like.

He had eyes, ears, nose, hair, and a mouth, but everything was unique. His eyes gleamed bright, no pupils, just a brilliant blue. They were also illuminated, as if light came forth from within him. His mouth, lips, and nose looked human in shape and very skin-like, but cut into his face was what looked like ornamental tattoos, similar to war paint. However, these tattoos changed colors, textures, and even patterns as he stood motionless. The 'tattoos' on his face combined with the brilliance of his eyes commanded such majestic wonder that Braxton had a hard time looking at anything else. His hair was dark, curly, and shoulder length.

His attire was accented with what looked like solid, light-emitting gems and jewels, but the material shifted color and radiance, just like the tattoos. It was as if his clothing was made out of a vibrant and translucent semi-solid liquid, or some sort of gelatin. His hands were huge, and at his waist hung a sword, the blade made of what looked like light. It wasn't like a light saber from Star Wars, but more of a thick blade made of light and semi-solid matter. He did not speak audibly, at least they didn't think he did, but when he spoke, they heard him loud and clear in their minds.

The presence walked toward Bax who steadied himself in preparation for a physical altercation. Three giant strides were all it took before Abele was upon him. Fear gripped every sense and nerve, as Bax swung a fist at the being. Abele, moving with lightning-fast speed, restrained the Brit by crossing his arms and turning Bax into a figurative pretzel. Initially, Bax tried to squirm, but searing pain shot through his body and he immediately stopped, vowing in his mind to not try that again. He was totally overcome. He simply settled into the giant's arms and waited. Abele slowly let him go and Bax obediently knelt to the floor.

Abele turned his gaze toward the attorney and held out his hand. Then he said with that booming voice, "Solomon Keyes, stand up."

Solomon put his hand in the alien's and stood to his feet, his knees still quivering. As he stood for a moment, a sense of restored confidence passed over him. Sully looked into the blue orbs of this creature's eyes. The experience was terrifying in ways that defy human understanding. At that moment, Solomon knew his life was fully in Abele's hands. He had no ability whatsoever to withstand the being's physical or psychological will. Abele smiled ever so slightly, and it almost brought Sully to tears. It was as though, through that simple expression, he assured Sully beyond any doubt whatsoever, that he was not alone.

"You have been chosen. He shall have a crown; you shall have Lux et Veritas, the light of wisdom and the truth of judgment." Abele was still holding Solomon's right hand. At that moment, he passed his left hand over Solomon's outstretched forearm. As he did, a hot sensation flowed through Sully and he flinched slightly. Abele commanded, "Retrieve it by night."

Abele let go of his hand and touched Bax on the top of his head. The Brit then looked up at the giant figure, smiled, and nodded, as if he heard something. Whatever it was, it was clearly private. Abele then bent down and touched Anny on the shoulder and she sat up. Sully saw fear get replaced with an expression of peace and thankfulness, followed by tears that rolled down her cheeks as she whispered over and over, "Thank you, thank you."

Abele then reaffixed his cloak and hood, and his face disappeared back into the shadow. He then started walking backward toward the windows on the far side of the room, and as he did, Solomon looked at Anny who was still sitting peacefully propped up against the wall. She appeared to enjoy the tears that remained. Bax looked contemplative, but he too was at peace.

Sully looked at his forearm. There, burned into his skin, was a series of numbers. They were emitting light and changing colors, just like the 'tattoo' markings on Abele's face. Finally, when Solomon looked up, he realized, not surprisingly, that Abele was gone. Anny sat in tearful peace, Braxton sat in contemplative silence, and Solomon sat down at the edge of the bed and looked at his arm. There was nothing anybody could say, for the experience defied any logic or reason. But they were at peace, and they now had orders.

Sully passed his fingers over the markings on his arm. It felt like the skin had been carved out, and the voids left behind had been filled with a substance never before seen on Earth. It was a bright, brilliant substance, a solid matter that glimmered like light passing through water.

He read the numbers in succession, *24537732531271*, before reclining back on the bed. There he laid, staring at the ceiling through a haze of wonder and amazement.

CHAPTER 41
A Bellwether Moment

Wednesday, July 4, 2012

The Cardinal sunk heavily into an overstuffed chair in Abdullah's suite at the Four Season's Nile Plaza Hotel. Abdullah sent the Hand back to the shaft to provide oversight while waiting for the arrival of the marine equipment they ordered.

"You look troubled, Cardinal." Abdullah handed the Cardinal a Jack Daniels, neat.

"What I say here stays here?" Cardinal Salah took a sip.

"Of course."

"There is trouble in the Vatican, the type of trouble that dwarfs sex scandals. The type of trouble that could mark the end of our order as we know it."

"Really? That assessment seems a tad dramatic for a man who avoids theatrics." Abdullah sat back into a chair opposite the Cardinal and took his own sip.

"All the more troublesome then. Since we last met, I've sought to identify the Vatican's role in these most worrisome days, but the more I look, the more I find. The more I find, the more I must ask deep and troubling questions. Honestly, such is the horror of some things I've uncovered that I am, for the first time in my life, actively contemplating a resignation of my duties as Cardinal."

"Wow," Abdullah's eyebrows rose with surprise at that comment. "Anything you can talk about?"

"Some perhaps," Salah adjusted his posture and cast a cautionary look around the suite. "Last week, I attended an ears-only meeting where it was announced that Benedict will be resigning. This will be made public at the end of the year."

"A Pope is resigning? That's tremendously uncommon, right? Does that even happen? May I ask why?"

"Officially?" the Cardinal chuckled. "Officially, for health reasons. Unofficially, it has to do with what some in the media are calling the Vatileaks Scandal. You can look it up online if you haven't kept up."

"I don't look anything up, online. I'd tell my Hand to do it, but since he's out, why don't you fill me in?" Abdullah was enjoying this, but kept his demeanor, intact. Vatican intrigue was always fodder for a fantastic story.

"Documents were leaked to the press. The culprits began leaking them last year, and slowly, the drizzle has become a full-scale storm. They speak of certain clergy who are jockeying for power within the Curia. The documents point to a longstanding culture of bribery and sexual cover-ups involving much higher-ranking clergymen than ever before thought. Worse still, some emails written by current and previous Popes discuss ongoing money laundering activities. It's a big scandal that the Vatican is doing everything in its power to keep quiet, but it's bound to come out sooner or later. You can read about the rest."

"I'm sorry to hear that."

"The Jesuits are making a move. I believe this is all being orchestrated by them."

"The Jesuits?" Abdullah took another sip. "Weren't they the ones you told us about, who run the telescope in the United States?"

"Yes, they are. The announcement of Benedict's resignation is stunning, and may bring about the fulfillment of Saint Malachi's prophecy." Salah could tell Abdullah had no idea what he was talking about, so he went a bit further.

"Malachi was a 12th century Archbishop of Armagh, Ireland. As the story goes, he came to Rome on official business and while there, had a dream. It was a prophecy about the final 112 Popes. John Paul II was number 110, Benedict currently is 111, and whoever comes next is referred to in the prophecy as *Petrus Romanus*, the final Pope of the Holy Roman Catholic Church."

"Really? Is the prophecy credible?"

"It is a matter of much debate outside the Vatican walls, but within the College of Cardinals, Malachi's prophecy is what's fueling the power struggle. I count no less than six of my colleagues who are currently vying for the seat of *Petrus Romanus*. They are so brazen and arrogant that they openly say as much." The Cardinal mimicked a spitting motion to express his disgust with them, "The egotism of these men is an abomination and it sickens me."

"That makes it sound like the prophecy is quite credible."

"If it is, we're in for a ride. I know the prophecy by heart, which says: *In the final persecution of the Holy Roman Church, there will sit Peter the Roman, who will pasture his sheep in many tribulations, and when these things are finished, the city of seven hills* — that's Rome - *will be destroyed, and the dreadful judge will judge his people.* I fear that the proponents of evil have already won."

"How is that?"

"Because if I told you how many of us within the Catholic order are beginning to conceive the eventuality that a non-Christ derived salvation is coming…"

The Cardinal looked off into the space between him and Abdullah, seemingly lost in a distressful thought. Then, in almost a whisper, he said, "It's not just the Jesuits who believe an alien species is imminently arriving here on earth. The power brokers in the Curio are wrestling for position and status so that they may inherit a seat as the vicar of whosoever or whatsoever shall arrive next and proclaim this salvation of souls. Some even say the worldwide religions will be reset in this hour. I truly never thought I'd see the day, and yet the evidence is compelling. So very compelling."

The Cardinal sat quietly for a moment, and then began to muse, almost to himself, "The most significant and important Catholic theologian of our time, Hons Urs von Balthasar, once wrote in his *Casta Meretrix*, 'the figure of the prostitute perfectly defines the Church of the New Covenant in her most splendid mystery of salvation.' You see, Abdullah, in taking the gospel of salvation to the ends of the world, we have chosen to be unified with the world, and unity was only attainable by harlotry or by intermarriage. This one world form is what Balthasar defined as 'the new apostolic union of peoples,' a phenomenon that could never have been avoided."

"We've known it forever though, haven't we?" he continued. "Even U.S. President Ronald Reagan once said, when he addressed the UN, 'how quickly our differences worldwide would vanish if we faced an alien threat from outside this world.' He was right, and the utopian, one world order will be the final vanquishing of religious thought and individual expression. Recently I've wondered, what did Mr. Reagan know when he said those words?"

"Cardinal, excuse me, but this seems like hopeful vindication for you. Have you not been the champion of unity? Has that not been your identified lifelong mission?"

"Unity of the human spirit, sure. United about our globally shared human exceptionalism, absolutely. But united in belief? Heavens no! This unity of mind and belief is but an erosion of what it means to be human. The worldwide progressive movement knows not what it's asking, I fear."

Abdullah nodded contemplatively. The Cardinal never failed to surprise him. Though he wasn't buying everything the clergyman was selling, Abdullah enjoyed hearing the perspectives of wise, learned men of the religious cloth. Their viewpoints were always filtered through the rather constant paradigm of faith, and that made for interesting discussions and debates.

Religious academics, by virtue of their need to protect their faith, always had to more thoroughly vet prevalent scientific data before publically accepting it. This was a safety mechanism to avoid mockery when advancements in technology inevitably change the traditional, religious status quo. It sounded to Abdullah like the Cardinal was afraid the Catholic Church was coming up on a bellwether moment, a moment when 2,000 years of religious nonsense was about to get turned on its head. If so, thousands of the world's powerful and wealthy elites were about to be made fools.

Abdullah Kahn, for his part, more closely aligned in character with the power-seekers the Cardinal described. If the world was about to unite under something as cataclysmic as an invasion of another species, there were always powerful parts to play and fortunes to be made. Posturing for that eventuality was not a bad business policy; at least in Kahn's mind.

Abdullah admired the Carnegies, Rothschilds, Vanderbilts, and other titans of the industrial revolution. The decisions made by these ruthless men launched empires and wealth that rivaled the riches of Solomon. It was that type of wealth and that sort of legacy Kahn pursued, and why not?

The two men heard a click at the front door and it swung open. In walked the Hand. He was panting softly, as if he hurried back to the hotel on foot. He was flushed too. In fact, he looked miserable.

"The shipment arrived. We'll be ready to dive as early as this evening."

"That's good news. At last, we find out what secrets lay beneath the Osiris tomb," Kahn touched rock glasses with the Cardinal and took a sip, without first offering the Hand a drink. Insulted, the Hand glared at him with beady little eyes and pursed lips. Kahn took no notice.

"Will you be accompanying us to the shaft later tonight, Cardinal?"

"No sir, I'll be enjoying a nice book in my room, eagerly looking forward to hearing what you find."

They raised their glasses again and had another drink. The two men carried on for another hour, eventually forgetting the Hand was even present. The Hand did not forget them, however, and sat stewing from a quiet corner of the suite. The whole time they talked, he glowered at Abdullah with a burning hatred, and hung on the man's every word.

Your time is coming Abdullah, the Hand grinned sadistically. *It's coming...*

CHAPTER 42
Elephantine Island

Wednesday, July 4, 2012

The pictures taken at the shaft, a brief description of that bizarre event involving Abele, and the numbers etched into Sully's arm were all sent to Con via encrypted email. Con's response came quickly. He asked for a couple of days to pour over the data, but suggested a Skype call for later that night.

"Still doesn't hurt, huh?" Bax asked.

"No, not at all. Strange isn't it?" Solomon ran his fingers over the illuminated numbers on his arm as they sat together, waiting for their dinners to be served. They were at a restaurant Anny found during their first visit called Kahn Mousa. It was a feel-good local joint that served good local food.

"What's really strange," Anny interjected, "is when we go to bed, his arm looks like a nightlight under the blankets. And it slowly pulsates, going from dim to bright, over like a ten or fifteen minute span."

"That's gonzo, mate," Bax too ran his finger across the numbers, his eyes inspecting the mesmerizing light. Sully suddenly retracted his arm as Braxton sat up straight to make room for the arriving plates. Since the incident with Abele, Solomon wore long-sleeved shirts all over blistering Cairo so he wouldn't attract attention. He even avoided Anny's favorite hangout spot, the pool.

After Abele disappeared and they came back to reality, a quick Google search revealed that the Latin phrase he used, *Lux et Veritas,* was translated to mean *light and truth.* It was actually a phrase Yale University adopted long ago as its motto.

After running a few simple algorithms in an old MI6 software suite, Bax was able to figure out that the succession of numbers on Sully's arm probably corresponded to GPS coordinates. However, it was not immediately obvious where on the globe they pointed. If the numbers coordinated south-by-east, they pointed to the wilderness of Mozambique. If south-by-west, they pointed to somewhere in the South Atlantic, off the coast of Brazil. If north-by-west, they pointed to the middle of the Atlantic Ocean. But, when fixed north-by-east, the coordinates pointed to the southeast corner of Elephantine Island, an established archaeological site in southern Egypt.

Based on current circumstances, Elephantine Island seemed like the most likely spot. The team decided to make the trip, unless Con came back with totally different intelligence.

If their assumptions were correct, the numbers on Sully's arm lined up as GPS coordinates for 24° 5'3.77"N by 32°53'12.71"E. If taking Abele's words literally, they were to go to Elephantine Island by night, go precisely to the location referenced by the numbers, and find a thing called *Lux et Veritas* there.

After dinner, they reconvened in the honeymooners' room to Skype Con. The connection went through on the second go, and like the first call from Istanbul, the picture flickered and the audio wasn't great.

"So, the way this works," Con explained, "I upload the subject's photo into the search program, and then assign a data range, telling the program to query any number of searchable domains with that data. My program then compares the subject's photo to those images that are returned, and if one ranks as a 90% or higher likely match, the image is retained for manual review. The problem is that there are hundreds of millions of online images, and a good fifty different large-scale public databanks. Say I pick the right databank, like Google Images. Even with my proprietary mark and search algo, there are multiple result variations."

"So, we still won't know who he is?" asked Solomon.

"We don't. Straight-up, I'd need a month to even make a dent in all the pictures that are online and searchable. It's the manual review of the final million that takes the time. With two days, I'm running a friggin' needle-in-a-haystack lotto here."

"Fair enough, what about the water being pumped out of the shaft?" asked Bax.

"Nothing yet. I did reach out to Leola's friend, Jennifer, the journalist at the Post. Because of her Middle East contacts, I asked if she's heard any rumors of activity at the shaft. She said she hasn't, but she'll call a few contacts and poke around. I'm supposed to hear back from her on Wednesday."

"Did she ask about Leola?"

"She did."

"And?" Solomon was nervous about old acquaintances poking around, especially inquiring minds like Jennifer Cox, who had a reputation for bringing secrets to light.

"And, I told her that after you guys broke up she quit the firm and moved out west. I told her she seems to be doing well, and promised to tell her hi next time she called. She seemed satisfied, but what do I know?"

"Con," Bax interjected, "don't take the photos to anybody else…"

"Rooter believes he's got a reliable contact at the NSA," Con interrupted. "I could have the guy looked at closer, and we could possibly get an answer on this much sooner. You sure you don't want us to ask?"

Bax paused and looked at Solomon with an inquisitive expression. Solomon told him that he never met Rooter's contact, but knew of him, and thought they were college buddies.

"Rooter there?" Bax finally asked as Rooter came into the picture.

"Your boy safe?"

"Hell yeah, he's safe. He was a roommate of mine for a semester back in college. Computer whiz. You know what you think of when you close your eyes and imagine an IRS worker? Pimple-faced, four-eyed, suspender-wearing schnookle? My guy is that, except he's at the NSA."

"Can you get the photograph to him from a remote location using one-and-chuck gear? We have a perfect place there with Papa Roger and I'd hate for it to get compromised."

"Are you kidding with me right now?" Rooter got close to the camera and they could see he hadn't shaved for a few days, "I'm an American you cheeky-jerkoff. We invented espionage, the bomb, and kept the Queen's vermin from saluting German sensei for the rest of their lives. You done?"

Bax looked at Sully, who smiled with amusement and shrugged, as if to say he took no responsibility for Rooter's belligerence.

"So, that mean yes?"

Rooter rolled his eyes, "Yes."

"Okay, then. Go for it."

"Rooter out," he abruptly left the screen. Con quickly reassumed the position of speaking into the camera.

"Obviously, you guys know that you're looking for a mystical set of stones or gems right?"

"No, what? What are we looking for?"

"Uh-huh. I think you're looking for the Urim and Thummim," Con began, slowly pronouncing the words Or-um and Tu-mim.

"They are ancient divination tools used by the Jewish high priest, said to decipher the will of God. Urim and Thummim are literally translated to mean *lights and perfections*. There isn't a whole lot of information about this artifact, but in the book of First Samuel, chapter 28, the Urim and Thummim are listed as one of three accepted forms of communication with the Divine. Dreams and prophecies round out the list. The best physical descriptions we have of the Urim and Thummim are from the Jewish Scriptures, and lead us to believe they are jewels or stones of some sort. There is a somewhat interesting connection to Marduk and Babylonian mythology as well. It's said that the high priest of Israel put the Urim and Thummim in a concealed pocket within the Ephod. The Ephod was a breastplate the priest wore as part of his official vestments. The Urim and Thummim would then somehow interact with the metaphysical realm and provide a communication vehicle between humans and the divine, the so-called 'God of Israel.' But in Assyrian and Babylonian mythology, the Tablets of Destiny appear to be very similar. Marduk put his seal on the tablets, and so long as those tablets rested on the breast of a mediating demigod, mankind could communicate with the so-called deities from beyond."

"So, you're looking for a really cool rock in a really old rock pile. Good luck with that…" they heard Rooter say, faintly.

"Which leads me," Con said, as he turned to give Rooter a sour look, "to the numbers. I'm sure you figured out by now that they're global coordinates, right?" Bax nodded to the webcam.

"Well, it's really interesting that those coordinates put you on the southern tip of Elephantine Island, which is the location of a modern-day dig. You have to look pretty deep, but one set of artifacts recovered from that archeological site is called the Elephantine Papyri. The Papyri consists of hundreds of scrolls and letters written by the people living there, including a Jewish population from around 650 BC. So, as it turns out, Elephantine was the location of a Jewish military outpost during King Nebuchadnezzar's sacking and burning of Jerusalem. Furthermore, the Papyri talks exhaustively about a replica temple to Yahweh - that's the name for the Jewish God - on Elephantine, which was evidently damaged by an anti-Semitic uprising around 480 BC. Anyway, the ultimate connection for us is that the Jews might have smuggled their precious artifacts out of Jerusalem before the Babylonians burned and pillaged their holy city. And if they did, what better place to hide those artifacts than in a secret replica temple to Yahweh guarded by a military garrison?"

Bax nodded, "Good work, Con."

"What sort of political/tourist climate are we looking at for Elephantine Island?" Sully asked.

"As far as I can tell, the tours available in the city of Aswan will boat you past the island, but access to that area is strictly off-limits. This is probably why E.T. told you to retrieve the artifact at night. I did find a hotel that's on an island just to the south of Elephantine called the Pyramisa Isis Island Resort. The Nile flows to the north, so you might be able to swim there with the current at night. It's a little over a quarter-mile."

"Okay, we'll figure that out. You got anything else?" asked Bax.

"Yeah, watch for alligators," again, Rooter's voice could be heard in the background.

"I do," Con said, elevating his voice over Rooters. "I noticed an etching in the rock by the opening to the shaft in that photo you snapped of the midget. It's over his left shoulder. I did a little research because it looked like a hieroglyphic image of some sort, but it's actually a burn mark. It's pretty cool because this mark has baffled archeologists for centuries. This burn corresponds to what some in the scientific community call zero-point or new energy. It's a bit complicated but let me try and explain." Con paused, presumably to look at his notes.

"That mark, actually, is called the Osirian symbol, and it's a perfect mathematical matrix. So check this out, the matrix starts with what's called a Vector Equilibrium, which basically indicates perfect uniformity and stability within a field of energy's inner core. This, according to some, is the building blocks of a theoretical energy source known as the Taurus. That Osirian symbol is constructed by taking 64 pyramids, that's 64 four-sided tetrahedron, and overlaying each one with a toroidal energy field. Next, you strip away the tetrahedron – pyramids – and what you have left is the exact symbol that's burned into the rock in the picture you sent me."

Bax looked at the others to gage their comprehension of what Con was saying. They too were lost. "Not sure we follow, mate."

"I don't know what else to say," Con said as he stretched. "The ancients never burned pictographs into the stone; they etched and drew them with pigment. Furthermore, the burn should have faded long ago, unless it was more recently put there, but scientists have known about this mark for hundreds of years."

"You got a theory?" Solomon asked over Bax's shoulder.

"Not yet. Just that we have a really strange marking at the entrance of an apparently significant tomb that indicates the existence of an unlimited energy source. You know, some conspiracy theorists say that the pyramids in Egypt are more than just eye-candy for tourists. A lot of what's out there is stupid, but one theory caught my attention. Long ago, the Pyramid-Complex there in Giza was actually built on the banks of the Nile, back before the Nile River was dammed up the way it is today. Originally, there were retaining walls built around each of the pyramids too, probably for flood mitigation. What's weird is, well below the levels of the historical water table, scientists have found rose quartz, which is not indigenous to Egypt."

"Yeah," Sully said, motioning for him to continue. "And?"

"And that seems to indicate that something is still down there. Makes sense in the context of the Phantoms' intrigue with the Osiris shaft. I just don't know what, though. I need to keep reading. I guess that's about all I have."

The conversation ended a few minutes later, and after some casual planning, Bax retired to his own room.

It was impossible to know where popular belief and conspiracy theory merged, so they decided not to worry too much about Con's Osirian symbol disclosure, and instead focus on the task at hand. None of them knew how fast the Nile flowed but didn't want to chance having to try and swim upstream, so they took Con's advice and booked their rooms at the Pyramisa Resort.

CHAPTER 43
An Artifact from the Deep

Saturday, July 7, 2012

At the time of their first entry, the dive team insisted Abdullah stay behind for safety reasons. Wise advice. While three men dove into the water-shaft, only two reemerged. The cause of the third diver's death and disappearance was a mystery.

The initial survey divers brought flashlights and strung underwater rope-lighting as they progressed down the long passage. They were trying to prep the hallway for future dives. As predicted, the waterlogged hall descended at a 30-degree angle, heading southeast, with an arched ceiling the entire way.

At just under 900 feet from the opening, the hallway ended and the surveyors swam into a huge underwater cavern. They could not tell how deep or how wide it was, but based on the horizontal arch in the cavern's bedrock, they surmised that if symmetrically cylindrical, the cavern had a diameter of at least a half-mile. Their explanation made little sense to Kahn, so one of the surviving divers explained it another way.

He tied a piece of string to a soda can and held it up, with the can in one hand and the string in the other, "This string represents the passageway that starts under the sarcophagus. The passage led us to a huge cavern that we think is shaped like this soda can. We were unable to find the other side though, so we're not certain how fat the can, cavern, actually is. Peter and I were marking the entrance back into the hallway with rope-lighting, and that's when JB said he was going to have a look around. About five minutes later we heard JB scream, and then silence."

"Precisely, what did you hear?" The Hand asked

"I heard what sounded like an earthquake, a loud rumbling noise. That was followed by the scream and then, nothing."

Since JB's untimely demise, Bernie Waite was now the dive leader, and he was the one explaining all of this.

"Also, a few minutes after he left our position, he said something about thinking he saw dim lights ahead. Peter warned him to be careful, and then the rumbling sound, a scream, and poof, as if his com shut off, we heard nothing else. That was it."

Circumstances being what they were, Kahn was forced to dramatically adjust the payment contract for the two remaining divers, Bernie and Peter. That was part of what had him so annoyed, but mostly he was weary of the succession of challenges they kept facing. It was as though something didn't want them to uncover the secrets from the deep.

Initially, Bernie and Peter could not be persuaded to venture back into that cavern for any reason. But after some convincing that involved adding two zeros to the end of each of their paychecks, they agreed, but not without other equipment.

They asked for top-shelf Hollis sea-scooters for efficient maneuvering and quicker escapes. They also demanded an infrared robotic camera, so they could peer into the black cavern without actually venturing in. In addition, they demanded a special underwater sonar navigation device that was typically used for underwater engineering ops.

Kahn acquiesced to all the demands and made one of his own. He was not going to be talked out of entering the cavern with them the next time around. Everyone agreed, and the required items were quickly procured.

After all the equipment arrived, the time came for Bernie, Peter and Abdullah to head back into the shaft. The mood was serious and somber as they geared up just inside the mouth of the Osiris tomb.

The pumps stymied the rising water some, but were unable to fully keep up. The water now reached the second landing and was almost to the ceiling of the room that housed the seven burial chambers. That's why the men were gearing up just inside the mouth of the shaft. They would have to climb down the first ladder in-gear, and swim down the second until reaching the Osiris tomb. From there, they would swim down another 30 feet to the mouth of the long passage. They would drop another 60 feet in depth as they traversed nearly 1,000 feet of passageway. That's where they would hit the cavern entrance and try to figure out what malice existed in there.

Once they were fully submerged inside the second level of the shaft, they conducted a final gear check of their coms, cameras and gauges. They set their dive computers for a mixed-gas decompression schedule, with an alarm system triggered at about 130 feet. When everything was dialed-in, Bernie led the way, Kahn followed, and Peter brought up the rear. Each of them was using a Hollis scooter, so very little energy was needed to advance. When moving through the vertical portions, they had to take it really slow because of the tight fit.

At the point where they cut through the basalt to enter the long hallway, the current of water was very strong. In fact, it was unnerving, though the less-experienced Kahn would never admit it. Once they were inside the hallway, the current was still and the world became a quiet and mysterious place. The water was crystal clear, and Kahn was surprised by how far ahead he could see with his mounted headlight. He also noted the glow of the rope lighting. The series of strung blue lights below him made the hall look like a runway at night, as seen from above.

"We have the length of almost three football fields to go," noted Bernie's voice in Kahn's ear. "Keep your eyes open and follow close."

With that, Bernie launched forward at the scooter's top-end speed, which was about 4 miles per hour. On the way, Kahn noticed the smooth walls of the passage. It looked as if the hallway had been cut straight out of a huge brick of solid granite. If he didn't know better, it might have even been metallic. The ceiling was indeed arched, and this too was smooth and appeared seamless. *The ingenuity of the ancients never ceases to amaze me...*

"We're getting close," Bernie said. "Slow your speed to level 4. Everybody still okay?" Both followers answered in the affirmative.

About a minute later, the cavern opened up in front of them. The floor of the passage gave way to an abyss of black water below. The scene pushed Kahn's heartbeat to the limit. Just inside the hallway, Bernie pulled the robot out of a mesh bag that Peter had been dragging, turned the little machine on, and used a control pad to maneuver the camera into the cavern. There was a color display on the hand-held controls, which all watched intensely. The camera was connected to a thin cable which allowed for a maximum reach of 200 feet.

The robotic device looked a lot like a bulging miniature remote submarine. The camera and LED lights were in the front with the rudder and propeller toward the back. It was balanced with a sensitive air pressure technology that kept the image steady.

The bot reached the end of its line, and nothing out of the ordinary happened. They maneuvered it up as far as it would go, then dove it down as far as it would go, before deciding they needed to reposition themselves further in the cavern to find whatever it was that had killed JB.

"It can't be much further," Peter blurted, "he wasn't gone that long. Let's reposition about one hundred feet into the cavern and try again."

From their new position, they started the same procedure. This time, when the bot reached the 127-foot mark, a distinguishable light showed up in the viewing screen. Bernie cut the lights on the bot and they immediately saw greens and blues, and what looked like boiling water. It was similar to surface wave activity, as seen from below, but in this case it was out in front of them horizontally.

"That can't be right," Bernie mumbled as the others watched with anticipation.

The bot inched forward as the men held their breaths and watched. It was another inch or two before the camera lens hit the churning water. Then, all of a sudden, the camera pushed through the wavy wall and fell. It was caught by the fiber optic cable that connected it to the hand-held, but Bernie felt a definite tension as the viewing screen flickered and blipped.

When the camera first approached the upset water, its depth read 113 feet, roughly equivalent to the depth on Bernie's dive computer. But after the screen flickered, the display showed that the camera was at a depth of over 300 feet.

The men sat in silence for a minute before Bernie said, "I think I know what happened."

"What?" Kahn blurted.

"The upset water has to be some sort of a waterfall. The camera went over the edge, was caught by the cable, and swung back into the water, and now is reading at a depth of 300 plus. This doesn't make any sense though…"

"What? That makes perfect sense. What do you mean?" Kahn was breathing heavy.

"Try to control your breathing, Abdullah. At this depth, we have limited time and air-gas according to our decompression schedule."

"What are you saying, damn it?"

"I'm saying, water falls when it's pushed off the edge of a hard surface. This is a waterfall to be sure, but it's not flowing off a hard surface, so what's making the water fall like that? Wait, I think have an idea."

Bernie then told the camera to dive to a depth exactly 200 feet below them and held it there at maximum tension. From there, while keeping the fiber optic cable taut, he maneuvered the camera back toward the waterfall wall, inching it up and further away from him as it advanced. When it got close, he kept the propulsion hard-over, and maneuvered the camera out into the fall to try and get a look at what was going on beyond the anomaly. He got the camera just right, the screen flashed and flickered, but the airy part of the cavern was too dimly lit to see anything and the mounted light was too weak to illuminate whatever was beyond.

They needed a new strategy.

"Look," Peter said. "There's a limit to how far we can dive, and I think it's safe to say this cavern is deeper than 200 feet."

"Agreed," said Bernie as he maneuvered the camera back toward them.

315

"So, the way I see it, we have a lateral window here ahead of us, which we can investigate, but unless there's a viable way to get into the open air part of the cavern at around this depth, we're going to need some different equipment."

"Roger that."

"Air check," Peter looked at his gauges. "Okay, we have time to fire up the Teledyne and get some initial readings, but we'll need to start working our way back in about fifteen, copy?"

Kahn was suddenly thankful the divers talked him into purchasing the navigation system, as expensive as it was. It utilizes multi-beam imaging sonar to give divers an adjustable view range of between 5 and 150 meters ahead of them. It can be used as a static device, but also has the capability to stream images while the divers are underway. If there was a way to get into the airy portion of the cavern, this little piece of high-tech gadgetry was sure to show them how.

Bernie fired up the Teledyne and said, "Peter, you spot me. Abdullah, wait here while we take a few readings. We'll bring you out if we find something interesting."

The two divers maneuvered further into the cavern and a few seconds later, were out of Abdullah's sight. As soon as they were gone, Abdullah's breathing heightened. It was an unsettling feeling to be hovering there, in the blackness of a mysterious subterranean cavern. Through his com, he listened to the others as they worked their way along a vertical grid to investigate the anomaly ahead.

Ten minutes into the investigation, Kahn heard what he hoped to.

There's something.

Yep, I see it.

Does that pass across the threshold?

Here, see if you can get a steeper angle on the shelf.

I got 'cha.

Right. That's better. Here we go. Yep, look there, it passes over the threshold!

Sure does.

Looks like an entry point.

"Gentlemen, where are you?" Kahn interrupted, "I want to see this."

"Negative Abdullah," Bernie responded, "We're noting the GPS now and are on our way to you in a few seconds. We need to refill the tanks and resume the operation on the next dive."

"Fine," Abdullah said, disappointed.

The guys made it back to Kahn and noted the air and depth on their computers. It was time to make their assent back through the halls and passages. They needed to leave time for two decompression stops along the way. The dive computers showed about 12 to 13 minutes of air left, probably closer to ten for Abdullah, who was sucking his a bit faster. They would need about six minutes for their combined safety stops. It was time to go.

Bernie was the first to surface in the Osiris shaft, just as Abdullah's final warning alarm sounded right below. Bernie smiled at Abdullah as he surfaced next to him, "No sweat, eh boss. Might as well use the whole tank, you paid for it all, anyway."

Once they had geared-down, the divers gave an overview of their findings. The sonar picked up a solid shelf that protruded out from the wall of the cavern. The landing was about 280 feet from where the tunnel opened up into the cavern, along the circumference to the right. As the divers scrolled through the saved images on the Teledyne, they noted how perfect and uniform the shelf was, as if it had been purposefully etched out of the wall of the cavern.

On their second dive, the three-man team immediately returned to the site of the shelf. Bernie volunteered to be the first to stand on it and pass the threshold of the wavy water. To be safe, the team first anchored a rope to a bolt they shot into the cavern wall. They affixed the rope to his diving harness. He was tied down and ready to go.

Peter and Abdullah watched nervously as Bernie stood on the ledge, which was only about six feet wide. He inched his way toward the waterfall threshold. First, he passed his hand through. Then, he inched closer and passed his face through. Once he did that, he stepped in more quickly and his com registered a loud rushing noise, like the sound of a huge waterfall.

"It's some sort of a pressure chamber," Bernie said. The others could hear him breathing heavily. "Wow, there's lots of pressure."

"Bernie, is it safe for us to pass?" Abdullah asked.

"That's affirmative. There's enough room on the ledge for both of you. I see a staircase leading down. Wow," he paused again and breathed deeply, "be advised, there is a lot of pressure in here, guys."

The others followed him onto the airy side of the ledge, and Abdullah gasped at the sights. The chamber was an extra-worldly place. The waterfall was not a waterfall at all. Incredibly, they found themselves enclosed on all sides by a circular wall of water, as if they were now inside a bubble – that is, with the exception of a small vertical sliver of exposed cavern wall behind them on the ledge. The water looked as though it was being held back by an invisible force. It was majestic and terrifying at the same time.

Bernie hadn't lied, the pressure was enormous and Abdullah found that breathing deeply kept him from feeling like his chest cavity might implode. All three men remained on all fours, trying to acclimate to this new world. Peter was the first to remove his regulator and test the air. He found that they could breathe normally, so the others followed suit and let their gear dangle.

After acclimating a bit, they looked around. There was indeed a staircase that descended deeper into the cavern. They could see without flashlights because the foliage was illuminated and cast a faint light. The most predominant "plant" seemed to be the vines that wrapped up in a tangle along the staircase. It appeared as though they were not plants at all, but strung together beads of tiny LED bulbs. All of the plant life cast a faint but clear glow throughout the cavern, shinning predominantly deep blues, greens and purples as far as they could see. The team decided to descend the stairs.

Everything about this cavern was foreign to anything the men had ever experienced. One continuous and circular wall of water surrounded them, all the plants appeared to glow, and the sounds of air and water set the backdrop for this truly magical place. The air smelled sweet in their nostrils, too, as if they were in a botanical garden or greenhouse. Bernie noted how surprised he was that none of the plant life had been seen floating in the water on their approach, but then again, everything seemed to be alive and, for lack of better way to describe it, *conscious*.

Due to the abnormal pressure of the cavern, their equipment readings were all out of whack, but they guessed that the stairs led some 300 or so feet down before they dead-ended on a flat landing. The landing appeared to be a half-acre or so large, and circular. At the landing, the diameter between one water-wall and its opposite side was much narrower than at the shelf above. It was as though the walls of water were not cylindrical, but elliptical inside the cavern; as if the team was inside the shape of a football that stood on-end. On the landing, the plant life was more diverse and abundant, and all of it shone with its own unique glow. In the center of the landing, Kahn noticed a thin beam of wavy light that stretched up and eventually disappeared out of sight. *What is that?*

"This looks like a Taurus energy field," Kahn said, as he advanced toward the beam of light in the center. He was more thinking out loud then addressing anyone specifically. "That's the only way I could explain the phenomenon with the water, and it might also explain the pressure. And if it is, this tech has been theorized about, and rumored to have been replicated on small-scales, but nothing to this magnitude. This is unbelievable…"

Bernie stood motionless at the base of the stairs, amazed at the peculiar sights while Peter inspected the translucent leaves of a nearby bush. Then, abruptly, Abdullah stopped, looked at the two and said, "You guys hear the voices?"

Neither Bernie nor Peter could.

Abdullah looked around, confused, and tried to pinpoint the origin of the peculiar sounds. He continued toward the center of the landing and there he found a hole in the floor. It was a foot in diameter and circular. The wavy beam of light seemed to come from inside that hole somewhere, but he couldn't see how deep it went. Abdullah was sure he could hear the sounds of voices speaking in strange dialects, like a marketplace bustling with activity. And it still seemed to be coming from that hole.

He got down on his hands and knees and crawled to the edge of the hole. He felt like a kid eavesdropping on his parent's private conversation carried through the air ducts of the house. As he got closer, he thought he could make out some words. There was a saying that he heard over and over, and it began to ring in his mind as he tried to aim his headlamp into the hole.

One of his companions called to him, but Abdullah could not, or would not, hear.

Abba-la mo nemi kei. Over and over the saying repeated in his mind. *Abba-la mo nemi kei*. *Abba-la mo nemi kei*.

When he was right on top of the hole, the voices suddenly became louder. *Abba-la mo nemi kei*. He finally whispered it himself, echoing the chant he heard in his mind, "Abba-la mo nemi kei," and as soon as he did, a loud crack pierced their ears and sent Bernie to the floor in pain, just as Peter covered his face and grimaced.

Next, from inside that hole, a pedestal made out of some sort of crystal emerged and elevated. The pedestal was bright and magnificent. It rose up mechanically somehow, and when it stopped, its shelf was six-feet above the ground. On it was a magnificent, huge, black crown.

The crown was at least 24 inches in diameter and hit 12 inches high at its peaks. It looked like it had been fashioned for a head the size of a rhino's. The crown was sculpted out of some sort of black material, with sharp, ornamental spikes and spires. It was inlaid with large gems that emitted a form of black light, which was dark and sinister. Just the sight of it shot a nervous shiver down Kahn's spine.

Amazed, he staggered to his feet and without thinking first, reached for the crown with a quivering hand. The chant was now replaced with a deep, guttural voice that spoke English, "Let a king rise in the hour of conquest."

Reaching, Kahn felt the smooth edge of the crown and grabbed hold of it. As he did, the plants came alive and began to wrap their vines around the legs of the three men. The vines tugged at them with ferocity, as if trying to keep them from disturbing the crown.

"Abdullah, stop!" Kahn heard someone say behind him, but the voice was distant and muffled, and he paid it no mind.

Determined and obsessed, Kahn pulled at the crown with all his might and it slid off the smooth surface of the pedestal, crashing to the ground near his feet with a weighty thud. It was much too heavy for him to lift. Abdullah's whole attention was on the crown. He couldn't take his eyes off it.

Peter and Bernie screamed as they kicked and struggled against the vines and undergrowth. Kahn didn't even hear them. The vines pulled them into the thickets, and their screams were replaced by a chilling silence. Even the noise of wind and water was quieting.

In the vicinity of where crown fell to the floor, the vines recoiled, as if unable to come near it. Kahn was now staring at the crown and listening to the noise that seemed to come from inside it. Then, a droplet of water caught his attention and he looked up. He first noticed that the wavy beam of light had begun to flicker, as if struggling to maintain its intensity. Within the walls of water, bulges came forth, like huge tumors that grew and shrank in the same instant.

Abdullah knew he had to move. He looked down at the crown, and noticed it was now much smaller in size. When he lifted it, he found also that it was now lighter, easily manageable. Clutching it tightly, he advanced toward the staircase. He didn't bother looking for his dive partners, for now he had a singular mission: get out! As he walked, the plant life slid away, enabling him to pass.

Why are the plants afraid of the crown? It was fleeting thought, but one he couldn't dwell on now.

At the base of the staircase, he quickly flung on his gear. As the airy part of the chamber appeared to be weakening, so also the pressure seemed to be decreasing and he found it easier to move now. His slow walk turned to a speedy one as he climbed stairs. Below him, he saw the water begin to assault the landing, crashing down with an enormous ruckus. He kicked it up a notch and jumped up the stairs, two at a time. The adrenaline launched him into survival mode; even with gear on his back and shoulders, he moved with remarkable swiftness.

The walls of water then started crumbling on all sides, and in that instant, Abdullah looked up and saw the shelf. He was getting close. He ran as fast as he could before a loud crack marked the end of the force field's existence, and the waters came crashing down on him. The water knocked him off the staircase altogether and flung him around in a violent torrent of chaos. His body slammed into the stairs once, then again, each time sending searing pain up his spine. As the violence subsided, he opened his eyes and reached for his regulator. He found an extra set of goggles clipped to his vest and fumbled around with his instrumentation. He still had the crown, and once the waters were still, he turned on a small emergency lamp and looked at it.

The noises and sounds of activity that emitted from inside the crown were maddening. Kahn wanted to tell the voices to shut up so he could think, but knew it was futile. He tried to blot them out, but they seemed to get even louder when he tried. Like an annoying fly buzzing for attention, the noise assaulted his consciousness with inexorable persistence. He thought about dropping the crown for the sake of sanity, and even tried to at one point, but found that he couldn't. His right hand would simply not let go, even if his mind instructed it so. *Stop loitering here, you're running out of air,* he thought. Or, was it the voice of another? He honestly couldn't tell.

The rest of his journey back through the tunnels and shafts was a blur, but he managed, taking care to mind his decompression stops along the way. When he got near the end of the arched-ceiling tunnel, just before the vertical shaft, he took one final decompression stop. He hit the edge of the water, which was now much lower in the shaft, and he pulled his headgear off with exhaustion. Looking up, he saw the Hand staring down at him from where the Osiris sarcophagus lay.

"Dear God, it was like a toilet bowl in here! Are you okay?" The Hand was manic, speaking with such a high-pitched and rapid tenseness that Kahn couldn't really understand a word he said. "What the hell happened? Are the others okay? What did you see? Oh my God, it was violent in here, so violent that I thought we were all going to die! Where are the others? You must have triggered some..."

"Hand?" Kahn pushed the word out with all the effort and volume he could muster. He was exhausted. His head pounded under the crown's auditory torment and his shoulder and back throbbed.

"Y-yes. What?" The Hand stopped short his frenzied rambling.

"Shut the fuck up, and drop me a ladder."

After a momentary pause, where the Hand looked confused, he hurried away.

Kahn looked at the crown, curled a lip, and closed his eyes in defiance of the sounds of fighting, selling, talking, laughing, buying, cheering, and whatever else. The noise was deafeningly loud in his head, and it seemed as though every voice was talking directly to *him*. He sniffed once, then again. He could smell something like sulfur and the rot of garbage coming from the crown and wondered about the dark magic that must be locked up inside it.

Somehow, he got the distinct feeling that the crown actually found him, not the other way around. He knew he was now inexplicably bound to it, but the feeling was dread, rather than joy. He didn't understand much about what just happened, but with every fiber in his being, he now regretted ever going down into the deep.

Some secrets should stay secret...

CHAPTER 44
Treasure Hunt

Sunday, July 8, 2012

On July 5th, the team checked out, rented a vehicle, and drove eight hours to the resort town of El Gouna, located on the western coast of the Red Sea. They chose El Gouna because it was a resort destination famous for good snorkeling and diving, and they figured it would be easy to rent some equipment.

Anny marked their arrival with an odd observation, "It's not so different looking than the Mayan Riviera, if you mentally exchange the jungle there with the desert landscape here."

Bax nodded in agreement, although he had no idea what the Mayan Riviera was, and Solomon kept his comments to himself. As soon as the words came out, however, Anny laughed at herself for the absurdity of the thought.

It took less than an hour to find a stout little fellow manning a Colona Diver's shop. His English was good, but more than that, as Bax put it, the man was *chuffed to see a man about a dog*. They gave him a handsome tip for renting them a few items not on the official rental menu, and checked in at the Club Med resort a few miles away. They decided to stay a night in order to get some practice with the gear, as Solomon had never used diving equipment before.

Bax was not convinced they needed the tanks and regulators. He rather hoped to get by with just the wetsuit, mask, snorkel, and fins. But they didn't know the lay of the Nile River along the Aswan corridor, so chose to rent everything just in case.

The Club Med had a private stretch of beach, and a sandy atoll that meandered out from the hotel grounds. The atoll formed a cove where the waters were especially calm. It was a perfect practice spot. Bax and Sully geared up as Anny found a nice bit of sand nearby, and got comfortable. She elicited more than a few stares from local venders peddling their wares nearby. If the stares and occasional catcalls bothered her, she didn't let on.

Braxton wanted to preserve the air in the tanks for the trip, so after he ran through the finer points of scuba above water, they spent only a few minutes underwater assuring that everything worked and that Solomon was OK with a shallow water dive. The rest of their afternoon was spent on the beach with Anny, where they talked as friends and made jokes about Braxton's ridiculous British idioms.

Just before heading in for supper, Solomon asked what the alien Abele had said to them individually. However, neither Bax nor Anny had any interest in talking about it. It was as though the alien had said something deeply personal, and even the mention of the event caused them both to suddenly become introspective. Solomon caught the cue and let the whole thing go.

The next morning they packed up and drove further south. From El Gouna, it took just seven hours to reach Aswan. They arrived at the hotel at 3 p.m., quickly checked in and decided to look for a tour that might get them close to the Elephantine Island dig site. They hit a few dead ends before Anny found an overzealous street-hawk heister who called himself Ben. Was it that Anny found Ben, or had Ben marked her for a sucker? Debatable.

Ben was all too eager to 'help' them find a tour, and offered his services with pushiness and broken English. He started by rattling off the typical lines, *I do this for you, only you, and nobody else,* and, *you are big, rich Americans, you can pay...* Bax had heard it all before, and wasn't impressed.

Ben was a ferocious salesman and didn't let up. He managed to cross over the inappropriate line once or twice during the exchange, which only served to annoy Bax more. Sully thought the young Egyptian was just trying to be funny, but it really wasn't.

According to the Brit, Ben was the quintessential *wanker.* In fact, he said it to Ben's face at one point, "You're quite the wanker aren't you?"

Solomon chuckled, Anny bit her lip nervously, and Ben smiled and nodded as if he had a clue what that meant.

Nobody believed he knew what wanker meant, and that was part of the joke. Oblivious to the insult, Ben doubled-down on his position that $50 per person was a fair price for access to his boat, which was really no more than a rusted hunk of junk.

In the spirit of peace and timing, Bax relented to the price. He wasn't happy about letting go of US $150 for a 20-minute ride on Gilligan's rust-tank, but he eventually capitulated and paid, telling the wanker to 'sod off' in the process. Ben told them to wait there, then jogged off and procured three generic tickets -- raffle tickets, the sort used at family reunions. He handed them their tickets and showed them a single, fifty-dollar bill. "This for Ben, all else go to ship cap'in, ok?"

"You mean you were only on the take for $50?" Anny asked.

"Yes, yes. Just $50 for Ben."

Now they all felt bad. Ben was a jerk to be sure, but part of it had to do with his broken English and a clear communication barrier. After all the fuss, he was only trying to scrape one-third for himself as a fee for getting them on a sold-out boat. That didn't seem so bad.

Bax chuckled, shook his head, and patted Ben's shoulder, "Right, so clearly I acted the giddy goat here didn't I? Sorry 'bout that Ben. Be on your way, then." Ben looked at Anny, then back at Bax, then waved and walked away with no concept for what he was just told.

The "cruise" was informative, but cheesy. The intelligence they gathered came primarily from their own observations, as the guide said very little about Elephantine Island when they passed. Initially, it was discouraging to find that large boulders ran along the Island's southeastern shoreline. They were big enough that climbing out of the water along that stretch of shore was going to be difficult. The terrain was not the only problem either. There was also a hubbub of activity just across the narrow strait, on the Aswan city side of the Nile to the east, where walkways and restaurants made for a natural gathering place for tourists and tourist industry nationals. Once the boat past Elephantine Island, it turned around and took them back upstream along the other side. This side, and especially the south and southwestern side of the island, seemed deserted. The river was much wider on this side as well, with far less activity than on the western shore of the Nile.

That evening, they got a late reservation at the Terrace Restaurant, an eatery at the beautiful Old Cataract Hotel. They dined on a terrace, which was part of a multi-leveled series of balconies looking west over the Nile. From there, they had a view of the southernmost tip of Elephantine Island. It was a perfect spot to monitor the ebb and flow of human activity well into the night. The food was good too, although expensive.

Egypt had a thing for lighting. At the Giza Plateau, lasers and powerful strobe lights choreographed to music brought the pyramids to life every night. It gave tourists a show that might have made Disney proud. Everywhere, in hotels, shops and ruins, there was always plenty of accent lighting, over-lighting, and bright lighting. True to character, it was no surprise to the team when powerful blue-green lights popped on and illuminated the southernmost tip of Elephantine Island.

The terrace closed at 1 a.m., and they were the last patrons to leave. They were relieved to find that human activity on the Aswan side of the shore, as well as boating activity in the river, diminished significantly after midnight. They now felt confident in the plan. They could float from the north shore of their hotel to the southwest shore of Elephantine Island with little chance of being detected. And, to Bax's relief, they could do it without scuba gear.

The next day, they slept in as late as they could. Once they were up and about, the team hopped a ferry to the Aswan shore, and retrieved their rental car. They needed to find a good rendezvous spot downstream from Elephantine Island, so the crew drove north out of the city to have a look around. Ten miles out of town, they found a bridge that crossed over the Nile, and followed the signs to the Edelgraven Tombs. There, they got out of the car to have a look around.

The tombs were a perfect meeting location due to the scarcity of human activity in that area. If Edelgraven was a tourist trap, the owners had a serious marketing problem. There was literally nobody in the vicinity. They could see the city of Aswan, across the Nile to their south. It was quickly decided that Bax and Sully would reunite with Anny at this location, after retrieving the artifact on Elephantine Island.

Their plan was set.

Around midnight, Anny left the men and took a water taxi to Aswan's main marina. She then retrieved the car and drove back to the Edelgraven Tombs, where she parked and waited for the men to show up. As Anny departed, Bax and Sully put their gear in a duffle bag and walked to the northernmost perimeter of the hotel grounds. There, just a few feet from the river, under the cover of the trees and bushes, they geared up.

They both wore full-length wetsuits, fins, neoprene hoods, and goggles. They had a waterproof GPS, small shovel, knife, rope, and other essentials in a canvas duffle bag, which Bax synched up and threw over his shoulder. They dipped into the water with hardly a splash, and floated forward into the lazy current.

The natural flow of the Nile kept them moving in the right direction, but it was slow. When they could afford to pick up the pace, Bax gave Solomon the swim sign -- four fingers in a pinching action with the thumb. Fist-up meant stop. Fingers pointed down meant dive underwater to avoid detection. If for some reason they got split up on the way, the plan was to evade detection and rendezvous at the southern tip of the island.

The night's sky was clear and bright and the air was comfortable. The Nile had a murky, mysterious quality to it. There was an unpleasant, musty smell coming from the water, so they cautiously kept from swallowing any of it.

To Sully, the whole experience was surreal. While lazily floating along, he thought about how many generations of people this great river had served throughout the millennia. It was an ancient river, and one that bore witness to some of the most important civilizations in history. *Never thought I'd be illegally floating down the Nile, like Moses, trying to escape the authorities... I'll have to cross this off my bucket list.*

Three quarters of the way, they approached a police boat idling in the middle of the waterway. It was not a large vessel, just a two-person motorboat. Bax and Solomon heard two men talking jovially.

Bax looked at Solomon and gave the fingers-down sign, followed by the pinching motion, and then pointed toward the other side of the boat. Sully figured out what he meant. They let the current take them to within twenty feet of the men, when Bax silently dipped below the surface, with Sully following close behind. Underwater, they kicked their fins as hard as they could. Solomon glanced up just in time to see the faint silhouette of the motorboat pass above. Though he tried, he could not keep up with the ex-British Special Forces operative, and quickly lost sight of him. At the end of his wind, Sully came up with as light a ripple as possible, and took a long, slow suck of the dry, night air.

Wondering how far he made it from the boat, he turned back anxiously. He was pleasantly surprised at the distance he covered. The Police were so far back that their voices were barely audible. Keeping his fins submerged, he lightly kicked to make up some water. A minute later he caught up to Bax, and they rounded one final bend of the stream together, before seeing the illuminated glow of Elephantine Island. About 100 yards... *So far, so good.*

From their vantage point, the river was quiet and the shoreline to the east seemed deserted. Keeping just head and nose above the water, they drifted to the shore and climbed out slowly. The first thing they did was lose the fins. In booties, they ran up the large boulders, over the crest of the dig site, and down into a small valley where the archeological remains of sundried brick homes and columns greeted them with unenthused stillness. The area was pitch black. The bright, ornamental lighting that hit the southern tip of the island came from the eastern shore. The ridge surrounding the dig site was many feet higher in elevation, so the effect was a long, dark shadow strewn across the valley floor.

They took cover behind the two perpendicular walls of an ancient structure. Bax gestured for them to stay quiet and listen. The place was as silent as a cemetery. The night-bugs even seemed lethargic. It was so quiet that Bax's whisper startled Sully, "OK, you good to go?"

"I'm good."

"Alright. Let's do this."

From the bag, Bax retrieved the GPS handheld and two small flashlights. "Try not to risk the light. Use it only if you must, and only if you're sure nobody will notice, copy?"

Solomon nodded as Bax gazed toward the east from a crouched position. "I'm going to leave the bag here. Let's just mark the spot, see what we need, then come back for it." Solomon nodded again.

They moved stealthily through the dig site and followed the GPS coordinates into an area where the dirt and rocks gave way to short, fat trees and undergrowth. Their spot was just on the edge of that vegetation. When they got to the exact location, Bax dropped a white sock on the sand and turned the GPS off. It was all rather anticlimactic. He looked at Solomon with an ironic smile and said, "Brov, did the earth move for you too?"

Solomon chuckled. "No. Not sure what I was expecting, but there's nothing here, is there?"

"Dirt, rocks," Bax knelt down and started pushing the sand away with his fingers. As he did, he saw out of his peripheral vision something that caught his eye. It was Solomon's right forearm. The light coming off the tattoo was shining so brightly he could see it through the wetsuit. "Sully, take off the top side of your wetsuit, but be careful about it. Those markings are really bright."

Sully unzipped the suit down to his navel and pulled his right arm out of the sleeve. Braxton shielded his arm from the eastern shoreline as he did, and sure enough, the tattoos were shining bright blue-green. The light was brighter than normal, to be sure.

"Look," Solomon saw something and pointed to the ground.

There was a beam of light, no thicker than string, visible in the sand. Remarkably, it was only visible under the light from Sully's arm. "Watch the direction you're pointing the light. I'll see what it is."

Solomon adjusted his stance so that his back was to the east and crouched down with the Brit. Bax found the light and ran his fingers along it. It looked as though a piece of white string had been laid down in the dirt and was shining brightly, as if under a black light. But this was not string and the light coming off Solomon's arm was not black light. This was something else. The GPS marked the spot where the string-light ended, but it continued onward in a northerly direction into the undergrowth. The men followed it carefully.

Fifteen or twenty feet into the undergrowth, the light on the ground ended and bent into the earth. Initially, Bax got on all fours and tried to dig with his fingers, but the dirt was coarse. He instructed Sully to wait there while he fetched the canvas bag. Inside the trees, Solomon felt more secure about the glow coming off his arm.

While waiting for Bax, he noticed something odd. When he moved his arm closer to the light-string, the two anomalies interacted. It was like a ripple effect. It seemed as though the light-string wanted to go into Sully's arm and join the light of his markings. *That's so bizarre,* he thought, as he moved his arm closer, then further away.

Bax returned and they took turns digging, following the light into the earth. It was actually hard work, as they encountered some thick roots and big rocks along the way. Eventually, they had a hole about six feet deep and that's when they saw light appear just below the remaining thin layer of soil. They looked at one another with anticipation. Abele was right. Something was here, and they were about to unearth it!

The light in Solomon's arm started to pulsate. Excited, Bax whispered, "Why don't you dig now, boyo; it's doing somethin' crazy with your arm there."

"What, big SBS guy is scared now?" Sully joked.

"Hell yes." Bax conceded and moved out of the way.

Solomon reached down and used his fingers to unearth a small box - half the size of a cigar box - and pulled it out of the ground. The light inside it was so bright that it bled opaquely through the creases and joints. The box was two half pieces stuck together, not a top and bottom, but a left side and a right side. The seam ran around the box entirely, and it was from that seam that the inner light was spilling forth. Sully cracked it open slightly, and such a flood of light started coming out that he thought better of it and pushed the two sides back together.

"Yes, good," Bax nodded. "I was going to say we should wait for a safer place. Let's get off this bloody rock then." He turned and led them back to the southwestern side of the island. There, they geared back up and put their fins on.

Bax put Sully's box into a dry-bag, and secured it into a flap on the inner lining of the duffle. He then shoved all the other tools and gear in as well, and synched the whole thing up.

"Ready to go?"

"Sure am," Sully said as he zipped the top half of his suit into place.

Once in the water, they had to cut across the flow toward the west bank of the river. The Nile was absolutely deserted on this side. The men kicked harder to assure they got across the wide side of the river before floating past the rendezvous location. They made it with over 50 yards to spare. When they got near the rendezvous location, they heard Anny whistle from the trees on the bank. They climbed out on a small, rocky beach, and Anny was there to meet them. She took the bag from Bax, "Did you find it?"

"We found something," Sully replied as he stood up out of the water, breathing a bit heavy. "Don't pull anything out of the bag yet, babe. Whatever we found is bathed in light, way too bright a thing to look at here. Let's dry off quick and go somewhere safe."

CHAPTER 45
The Magic of the Crown

Sunday, July 8, 2012

Abdullah woke with more than a few old-man aches. It seemed as if every muscle in his body hurt. His left shoulder in particular throbbed deeply. After laboring for a moment to sit up, he massaged his shoulder and tried to work the range of motion a little. Motion transformed the deep throb into a searing pinch. Wincing, he decided to leave it alone and let a doctor handle the assessment.

The sounds of extra-worldly marketplace commerce were ever present, although the crown itself was out of sight. Kahn looked at his duffle bag in the far corner of the room and shook his head. He knew the crown was inside it. The effect of the noise on his psyche was like an annoying tickle-me Elmo doll that wouldn't shut up.

Kahn was surprised to find that nobody else could hear the noises coming from the crown. The various members of his team marveled at it, wondered what it was, and each took a moment to hold and admire it, but nobody could hear *through* it the way Abdullah could. Nobody smelled anything on it the way Abdulla could. In addition, soon after emerging from the shaft, Abdullah discovered something else that was fascinating – he could 'hear' the thoughts of people standing near the crown. He quickly realized that if he wasn't careful, others could hear his thoughts too. He didn't know for sure, but it appeared that he needed to think something coherent in order for anyone to hear him; as though talking without using words.

The scene just outside the Osiris shaft had been overwhelmingly difficult to manage. Abdullah simultaneously had to try and ignore the noise from the crown, not think about the pain in his body, not listen to the thoughts of those around him, and not think anything overt himself for fear of being *heard* by his subordinates. It was exhausting and terribly uncomfortable. That's why he opted for a quick and perceptively rude departure.

Just before climbing into a cab that was staged behind the construction barriers, an Egyptian national who worked off and on for the Phantoms jokingly went to put the crown on his own head. That's when Kahn exploded with an outburst of anger and lunacy. It was an extraordinary response to a seemingly small infraction, and everyone present agreed it was over the top. It's not as though the young Egyptian had meant any offence, he was merely joking around with the others. But Kahn's reaction to the joke stoked the Cardinal's curiosity, as he was watching the scene silently from the outskirts of the mob. The response was nothing short of violent, primal, and animalistic. It was a reaction more appropriately reserved for the betrayal of honor or the murder of a firstborn.

The Cardinal noticed other things as well. For one, since emerging from the hole, Abdullah seemed irritable. Normally, he was a good-humored man. Sure, he could be cynical and crass, but happy and well-intentioned, nevertheless. But on the pathway leading to the cab, he barked angrily at the people around him, the Hand in particular. He kept justifying his agitation by telling the Hand that he had a terrible headache. He asked incessantly to be taken to his hotel room and left alone. At times, he closed his eyes as if trying to shut out the world. But when his eyes were open, they darted this way and that, as if responding to every little piece of stimuli in the vicinity. *How peculiar,* the Cardinal thought.

That night, the Cardinal and the Hand ate dinner without Abdullah and said very little to one another. They were both wondering what happened in the hole? How had the other two divers died? What was tormenting Abdullah, besides bodily aches and pains? Why had the water in the shaft suddenly emptied? And the most important question, did Abdullah find Nimrod's ancient crown? Was this the link that proved Nimrod was the same person as Osiris? If this was Nimrod's crown, it certainly did.

Cardinal Salah thought about all the connections he made while researching Malcolm's book. A clearer picture was beginning to emerge, even out of the mosaic that is myth and fable. He chewed his food slowly and thought about it all. *Greek mythology tells stories about celestial deities having demigod offspring with humans. This is the same story as found in the Bible, the Apocrypha, the ancient Epics, and nearly every other myth from that era around the world. All these stories, to include those found in Christianity and Islam, make reference to a singular earthly ruler after the Flood. A demigod. A hero. Part man and part immortal alien. Nimrod. Nimrod is called by different names depending on region, but his name always translates as "son of…" Abdullah finds the crown of Nimrod… The demigod ruler of this earth is returning…?"*

The Cardinal stabbed at his fish and closed his eyes. Before that night, he never put a whole lot of stock in the authenticity of Islamic texts such as the Book of Rolls. He rather audaciously believed that most of the so-called inspired works of Islam were merely renditions, or outright plagiarisms, of much older and more authentic works. But now he had to deal with an artifact first referenced in a Muslim text thousands of years after the life and death of Nimrod. If this thing was actually discovered, the ramifications were startling. *Abdullah emerges with a black crown… the crown of the demigod king of the earth. The demonic king of the earth is coming to rule once again…*

After dinner, they both retired to their own rooms. They agreed that the Hand would attempt to interact with Kahn in the morning and advise the Cardinal as to when it would be appropriate to meet.

Splice

Though physically pained and psychologically irritated, the morning brought him a renewed sense of strength and vigor. Gingerly stretching his lower back and legs, he cast another glance in the direction of the crown. Whatever else might have been interesting to explore in that airy cavern was now under water and probably destroyed. Thinking back on the experience, he felt lucky to be alive.

It's time to leave Egypt. I need to get out of this dust bin...

He moved stiffly toward the bathroom to freshen up. Once he was in the shower, he noticed that the volume of noise in his head was down a little. As if leaving a room where a television is blaring, the sound from the crown was muffled by distance as well. That was encouraging. At least he could get some separation from the endless racket.

What normally took fifteen minutes took thirty. He knew something was wrong with his shoulder and thought about seeing a doctor before getting on a plane. *Surely, the Hand could fetch a doc and bring him to the hotel...*

After he dressed, combed his hair, and put his shoes on, he walked over to the duffle bag and opened it. There it was, his crown of splendor. He felt his heart race as he reached in and took it out. The crown was definitely smaller now than when he first experienced it on the pedestal. There were six spires, each about nine inches long, symmetrically distanced from one another. One of them marked the front of the crown since it was almost twice as thick as the others. Each spire was ornamented with jewels, but they were not jewels Kahn could recognize. They were cut like traditional gemstones and firmly affixed in the crown, but they had a gelatinous bounce to them when he touched them with his finger. They emitted light as well. Not bright and radiant, but light similar to black light used in a Halloween decoration. The black material was hard and dense, but it had undoubtedly shape-shifted since the time Abdullah first interacted with it deep below the surface of the earth.

There were other oddities as well. For one, its mass seemed to be changing. Though he was not a physicist, Kahn knew it was impossible for a fixed object to go from being as heavy as a 25-pound dumbbell to as light as a plastic toy, all within a few minutes.

A knock at the door startled him. "Who is it?" he barked.

"Me," came the high-pitched voice of his Hand. "May I come in?"

Kahn rolled his eyes and looked back at the crown. *Am I ready to talk to that little gremlin about this? Suppose I have to if I'm going to get out of Cairo today...*

"Hang on, I'm coming." He finally said, and shuffled to the door to let him in.

"How are you today?"

"Sore, really sore," Kahn said as the Hand, ignoring him, walked straight past him and toward the crown at the foot of the bed.

"Really? Sorry to hear that…" Kahn mumbled, sarcastically. The Hand appeared as though he hadn't heard.

"I did not get a chance to look at this yesterday." The little man got close and inspected the crown. "Is this a metal or a stone?"

"Maybe neither." Abdullah limped over to the bed.

"They were saying that it grew and shrank, depending on who held it. Have you found that to be so?"

How do they know that? Kahn thought.

The Hand responded as though he heard Kahn's voice audibly, "As I said, they said it grew or shrunk depending on who was holding it. This happened behind the construction barrios, when the men were passing it around. Don't you remember?"

Abdullah walked up behind him and heard the Hand's thoughts as if they were spoken words. *I wonder what it feels like? What if I just touch it? It's so beautiful…*

Abdullah sighed. He'd forgotten about that mind-reading thing. It was a disaster waiting to happen. Sooner or later someone was bound to think something inappropriate. He rubbed his forehead and said, "Go ahead and touch it. Your head is smaller than mine. Maybe it will change sizes or something."

The Hand reached out and touched the top of the thick spire. Sure enough, the crown shrank in diameter just a little, ever so slightly, as if it knew intuitively how to fit the head of the person who last touched it. Seeing the phenomenon, Kahn pushed the smaller man aside and touched the crown again. It immediately grew and returned to its previous size. "Fascinating. So, as the men were passing it around yesterday, the crown was changing sizes?"

"That's right," the Hand responded. "They said the size changed, and the weight too. But the size change didn't always correspond with the weight change. What an odd piece of headgear."

"Hand, do you hear anything?"

"No, why?"

"Hand, look at me." When he did, Abdullah thought the words, *I can hear your thoughts, and if I want, I can talk to you in an extra-sensory manner, as I am now.*

Splice

The Hand's mouth opened agape. *Can you hear my thoughts?* He thought, just as Kahn silently replied, *I just told you I can.*

"Holy Shit!" his squeaky voice shrieked as he reacted by jumping backward and looked around suspiciously, as if expecting someone to pop out of a hiding place and say he'd been *Punked.*

"Calm down. This is why I had to get home yesterday. When the men were passing this thing around, I heard their thoughts and it was all jabbered together with their audible voices. That's not all either."

"What else?" The Hand looked at the master with nervous suspicion, reflexively crossing his arms across his chest, as if trying to hide his transparency. "What else can you do?"

"I can hear something in the crown," Abdullah said, looking at the object. "I can hear the sounds of a marketplace, a blacksmith, laughing, talking, even singing. I can hear the sounds of another world. The languages are strange, unlike anything I've ever heard before. I can smell it too. It smells thick, like when you're in a really humid rainforest, but the odor is not very pleasant. It's rather rotten, especially on the exhale."

"So, you can hear my thoughts?"

Kahn nodded.

Can you hear me now? The Hand thought, testing it again.

"Yes, already. What are you, stupid?" Kahn barked. He then sat on the edge of the bed gingerly, pressed his thumbs into his temples and closed his eyes, as if trying to blot the world out, "Everything gets muffled the further we go from the crown. Right here, next to it, everything is so loud. The sounds of the world beyond, your thoughts, my thoughts, everything is deafeningly loud in my mind. But if we go out into the hallway, the sounds become distant, and sort of muffled."

"Can you still read my thoughts in the hallway?"

"I don't know."

"Can we go see?"

Kahn grinned, "What's the matter Hand? You don't like that I can read your mail?"

"Frankly, no. I don't like it at all. It's a terrible invasion of privacy."

The Hand walked to the front door, keeping his arms crossed. Kahn too was curious, so he followed him into the hallway. They soon learned that the range of

334

Kahn's ability to hear the crown was roughly the same as a person's range of hearing someone talking in a loud voice. Not yelling, but speaking loudly. Abdullah reported he could no longer hear the crown's noises when they got down the hall about 50 feet from the door. Obstructions like doors and walls also affected the sound volume and quality.

In the process, they also found that the further they ventured from the crown, the more difficult it became to communicate telepathically with one another. The volume never faded, but the person thinking the intentional thought had to concentrate harder in order to communicate. The further they walked away from the crown, the worse their connection, and more broken the conversation became. It was similar to a phone call under a poor cell signal. After a few tests up and down the hallway, they decided the range for telepathic communication extended to a little more than 150 feet from the crown. Obstructions like doors and walls did not impair their ability, only distance.

Once the investigation concluded, the Hand was more at ease. He was comforted by the limitations of the artifact. "Do you find that you can only hear emphatic, coherent language?"

"What do you mean?" Abdullah asked.

"I mean, you can't hear me when I'm thinking about walking my dog, right?"

"That's true, "Kahn agreed. "When I want to be heard, I have to actually formulate the language of my thought in my head."

They both returned to the crown. The Hand picked it up and inspected it. "So, what do you think it is?"

"It's got to be that crown the Cardinal talked about, right? The one from the old stories?"

"Nimrod?"

"Right. Nimrod."

"This could be a powerful weapon," the Hand mused. "Would you mind if I put it on?"

"No, go ahead," Kahn said, and then felt a twinge of anger, even jealousy, as the Hand put it on.

He went to look at himself in the bathroom mirror, but before he got there, he bent forward awkwardly and the crown slammed to the ground. Massaging his neck, the Hand turned to his master, embarrassed.

"Ouch, it got really heavy the second I put it on. That hurt my neck."

Inside, Kahn was pleased. He flashed a condescending look and shuffled past the little man, bent over, and picked up the artifact. The minute he touched it, it grew slightly. It was *his* crown after all. Kahn felt it had appropriately rejected the witless Hand, though he knew better than to formulate that thought into words.

"Have you put it on yet?" the Hand asked, still rubbing his neck.

"No."

"Why don't you put it on?"

Kahn looked closely at the jiggling, gelatinous jewels and admired the soft glow they emitted. As he did, he felt the temptation to put on the crown, but that temptation was coupled with a strange fear and reluctance. He heard the Hand say something behind him, but paid no attention. His eyes were fixed on the smooth black material. He sniffed and smelled the scent of something burning in the distance. It wasn't wood or tobacco, but something more exotic. He liked the smell, then exhaled and grunted, as a sour sense exited his nostrils.

Then, he heard deep throaty voices begin to carry a beat, and high-pitched voices sang along. He closed his eyes and was taken to a place, far away. He ventured deep into a world where the plants, rocks, and water all emitted their own light and life force. There was a musical charm in the air, a sense of euphoria. Kahn felt it and was swept deeper and deeper into the bliss. It was aroma, sight, sound, and the feel of tranquility that carried him up and beyond, further and further…

"Sir!" the Hand's scream jarred him out of whatever he was going through. Abdullah sat down. He was dizzy, very dizzy. Sore too.

"What happened?" he was breathing heavy, as if stepping off a treadmill.

"You started dancing," The Hand said slowly. He looked curiously at Abdullah. "It was a very strange and exotic dance. You couldn't hear me. I tried tapping you on the shoulder and you couldn't feel my touch. You weren't here."

As the room stopped turning for Kahn, the Hand came into focus. He was staring back at Kahn, a look of wonder splashed across his face. Kahn tossed his head, as if trying to shake a sleepy fog, "What?"

"That was wild. I asked you if you'd put the crown on yet and you did not answer me. You just brought it up to eye level, looked at it, and a minute or so later, you started dancing with it. You were moving like a professional on Broadway, with grace. You obviously heard a rhythm that I could not hear. It was very queer indeed. I would pay to see it again. It was magical."

"Keep your money," Kahn scowled. "How long did I dance?"

"Three or four minutes, I guess. You've been moving gingerly since coming out of that pit, but when you danced, it was like you were weightless. Do it again."

"Don't be ridiculous…" he was going to say something, but the Hand cut him off.

"I'm not, sir," the Hand was getting excited so his pitch became shrill. "It was magical. No man has ever moved like that. I insist you do it again."

Kahn shook his head again and chose not to dignify the request with an answer. Just then, the fog of sleep came over him and he felt he needed to close his eyes. "Hand, I need to rest. Please leave."

"Okay, but what about the Cardinal. He seeks an audience with you."

Kahn shuffled toward the head of the bed, still holding onto the crown, moving especially slow now. "We'll do dinner. Come back at five. We need to talk about how we're going to get this thing out of Egypt.."

CHAPTER 46
Awake and Alive

Sunday, July 8, 2012

Bax and Sully hastily changed out of their wetsuits as Anny put the duffle bag in the trunk of the rental. After changing, Solomon retrieved the box and wrapped it, along with his left arm, in a towel to conceal the bright light that emitted from both. Bax drove, Anny sat shotgun, and within five minutes of swimming up to the shore, they were on the road again, this time heading back toward El Gouna.

They were amped for the first two hours of the drive, and talked and laughed merrily. It was the regular old mutual admiration club, each person congratulating the others on a job well done. Anny had to hear the whole story from beginning to end twice. She asked the same unanswerable questions over and over. They knew that whatever they found somehow interacted with Solomon, or at least the stuff Abele put into Solomon, but little else. Everything was a mystery, and for their northbound commute, the mystery kept things exciting.

A couple hours in, the sun ignited the eastern sky, and that's about when Solomon and Anny both fell asleep. With little traffic on the road, and an unending desert landscape, Bax's eyelids got pretty heavy as well. At one point he jerked the car back into the appropriate lane and tried to shake off the drupe. Anny slept on, but Solomon stirred and asked if he needed a break.

"I dare say," Bax yawned, "I'm too pooped to pop. Fancy a cup of coffee in the next town?"

"Sure, where are we?"

"North of Luxor," he said, yawning a second time. "Place called Qena is up ahead. I probably butchered the Arabic pronunciation, but it's something like that."

They came to the outskirts of Qena just after 7 a.m. and drove into the downtown corridor. They found a surprisingly large and modern city situated on the eastern bank of the Nile. It was not hard to find a café. Their server, surprisingly, spoke good English and explained to them that Qena exploded when westerners began visiting Luxor as a tourist destination. That's why the city was so tourist-friendly.

Qena was the midpoint for anyone driving to or from Luxor and the Red Sea resort district. There were a few hotels, but shopping was the main draw. There were hundreds of shops and merchant carts everywhere. Most sold Qena's famous pottery, as well as other artifacts and cheesy replicas. Restaurants and cafes were plentiful. A couple tourist traps dressed up and disguised to look like museums dotted the corridor as well.

They took their time, had a nice breakfast, and downed lots of coffee. Beyond the windowpane that peered into the street, Anny noticed a merchant get into a heated argument with a teenager who stepped out in front of his pushcart. The others didn't notice. They talked about Dotty and toasted his foresight in originally making the recommendation that they come to Egypt.

Or, was it more than Dotty's foresight? She wondered, yawning.

Somewhere along the journey, Bax and Sully had become friends. Not just friends, but brothers. *When did this happen?* She watched their interactions with amusement and smiled, happy that Solomon seemed so happy. Slowly, she let herself get pulled back into their conversation…

On the one hand, they could not deny that some sort of invisible guidance had led them up to this moment. How else could they explain being in Egypt in the first place? How else could they explain Malcolm, Sully's interest with his journal, or any of what had happened since? On the other hand, the concepts of fate and destiny were too farfetched to even define or defend. The three of them debated it casually as the coffee refills came.

Solomon had never been one to entertain mystical concepts, conspiracy theories, fables, or any such 'hebejebe-voodoo.' He was an empirical evidence guy, a pragmatist. He appreciated the scientific method. Logic and reason were the backbone of his understanding. He never felt threatened by, or anger toward, those who chose to live in what he called the 'pink-fuzzy haze of arcane belief.' At times, he even felt pity for them and tried to help them see reality. Indeed, he even made a living off these kinds of people.

However, things were changing. Nothing Sully experienced since going to his mother's funeral unfolded the way it was supposed to. The world at large seemed to be less structured now, more of a mysterious place than he once believed. *Is the world changing, or am I? Am I witnessing a new collective consciousness, an awakening of some sort? Or am I just waking up, personally?* While he had no answers to the questions, he did have evidence of some kind of metaphysical change, and it burned with intensity across his forearm.

With full bellies and caffeine-twitchy temperaments, they finally got back on the road. Solomon drove while Anny held the little box under a blanket in the back seat. Thirty minutes into the drive, remarkably, Bax fell asleep in defiance of the java's stimulating effects. Sully's arm was less of a distraction now, for though it was still lit up like Times Square, it was camouflaged by the bright sun and endless reflections cast by the desert-scape.

Splice

In El Gouna, the first thing they did was drop off the rented scuba equipment. Next, they promptly checked into the first hotel they found and congregated in Bax's room to finally open the little box and inspect the contents.

With the curtains shut, Solomon withdrew the box, and as he did, the markings on his arm lit to attention. Slowly, he separated the two halves of the box and a brilliant light blasted through. This was not a light defined by color, it was a light defined by the color spectrum. It was like the fire that comes off a perfectly cut diamond. It was brilliant and radiant and took their collective breath away.

The box slid open, and in each half rested an orb. The core of each orb was the size of a marble, but each was surrounded by multiple layers of radiant light. So powerful was the light that each core was literally suspended in air, as though floating within the light that enveloped it. One orb's core was jet-black, the other was pale blue. Solomon picked one up. When he closed his fingers around the orb, he could feel the core of it. Balling a fist around the core of one, the light caused his hand to become transparently red, and they all saw the bones, cartilage, and muscles through his skin.

When he opened his fingers and let the orb rest in the palm of his hand, the core again elevated on the wings of its light. As it levitated, he could not feel anything solid. Like magic, the orb's core floated about an inch above his palm. They all squinted at the radiance, amazed by what they were seeing.

Stranger things happened when Sully reached for the other orb. When one orb was in each hand, his forearm began to twitch, as though a muscle spasm was taking place throughout his arm and shoulder. Then he started breathing in short gasps. Anny said something, but he couldn't hear her. Through blurred vision, he saw Bax hold Anny back and as if in slow motion, saw a worried and terrified look on Anny's face.

He felt a fluid-like, tickling sensation though his body, and then the illuminated numbers on his arm merged together, forming a zigzag pattern like a bolt of lightning. That single strand of light then split in two, and one of the new strands traveled up his arm and crept past his neck and face. It illuminated his eyes with a brilliant blue and poured light out of his mouth, nose and ears as the light traveled past his neck and face region. It was a terrifying sight to the others. The light then traveled down the other arm and finally came to rest in an identical pattern on his other forearm.

For a moment, things were quiet. Then, Sully started to laugh and cry simultaneously, as though overcome with raw emotion. As he was babbling, the two strands of light on either forearm slowly crept to his hands. When that happened, he unclenched his fists and held the orbs, palms-up, one in each hand. They floated again, just as before. Next, the light in his forearms flowed through his hands and was swallowed completely by the two orbs. As soon as that happened, his body relaxed and his breathing returned to normal.

"What is it?" Bax said, still holding Anny by the shoulders. "What happened?"

Solomon's face was stern, but calm. He wore the hint of a smile at the corners of his mouth. In response to Braxton, he shook his head as if not able to articulate it, and let the orbs fall into the two halves of the box. The light surrounding the two cores then extinguished completely, leaving only the small marble-like objects behind, one black and the other pale blue.

"So? What?" Anny asked again.

"It's hard to explain," Solomon started. "It didn't hurt. It was a little uncomfortable at times. It felt... overwhelming."

He looked at the two orbs. He picked them back up, and as soon as he did, they lit up again with the same diamond-like fire. He held them palms up and they all stood there, staring. Anny suddenly said, "So what? Does this mean we're going home?"

Just as soon as she asked that question, the orb with a pale blue core jumped and pulsated with bright light, while the other one dimmed and sunk lower toward Sully's palm. The three companions looked at one another in amazement.

"It's like an Ask the 8-Ball," Bax mused. "A hand-held fortune teller. That's wild."

When he said that, the black marble shone bright and the blue one dimmed.

"Hang on," Solomon said, as he closed his fingers around the orbs. "We need to see what's going on. Let's ask a question that we already know the answer to."

He opened his palms and the two orbs bounced into the air with identical light. Solomon asked, "Did Dotty die?"

The blue orb bounced and lit up as the black one dimmed. Solomon followed with, "Did Dotty die in a car accident?" Predictably, the black one lit up as the blue one dimmed. Sully then put the orbs back in the box and the light extinguished once again. He immediately knew something that his companions didn't. The orbs were only mimicking a knowledge he had locked inside him. He didn't know how to articulate what he knew, but he just knew. Something was happening on a deeper level, but he kept this part to himself.

Both Anny and Bax tried to use the Urim and Thummim, but the marbles did not respond to them. To the others, they looked and felt like smooth stone balls in their hands. Only Sully could use them. They sat in the room and talked for some time, trying to guess at what was going on. Solomon tried to explain what happened to him during the initial blitz of activity, but it was hard to put into words, and served to mildly frustrate him. The simplest and best explanation was that he now felt *awake and alive*.

"That's the best way I can describe it. It's like I have new vision, new understanding. It's not like I have new facts or intelligence, but just deeper awareness. I can't explain it in tangible terms…"

"That's hard to understand, brov."

He tried to explain. It was as though he was sleepwalking through life, and now suddenly felt alert and aware. He knew things that defy explanation. It wasn't like facts or book knowledge, but he knew certain things as truth against lie, reality against deception.

The more he talked, the more he confused the others. Clearly, something big happened to Solomon, but he was unable to articulate it. As Sully's frustration grew, he tried using more emphatic language, and this only put his companions further on-edge.

"I know that these Urim and Thummim are not of this world, and I know they are tools given to humanity for the purpose of knowing truth and administering justice. I can't tell you how I know that, I just do. I also know that these are not for my benefit. I don't need them to administer truth and justice because now, somehow, truth and justice live inside of me. That's what happened back there in simplest terms. Truth and justice now lives inside of me. These marbles are for you, for mankind. They are two witnesses, each testifying to the authenticity of truth, in singularity. Their purpose is so that the decrees of truth and justice administered over mankind will be proven authentic beyond doubt, and accepted without question."

Solomon had clearly changed. He was no longer the collaborative 'leader-from-behind' that they knew and loved. He now spoke with the confidence of verdict and portrayed an all-knowingness that, frankly, rubbed Bax and Anny the wrong way.

"You can't know truth in singularity," Bax objected. "Nobody can."

"I can and I do. How would you know? You're still asleep."

"You're beginning to sound like a dirty Yankee, mate. I liked you better when you had a sense of humility about you."

When the conversation deteriorated, Solomon backed off. He wasn't being fair. He decided his friends would have to process and understand this entire event, over time.

342

He knew he had changed and he knew the changes would be hard for his friends to accept. At times, he knew they would wish for him to revert back to the old Sully. He fought against the urge to feel guilty for never wanting to go back to *being asleep*. His understanding was now so clear and vivid that it even overpowered his sense of human emotion. In other words, he would sooner let his friends and family abandon him than go back to being asleep. The deep knowledge he now possessed was too compelling and real.

In his mind's eye, the light of Lux et Veritas burned with ferocity. Solomon had already abandoned the idea of a quiet life in Middle America. He now understood clearly that the world was about to be turned upside down. He knew humanity was on a crash-course with hell, and he knew earth was the battlefield for a coming war, the likes of which has not been seen since time immemorial. Although he didn't choose any of this, he knew he was chosen, thrust into the center of a terrible epic between light and dark. Solomon now understood what Abele meant when he said, *you've been chosen.*

CHAPTER 47
True Telepathy

...

Abdullah Kahn made an important decision before dinner with the Cardinal that last night in Cairo. Although he wanted to return to his Long Island estate and get some rest and relaxation, he decided to take the private jet to Rio instead. He needed to return to BSA so that the crown could be inspected, tested, and analyzed in a controlled environment, under his personal supervision. He needed to better understand the ancient artifact to try and ascertain what they were dealing with.

A primary question related to safety. Privately, Kahn wondered if the crown was emitting some sort of radiation. He felt pretty awful, even poisoned, since its discovery. He also questioned whether it was interacting with his brain in a way that might be damaging. Kahn really struggled with the crown's power over his mind. He lived in a constant state of being both attracted to and repulsed by this dark artifact.

After Cairo, they flew to Rio and spent six weeks at BSA. Day and night, a team of scientists headed by Doctor Michael Monroe studied the crown. They used every piece of high-tech equipment they owned. The research delivered a variety of scientific answers. However, Kahn wasn't any closer on the deeper philosophical questions surrounding, *who* and *why*.

The team quickly determined that the crown was made of something new, never before analyzed. The material defied physics because it had mass, but the mass was always changing. Gravity remained constant, so the changing mass of the object was responsible for its fluctuating weight, relative to the handler.

They found that the crown's molecular structure was always changing. It was like all the quantum theories of the last two decades came together in one tangible object. The number of atoms that made up the structure, shape, and mass of the crown was always in flux, materializing and disintegrating by a factor of billions per second. It was 'mathematically impossible,' but in the theoretical world of quantum strings, it made crazy sense. At the molecular level, it was like the crown was dying and resurrecting itself trillions of times per second.

The BSA scientists began calling the crown's mass, "black matter." Since it was always disappearing and reappearing, it never fully interacted with the physical world. In fact, the metaphysical nature of the crown's mass placed it outside the earth's space-time continuum. While the crown appeared as a tangible object within earth's three dimensions of space and one dimension of time, it actually transcended all four. Theoretically, the crown acted as a portal to the metaphysical, a wormhole of sorts. Eventually, the BSA researchers surmised that it had to be the properties of the black matter itself that allowed a look into other realms. Telepathy happened if two or more people learned how to use the crown to 'peek through dimensional limitations.'

"Simplistically," Monroe explained, "speech is a process where the brain transmits thoughts and converts them into coherent, linguistic noises. Those noises transmit by sound waves through a single space-time, which others in that space-time can hear and essentially decode. Speech is truly a miraculous thing, but in the context of telepathy, we've found speech and its bio-mechanical transmission to be a primordial adaptation, a very basic and elementary evolutionary trait compared to the crystal-clear telepathic uplink the scientists are enjoying in the presence of the crown. One of the scientists likened it to the difference between a 56k telephone uplink and a fiber-optic, 100 megabits per second channel. It is hardly comparable."

"Well, it's just thoughts, right? Words put into thoughts?"

"No, it's much more," Monroe said with an uncontainable smile. "Having spent six weeks in its presence, my team has learned to communicate with one another telepathically, but without using words at all. Though difficult to describe, we now send and receive new packets of data comprised mostly of feelings and ideals, or concepts and ideas too abstract for words. As we studied the crown, we have learned to prefer this method of communication because words are so limiting. True telepathic communication is perfect and exact. No longer do we experience misunderstanding between the members of the team. Nobody ever falls behind. It is the most euphoric working environment I've ever known."

"I don't get it," the Hand said in response. That's when Monroe telepathically communicated what he was trying to say in words, and at that instant, both the Hand and Abdullah both realized what the scientist was trying to convey.

Monroe explained how the science of telepathy was cracked with the help of the Anima Imperium. After they had established that the crown was not giving off harmful radiation, but before they knew what they were dealing with, a startling discovery was made. In the minimum-security wing of BSA, a 12-year-old trafficked-in slave boy was being experimented on with the Anima Imperium. While *under the light,* and during the time his Life Essence was detached from his brain, he was somehow able to eavesdrop on the telepathic conversation that the scientists were having while researching the crown all the way over in max-sec.

With that realization, the team drove the crown well outside the city limits of Rio de Janeiro and began to communicate telepathically with one another there. They did this while the Anima Imperium was used on the same boy back inside the BSA labs. There again, the boy recalled hearing the telepathic conversation in its entirety and could even recount what was said after the Anima was turned off.

It was these and similar experiments that caused the team to conclude that most of what humans identify as attributes of being uniquely *human* are just evolutionary biomechanics. There's nothing all that unique about any of it. From the expression of thoughts or feelings, speech, being able to talk and comprehend, being able to walk, shake hands, have sex, love someone, eat, urinate; everything happens at the bio-mechanical level. The biomechanics prompt the secretion of adrenaline before a fight, and the biomechanics prompt the secretion of hormones while in the company of an attractive someone.

With the help of the crown and the AI, the team identified a much higher intelligence locked within the human being, one that's never before been tapped and documented. They found that the humans essence is more closely related to a conceptual *alien being* than, say, ape or monkey.

Eventually, they agreed that extrasensory perception and telepathy had not evolved in mankind because these traits are inherent components of the life essence or soul. This conclusion was now beyond refuting. The boy under the AI did not have to learn how to use telepathy, as though he was a child learning to walk. It just naturally happened whenever the conditions supported it. He could hear – or more accurately, feel and fully comprehend – the telepathic conversations scientists were having a hundred miles away.

It was harder to communicate telepathically when not using words. It was not as though they had to learn a new skill; rather, they had to unlearn their heavy reliance on verbal communication. Abdullah and the scientists each practiced, and some of them got the hang of it within a few days. For others, it took a week or more. Predictably, those who were naturally quiet or shy were faster to grasp wordless telepathy.

While at BSA, Abdullah forbid the scientists from putting on the crown, though one or two of them defied the order and tried it on when nobody was looking. What they experienced was similar to what the Hand had experienced -- the crown's mass grew more and more until it was so heavy that they bent at the waist and let it slide off. Both men who put the crown on regretted doing it. There was no positive outcome. All they got for defying the order was a kink in the neck.

When the research at BSA ran its course, Abdullah took his crown and his trusted Hand, and flew home to Long Island for a well-deserved break.

CHAPTER 48
Reunion

…

"Hey, yo, fatal systems error," Rooter shouted and slammed his hand on the wall separating his room from the living area, "Fetch me a brewski, will ya?"

"Hey, double-stack," Con retorted, "you want a beer, fetch it yourself!"

Rooter rolled his eyes and slammed a hand into the wall a second time, "I told you once gigawatt, ease up on the fat jokes, I'm sensitive."

"La-la-la, I can't hear you, my headphones are keeping the…"

Rooter's door suddenly opened and Sully walked in with his arms spread wide, wearing a million dollar smile. "You miss me, Rooter?"

"Sully! Hell yes I missed you! You didn't say you were coming back today," the PI stood stiffly and embraced his friend.

"You tear into one another like this all the time?" Bax asked, as he pushed into Rooter's bedroom with Anny following.

"Nah," Rooter replied as he dished hugs around. "You just caught us on our best behavior is all. Normally, I'm breaking lamps and tire irons over that idiot's head."

Con heard the commotion and came out of his room to a chorus of laughter and good cheer. The group was ecstatic to be back under one roof. Although he didn't say much, Con's joy was evident in his expression. It was the widest Sully had ever seen him smile.

Bax had planned to stay in the UK and not return to Texas with the others. He knew work had to be done at the government level, and felt some measure of anxiety to get moving on that. The Phantoms were too large and organized an entity to leave alone. But before that, he wanted to be a part of the debriefing between Solomon and his team, and not just for the information he might gather. He wouldn't openly admit it, but Bax felt as close to these people as he had ever felt to anyone. These random *yanks* were like his family now.

They congregated in the living room and opened up. Predictably, Rooter and Con were most interested in seeing the Urim and Thummim. Solomon opened the little box and passed the two marbles around. They were plane and ordinary, somewhat of a letdown to Rooter. He looked at Con and said, "These marbles are as ordinary as motherhood and apple pie. What gives? Didn't you say they were soothsaying tools of some sort?" Con shrugged, visibly disappointed.

"Give 'em here," Sully grinned as Rooter handed them over. When he did, they lit up like diamonds with their own sun-source. The fire took their breath away. The stones hovered a few inches above his palms and Solomon told Con to ask a question.

"What time is it?"

"That's open-ended. I get the answer, and I can tell you its 11:52 without looking at the clock, but the orbs only respond to closed questions. As in, yes-or-no questions."

Rooter looked at his wristwatch suspiciously. Con thought for a second and asked, "Is Rooter fat?"

The light-blue orb lit up and bounced as the black orb dimmed and ducked. Bax chuckled, pointed, and said, "That means, yes."

"Hey orbs, look over here," Rooter chided, gesturing to himself. "Is Con so smart that he lacks social grace?"

The orbs didn't change at all, and Anny said, "That's what happens when the question is so stupid, the orbs choose not to dignify it with an answer."

Everyone had a good laugh as Rooter thought about his phrasing and realized how poorly worded his question actually was. He had to laugh at himself too.

Sully dropped the Urim and Thummim back in the box. It was good to be home. Next, the guys wanted to know more about Abele and that whole experience, so Sully gave a full report. Bax and Anny still remained mum as to what the being had told them individually. They told the story of how they retrieved Lux et Veritas in the middle of the night, and got into how the artifact changed Solomon in some mysterious ways.

By the time they reached Texas, Anny and Bax had accepted the changes in Sully. They were reluctant to fully embrace the new him, but something had happened in the Cairo airport that made believers out of them.

Anny explained, "In the Cairo airport, after passing through security, on the way to the gate, Sully told us we needed to be on the lookout. Bax and I were like, 'What? What are you talking about?' But he was adamant and led us into a duty free shop.

A minute or two later, that little pale man who was standing outside the Osiris shaft came and walked straight past us."

Rooter straightened his posture as Con's eyebrows jumped. Bax took the story from there, "Our boy got a pass from me at that point. That ghostly little man has a queer cut jib. You know, you saw it in the photos. He was not misplaced. It was definitely him and somehow Sully knew he was coming up on our six, and warned us before it was too late."

"What did you do? Was he on your flight?" Rooter asked the obvious next question.

"No. I tailed him to a door in the concourse where he and his companion were screened through. We asked around and think they were flying private. One security person who spoke broken English said 'private passengers' while pointing to that door. Anyway, he was with an older guy, maybe mid-to-late fifties. Familiar face. I tried to snap a few shots of him, but only got partials."

Bax pulled out his little spy camera and asked for the security code to link into the home's wifi. Con gave the code, two alphanumeric units at a time: *Gr3asy1ta1ian*.

Bax entered the code and chuckled in Rooter's direction. Rooter shrugged, "What, you got a problem?"

"No, no problem. Your mate has a funny wit."

Braxton transferred the photos, including the 22-second video he took of the two intrigues in Cairo. The boy-genius then excused himself to initiate the facial recognition software, while Rooter gave a brief and uninteresting report of their time together since moving to Texas.

"We'll go into Houston here and there because it gets so damn boring in this house. We went up and caught a Ranger's game last week. That was nice."

"You stay under the radar?" Bax asked.

"'Course. We only use cash or prepaids, always go with the hats and sunglasses." He paused and thought about it for a few seconds, "But frankly, nobody in this state seems to give a rip we're even alive. It's been a whole different experience from the time in Edgewater. It's sort of hard to keep your damper up when day-in and day-out, nobody knows you even exist."

"Somebody knows we exist, but you're right." Solomon interjected. He had that look, the look that said he knew something that nobody else did. "We're safe here and it's OK to let the guard down a little, for now anyway."

"See, there you go," Bax started in on him. "That may very well be true, and since Cairo I've committed myself to giving you the benefit of the doubt, but why say it? We let our guard down and something happens that you didn't expect and then what?"

"We've had this discussion," Sully smiled, "truth is irrevocable. When the climate shifts and life becomes more dangerous, I'll know that too and I'll let 'cha all know. It's hard to explain."

"I think I get it," Rooter piped and pointed to Bax first, then Sully. "You operate on logic and statistical probabilities. It's what informs your decisions. But you've changed, Sully. You now operate on gut and instinct. The two conflict with one another, so you guys are not seeing eye-to-eye on things."

Rooter was right, and it was pointless to argue from those opposing paradigms because even hard-pressed, they'd never really align. Bax saw the world through the lens of action and reaction; tried and tested probabilities which were conditioned and learned. Sully was now different. He somehow went from being an analytical legal mind to innate instinct, intuition, and sensation.

Bax was trying to embrace the newfound psychic abilities of his friend. Logically, if the skill was real, Bax knew that Sully's psychic powers would prove remarkably useful against the type of evil they experienced. *Indeed, they already had…*

But breaking old habits is tough. Assessing and moving on gut instinct was even more difficult for Bax.

Though it pained him to do so, Bax extended the olive branch this time, "He's actually right. His 'danger-dar' appears to go off when it needs to, so if he says it's safe to be easy in life these days, then it probably is. Honestly, I've seen enough to agree with that much."

"Yeah, we got Frodo's elf-sword here. It's bound to light up when goblins are near, right?" Rooter had his way of putting things.

Changing the subject entirely and doing so without notice, Anny pointed to her and Sully and said, "We're together." The announcement was followed by silence.

"Wow, really?" Rooter finally said, staring down his attorney friend with a conflicted glare, "Huh. That's a gut punch if there ever was one."

It was an awkward moment. Had Anny thought there was even a remote chance that Rooter would have responded that way, she wouldn't have been so brazen in the announcement. She felt a pang of embarrassment, as Sully sat quiet under his best friend's accusatory gaze.

"So, you two are together," he said, just as the corners of his mouth twitched and signaled his loss of containment, "That's crazy, because here I thought that only me 'n Con ever actually saw that coming!"

They broke into a relieved chorus of laughs as Rooter stood up to give Anny a hug. He followed that with a formal handshake with Sully and said, "And you. I can't tell you how many nights me 'n Con sat here and talked about what a window-licker you were. You were so dense back in Edgewater even Con felt sorry for you, and in the relational context, that's sayin' something." They heard Con deliver some inaudible barb from the other room.

"Seriously though, congratulations, kids. I'd be lyin' to ya if I said I didn't see it comin' for what, a year or more? Really, I'm happy for you both. You two are a good match. You'll have to fight over which side of the wedding I'm in but there's time to figure all that out..."

"We're thinking about going to Kansas in the next day or two," Sully said. "I want to meet her folks and get acquainted. I was thinking about all our stuff back in DC, and thought maybe you could go settle those affairs."

"Sure, what'd you have in mind?"

"Well, Bax and I were talking about this, and if the Phantoms got what they were after in Egypt, there's a chance they may not be looking for us anymore, me in particular. But in case they are, we should hire an attorney to close the business, settle individual accounts, and whatever else it takes to disappear from our old lives, without dying. I was thinking Boardman. We've known him forever, he's a sly fox, and I'm sure he'll do the business quietly."

"Do we bring him in?"

"I wouldn't personally have a problem with that. When I think about him, I feel like he's an ally in all this, especially on the business end. I don't know. It's open for discussion, I guess."

"So, no emphatic 'inside' word on this one, ey?" Bax mocked. "This a case where the marbles are both dark, is it? Because, if so, we should defer to logic, predicated on analysis, and that tells me not to bring unnecessary anybody's into the circle of trust now, or probably ever."

Solomon shrugged, as if to say Bax won that round, "So, just tell him whatever he needs to know then. Let's keep it vague."

Con walked out of his room and looked at Braxton with a wide smile. "His name is Abdullah Kahn. This one was easy. This guy is all over the net, been a playboy for some time. Lots of mystery and intrigue, too."

"Really? Lord's wig and all?" the Americans had no idea what that meant, so Bax rephrased, "Is his identity confirmed?"

"Yup. It's as confirmed as my program will confirm anything. He's not lived a quiet life, and like I said, he's all over the Internet so I got images of him everywhere. It was an easy match."

Bax spent twenty minutes with Con going over his findings before returning to the larger group. He was satisfied with both the procedure used and the conclusion reached. It did indeed appear to be the infamous Abdullah Kahn. A number of questions now surfaced. Bax knew he needed access to data of a less accessible nature, back in the UK.

As dinnertime approached, they put the business aside and fell into old relational habits, poking fun at one another, making crude jokes, talking over one another, and catching up on life's many oddities. It was easy to settle back into the K&A comfort-zone. For dinner, they fired up the grill and cooked a few nice cuts of beef. They found some camping chairs and set up under a huge backyard tree. It was hot outside, but this was real therapy.

It wasn't one specific thing that brought bliss to Manvel, Texas that night; it was a combination of many things. It started with good company. Good people are always the bedrock of worthy memories, but these good people also had good attitudes. Through the refinement of intense circumstance, they learned to not take for granted the little moments of light-heartedness that creep up unexpectedly. Then, there was the familiar American sizzle of burning fat, and the aromas of sizzling meat, and the crisp taste of cold beer on a hot midsummer's dusk. It didn't get any better than that.

In one another's company, they truly found Gene Austin's *Blue Paradise*, or was it *Blue Heaven?* Bax couldn't remember.

"So, I got a question," Con mused from a reclined posture in his patio lounger. "We found a thing that an alien told us to go find, but what about the rest of Malcolm's journal? It doesn't say anything about magic marbles."

"We have to figure," Bax said, "that the Phantoms also found something in that Osiris hole."

"Con brings up a good point," Anny said, "where is this all going? I'd like to think that life is slowing down and recalibrating, but something in my gut tells me that this is only just the beginning."

Sully's attention piqued when she said that. *What is it about gut and feeling these days?*

The group talked, but Sully stayed quiet and listened to his friends intently, pondering. He had profound insight into many of the questions they asked, but kept them to himself. Had they considered asking the Urim and Thummim their questions, he wouldn't object, but they never did. It was not in their nature to submit in that manner, even if they knew the truth was at their fingertips.

Though he intuitively felt confident he knew the answers to some of their questions, something told him to sit silent. He had a deep realization of fate. The knowledge he now possessed was trumped by the ultimate power of destiny. Much of the conversation among his friends was futile. They would not be able to alter most of what approached, even with good planning based on accurate foresight. Control was not the answer.

This beautiful night and these beautiful people mattered more than answers right now. The camaraderie, the friendships, and the bonds that tied them together – his engagement with larger truth would only tear them apart, so on this occasion, Sully chose to simply enjoy his friends.

CHAPTER 49
The Hand of Kahn

...

The Hand stood on a second story balcony overlooking the pathways that zigzagged through the gardens. Kahn's home on Long Island was a testimony to finely manicured grounds, with impeccable attention to detail throughout the curtilage. The view's serenity should have inspired a sense of calm, but instead the Hand's pulse quickened as he watched his master agonize. It was finally about to happen. A malicious grin crept over his face as he resolved to keep quiet and remain undetected.

Before leaving BSA, many on the team investigating the crown learned how to withhold thought. The skill was cumbersome at first, but like riding a bike, once you get it, you get it. Primarily, the technique is about *will* – essentially *willing* thoughts to not be heard telepathically.

Some were better than others at keeping their telepathy 'quiet.' The Hand was better than most.

Kahn wondered about the Hand. Though he hadn't questioned his loyalty for some time, an old concern crept back into his consciousness. Since the Osiris shaft, and especially since BSA, Kahn was concerned, *am I calling the shots or is this little fellow playing me?*

Abdullah had squashed his paranoia about the Hand years ago, but something was now off. The old worries invaded his mind like bees to a hive. Something about the Hand's demeanor was different, but he couldn't put his finger on it.

The Hand had quickly mastered the ability to mum his telepathy, something that most others on the team struggled to do. Kahn figured his telepathic proficiency had to do with his character. The Hand was always cloaking his personal agendas behind masks and mirrors. It was precisely this knavish behavior that had the billionaire so concerned. *I can never tell what he's doing or thinking...*

Mister Jones is how he first introduced himself. He'd appeared out of nowhere one day while Abdullah attended a summit in Budapest on worldwide energy demands. Kahn was on official family business at the time, attending on behalf of his wealthy new father-in-law. One night, while sipping a cocktail in the hotel bar, Jones suddenly appeared and introduced himself. He was short and pale, but back then he carried more weight in the cheeks and more pigment in the skin and hair. Socially speaking, he was more charismatic too.

After some casual conversation, mostly about the summit, Jones abruptly leaned in and informed the to-be-billionaire, "I make things happen. My job is to take ordinary people and make them extraordinary. I can make you extraordinary."

Kahn never suspected a relationship between he and Jones would develop, much less last as long as it had. But Jones knew things. Private things. From the start, he knew that Kahn's marriage was less about the woman and more about a union with the Karafi's money. Jones easily pegged Kahn's true motivations in that first encounter. Truthfully, Jones pegged a lot of things. He had a talismanic ability to know the secret motives of one's heart, and a cunning that enabled him to use that knowledge to further his undisclosed agendas.

A few months after the fortune was transferred into his name, the Kahns got into a fight, and their discord led Abdullah to check into a Sheraton in downtown Kuwait City. There, at the hotel bar, Jones miraculously appeared once again. Of course, this was billed as irony, and oh, what a small word after all.

The meeting started off casually. They discussed stock portfolios, investments, and other items as Kahn pulled hard on the business-end of an expensive bottle of whisky. As the night darkened, they ventured into other discussions. Jones led the way. One such topic involved how Abdullah might – should he ever so desire – consolidate his newfound wealth under his sole control. This led to quieter talks about murkier alternatives, and it all took place while the thick numb of booze settled in on Abdullah's senses.

After Jones orchestrated her 'accidental' death, he humbly asked Kahn for a job. Feeling indebted at best, a mark for blackmail at worst, he gave Jones a job and called him his *Personal Manager*. But Jones started introducing himself as "Mr. Kahn's Right Hand" and that title began to stick. Predictably, it morphed into all sorts of titles, but Kahn started calling him plainly, the *Hand,* after Mister Jones asked and then insisted that he did. At first, it was a knotty title coming off the tongue, and then it got easier. At some point, the title became his name, and then his name became his whole identity. But if Abdullah was honest, especially in those early years, it was never he who called the shots. It was Mister Jones.

The Hand's dark, beady eyes strained to see, as Kahn looked around his garden suspiciously. Kahn wanted to know he was alone. The Hand licked his thin pale lips and leaned forward. *It's happening. It's finally happening.*

Abdullah brought the crown to eye level, then hoisted it up and set it on his head. The Hand could hear him laugh, as if overjoyed. Then the laugh changed and became hysterical, like the shrill of the Joker. Then the laughter bellowed like a loud, deep, bass drum. At that instant, the Hand could hear, by telepathy, a conversation Kahn was having with the owner of that deep and terrible voice.

"You are Abdullah Kahn, but I only know you by the name *Weasel.* What makes you think you are worthy of me?"

"Lord, are you God?" Kahn's telepathic voice sounded frightened.

"I am."

"Then I am Abdullah Kahn, weasel, and live only to serve you."

"Then kneel."

The Hand watched as Kahn knelt down to one knee and dropped his head slightly. It was an odd sight to behold, as Kahn had always been a defiant, arrogant jerk. This posture was different. The Hand's upper lip curled, *this posture is pathetic. That's why you could never be worthy, wife-murderer.*

"Weasel, your purpose has been served. You are unworthy of me. Take the crown off your head."

"No, Lord, make me worthy. I beg this of you."

A chilly, derisive laugh followed, "You've never been worthy. You're nothing but garbage. You are a weasel, nothing more."

"Lord, I insist…"

"Take off the crown, or be burned from the inside out."

"I can't, Lord. The power in it, in you -- I'd do anything for it… for you. Just name it."

The Hand's eyes widened with horror at what he witnessed next. First came the laugh, loud and powerful. Then, Kahn let out a bloody scream. He reached for the crown to try and get it off, but now it would not come off, it just rattled and moved on his head as the old man lunged and heaved under the pain of an unseen torture.

Suddenly, the crown's spires that pointed upward turned upside down, and formed into what looked like the fingers of a powerful black hand, palming Abdullah's head. They dug deeply into his scalp. From his vantage point on the balcony, the Hand could see splatters of blood and chips of bone coming off Abdullah's head.

The Hand's eyes narrowed and the thin-lipped grin returned. It was all so satisfying. *Well worth the long wait. Keep hurting him. Keep squeezing. Kill him!*

The Hand felt an emotional, even sexual satisfaction at the sights and sounds of Abdullah's torment.

Eventually, the incoherent sounds of agony died down and became a coherent cry for help. That's when the Hand jumped up, ran inside the house, down the stairs, and out into the backyard. On approach, he saw that Abdullah's eyes were bright red. Not just red, but candy-apple, sports car red. They looked so bizarre that the Hand grimaced and stopped short. Pushing through the momentary fear, he approached the broken man lying in the spattering of his own blood, vomit, and mucus. Both arms were hyperextended at the elbows, both legs the same at the knees. Every muscle in his body appeared tense and rigid. The veins in his neck and forearms were protruding through the skin in such a way that they looked like a three-dimensional concept design for a subway system. Kahn was a mess.

His jaw was locked. He swallowed hard without closing his mouth as his red eyes rolled back into his head. "Crown. Cr-Crown." He pushed the words through clenched teeth.

The Hand knew what he needed, but was enjoying the moment far too much. He responded with forced trepidation, "Wh-what? I'll call a doctor."

"Get the cr-crown. Get it off me."

The Hand didn't immediately move. Kahn tried to articulate his need again, but he couldn't. He then tried using telepathy, but the pain made it too difficult to think coherently. No words or communication of any form would come.

His eyes rolled back to the front and he focused. There, standing over him with a peculiar look of satisfaction, was the Hand. It was a moment of calm and clarity amid the Devil's vitriol. At that instant, Kahn knew beyond any doubt that his prior suspicions were finally realized. Indeed, all this time, it was never he, but the Hand who called the shots and dictated events. 'Betrayal' doesn't even begin to describe what Abdullah felt. It was almost worse than the physical anguish.

Though the moment only lasted an instant, Kahn felt a lifetime of emotions. Embarrassment, anger, confusion, and worst of all, shame. He felt shame for letting greed cloud his judgment, for selling his soul for material wealth.

The moment didn't last. The Hand suddenly leaned down and knocked the crown off his head with casual indifference. As soon as the crown hit the ground, his muscles relaxed and the pain subsided some, though his body remained broken.

The Hand picked up the crown. When he did, it started vibrating, and a few seconds later it contracted on itself, morphing into a sphere the size of a baseball. It was smooth and shiny, and dotted with tiny glowing spots of other material.

Leaning over, he placed the little ball on the ground in front of Abdullah's contorted face. He then sighed, stood, and stuffed his hands in his pockets. Abdullah was still speechless. He was trying to avoid passing out from the pain and exhaustion. His eyes jogged from the ball to the Hand, and back to the ball again. Dirt from the sidewalk stuck to his bloodstained face, and open wounds gushed dark, sticky blood around the crown of his head.

"I'll call a doctor for you," the Hand finally said, sympathetically. Without another word, he turned toward the house as if on a Sunday stroll through the gardens of the estate. He was in no hurry, and made no attempt to pretend he was. Had Abdullah not been in such anguish, he might have heard the Hand whistling, casually reenacting the theme to 'The Andy Griffith Show.'

CHAPTER 50
New Hope

...

Kahn sat up as the Hand approached with a tray of delicacies, "Shouldn't we talk?"

"There's nothing to talk about."

"The hell there isn't. I was in pain, not dead."

"What do you need, Abdullah, an apology? Some sort of recompense for the wrongs you've suffered? The past is the past, and you, of all people, should know how to let it go."

"You used me. Why?"

"I was seven when my dad taught me a very valuable lesson. Funny, it happened while dad used me like a blow-up doll one night. He said, 'you'll never amount to anything, dwarf. In this world, you'll always be garbage, a weasel.' That's the pet name he used when raping me, *Weasel*."

The Hand put the tray down on the bed next to Abdullah, who had plaster casts on all four limbs.

"Just imagine my surprise when the voice in that crown called you a weasel too. I've been called a weasel my whole life by my dad, but the other day when you put that crown on, I felt my dad's presence for the first time since I rammed the sharp side of a peeler through his eye socket. That happened, by the way, when I was seventeen. I didn't spend much time in lock-down, though. They tried me as a minor, and the judge felt bad for me."

Kahn looked at the little man reluctantly. There was certainly more to him than he previously knew. Through the years, Kahn had never bothered asking the Hand about his personal life or parents. He never much cared about anyone besides himself. The Hand took one of the crab cakes and fed it to him. Kahn chewed slowly.

"So, we're both weasels, and we've both killed for personal gain. You can feel betrayed all you want, but take my advice, wear the weasel. Own it. It's better that way." The Hand flashed a cruel grin.

"Where's the crown? I can no longer hear the voices."

"Really? I had it put into a glass cube." The Hand nodded towards the far wall, "It's in your armoire just there. You should be able to hear it fine."

Kahn looked downcast and shrugged, "Truth is, I've not heard it since the day I put the damn thing on."

"By the way, I heard from the Stable Keeper, Alicia Zieda."

"Yeah, when?"

"Few days ago, the day you came back from the hospital, I think."

"And?"

"She's well, good of you to ask," the Hand said sarcastically as he fed Kahn another bite. Abdullah didn't have the energy to quarrel, so he chewed slowly and just waited for the Hand to keep talking.

"Anyway, she was excited about a new specimen." Kahn's eyebrows jumped as the Hand grinned and said, "A tri-animal species."

"Yeah?"

The Hand grinned wide, unable to conceal his own excitement, "The torso and legs of a lion, the head of a big-horned sheep, and the best part, the tail appendage of a full and functional viper of some sort."

Kahn whistled and scrunched his face, "That's nasty."

"She wants to ride it."

"Come on!"

"Really, she thinks she'll get there too."

"Why? How? Do we have any clients needing to ride lions, goats, and snakes, or all three at the same time?"

"I don't know," the Hand shrugged and put up a defensive gesture, "I'm just the messenger."

They sat there for a few moments in silence before the Hand gestured to the trey. Abdullah declined the food but asked for a swig of water. The Hand carefully helped him with a drink.

"It wasn't all bad, was it?" Abdullah asked, almost in a whisper.

The Hand shook his head.

"Why the malice toward me? Why did it please you to see me suffering the way I did that day in the garden?"

The Hand shrugged and agreed, "It hasn't been all bad. Honestly, you've been the closest thing I've ever had to a friend, even though you were an abusive asshole for most of it. But in the end, my pedophile father was probably right. This world is no place for a pasty dwarf, and I'll probably always savor the pain of others. I don't know. It sort of helps me cope with my own."

Their relationship had changed, and changed dramatically since the incident in the garden. Abdullah now relied on the Hand for everything, and therefore, gave him whatever he desired as payment for sticking around. The Hand got to do whatever he wanted, see whoever he wanted, and give the Phantom organization any command or dictate he wanted. During the time Abdullah was on the mend, the 'understanding' was that the Hand got to play God.

He particularly enjoyed Abdullah's centurion card from American Express. He used it to order up some of New York City's most exotic call-girls. He found it amazing, what money could get a desperate person to do.

Abdullah learned that the Hand was a deranged sexual deviant, and got the girls to do things that most deviants don't even fantasize about. One girl, in fact, might have even died. The Hand didn't know because he only went so far as to summon a car service to take her to the hospital, and didn't bother to follow up.

"The girl from the other night. She gonna be okay?"

The Hand shrugged flippantly.

"You don't care?"

"Why should I? She's a whore."

The Hand lifted the glass to Kahn's mouth again. Abdullah took a big drink this time, as he did not know when the Hand would return to offer him food and water. There was no set schedule.

The Hand was a calloused and hardened individual, much more so than Abdullah. Both men had skeletons in the closet, but Abdullah was able to live and enjoy life, whereas the Hand seemed to live life solely defined by the atrocities of his past. It made the small man unpredictable, dangerous in a sneaky and cunning sense.

"Any ideas on what to do with the crown?" Abdullah changed the subject.

"You say you don't hear it anymore?"

Abdullah shook his head.

"We could see if someone else does. Set up an experiment. Put it in a bathroom behind a counter and have people over. When they use the bathroom, if they hear it, they'll look around for the voices. Something like that?"

"That's a good idea," Kahn agreed. "Why don't you set up a few parties then, and we'll start having people over. See if we can find someone who might be able to help us crack this riddle."

"Isn't that what I just said?" the Hand's face suddenly became rigid.

He seemed upset, so Kahn retreated and nodded sheepishly. "Yes, sorry. I'm used to being an asshole, remember? You had a good idea. Let's do it."

For the next many months, the Hand set up party after party, inviting the world's social and political elites to the Long Island mansion for an evening among their fellow cream. But party after party yielded no suitor for the crown. Like an obsession, they both fell into a routine where all they did was scour the world's headlines for any clue that might help identify someone with the gift.

While Kahn was in recovery, they kept others in the Phantom organization at bay by making up excuses for why they couldn't meet. The General, the Scientist, the Cardinal, and an array of other big players were sidelined while the Hand worked to find a suitor for the crown.

In time Kahn's body mended, but the crown did more to him than break a few bones. The reproductive capabilities of his cell tissue were damaged somehow, and he began to age at an accelerated rate. His personal doctor guessed that age was descending on him at the rate of one full year for every month he lived. Abdullah made one brief trip to BSA in October, hoping the scientists there could diagnose and figure out how to reverse the damage, but the case defied their best attempts at a workable theory.

As soon as he returned to his estate he came down with the flu and was bedridden for a month. Around that time he emotionally accepted the fact that he was going to die much sooner than he expected, and stopped trying to fight so hard for a cure. The Hand let go of his vitriol during Kahn's rapid deterioration too. He actually did his best to make him as comfortable as possible through the dying process.

By early December, both of them wondered if they would ever find another person who could hear the world beyond that space-time portal. The crown was no longer a crown, but a ball of black matter concealed in a glass box. It had been that way since the garden. By late December, it was becoming apparent that Abdullah would likely not live to see the day the riddle was broken. But then, quite unexpectedly, a young man of mix-racial descent entered their world. His name was Leonardo Khalpana.

Had they found him, or had Leo found the black matter? They didn't know for sure. What was certain, however, is that Leo heard those noises as clear as a bell. Remarkably, when Leo heard the world beyond the black matter, Abdullah also got his own special hearing back.

After his brief encounter with Leo, Kahn shuffled into his private study, still cradling the little glass box. His face was strained, annoyed somehow.

"What's the matter? You look aggravated," the Hand commented.

"I am. That kid out there unlocked the noise from this thing. I forgot how annoying this is."

"He did?" The Hand jumped up, knocking over his rock-glass in the process, and shattering it on the wood floor, "You mean we found our man?"

Kahn nodded reluctantly, "He's hardly a man. More like a boy, spoiled kid at that. It's that Leo Khalpana."

"Leo Kha, you mean the son of that Jordanian, Toby May? The guy with the boy-toys?"

Abdullah nodded. "I guess. I don't know his history…"

The Hand gestured for Abdullah to sit down, and proceeded to set the black matter on the mantle. But Abdullah pointed at the door and signaled for him to put it somewhere much further away.

"All along," the Hand was saying as he returned to Abdullah, "we were looking for esteem and honor, and this kid's been on the outer fringe of middle-class since he wore short pants to weddings. Come to think about it, he's just like you."

"Come again?" Abdullah pressed his fingers into his forehead.

"He's like you," the Hand repeated and shrugged. "I don't know. Got a pile of money from elsewhere, but never had to work for it. He's ambitious. I don't know."

"How's that?"

"I read he got a big inheritance from his donut punching father. He's been living off it his whole life. Just seems odd that the crown only talks to trust-fund recipients."

Abdullah frowned at the characterization, and then grinned, "Hey, I worked for mine. Even had to kill for my supper, am I right?"

They laughed and the Hand poured new drinks, "So what are we going to do with him?"

"Whatever we do, we should do it at BSA. Somewhere we can contain him and the experimentation." Kahn sipped the golden liquid, "Any luck, something will happen and give us some insight into how to reverse my condition. One can hope, anyway."

"You can't get there, how you plan on…"

"Oh, I'll get there," he interrupted. "We'll use the private jet and I'll get to Rio one way or another. Oh, you better believe it."

They sat and drank, and soon noticed the sphere flexing inside its glass encasement. Something was happening.

CHAPTER 51
Hutchinson

...

Manvel, Texas to Hutchinson, Kansas is an eleven-hour drive. It's certainly doable in one sitting, but that seemed rushed to the traveling couple.

Since arriving in Texas, both Sully and Anny inadvertently fell into a Jamaican *ire-ire-mon* pace of life. Nothing needed to be rushed. On the contrary, life needed to be savored and taken in sips. For this reason, they ended up staying in Manvel almost a month.

Manvel was a perfect place to decompress. They had more than a few 'therapeutic barbeques' out back. They got to know Roger Weaverly, who turned out to be a great host. They even got to know a few of Papa Roger's friends as well. One Sunday, Anny and Bax attended a church service with Papa Rog's Texas brethren, though the rest of Sully's crew politely declined.

On Solomon's request, the team kept Lux et Veritas from the men and women of Crossroads Foundation. Practically, he didn't mind them knowing about it, but the timing didn't feel right. There was a light, wispy barrier between the two groups that seemed to be fixed there by some unseen power. That barrier prompted men on both sides to conceal and hide. It encouraged them to distrust and question.

The Crossroads folks found the K&A crew to be odd, not what they expected. They always expected to have long-term guests show up, at a day and hour such as this, but they pictured those guests to be something else. Something less worldly. Something less urban. Something more like them, to be frank.

From the K&A perspective, the tight-lipped murkiness surrounding what Crossroads Foundation was, why it existed, and what purpose it served caused a level of distrust. Therefore, both groups labored under a cloud of intrigue, at least for the time being.

Braxton said his goodbyes as autumn's foliage turned into full brilliance. He planned to be in touch, but nobody knew when that might actually be. His strategy was to get back home and figure out who Abdullah Kahn was, as well as identify and build a team he could trust. Ultimately, his goal was to ascertain the Phantom's identity, and he had an idea about how to accomplish that task. It was an idea that Abele gave him in the hotel room in Cairo. It fit perfectly with his skillset, and if executed the right way, it had a high probability of success. If he executed well, he might eventually find himself at the center of the Beast.

The Beast... Why did Abele refer to the Phantoms as 'the Beast?' Bax thought and calculated. But ultimately he decided to head back to London to begin executing his plan.

Rooter and Sully both wanted to drive him to Bush International, but Braxton would have nothing to do with that plan. *Why risk the surveillance at this point?* So, on an unseasonably hot day in Manvel, handshakes and hugs were given on the front porch of their Manvel residence instead, while Papa Roger's car hummed under the strain of its AC in the driveway.

The weather was much cooler the day Sully and Anny finally got in her car and drove north. That same day, Rooter drove his rig back to DC in order to begin organizing the complete dismantling of the K&A assets. Not just the K&A business, but he was also tasked with securing and finalizing the team's individual accounts and personal effects, as well. By the time he was done, Rooter hoped to assure no crumbs led to Texas, Kansas, or anywhere else for that matter. He figured on returning to Manvel by mid-December at the latest.

Con had the place to himself for a few weeks. Papa Roger offered to increase his visits, but the computer hacker assured his host that he'd thrive by himself. Quiet's company was something he'd desperately missed during the last year of chaos.

* * * * * * * * * *

As Sully crept up Briarwood Lane and saw the large, stucco-and-brick home, he actually began to panic. His disposition took Anny by surprise.

"Maybe we should have called, you know, and warned them we were coming."

He stopped the car a half-block before the Boyle residence. He felt her hand on his arm, "It's gonna be fine. These are my parents. They are good people. Just regular, charming, old-fashioned people. You'll see."

Two minutes later, they were at the front door, Anny's arm looped in his "You gonna ring the bell?" he asked, nervously.

"Nope. You do it whenever you're ready. We can wait here as long as we need to."

He took deep breath and wondered why he was so nervous. This was not like him. He was the guy who went into a hostile courtroom and made everyone see it his way. *Cowboy up Solomon, you're being pathetic.*

He reached across Anny and pushed the doorbell button with a swift motion.

"Just a minute," he heard a woman say.

A few seconds later the door opened and Anny's mom, a radiant lady in her early 50's, put her hands over her mouth and fought back an immediate onslaught of tears. The tears must have been contagious because Anny followed suit, and they embraced with squeals of glee.

Anny's mother had two glows. First, the glow that comes from affluence. Anny's mom had the purchasing power to buy cosmetics that slow the aging process and promote healthy skin. Second, the glow that comes from the inside. It was an inner light that testified to a life well lived. It was the second glow that mesmerized Solomon. It was the second glow that he knew like an old friend, for it was the same glow he saw in Anny.

Bill came down the main stairs and into the foyer. Though not as theatrical, his overjoy was apparent too. These people were real. Bill and Jesse Boyle were a hometown husband and wife, not afraid to show joy when they felt it, and not afraid to be foolish when the time called for it. There was no pretense in them, no fakery. Anny was right when she said they were good, traditional people. Within minutes of their arrival, Solomon felt like a longstanding member of the family.

During the weeks they stayed in Kansas -- Anny in her childhood bedroom and Sully in the guest bedroom -- Sully got to cross off a few bucket-list items.

For one, they enjoyed Kansas-style barbeque, something he'd always wanted to try. The Boyle family's favorite BBQ was Dannyboy's Smokehouse. Another was pheasant hunting. Not really on his bucket-list before arriving at the Boyle's, but something he became fascinated with while there. While on his first hunt with Bill and the dogs, bundled in layers of clothing to ward off the chilly drizzle, Bill decided it was a good time to say a few things.

"Anny 'n the missis always had an open relationship. My little girl never realized that everything she told her mother, and told her mother to keep from me, was blabbered about within hours of the hearin'." Bill chuckled to himself.

"Anyway, I've always been kept in the loop. Had to pretend I wasn't cause that was what kept the balance in our home, you see. But truth be told, I always knew. I knew when she got picked on. Knew when she had her first kiss. Knew when she first climbed into bed with another man. My little girl's always been so honest with the missis that I know what she says now is true. And I'm... I'm just so..."

Bill swallowed a lump and looked away momentarily. There, standing in the tall grass, Sully saw something that very few others ever did, Bill's emotional side.

"Ah hell," he finally pushed the words out, "you never stole her dignity from her. Why?"

Solomon chuckled, "That, sir, is a long story. However, it takes two to agree on a thing that involves two people. She kept our commitment intact as well, so I can't take all the credit."

"I understand, but you showed leadership. You showed courage. You showed self-control." Bill smiled and shook his head, "I've not always been a prayin' man. Lookin' back I should'a done more of that. But the missis, by heaven, she prays. She prays to God Almighty every day. One thing she's always prayed is for an honorable man for her daughter. I guess what I'm tryin' to say here is, I believe her prayers have been answered. And it does somethin' to me, knowin' she's with a man who loves her enough to do right by her. A man who loves her as much as her daddy, even."

It was the first time Sully had brushed so close to the love a father has for his little girl. There, in the tall grass, it all made perfect sense. *As young men, we hunt for easy relationships and we prey on the loosest among them. Then, we become fathers and wonder, 'Does a better man than me exist out there? Will he find my little girl before the wolves do?' Leola, I'm so sorry.*

Sully heard the dogs bark ahead. Bill was moving on, but before he got too far off the subject, Solomon had something he needed to say as well.

"Bill," he tapped the older gent on the shoulder, "before we start shooting guns, I came here to Kansas to ask your blessing. I've fallen for Anny in a way that's hard to explain. In my youth, I was afraid of absoluteness. Singularity, as it were, scared me because it felt confining. But this past year a lot has changed for me, and now I find comfort in the things I used to fear. So, I don't want to date your daughter. I want to marry your daughter. If you'll give me your blessing, I'll honor and cherish her for the rest of my life."

"Solomon," Bill's smile-wrinkles deepened, "giving you my blessing is the easiest decision I've ever made. But, there's one condition."

"What's that?" Sully replied.

"We need to shake hands on your promise. That's all the commitment I need from a man with honor."

CHAPTER 52
King of the Earth

...

Abdullah Kahn's servant-fellow was being shifty and vague about the purpose behind the need to go to Rio. So much so, that Leo declined the invitation, and asked the pale host to call a sedan. He and his wife were ready to return to their Manhattan hotel. There was something peculiar about the Hand, and Leo couldn't shake the warning in his heart.

Why Rio? Why the subterfuge? What's so important about that black blob that these guys can't, or won't, talk to me straight-from-the-shoulder?

As he and Ali sat patiently waiting for the sedan, Leo felt a curious regret settle on his mind. He wondered if he'd been too quick to decline the invitation. He could not deny the longing he felt, just to be in the midst of that strange relic one more time. Like the night prior, the matter seemed to call to him at a deep and subconscious level. There was something powerful and intoxicating about it.

At the impasse, the Hand realized he needed to disclose more to the young aristocrat. Having Leo and Ali depart in a sedan was not an option, so he quietly formulated Plan B with Abdullah in a nearby room. They had to get Leo to Brazil.

The Hand returned to the Atrium where the Khalpanas sat, quietly chatting about nothing important. He chose his words carefully and explained that they were going to an off-books laboratory on the outskirts of Rio. There, they intended to figure out what the black matter actually was. They needed Leo's help because he was one of only two people in the world who could hear its metaphysical elements within the matter. He also disclosed that according to prevailing wisdom, the black matter was some sort of portal to another space-time realm. Those two details piqued Leo's interest and, relieved, he agreed to accompany them.

Though Ali sat beside him, he made the decision to go to Rio without consulting her in any way. He hadn't even bothered to look at her facial expression to gauge her feelings on the matter. The whole thing did not go over well. Later that evening, they got into an ugly fight about the ordeal, and Leo dealt with the discord by letting Ali fly to Madrid instead. Leo could go to Brazil, while Ali spent a week with her mother in Spain; they'd reunite in a week.

The next morning, they parted ways at the airport amid a thick air of tension. Ali was not fond of Abdullah, and detested his "Hand" even more. Something told her that her husband was walking into a terrible trap, but she had no way to articulate those feelings logically. Her options were to throw an emotional tantrum in the hopes of levying a guilt trip, thereby causing Leo to opt out of going to Rio, or to grin and bear it. Her deportment at goodbye had mostly to do with an indescribable fear for her husband, coupled with no small measure of anger toward the two strangers who, in her opinion, had seduced his will.

Leo leaned in to give his darling a peck on the cheek just as she turned her back and walked to another area of the airport. It was a blatant act of disrespect, and he clenched his jaw involuntarily. She wasn't like that, normally. Ali took great care to avoid being publically disrespectful to him, and her behavior agitated his masculine, Muslim sensibilities to the core. He tried to control his breathing as he took a nervous glance around the concourse. *Good, nobody saw that.*

* * * * * * * * *

First, Leo got a tour of the minimum and medium security wings of BSA. At Leo's pressing, the tour guide, Dr. Monroe, reluctantly admitted to purchasing humans on the black market and using them in biological experimentation. He forcedly justified this action on two levels. First, human trials were a necessary evil in the pursuit of genetically engineering a higher species, and of curing disease. It would have taken BSA an extra 75 years to get where they were if they'd complied with the UN's prohibitions on human testing. His second justification simply came down to sex and vanity, and had to do with the beautiful, sexual people of the Zoe Ginosko Laboratories in the mid-sec wing.

"We buy them from sex slave traders and give them new identities. This is what they become. So, you tell me Mr. Khalpana, do you suppose our therapies hurt, or benefit these men and women?"

Leo knew the excuse was bogus, but he was tantalized by their beauty nevertheless. Monroe saw Leo's fascination and called one woman and one man into a room, and had them undress in front of them. Both bodies were perfect - still uniquely their own, but perfect.

"Would you like for me to have them perform sexual intercourse in front of you?"

The question caught Leo off guard. "Um, no. That's not necessary. Thank you both, please put your clothing back on."

"It's nice though," Monroe said uncaringly. "If you ever want to see it, or participate with some of them while they do it, just say the word. That's what we breed them for, after all."

That's what we breed them for? What's that supposed to mean? The Doc's hubris was jarring and Leo shook his head, offended.

… Jarring, sure, but powerful, no?

Leo looked around. Had he just thought that second part, or had someone corrected him? Nobody was paying attention to him, and he thought about the black matter. Suddenly, he felt exposed.

Later that night, while sipping a nightcap in his room, he was thankful that Ali chose not to come to Rio. She was a humanitarian at heart, and not like her contemporaries and fellow trust-fund kids, who used humanitarianism as absolution for the guilt of their affluence. Ali would be appalled by this place. Not only would she be deeply offended, but she would probably make a public media spectacle.

Leo's room was simple and clean. He didn't know he was under 24-hour surveillance and that even as he grabbed the in-room phone and dialed his mother-in-law's residence, eyes watched while ears listened to his every ensuing conversation. BSA left nothing to chance. Whatever he did in supposed privacy was recorded and chronicled, and filed away for safe keeping.

Life at BSA was a game of cat-and-mouse. Whenever they talked, Leo told Ali the stuff he figured she could handle. He kept the danker stuff to himself, just as the brass at BSA did with him. Moral and ethical outrage was kept in check by everyone, and keeping the atmospheric balance was considered a team sport by the lab's employees.

On day two, he was whisked to a room in the max-security wing bright and early. There, a team of scientists were analyzing and inspecting the black matter, which had been removed from its glass box. Donning a lab coat like the rest of them, Leo spent the day learning and getting caught up on all that the scientists had discovered so far. He was taught how to comprehend and communicate with pure, wordless telepathy. They were astonished at how quickly he mastered that illusive skill.

The black matter interacted with Leo in one unique way. When he got within a few feet of it, the matter destabilized. It vibrated and changed form by stretching and contracting on itself. It looked like an insect cocoon beginning to lose the containment battle.

The team was eager to see more and wanted to conduct further experiments with Leo, but Abdullah forbid it. The scientists strongly recommended that the matter be allowed to interact with Leo, but Abdullah was unrelenting. When they insisted, Abdullah became irate and nearly violent. Over the course of a few days, the conflict grew. The stalemate began driving everyone insane, and then, just as suddenly as Kahn prohibited interaction between the matter and Leo, he caved in and gave his blessing. It was as though he'd lost the will to fight about it any longer.

Immediately, a conference room was prepped and Leo was summoned.

At the head of the table sat Kahn. He looked old and decrepit. He was flanked by the Hand and Dr. Monroe. At the other end of the table sat Leo. The scientists were gathered in the remaining chairs and standing against the walls.

As he sat in the conference room, Leo could hear the sounds of the other world, loud and intense in his head. Everything that happened from this point forward happened telepathically, and most of it without the use of words.

"Where's the black matter? I hear and smell it, but I can't see it." Leo's question was not accusatory, just matter-of-fact.

Abdullah set it on the table. It was encased in its glass box. "Here it is."

"Give it to me," Leo said. Everyone in the room, except the Hand, was shocked by his sudden *voice* of confidence. Leo's mouth curved upward as a grin overtook him, "Hand it over, Abdullah."

"What did you say?" Abdullah's face turned rigid. A standoff ensued as the onlookers held their breath.

"Give it to me, or be burned from the inside out." Kahn shot a look at the Hand with horror and fury.

"You told him about that?"

"I did not, I swear it," the Hand defended, before looking at Leo with a puzzled gaze. "But he clearly knows about that."

"Clearly," whispered Kahn in an actual voice. Beads of sweat formed on his forehead at the mere thought of that experience in the garden.

Kahn pushed the glass box and it slid along the smooth table finish, stopping in front of Leo. As it drew near, the matter inside began to expand, contract and vibrate. When Leo touched the top of the box, the matter broke the glass and spilled onto the table. Some in the room stood involuntarily, startled. Others pushed their chairs back and away from the table. Leo simply closed his eyes and crossed his arms over his chest. He waited, calmly, with a look of serenity and contentment splashed across his face.

As if choreographed, the matter inched to the edge of the table and then jumped onto his chest. It climbed up his chest and face, and settled on his head. There, it morphed into a crown, a beautiful, sharp, powerful-looking crown. It was stunning.

The black matter now gleamed with a frosty brightness. Huge, inlayed, exotic jewels tempted the onlooker's eyes. There was sensuality about the crown, something that tickled the lust of everyone present.

Leo opened his eyes and a sense of terror overtook the others. He was suddenly a great and terrible presence. As if a heavy hand pushed down on the back of every head, each person in the room bowed in reverence. Even Abdullah - who struggled mightily against the downward thrust of the unseen force - eventually dropped his head in a posture of worship.

Only the Hand was not compelled to bow. Just as the crown settled on Leo's head, and before his presence had changed, the Hand preemptively got off his chair, stepped back, put one hand over his heart, and bowed low. He did it with lurid flamboyance and pride. As if he knew what was coming. As if this event marked the long awaited, triumphant return of the King. He preempted the others by almost a minute, but the others were in such shock of what was going on that they failed to notice.

Then, suddenly, Leo vanished and the compulsion to bow was gone. Right before their eyes, Leo was sucked into the crown, head first, and disappeared. It was hard to explain in physical terms, but he and the crown both simply vanished.

* * * * * * * * *

When Leo opened his eyes, he was in a different place altogether. It was a place beyond planet earth, a place somewhere among the stars, maybe.

His lungs burned, and the taste in his mouth was putrid and awful when he exhaled. However, when he inhaled, it was sweet and neutralized the rot. It reminded him of the sickness he felt the first time he saw the matter at Abdullah's party.

On the second exhale, he coughed and vomited. A hand on his back caught his attention and he looked up. There he saw, standing above him a being, having the form of a man, who was cloaked and hooded. His face was veiled by the shadow of the hood.

"Don't be afraid, my name is Abele. You're here because you've been chosen. The illness you feel is your body acclimating to this place. You'll find power in the things you're inhaling, eventually."

"Who-who are you?"

"I'm Abele. When you are ready, stand and follow me."

Splice

He couldn't. He felt too sick.

After a few minutes, Leo could sit up and look around. He was in a great and desolate expanse, and he could see hills and valleys everywhere. In the far distance he saw mountains stretching high into the sky. There were three suns of varying sizes, each casting a reddish-purple hue. *Are they suns, or are they just reflecting a powerful light?* Leo couldn't tell, but together, they gave off less light than Earth's single star.

In the sky he saw flying things going this way and that. Some of them looked like stereotypical UFOs and some had longer and sleeker shapes, but each was unique. He soon realized that the flying objects were not machines at all, but biologically alive-and-aware transport beings. Nothing was mechanical -- everything had life.

He blinked and looked around, and then noticed that most everything that walked, crawled, or grew on the ground was somehow awake and aware as well. The trees even, though few, seemed to have higher intelligence than mankind.

The upturn in his stomach settled as a jolt of energy began pumping through his system. Abele noticed he was better and said, "Master Khalpana, you have an appointment. We need to be off."

Leo nodded. With Abele's assistance he stood up. He felt light on his feet as Abele looked into the sky and raised his arm. From above, one of the flying-things -- having the form of a spacecraft, but the skeletal structure and intelligence of a living organism -- descended near them. As if it was some kind of taxi, they climbed aboard.

It took off with blazing speed. Leo tried to look out a window, but they were moving too fast to see much of anything. It was a blur of light. Then, Abele said something in another language, and suddenly, the whole skeletal structure of the craft became transparent. Leo felt as if they were flying through space and time in a glass bubble.

"You want to see out the window, fly inside the window," Abele said, reclining in his seat.

"Where are we?" Leo asked hesitantly.

"We are in eternity, in the Kingdom of the First."

"Who's the First?"

"He's known by many names among humans. He's lord of the pantheon, overseer of creation, the originator of form and material reality."

"Allah?" asked Leo.

"It is as you say. That is one of many names."

"What am I doing here?"

"A stockyard breeds cattle and raises them. When the cattle mature, they are led to the slaughter, so that they may fulfill their ultimate purpose in life. The human race is approaching maturity. At maturity, they will be led to fulfill their ultimate purpose in life as well."

"You mean we will be slaughtered?"

"Not precisely," Abele's pitch hinted toward amusement, although Leo could still not see his face. "But led to fulfill your ultimate purpose, yes."

Abele leaned forward and took a cautionary glance around. Then, carefully, he got near Leo's face. Leo could see faint points of light marking Abele's eyes under the hood. The eyes became large, and in that instant, a message was transmitted to Leo, privately.

"There will be two kings, two kingdoms, and two paths. All roads lead to death, but one, also to life. You are a chosen king. You will lead one of those kingdoms, and fulfill the rite of passage along one of those paths. The rest is up to you."

The alien leaned back and cut the 'private link.' Leo gasped and swallowed, as if he'd been holding his breath. *What did he say?*

"I don't understand you," Leo pushed the words out, "I don't und..."

"You will, in time," Abele's voice was authoritative and prompted Leo to stop asking questions. "Look, ahead. We are now approaching your appointment."

The craft slowed, and as it did, the transparent membrane morphed back to its original form. Once the craft came to a stop, a bridge extended to the ground below.

"Follow me," Abele said as he led the way.

Upon exiting the craft, a large company of beings congregated on the precipice. There were beings of every size and shape, some two-legged, some four, some six, and some with many more. For the most part, the beings that most closely resembled humans seemed to be highest in the pecking order.

Their attire was noteworthy. Some were dressed in cloth, similar to humans, while others were adorned in garments made of water, fire, ice, or exotic materials that lack earthly comparison. As Leo watched, he realized that many of the beings could shape-shift.

When Abele got to the edge of the ramp, he called out in a loud voice, "Hail, Leonardo Khalpana, King of the Earth."

"Hail!" a loud rumble pierced the atmosphere as every being echoed the salute. Then everyone uniformly knelt to one knee as Leo passed. He was filled with a pride and sense of belonging he never knew, but always knew he wanted. He felt as though he was home, at last.

Abele threw off his hood and extended his large hand to him, "Come."

Leo took his hand, paying particular attention to the markings along Abele's face and neck that ever-shifted into exotic symbols. They were black, just like his eyes.

They came to a huge door at the mouth of a mountain. They passed thorough and walked along a corridor that seemed to stretch forever. As they ventured inward, more beings approached and bowed down as Leo passed. The sense of power and acceptance was everything he'd ever dreamed it could be. Soon he heard a rushing noise, like a waterfall, in the distance.

They came to a throne, massive in size. In earthly terms, it was the size of a 20-story building. Someone sat on the throne, but all that was visible were two enormous feet. The rest of the throne was veiled by an incredibly thick waterfall. The one who sat behind the water was huge, radiant, and the color red.

"Who stands before me?"

Leo fell to his face in terror, as Abele knelt on one knee. The voice was like the crack of a thousand cannons. When the being on the throne behind the water spoke, steam rose amid a sizzle of what sounded like the colliding of heat and water.

"Lord, I bring before you, Leonardo Khalpana, King of the Earth."

"Stand, Leonardo Khalpana."

"I c-can't, Lord," Leo was shaking with fear.

"That's right. You can't."

Abele looked up at the waterfall and waited for his cue. It came in the form of a hiss, at which point he took Leo by the arm and hoisted him to his feet, saying, "In trepidation, you must stand and claim what's been given to you."

His knees were weak, so Abele kept a steadying hand on him for support. Leo willed his eyes up toward the waterfall.

"Leo, do you accept the responsibility of kingship over the earth?"

Leo gulped and glanced at Abele, who had a peculiar look to him, almost sad. Leo cocked his head and Abele shook it off, then smiled and nodded, as if encouraging him to take the charge.

"Yes, Lord."

"Then, I give you my power." Leo couldn't help but squint when the being spoke, for his voice was bone-shaking. Then, suddenly, Leo let out a scream and fell back to the floor. Abele took a step back and crossed his arms.

Leo curled up on the ground in pain for a couple minutes. Then, as quickly as it began, the pain subsided and he opened his eyes. His legs were no longer shaky. He stood up. There was something magical about him. He looked at Abele and asked with surprising authority, "Do I look the same?"

Abele cocked his head and smiled, as if to say, *sort of.*

Leo's eyes burned with red fury. He felt unable to contain the power he now had inside him. By his will, he levitated into the air. Then, by his will, he breathed hot coals on the ground from where he floated. He now had powers and abilities that had only been conjured up in comic books, and he felt an elation that transcended human thought or understanding.

What happened to me? He thought, then an answer came, also from within his psyche. "I have become lord and king of earth."

A deep-throated, rumbling laugh came from behind the waterfall. That voice no longer seemed so powerful. Rather, it now seemed like a representation of Leo's own voice. Leo tossed back his head and laughed alongside the one on the throne. He floated back to the ground next to Abele. After the moment passed, Leo looked back at the waterfall and waited for instruction.

"There is a book, and you need to destroy it. It contains a cypher that cannot be found by our enemies. You have a copy of it in the laboratory. Do not read the cypher."

"Understood. What then is our mission?"

"To unify the people of earth. There is a rebellion coming, one that, if it gains momentum, will effectuate a terrible war. That war will end with the extinction of the human race. Therefore, you must root out the troublemakers and unify the people of the world before that happens. We must destroy the unenlightened ones before they gain strength and numbers."

"Understood."

"Then go."

* * * * * * * * *

Those were the last words Leo heard before falling back through the crown's portal. With a buzz and a thud, he plopped into his chair at the conference table. *Was it a dream? Had it really happened?*

"How long was I gone?" he asked.

"A couple seconds. Maybe three. What happened?" The Hand was the only one in the room not sitting stunned and gape-mouthed.

"Where's the crown?" Abdullah demanded.

"Bring me the book," Leo said to the Hand.

"The book?" the Hand was confused

"Where's the goddamned crown!" Abdullah demanded a second time.

Leo cocked his head in Kahn's direction, put his hands up to his mouth, and spat hot coals into them. Everyone in the room gasped. Leo then threw two balls of fire on Abdullah who, in front of twenty people, burned alive amid a *katzenjammer* of screams.

One scientist tried to exit the conference room while it was happening and Leo asked him not to. He complied, and then vomited. Leo glanced at him and thought, *that's a strange reaction, considering the unholy things they routinely create and discard here in the halls of BSA.*

Everybody heard his thought, but nobody responded.

The flame engulfing Abdullah dissipated. Only slight convulsions of his leg muscles marked the fleeting life that was once so dominate. Slowly, the team took their seats again. With Kahn's corpse lying in a smoldering heap of scorched bone and simmering flesh, Leo reiterated, calmly, "Hand, bring me the book."

This time the Hand understood what he wanted and ran to fetch it. Within a few minutes he returned, panting, "Here, here it is."

Leo took the copied pages from Malcolm's journal and flipped to the Eteocypriot script in the third section. As he looked it over, his upper lip curled, and they heard a gurgling sound come from inside his chest and throat.

378

"Can you read that?" the Hand asked excitedly. Oddly, the Hand was the only person who seemed unfazed by Leo's metamorphosis. It was as though he knew all along that this was the end game.

"No," that was a lie, but the one behind the waterfall told him not to read it, and now Leo knew why.

"Are there any other copies of this book in our possession?"

"Yes."

"Burn them all."

Even as he gave the instruction, the pages in his hand burst into a hot blue flame. Within seconds, it was consumed entirely. Only a whiff of ash and smoke remained. Leo rubbed his fingers together and looked at a picture on the wall. He walked over to it and looked at his faint reflection in the glass frame.

Good. I look like Leo… except for that lazy eye.

He poked gently at his left cheek. There was a slight droop just under his left eye, and his eye was indeed sagging. He let it go and straightened his posture, pleased with how he looked otherwise. *Now to taper this authority a little, and make some new friends...*

"Hand, gentlemen," he telepathized, as he turned to face the table. His telepathy was now delivered with less authority, more commonality. Immediately the room felt safer. "Our mission at BSA has changed, and I've been given instructions from the Lord of our celestial brethren as to where we go from here. Abdullah Kahn has fulfilled his purpose, and he will be honored for his accomplishments among those who have gone before him."

Cunning, the Hand thought without disclosing his musing telepathically. *The lord of our celestial brethren' instead of Allah? Very cunning indeed.*

The Hand spoke for the group, "What are we to do?"

Leo looked at him and smiled. It was a comforting smile. Leo now looked completely normal, but for the unequivocal authority he was able to turn on or off at will.

"You can start, Hand. Start by pledging fealty to me, and come under my protection. When the Hand is through, you all may join him. That's where we begin this journey..."

CHAPTER 53
Revelation

...

An unexplained anxiety grew in Solomon's heart. He was having the time of his life with his new fiancé and her parents, but something was calling him back to Manvel, Texas. At his urging, Anny helped make preparations to leave, even amid Bill and Jesse's insistence that they come back for Christmas which was just a few weeks away. Sure, he wanted to commit to more family fun during the holidays, but the feeling tugging at his sense of purpose told him something else. He heard the word deep inside his soul. He was embarking on a new journey, a pursuit of ... *singularity?*

They beat Rooter to Manvel by two days. When he arrived, the group instantly fell into a routine of good cheer and frequent barbeques. An onlooker might have perceived a casual atmosphere among them, but Sully couldn't shake the growing fear that something lurked behind an upcoming bend in the road of life. He felt as if some impending peril sought to ambush them. He did his best to feign casual contentment, but Anny and the others sensed that something was off, too.

He couldn't put his finger on anything specific. *Do we need to move again? Are the Phantoms after us again? Are we safe?*

There were no clear answers this time. No specific directions. A defined sense of intuition was undeniable, but the non-specific nature of it was vexing to his core. Privately, he even tried to consult the Urim and Thummim, but he should have known better. Those marbles, after all, just reflect whatever truth already resides in him.

One evening, Papa Roger brought a young couple to the house for dinner. They must have been late teens or early twenties, but they were married with one on the way. They were a happy team and blissfully naïve. After dinner but before dessert, they launched into their story...

Papa Roger's organization had been instrumental in helping them get off the streets of New Orleans a year ago. At the time, they were both addicted to drugs and were doing anything they could to make enough money for the next fix. They were caught in the throes of addiction, desperate and homeless. It was a sad story, but one that ended with a testimonial about the power of redemptive love. It was their story that lit the bulb in Sully's head.

On their conclusion, he jumped up and said, "Of course!"

Without another word, he ran to his room and quickly reappeared with the orbs. Papa Roger had not been told about these yet, so with predictable agog, he demanded a full account of what they were and how they came to belong to Sully. After some explanation and processing, Solomon pushed through to the point of why he'd brought them out.

"You all believe truth is singular, right? I mean, there is only one truth?" The guests nodded. "Well, I never believed such a thing until these orbs came into my life. But they can only answer yes or no. In other words, there's no gray in their ability to respond. If they don't respond, it means the question is poorly worded. These only react to questions of singular truth. Now, if there is singular truth in our little world, there is also singular truth in the entire cosmos. It has to be that way. The question is, where does this truth come from? How do we find it? Who embodies it?"

"I'm lost" Con said, "and frankly, if I'm lost, so is Rooter. That means, at least half this group has no idea what you're talking about."

Rooter nodded in agreement.

"Think about it," Sully pursued, slightly frustrated. "Muslims believe Allah embodies singular truth. That's why they can't conceive of infidels comingling with their belief system. Christians too, Judaism, same thing."

The group sat and blinked. "What I'm getting at is, we have to strive to discover truth in singularity. See, asking a question on the basis of religious faith or ideological passion is inherently the wrong way to ask a question."

Solomon took the dead marbles out of the box, and as soon as he did, they lit up with absolute brilliance. The guests looked on, mesmerized by the radiance.

"A question of singularity, observe. *Are rocks transparent?*" The orbs didn't adjust at all. Sully looked at his companions to discern whether they were getting the point.

He continued, "See what I mean? They may be, they may not be. We know that the transparency of a rock depends on its chemical composition. So, 'Are rocks transparent?' is inherently the wrong question. We need to learn to ask the right questions, such as, *Are some rocks transparent?*"

The second he asked the follow-up question, the blue orb lit brighter and bounced, signifying 'yes.'
Solomon put the orbs back in the box and they immediately dimmed. He then looked at Roger Weaverly. "You people, Christian people. You believe in singular truth. You call him God. You also believe that God communicated that singular truth through his son, Jesus, right?"

"Right." Papa Roger adjusted his posture.

"Okay then, are you prepared to ask the orbs *the* question of your faith? Are you prepared to have them either confirm or deny the authenticity of your faith?"

Papa Roger nodded slowly, "Okay. I get what you're asking…."

"Will you do it? Will you ask, 'Does the Christian belief in God and his son, Jesus Christ, reflect singular truth?' And will you accept the response given by the orbs?"

Weaverly sighed and took a cautionary glance at his guests, "I'm not sure I'm willing to do that."

"Why?" Solomon grinned. He knew Weaverly wouldn't and he also knew why.

"Because I'm not willing to accept that it's not true. That my faith is misplaced."

"I get your fear, but that doesn't make sense, intellectually speaking," Solomon retorted with as much grace as he could muster. "Isn't faith, in essence, *your* pursuit of truth? If you have the opportunity to confirm it, would you honestly choose not to?"

"Yes sir, it is. But if your orbs come back and tell me that my faith is not real, then, well, I don't know. I might think your orbs are full of it, or… I guess I have to think about this a bit more before taking that plunge."

"I understand, I do. But with all due respect, that's exactly why I believe Christianity is false. It's just as false as atheism, Islam, or Judaism."

Rooter even swallowed hard at the hearing of those words. Telling a Christian his premise of faith is a falsehood is akin to shooting your neighbor's dog. Con too felt the same, and adjusted his posture nervously.

"Don't take this personally, Papa Rog, but I submit to you that we, humans, are married to form and function, tradition and ceremony. Inside, if you have the light of Lux et Veritas, you know that the pomp and circumstance of religious premise is false. It's a lie. Even if you're almost right, or even if 99% of your belief structure is right, the 1% whiff of grey renders the whole thing a lie. But even unto death, you're willing to hold onto that lie because the truth is scary and absolute. That's what I mean by, *singular.*"

He looked at his fiancé and continued, "I had to learn this the hard way, but that's why the orbs were given to me, I think."

"Wait just a minute," Rooter came to the guests' rescue. "You're making Christianity and Islam, religious and moral equivalents? I don't know boss. I haven't seen much in the way of suicide bombers on the Christian side of things lately…"

"No," Solomon shook his head emphatically, "I'm not equating the two messages. I'm equating the form and function of religion, any religion. They are all one and the same. You see, in my mind, the pursuit of truth is both as subjective, and simultaneously as affirmative, as say, my love for Anny. Religions seek to point people down the path of truth from a defined, formulated standpoint. But truth is less controlled, more ambiguous, and much larger than the definition we try to contain in it with. . Don't believe me? Just look at these." Solomon pointed to the Urim and Thummim.

"Therefore," he continued, "there needs to be a spiritual pursuit, in addition to a religious one, a pursuit that's birthed in love and relationship and submission. Where it gets tricky for religious people is, when they hear a guy like me say, affirmatively, that I've seen the true pursuit of Truth in the lives of Christians, Jews, Muslims, Hindus, and Pagans alike. You see, I'm right in my statement, but that comment just made me a heretic in *their* eyes, regardless of whether *they* are from here or the Middle East."

Weaverly and his companions sat quietly, thinking. A sudden flash of lightning bled through the window from the evening beyond their little house, and almost immediately, a torrent of rain began pounding the roof and siding. It was only mid-40's outside, and the wind and rain brought a cold chill into the air.

Weaverly poured himself a glass of Knob Hill, forgetting completely to offer any to the others. He was lost in thought. Eventually he asked for a full accounting of how Sully came upon Lux et Veritas. The story was retold. The group settled back into discussing Sully's notion of singularity; however, the concept remained outside the others' wheelhouse of understanding.

Faith, truth, singularity? Sully's lost his mind, concluded Rooter.

The time drifted away. It was coming up on midnight when a sudden knock at the door startled them. Cautiously, Rooter approached the front door with one hand on the pistol jammed in the small of his back.

He cracked the door and the others heard him ask, "Who the hell are you?"

No answer came, but as if under some sort of mind-control or spell, Rooter lazily stepped aside. Seemingly under its own power, the door then swung open. There, in the midst of the downpour stood Abele, cloaked and hooded.

Sully and Anny both jumped up as he entered and tossed off his hood. Weaverly gasped, the pregnant gal covered her eyes, and Con jerked his seat backward. They were all speechless, and terrified.

"Be at ease, please," Abele said, as the exotic markings on his face lit up with a brilliant blue. Similar to before, they were shifting along his face and neck. "I come on behalf of others, and bring revelation."

As Abele prompted them to be at ease, the atmosphere in the house quieted and they were immediately able to relax. There was a special power in his words. He entered the room and pulled up a chair, just as casually as a relative might. He smiled at the others with genuine familiarity. Nobody knew what to say, so Rooter fumbled with his words and asked, "S-so, then, how would you drink like?"

Abele chuckled and looked at him, "Pardon?"

Rooter cleared his throat, "Would you c-care for a drink?"

"Thank you, yes. I'll have what Mr. Weaverly is drinking, if you don't mind."

Rooter was so dumbfounded he didn't move. The others just stared. Anny came to her senses first and poured Abele a glass.

"Rocks?"

"Yes, please. Thank you."

The alien being sipped his drink and appeared to enjoy the flavor. Licking his lips he said, "I see you found Lux et Veritas."

"I did. Yes, thanks."

Con, who was sitting next to Abele, leaned way back in his chair, as if trying to create as much distance as possible between he and the visitor. Anny thought Abele looked smaller in stature, compared to when they first met him in Egypt. Weaverly remained silent, while the young couple fidgeted. Rooter was still standing near the front door.

Anny also noted a marked difference in the being's demeanor. In Cairo, Abele was a menacing figure full of power and authority. Here, in their dining room, his aura was less scary, even a bit gentle and comforting. She was in no danger of fainting this time.

With a deep breath, Sully finally broke the silence by putting up his hands, "Well, you're obviously not here to kill us…"

Con and Abele both chuckled at the abruptness of that statement, the others just looked on.

"…so maybe you can tell us why you've come?"

Abele sipped the bourbon again and closed his eyes with satisfaction. Then, without forewarning, he began talking to nobody in particular. "I am known by the name, Abele. I am what my people call a *courigon*, a messenger. As you can see, I am able to interact with humans, which is why I'm here. Humans view me and my people as an alien species. We view you and your people as our relatives, sort of. You ask why I've come. I've come to offer some counsel and revelation."

"An alien species?"

"Courigon, what's…"

"Hang on just a sec…"

Everyone started talking at once, so Abele put a gentle hand up and said, "Friends, one at a time would be easiest."

"I got this then," Rooter said, pushing to the front of the line. "So you're from another planet?"

"No, Mr. Patchouli, not another planet. We abide in another dimension. The universe as you know it, and everything in it, was made for and given to you."

"Who's Mister Patchouli?" asked Weaverly, dumbfounded by the enormity of what was going on.

"Please, call me Rooter. I left Patchouli behind a long time ago."

"As you wish," Abele conceded. "Most of my people are unable to freely cross dimensions. As I said, I'm a *courigon*. A messenger is able to freely move between the dimensions."

Con tossed up a hand and mused, "How about if you just elaborate on that for a minute?"

Abele smiled. "Let me start from the beginning then."

Abele took another sip. His language was remarkably pointed, and the others were struck by how few words he wasted. "Elohim sits at the top, and Elohim is the beginning and the end. In Elohim, all resides in equilibrium. The many faces and facets of Elohim were made manifest, and the manifestation of those innumerable qualities are represented by the entirety of all creation, in this dimension, as well as all others. That which is defined by human conception was first defined in the eye of Elohim. Nothing is unique to the human experience, save this one thing – your free will.

"Elohim is not a being, Elohim is all beings. Elohim is not a concept, Elohim is all concepts. Elohim is singular, and also eternal. Elohim defies yours and my concept of good versus evil, right versus wrong, just versus unjust. Only in Elohim's eyes do antagonistic forces coexist in perfect balance. Therefore, when Elohim allowed his essence to come into existence, everything came in twos. War was born alongside peace. Right along with wrong. Light came with darkness, and so it was with the creation of my civilization. So it was later, with the creation of yours.

"My people are the manifestations of Elohim's thoughts. We are limited by our purpose and use, and lack the ideal of self-governance that can only exist alongside free-will. We are all the hand of Elohim, the eye of Elohim, the will of Elohim. Some of us were made to represent love, while others were created as the embodiment of hate. Some were made to represent war, others peace. Every face and facet of Elohim was given the breath of life at conception, and we exist in eternity."

Abele took a moment to sip and savor again before continuing, "War, therefore, is merely a concept to you. An idea. But in my civilization, it is not just a concept, but also a manifest entity, and innumerable slightly differing entities. In my world, all things, even concepts, are given the breath of life. Your species was created by Elohim. Your purpose is to become the realization of Elohim's counterpart. Don't you see? Your free-will rendered unto you a form of *deification* that my people could never experience. By free-will, every man and woman has been granted the right and responsibility of self-determination, thereby becoming, in essence, what Elohim is, by nature."

"Is Elohim God?" asked Anny.

"Yes, Elohim is known this way."

"Right, but is Elohim Allah?" Sully retorted, knowing the answer.

"Yes, Elohim is known this way."

"Wait, wha?" Rooter started, but Abele cut him off.

"Allah, God, Yahweh, these are all words for Elohim, adopted by mankind at the behest of my species, the Abiforites and Xenolites. But my people are merely manifestations of Elohim's qualities, so they depict Elohim through the paradigm of their own design. Do all these words sum up Elohim in totality? No. Are they nevertheless, the best descriptors of Elohim for your purposes? Yes, I believe so."

"Why are you here, exactly?" Sully asked.

Abele looked at him with a curious gaze. "I'm here to bring revelation. The world as you know it is changing fast. Things that were locked away long ago are about to be let out. The human experience is about to be redefined in ways that I could not begin to explain. All of you have a central part to play as a calamitous season approaches."

"What's the revelation?" Sully asked, unsure of whether or not Abele could be trusted.

Abele swallowed the last few drops of liquor and stood up suddenly. He looked straight at Sully and stretched out his hand, "Come with me and I'll show you."

Sully was conflicted. On one hand, he had no reason not to trust the alien, but on the other, something told him to be very careful. Abele stood motionless with an outstretched hand, waiting.

He looked at his friends, all of whom were staring at him and wondering what he was going to do. "Okay then," he said, and leaned over to give Anny a kiss. Her eyes told him to go and see what Abele had to show him.

"Okay then," Sully said again, and reached out to take the being's hand.

As they touched one another, Sully's vision blurred. Soon, all he could see was white light. Where was the alien taking him? Where had the dining room in Manvel gone? Where were his friends? He felt the tight grip of Abele's hand, but all he could see was bright white light as far as his vision would allow. Was he falling? Was he floating? Was he still, or was he moving at all? He couldn't tell; it was as though he merely *existed* somewhere in the fabric of time without space providing any definable point of reference.

Was it like that for a long time, or just an instant? This too, Sully couldn't tell. He heard nothing until the sounds of activity started echoing from far away. He smelled nothing until the scent of dust and manure tickled his nostrils. Slowly, his senses began to pick up the scene, and vision returned to his eyes. As it did, he knew immediately that Abele had taken him to a different time and place entirely. The peace and tranquility of white light was replaced by jarring exposure to a mad frenzy of activity.

"Wh-where are we?" he shouted over the ruckus, just as a by-passer who was screaming something in another language bumped shoulders with him, flinging him around. Everywhere he looked, shirtless men carrying birds and animals of every sort were chanting and marching toward a structure in the distance.

Sully kept getting bumped by the pedestrians, but it appeared they couldn't actually see him. It's as though they were looking through him and advancing in a drove toward something in the distance. Sully regained his balance and started moving with the flow, more as a self-preservation measure. He looked for Abele, and found him a few feet away and on the fringe of the human current. Sully made his way to him.

"Where are we?" he asked again.

"This is ancient Babylon, Sully," Abele sidestepped and dodged a chanting man. "These people are under an intoxicant, and march to Etemenanki, the Temple of Marduk up ahead."

"Why are we here?"

"Because what's about to happen down there," Abele pointed in the direction of the structure, "is very significant to what you must endure, even as the human saga draws to a fantastic end."

* * * * * * * * *

In Manvel, Rooter and Con jumped to their feet, just as Anny screamed. One minute he was there, the next he was gone. They looked at one another, dumbstruck. *What just happened?*

Anny's hands fluttered as she started to hyperventilate. The pregnant guest reached over and put a comforting hand on her shoulder.

"What the…" Rooter started but stopped short. He was totally confused. Instead of talking, he looked at Weaverly and the young couple. The three of them sat like stones with loose jaws, amazed at what they'd just witnessed.

Solomon was gone, and so was the alien. All they could do was hope that Sully was okay, wherever he was.

Bellwether
SD

www.BellwetherPublications.com